BY THE UNHOLY HAND

A Medieval Romance

By Kathryn Le Veque

Book One in the Unholy Trinity Series

© Copyright 2019 by Kathryn Le Veque Novels, Inc.
Print Edition
Text by Kathryn Le Veque
Cover by Kim Killion
Edited by Scott Moreland

Reproduction of any kind except where it pertains to short quotes in relation to advertising or promotion is strictly prohibited.
All Rights Reserved.

The characters and events portrayed in this book are fictitious. Any similarity to real persons, living or dead, is purely coincidental and not intended by the author.

Kathryn Le Veque Novels

Medieval Romance:

De Wolfe Pack Series:
Warwolfe
The Wolfe
Nighthawk
ShadowWolfe
DarkWolfe
A Joyous de Wolfe Christmas
Serpent
A Wolfe Among Dragons
Scorpion
Dark Destroyer
The Lion of the North
Walls of Babylon

The de Russe Legacy:
The Falls of Erith
Lord of War: Black Angel
The Iron Knight
Beast
The Dark One: Dark Knight
The White Lord of Wellesbourne
Dark Moon
Dark Steel

The de Lohr Dynasty:
While Angels Slept
Rise of the Defender
Steelheart
Shadowmoor
Silversword
Spectre of the Sword
Unending Love
Archangel

Lords of East Anglia:
While Angels Slept
Godspeed

Great Lords of le Bec:
Great Protector

House of de Royans:
Lord of Winter
To the Lady Born

Lords of Eire:
Echoes of Ancient Dreams
Blacksword
The Darkland

Ancient Kings of Anglecynn:
The Whispering Night
Netherworld

Battle Lords of de Velt:
The Dark Lord
Devil's Dominion
Bay of Fear

Reign of the House of de Winter:
Lespada
Swords and Shields

De Reyne Domination:
Guardian of Darkness
With Dreams
The Fallen One

House of d'Vant:
Tender is the Knight (House of d'Vant)
The Red Fury (House of d'Vant)

The Dragonblade Series:
Fragments of Grace
Dragonblade

Island of Glass
The Savage Curtain
The Fallen One

Great Marcher Lords of de Lara
Lord of the Shadows
Dragonblade

House of St. Hever
Fragments of Grace
Island of Glass
Queen of Lost Stars

Lords of Pembury:
The Savage Curtain

Lords of Thunder: The de Shera Brotherhood Trilogy
The Thunder Lord
The Thunder Warrior
The Thunder Knight

The Great Knights of de Moray:
Shield of Kronos
The Gorgon

The House of De Nerra:
The Falls of Erith
Vestiges of Valor
Realm of Angels

Highland Warriors of Munro:
The Red Lion
Deep Into Darkness

The House of de Garr:
Lord of Light
Realm of Angels

Saxon Lords of Hage:
The Crusader
Kingdom Come

High Warriors of Rohan:
High Warrior

The House of Ashbourne:
Upon a Midnight Dream

The House of D'Aurilliac:
Valiant Chaos

The House of De Dere:
Of Love and Legend

St. John and de Gare Clans:
The Warrior Poet

The House of de Bretagne:
The Questing

The House of Summerlin:
The Legend

The Kingdom of Hendocia:
Kingdom by the Sea

The Executioner Knights:
By the Unholy Hand
The Mountain Dark
Starless
A Time of End

Contemporary Romance:

Kathlyn Trent/Marcus Burton Series:
Valley of the Shadow
The Eden Factor
Canyon of the Sphinx

The American Heroes Anthology Series:
The Lucius Robe
Fires of Autumn
Evenshade
Sea of Dreams
Purgatory

Other non-connected Contemporary Romance:
Lady of Heaven
Darkling, I Listen

In the Dreaming Hour
River's End
The Fountain

Sons of Poseidon:
The Immortal Sea

Pirates of Britannia Series (with Eliza Knight):
Savage of the Sea by Eliza Knight
Leader of Titans by Kathryn Le Veque
The Sea Devil by Eliza Knight
Sea Wolfe by Kathryn Le Veque

<u>Note:</u> All Kathryn's novels are designed to be read as stand-alones, although many have cross-over characters or cross-over family groups. Novels that are grouped together have related characters or family groups. You will notice that some series have the same books; that is because they are cross-overs. A hero in one book may be the secondary character in another.

There is NO reading order except by chronology, but even in that case, you can still read the books as stand-alones. No novel is connected to another by a cliff hanger, and every book has an HEA.

Series are clearly marked. All series contain the same characters or family groups except the American Heroes Series, which is an anthology with unrelated characters.

For more information, find it in **A Reader's Guide to the Medieval World of Le Veque.**

Author's Note

It's been a long time since I've had so much fun writing a story.

I came up with the Unholy Trinity when I write the novel Lord of Winter in 2015. Maxton, Kress, and Achilles were three loners who essentially liked to work as a team and who hated the de Lohr brothers, including Marcus Burton, so Lord of Winter was fun to write in that sense – pious, righteous Christopher and his antithesis, Maxton of Loxbeare. They were exactly enemies, but they didn't approve of each other, and Maxton felt as if Christopher was a goody-goody. No other way to put that. Maxton did hard work, underhanded and dirty work, while Christopher knew the right people, made the right moves, and received all the glory.

In this novel, we're at least ten years after Lord of Winter, when everyone has gone on the Crusades with Richard the Lionheart, although the path home after the Crusade ended has been different for all of them. Maxton and his companions didn't come home directly, but rather spent time (how can I say this…?) goofing off, being mercenaries and killers, whoring, and being basically directionless.

It got them into trouble.

There are quite a few secondary characters in this novel, so you may have to read passages over twice two pick up on all of the nuances. Not only do the de Lohr brothers make a brief appearance, but so does a very young Sean de Lara just as he assumes his spying against King John (you'll read his full story in Lord of the Shadows), and we also briefly meet Dashiell du Reims and Bric MacRohan – again – both when they were very young. Their stories happen a good fifteen or more years after this novel, so think of them as young, handsome, and hungry for glory.

Another prominent secondary character is William Marshal, Earl of Pembroke. William has made appearance in a few of my novels, including The Whispering Night, and he has often been described as England's Greatest Knight. Considering I'm writing about some of England's greatest (fictional) knights, I put them in good company by working with, and serving, the man who was referred to as The Marshal.

One of the fun things about this book was researching Medieval poisons. There are many plants that were known in Medieval times for their deadly quality, a few that are mentioned in this book. One of those is called *Dwale* – what we now know as Belladonna, or Deadly Nightshade. Historically speaking, it makes an interesting read to see how the poison was used. Deadly Nightshade has been around for thousands of years and was even used by the Greeks who wanted to do away with their enemies. Beware of Greeks bearing gifts (or inviting you to their feasts!).

Another fun bit of research I did was about Medieval banking – and yes, there was such a thing, really emerging strongly in the 12th century. They had 'deposit bankers' (which were just what they sounded like), and 'merchant bankers', etc. Italy, specifically Genoa, was the center of the early banking world around this time. Makes for some fascinating reading.

There's quite a bit that goes on in this book – there are some very bottom-of-the-barrel moments. There is angst and real fear in some parts. But there is also a lot of soul-searching and growth on the part of our hero, as well as our heroine, so I believe this story is mostly about hope and redemption. Can a man change his stars? Can he right the wrongs of the past? And can he find within himself compassion and understanding that he always believed he lacked? All valid questions, and works them out for himself with a little help from our heroine.

A short pronunciation guide and things that are real/fictional:

Blitha – Pronounced with a short 'I' sound, as in bliss. (Blitha is not actually a saint; this is a fictious figure)

Achilles – uh-KILL-eez

Ceri – Like Sarah, only with an "ee" on the end – like Sar-EE

Bishop of Essex – fictitious

William Marshal – Real. Literally, the greatest (real) knight England has ever seen.

Farringdon House – Fictitious, though there is a very large Medieval district called Farringdon, basically where Trafalgar Square is in present day.

Bishopsgate (part of the London Medieval wall system): Real.

Landmarks outside of the wall at Bishopsgate: Except for St. Blitha Abbey, real.

I don't normally include drawings or charts, things I use when I work on my stories, but in this case, I am. I'm a very visual thinker, so I often draw floor plans and such when I write to help me figure things out (like chambers and character movement), so I'm including the floor plan of St. Blitha (drawn by our heroine towards the end of the tale), and also of Farringdon House's lower level. Hopefully it gives you a good visual like it did me, but I'll make the disclaimer here that I'm not an artist. Still, I thought it would be fun for the reader to see my original drawings.

Love,

Kathryn

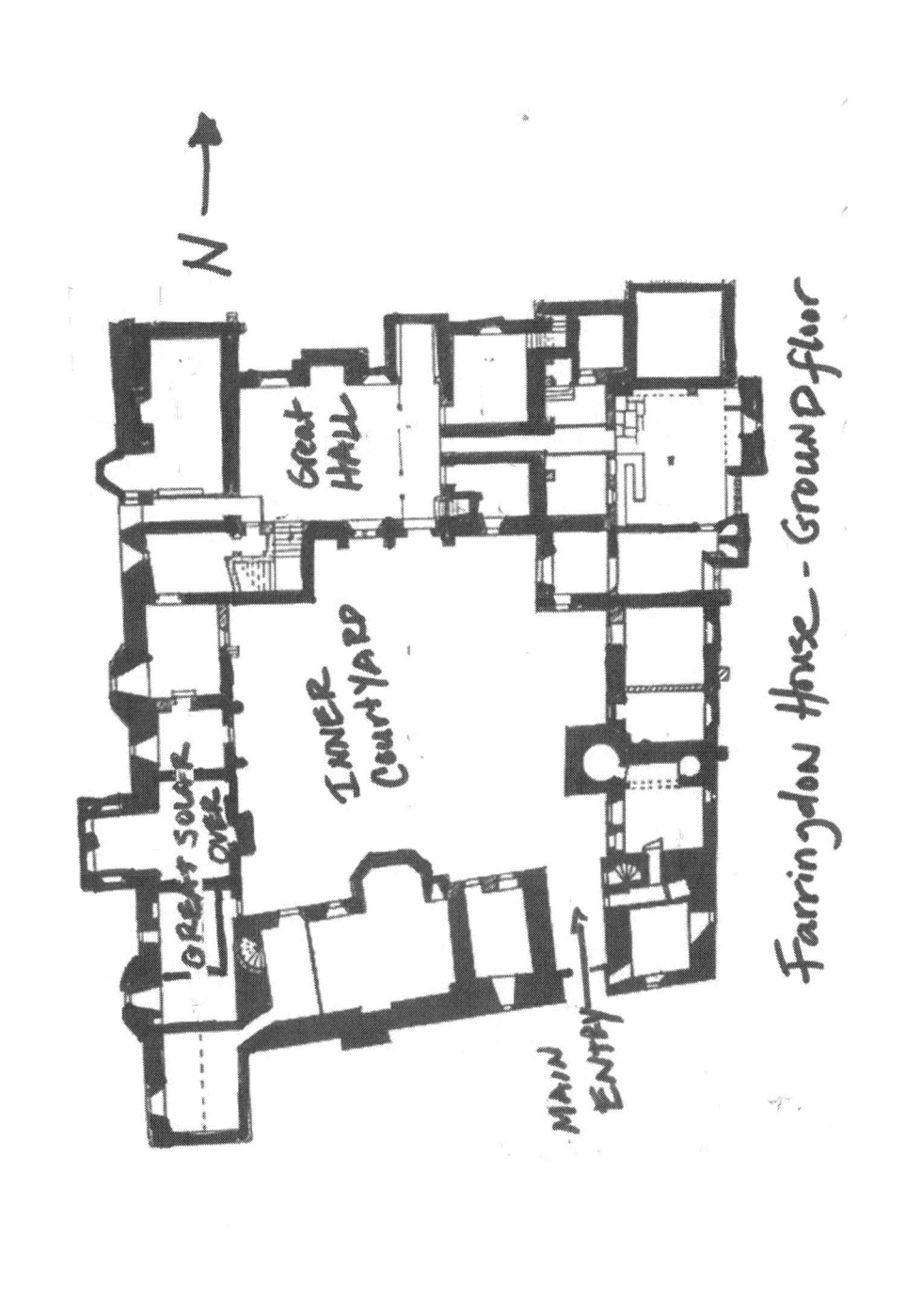

Farringdon House – Ground floor

St. Blitha Map c. 1200 A.D.

Not to scale

← N
To London →

Church
Abbot lodge
Mother Abbess Solar
Entry
Barn yard
Cloister
Garden
Cloister
Cloister
Entry
Cells
Walk
Oven
Oven
Kitch.
Laundry
Dormitory
Dining
Stairs
To chapel
Stream

Love is all truth;
Lust, full of forged lies
~ *William Shakespeare*

~ MIHI CREDE (TRUST ME) ~

Year of Our Lord 1199 A.D., The Month of August
Near the convent dedicated to St. Blitha of the Order of St. Dominica
North of the city walls, Bishopsgate

*H*E LOVED HER.
He said he loved her and that made this happening a right and true thing, consecrated by God. If God was love, then Rhyne de Leybourne was possessed by the Holy Spirit, and all things fine and good in the world.

He said he loved her.

She had believed him.

It had been soft and dark and quiet in the sod barn where he'd taken her, just to the east of St. Blitha where she served as a pledge. Dumped there was more like it, deposited by a greedy aunt who wanted nothing to do with her wealthy niece. She wanted the girl's money, though.

That made it okay, in her mind.

But there were those who had cared for the niece. Rhyne did, in fact. Or, at least he told himself that. The truth was that he loved her money, too, and he wasn't so willing to let it go. It had taken him so very long to discover where her aunt had sent her, and when he finally located her, all he could speak of was his longing for her, and she in turn declared her longing for him. He'd come for her now and would make everything right between them, as he promised.

But first, he would demonstrate his love for her so there would be no doubt in her mind that he was sincere.

She'd been by the gently bubbling stream just outside the abbey walls, drawing water for the wash, when he'd come upon his shiny brown stallion. It wasn't unusual for her to be outside of the abbey walls because that's where the main water source was, so when he pulled her to the sod barn, no one noticed.

No one even looked for her.

At first, he had been gentle, and their hugs of joy had been innocent. But that innocence was short-lived when he pinned her against the stable wall and his mouth began to wander, his tongue invading nearly every orifice on her head. She'd resisted at first, fearful of this very intimate attention, but he had ignored her resistance as he continued to speak of his love for her. His passion rose to frenzied proportions and his tenderness soon turned rough.

Now that he had her, he wasn't going to waste any time.

He continued to tell her how much he loved her, which made her uncertainty fade. If he loved her so much, then surely what he was doing was his right. He was demonstrating that love. When he was finished pawing her, he grabbed her by both arms and pushed her down onto the cold, dirty floor.

The straw beneath them was at dry but dirty as he pushed her onto her back and began fumbling with the bottom of her long woolen robe, the same woolens that all pledges of St. Blitha wore. His body was heavy atop her, squirming on her, and her uncertainty returned. *We should not be doing this*, she said, but he assured her that this was what people who loved each other did.

She believed him.

The woolens were shoved up, past her knees, to her hips, as he tugged and pulled, trying to expose her white body beneath him. When she tried to protest, he captured her mouth with his lips, his tongue pushing into her pink recesses. With his mouth keeping her occupied, his hands continued to yank up the woolens, exposing her belly. He couldn't pull it any further, so his hand snaked underneath, fondling her round breasts and feeling her nipples harden against his palm.

This is what people do who love one another, Andressa. Trust me.

But she couldn't relax, not when he was pinching her nipple, running his hands all over her breasts. His mouth continued to feast on her face, all over her face, distracting her from what he was doing with his hands as he continued to tell her how much he loved her. She tried to push him away one last time, but she didn't do a very good job of it. It was true that she loved him, and she'd missed him as much as he missed her.

This is what people do who love each other.

She wanted him to know she loved him, too.

She stopped resisting.

Then, he was fumbling at his own clothing, lowering his hose and rubbing his stiff erection against her thigh. She felt his hardness, greatly apprehensive. His mouth moved across her face again and he shifted his body, pushing himself between her thighs. Without hesitation, he slid his manhood into her virginal body.

She gasped with surprise as he thrust into her. It stung and was uncomfortable. But he ignored her gasps of pain and thrust into her one more time to completely seat himself. In that action, her virginity became a memory, but he didn't care. His mouth was on her ear now, groaning of his love for her once more, telling her how slick and warm she was, and how his love for her was now complete.

But she wasn't at all at ease with what he was doing to her, love or not. He was heavy on her, and her woolen garment was around her neck and mostly covering her face now as he repeatedly thrust into her, lifting her legs up to allow him more room to move. She lay there, motionless and overwhelmed, but she kept telling herself over and over that he loved her. He was doing this because he wanted to show her how much he loved her.

And she was letting him.

She loved him, too.

… didn't she?

His pace quickened and the thrusts became harder, more forceful. She could feel him grinding his pelvis against hers, their bodies joined as closely as a man and woman could be joined. Every contact brought a shock of sensation that bolted up her body and she wondered if this was what love really felt like. It was painful and uncomfortable, and the more he thrust into her, the more she questioned his love.

Is this really what love feels like?

She was coming to wish it would soon be over.

He gave one last, hard thrust, and his entire body shuddered. He was panting, breathing heavily, his body weight squeezing the breath from her. She couldn't see with her woolens up over her face and everything below her waist felt cold and exposed. When he finally withdrew from her body, he pulled the woolens off her head and she found herself looking into his smiling face.

You did well, he said.

I did? She asked.

He nodded, pulling her woolens all the way down, helping her cover up.

I'll return for you, he promised. *I swear I'll return.*

When? She asked.

Very soon, he said. *By the next full moon, I shall return and I shall take you away.*

She believed him. He said he loved her, didn't he? They had known each other for years and although he was a little flighty, and saw in appropriate humor in situations where there was no humor to be had, she'd never known him to be a liar.

He'd return for her, he'd said. She clung to that belief until she received a missive from him two months later announcing his marriage to a French heiress and a relocation to his wife's estate in France. It was a blow beyond belief.

She would never see, or hear from him, again.

This is all my life is ever going to be, she thought dismally. Light, and love, had left her, and all she had left was a former shell of herself. The woman before Rhyne had promised her the world didn't exist any longer. All she would ever have, and all she would ever know, were the stone walls of the dreary abbey and a life of piety she surely deserved, for on top of being blindingly foolish about Rhyne's declaration of love, she had sinned as well.

She deserved everything the hell of St. Blitha brought her.

It was a hell that even the Devil would run from, but little did she know that God had taken pity upon her. He was about to send her help in the form of a man known as an Executioner Knight. A man who had sinned far worse than she could ever imagine.

It would be a chance meeting that would change her life forever.

PROLOGUE

Five months later
Year of our Lord 1200 A.D.
Caversham Manor, Berkshire
A demesne of William Marshal, Earl of Pembroke

IT HAD BEEN a very bad winter.

The sky was the color of pewter, creating casts of dark and shadowed doom upon the winter-dead landscape and bringing to bear all of the unsettled mood that was so prevalent across the country. A new king had taken the throne less than a year before and now, in this dead and colorless winter, the land reflected the soul of the people.

Dead and colorless since John ascended after Richard's unfortunate death.

But death was a part of life and those left behind were forced to deal with the aftermath. As William Marshal sat in the small but cozy solar of Caversham Manor, he could see the fire snapping and crackling before him but he swore he could not feel the heat.

All he felt was the cold of an uncertain future.

The Marshal's world was one of trouble these days and as his mind wandered through the vines and thorns of the complex news he had received earlier in the day, it made less sense now than the moment he had first heard it. In fact, the bearer of the news was seated beside him with a cup of watered wine in his hand and the air, though stagnant with the smell of smoke and stale rushes, was filled with tension.

Doom surrounded them.

William knew the deliverer of the information, a strong and true knight William had known for several years. There were few finer men in the world than Sir Gart Forbes. Forbes had spent the past several years traversing through France and the Teutonic princedoms, fighting for the very rich lords who could pay for his sword. He'd gone on Crusade with Richard, and he'd remained after the fall of Acre, trying not to get caught up in the battle between the western church and the eastern church. There was Rome, there was Constantinople, and then there was the ominous suggestion that the Holy Father, the Pope, was no longer satisfied with waging conflict against his brothers in the eastern empire. Now, he was turning his suspicious and shrewd eyes westward to England.

It was a horrifying thought. According to Forbes, rumors of pure madness were flying fast and furious along the Pilgrim Trail, along the roads that led from the east to the civilized west. Forbes, a man who knew many but called few friend, had come back to England after eight long years away bearing tales of such insanity that William was still having difficulty believing them. It wasn't as if he didn't have enough trouble these days, with the French king raising an army in an attempt to regain Normandy. In fact, William had been in the process of planning a return to Normandy when Forbes had appeared with his news. It had taken William all afternoon to swallow the information, digest it, and understand the validity of it. Now, the information was consuming him from the inside-out.

"I had forgotten how bitter the winters are in England," Forbes said quietly, breaking the stillness of the room. "I had become accustomed to warmth all year 'round."

William turned to him, smiling weakly. "You prefer the heat of the savage kingdom, do you?"

Forbes laughed softly. "It has its advantages."

William's yellowed eyes moved over Forbes; he was a big man with a shaved head, young and handsome. He was also darkened by the sun from his years away from England, his skin tan as a cow's hide.

"Mayhap," William finally said, sighing heavy and sitting forward in his chair, hoping to catch some of the heat from the crackling fire. "Gart, we must speak again on the information you delivered to me this afternoon."

"Aye, my lord?"

"You are certain that you heard this correctly?"

"Aye, my lord."

"Explain it to me again. I want to make sure I did not misunderstand you."

Forbes cleared his throat softly, almost nervously. He wouldn't look at William as he spoke, mostly because the news he had delivered to William Marshal had been received from a whore and Forbes was ashamed of the fact. Whores were not the most reliable of sources and for a knight of his status to have not only listened to the woman, but to have repeated her words, was somewhat shameful. But on the chance she was telling the truth, Forbes didn't want to be left with guilt for not having relayed her information.

"You did not misunderstand me, my lord," he said, lowering his voice. "I told you the truth of what I have heard. In fact, I have a witness to what I was told – Alexander de Sherrington was with me at the time. I am sure you know Sherry; he is one of the most elite and powerful knights I have ever known, and he became a good friend whilst we were in The Levant. We even traveled together for a while."

William nodded faintly. "I know Sherry," he said. "A frightening man, in fact. He is also something of a loner."

"He works alone for the most part."

"So do you."

"I do."

"But you say he was witness to this information? Where is he?"

Gart shook his head. "This I cannot know, my lord," he said. "We were together in Rome and then he left because someone in The

Lateran Palace, a high-ranking priest, paid him a princely some to eliminate an enemy. I've not seen him since."

William pondered that for a moment before flicking his wrist at Gart. "It is of no consequence," he said. "I believe what you have told me. I simply want to hear it again to make sure I understood correctly. A woman gave you this information, you say?"

Gart nodded. "A courtesan, my lord," he said. "A woman who is a favored of one of the Holy Father's advisors, a man by the name of Abramo. She told me that she had been warming the man's bed for two years. Others confirmed this to me."

"Others you trust?"

Forbes shrugged. "One was a papal knight," he replied. "Another was an old man who was a servant of the body to Abramo."

William looked at him, seriously. "I see," he said. "And whilst in Rome, you entertained this courtesan."

"I did."

"How did you meet the other two men who confirmed who she was?"

Forbes started to look nervous again. "I wanted to see her before I left Rome to return to England," he said, not wanting to admit he liked the woman because she was sexually clever and stimulating. "I went to the Lateran Palace where she said she lived to see if I could send a missive to her, to draw her out so that I could bid her farewell, and I was told by a papal guard that she was a favored of Abramo, a man close to the Holy Father. When the guard sent the missive inside the palace, the servant of the body returned to tell me that the woman belonged to Abramo and that I was forbidden further contact with her."

William was listening carefully, moderately satisfied with Forbes' explanation. "And it was of Abramo that the woman spoke."

Forbes nodded, seemingly impressed or overwhelmed, or both, by the news he bore. "Indeed," he replied. "She said the information regarding King Richard had come directly from Abramo."

"And she was certain?"

"She was certain that Abramo was certain, and the man was certain enough to act upon the information."

William sighed heavily, sitting back in his chair and gazing into the hypnotic flames. "So Richard Plantagenet had a liaison with a woman in Sicily when he wintered there ten years ago in route to The Levant," he muttered. "And from that liaison, a son was born."

"Aye, my lord."

"A lad that Lothar has in his custody."

William always referred to the pope by his birth name – Lothar of Segni. It was a sign of the animosity that William had long been part of, something that had eroded whatever inherent respect the position of the pontiff required. Especially in this situation, there was no respect – only the presence of an adversary.

A war was on the horizon.

"Aye, my lord," Gart replied.

As the news sank in, William rubbed wearily at his forehead. Even the second time around, the information still shocked him. "So now he has Richard's son," he muttered. "Worse yet, he plans to supplant John with Richard's offspring?"

Gart nodded, watching William for any sign of what the man's thoughts were on the matter. All he could see were veins throbbing on the man's temples. "According to the woman, Abramo told her that assassins were being dispatched to England to kill John," he said. "There is no love between John and Rome, my lord. If the Church rids England of John and then lays claim to the throne with Richard's son, then England ceases to become our country. It will become part of Rome."

William already knew this. He shook his head, exasperated. "Already this plan is madness because the boy is Richard's bastard," he pointed out. "They cannot lay claim on behalf of the boy."

Forbes sighed. "This I said, as well," he said, somewhat sadly. "However, the woman told me that the Holy Father is prepared to swear that Richard married the boy's mother, a minor noblewoman, prior to his marriage to Berengaria, and that the Holy Father personally performed the ceremony. The Holy Father intends to legitimize the boy's claim."

William looked at him, hints of horror crossing his weather features. "Is this really true, Gart?" he asked, almost pleadingly. "This is truly what you were told?"

Forbes nodded. "I swear this is what the woman told me, my lord," he said. "That is why I traveled in the dead of winter to reach you. This is something you must know. John, as much as we dislike the man, must be protected."

William rolled his eyes, rubbing at his head more forcefully now. "Great Bleeding Christ," he hissed. "John may be an undesirable king but at least his is the legitimate king and if there is to be any removing of the man, I would do it and not the fools in Rome. Do they really think they can get away with such a thing?"

Forbes shrugged. "It would seem that they intend to try," he said. "My lord, I cannot swear to you that what this courtesan told me was true, but we cannot take the chance that it is. In any case, John must be protected against those who seek to supplant him. My information is over a year old and if the Holy Father has already sent assassins to England's shores, then the king is in great danger. It is not simply a matter of protecting him; it is a matter of eliminating the assassins. Only when the threat is eliminated will the king, and the throne, be safe."

William knew that. But he also knew something more. "As long as that boy is alive, John will never be safe," he muttered. "It is the boy who must be eliminated as well, or at the very least, brought back to England and placed under protection so he can never again be a threat."

Forbes nodded faintly. "There are knights who will do such a thing, my lord."

"You?"

Gart shrugged. "I would be willing to go after the boy and bring him back to England," he said. "With the connections I made in Rome,

I am fairly certain I would be successful at getting my hands on him. As for the assassins trained on the king, however, you need men with a special set of skills for that task. Assassins are a different breed of men."

William was well aware of that particular fact but he still pushed for Forbes. "You are an excellent knight, Gart," he said. "You have returned to England with this information so your loyalty is unquestionable. Therefore, you should be the one to protect the king. You are called *Sach* when you are in the heat of battle, a term for madness. Who better to kill the king's assassins than someone like you?"

Forbes immediately shook his head. "I am at my finest in the chaos of a battle," he said. "But what you need are men who are well-versed in espionage and silent death. I am not silent about anything, my lord. As I said, you need men with special skills. You need assassins to kill the assassins."

William pondered that statement, which was true in any case. "Assassins to kill the assassins," he repeated. He stopped trying to push Forbes into the duty. "I know many fine men who would be up to the task but I will have to give the matter some consideration. The right men for the right job."

Forbes' gaze lingered on William a moment, his dark green eyes reflecting the firelight. "I know men who would be perfect for the task," he said quietly.

William glanced at him. "Who?" he asked. "Do I know them?"

Gart shrugged, returning his attention to the smoking hearth. "You might," he said. "They are men who were with me in the Holy Land over the past few years, men I trust with my life. But these men… they are not ordinary knights, my lord. They think like barbarians, fight like savages, and move as silently as a hawk. Whilst fighting Saladin, they were used by the Christian commanders as a strike force, as assassins against their enemies, and these men never once failed. Their reputation was so perfect that even the Holy Father heard of them and summoned the men to complete a task for him."

William was interested. "Who are these men? Are they English?"

Forbes nodded. "Aye," he said, eyeing William hesitantly a moment before continuing. "My lord, you may as well know the truth of the matter. When I came to tell you of the rumors of Richard's bastard son and what the Holy Father intends to do with him, it was with these men in mind to prevent such a thing from happening. They are my friends, men I trust, and men who are currently in a great deal of trouble. They need your help."

William's brow furrowed. "What do you mean?"

Gart's gaze grew intense. "I mean that the task the Holy Father summoned these men for was, in fact, the assassination of the English king," he said. "The Holy Father assumed these men could get close to the king because they were English themselves. In any case, the Holy Father ordered them to comply and when they refused, he arrested them and sold them to his allies, the Lords of Baux, where they are now prisoners at Les Baux de Provence. I tried to find out what I could about the state of their captivity, or if they were executed, and I was able to pay a Capetian soldier for information that leads me to believe the Lords of Baux intend to ransom my friends to other allies as captive fighters. They are very valuable warriors and will command a great price."

William was looking at Forbes rather strangely. "How did you discover all of this?"

Forbes lifted his eyebrows in a gesture that suggested the answer was complicated. "They are my friends," he said, repeating what William already knew. "Much like me, they have been traveling the world since the fall of Acre, fighting wars and doing unpleasant deeds for the highest bidder. It is that reputation that attracted the attention of the Holy Father. After he approached them with this mission, they were given a nominal amount of time to consider the task. In fact, they discussed it with me."

"But you advised against it, of course?"

Gart nodded. "I did, but they did not need much prodding," he said. "However, when they refused the mission, the Holy Father had them arrested and the next I heard that they had been moved out of Rome. It was in my determination to find out what had become of them did I come upon the courtesan who told me the story of Richard's bastard son and the plans to eliminate John and put the boy upon the throne. Then, and only then, did I realize the greater goal the Holy Father had in mind when he asked my friends to assassinate their king. I doubt my friends even knew the reasons behind the Holy Father' request. Men such as they are often given a task without the reason behind it."

It was a complex and convoluted story that only grew in depth and difficulty. Every time Gart opened his mouth, the story grew arms and legs and heads in all directions. It was truly astonishing. William, as seasoned and wise as he was, was still having difficulty comprehending it all but, as Gart spoke, the complexity began to form a pattern and the pieces began to fall into place. Things, as dark as they were, began to make sense. Aye, a great deal of sense and William was starting to see the situation, and the solution, just as Forbes was.

"And you have come to me to ask me to ransom your friends' freedom?" he asked.

Forbes nodded, sighing, as if a weight had been lifted off his shoulders. "I have, my lord," he said, relieved that William understood the point he was making. "They would be perfect for the task of eliminating John's assassins, whoever might come on behalf of the Holy Father. There was a name for these men among the Christian armies."

"What name is that?"

"The Unholy Trinity. Men known as the Executioner Knights."

William cocked an eyebrow. "A seemingly ominous moniker."

"They would make the perfect weapon."

William drew in a long, thoughtful breath, peppered by bouts of coughing. When the weather turned cold as it was, he often suffered issues with his lungs. Winters made him ill. He patted his chest to loosen the phlegm.

"Mayhap," he said, "but how long have they been prisoners?"

"At least nine months."

William sighed heavily. "Nine months in the vaults of Les Baux de Provence," he muttered. "I cannot imagine the hell of it. And even if they are still alive, the Lords of Baux may refuse my offer of ransom. We are not exactly allies."

"If you offer enough money, they will not refuse."

William cast him a side-long glance. "How much money do you speak of?"

Forbes pretended to think on the matter but the truth was that he had already arrived at a sum and a plan. He had an idea in mind. "The knights I speak of are Maxton of Loxbeare, Kress de Rhydian, and Achilles de Dere," he said. "The family of Loxbeare are major landholders in Devon and the House of de Rhydian controls much of the lands near Manchester. De Dere has rich holdings in York. The point is that I am quite sure they would be willing to pay for their sons returned and you would not be out any money in the matter."

The light of recognition went on in William's eyes. "I know Hugh de Rhydian and Magnus of Loxbeare," he said. "They are both friends and allies. *Their* sons, you say?"

"Aye."

William turned towards the half-open solar door and called for his man-servant, a valet who did everything from dress the man to write his missives. William could write, and do it well, but his joints ached when it was cold and made writing difficult. As the servant scuffled in, he motioned the man towards his large, cluttered desk.

"We have missives to send," he told them servant, a sense of urgency in his voice. Then, he turned to Gart. "It will take time to send the missives and receive a reply. If papal assassins are already in England, then it may be too late."

Forbes' angular face was serious. "It is possible," he said. "The last I saw my friends was close to a year ago. I then spent two months in Rome searching for them and then I traveled home to inform you of the news. There has been time for the Holy Father to hire more men to do the job."

William digested the information before moving swiftly into action. He could no longer linger on surprise or dismay, and he wasn't a man who was prone to inaction. His entire life was proof of that. Under his expert guidance, missives were soon being sent to Hugh de Dere and Magnus of Loxbeare, and both William and Forbes were heading to Winchester Castle where the king was in winter residence. The time for talk was over.

It was time to take action.

Regardless of how William felt about John personally, it was imperative that the man know of, and understand, the threat against him. But there was someone else who needed to know, someone more powerful than even John. William sent Forbes to personally deliver the news to Eleanor of Aquitaine who, upon receiving the information of the papal plot against her son, donated money to the ransom cause.

Eleanor did not want to lose yet another son and with hope presented, she would do what she could to preserve John's rule. The Marshal had a plan for John's survival and Eleanor was more than eager to support it. Eleanor even sent men to ride to the Lords of Baux, led by Gart Forbes himself, to deliver the ransom. Both she and William had decided that it would be much better to send the ransom under her banner because as so many knew, she and John were always in contention with each other and Eleanor was far more French than she was English. Therefore, her banners were more suitable when dealing with the Lords of Baux.

Seven weeks, four days, and sixteen hours after Forbes delivered the information on that cold and snowy night to William Marshall, Gart Forbes and a gathering of armed men bearing the standards of Eleanor of Aquitaine arrived at Les Baux de Provence with a chest of gold and silver marks and a request from Eleanor to deliver the three English knights in the fortress vaults to her custody.

The Great Lord of Baux, a greedy man named Estienne, happily agreed at the sight of so much coinage. His purpose had been to ransom the knights off, anyway, and if *la subvention Anglais reine* wanted to pay handsomely for these men, then Estienne would oblige her. The deal was struck and the three dirty, beaten, and weakened knights were purged from his vaults after months of captivity.

In truth, it had been a slick operation and one that Gart had been quite proud of. Finally, his friends had been released and were very quickly heading back to England, fearful that the Lords of Baux would change their minds. They rode very hard for weeks, in nasty weather and constant storms, only to take an old cog from Calais on one of the very few clear days they'd seen in all that time, a cog that headed straight for the white cliffs of Dover.

To the three English knights who never believed they'd ever see the light of day again, it was a beautiful sight. But their duties, as explained to them by Forbes over the course of their travels, somewhat dampened that joy. They hadn't simply been ransomed; they'd been ransomed with a purpose, a purpose that would be revealed when they met with William Marshal.

However, Gart had hinted at something ominous behind The Marshal's meeting, leaving the three knights wondering if remaining in the vaults of Baux would have been preferable. Gart wouldn't give forth any further information, and in the weeks leading up to The Marshal's meeting, Maxton and Kress and Achilles were feeling some trepidation.

With good reason.

Little did they know that the fate of a country would soon been placed in their hands.

The Executioner Knights would become England's only salvation.

CHAPTER ONE

London
Convent dedicated to St. Blitha of the Order of St. Dominica
North of the city walls, near Bishopsgate
Almost Three Months later

THE WALLS OF the old convent were ancient, hundreds of years old at the very least, and emitted an odor that smelled much like Time itself, something like dirt and mold and stagnant water. It was an odd scent, once that inevitably created a mood of both religious piety and the inherent doom.

This must be what sin smells like.

That was what the man thought as he stood just inside the door of the old convent, his eyes adjusting to the weak light. There was no furniture, a dirt floor, and the ceiling was low to accommodate the short nuns who inhabited the place.

For a man of normal height, the ceilings weren't so obliging – he'd already hit his head, twice, the last time being on a beam that smacked him straight on the forehead. The least bit frustrated, he simply stood in one place and wait. He'd come with a purpose and, low ceilings notwithstanding, he would accomplish what he'd been ordered to do.

But the wait became excessive and he was exhausted. Months of travel had seen to that, and with no place to sit, his legs were beginning to tremble. He also hadn't eaten in some time. Dirty, worn, and unkempt, he wiped his nose with the back of his hand as he wait for the Mother Abbess to make an appearance.

It was her he'd come to see.

But it was a woman who was evidently too busy to see him immediately or had no real desire to. The man with the ragged beard wasn't beyond charging through the convent looking for the woman; therefore, he hoped, for their sake, that the nun who had answered the door had genuinely gone in search of the abbess as instructed. Men like Alasdair Baird Douglas were not men to be trifled with; he'd killed his share of women right along with his share of men, and even though he was in a holy house, it made little difference to the career killer. If the Mother Abbess didn't show herself soon, he'd have to go looking for her and eliminate anyone who stood in his way.

Fortunately, his murder rampage was suspended when the little nun he'd sent to fetch the Mother Abbess returned with three women in tow. They were all wearing unbleached wool habits, heavy and uncomfortable, and the only thing showing was their faces. They all looked the same to him; small-featured, brown-eyed, and dull.

One of the women, rounder than the rest, gestured to the cold hearth in the chamber and one of the other sisters scurried over to it and began to prepare a blaze. Alasdair glanced at the woman kneeling next to the hearth but he didn't give her further regard; he was more interested in the women that were standing before him. He looked at the small nun whose features he recognized.

"Where is your Mother Abbess?" he asked.

The young nun pointed to the round woman who had ordered the hearth lit. "It is she."

Alasdair turned his full attention to the woman in white, now seeing that she was older than the others, her dark eyes sharp and glittering. She made her way towards him slowly, with a massive staff in one hand, like a walking stick, but heavy enough to beat a man to death. She was gazing back at him in an appraising manner.

"Are ye Seaxburga?" Alasdair asked.

The woman nodded, once. "I am the Mother Abbess of St. Blitha," she replied. "Who are you?"

Alasdair eyed the woman. "Do ye swear this?"

The woman cocked her head as if insulted by his question. "'Tis thou who has sought me," she said in a heavy accent that was not Scottish or even French. Alasdair had heard it before; it was Italian. "If thee does not believe I am who I say I am, then I shall bid thee a good day. Thou will leave."

Alasdair didn't move; he continued to regard the woman, carefully, as if trying to determine if she was truly Seaxburga, the woman he'd been told to deliver the missive to. He caught sight of another nun in his periphery, a woman who was simply passing by the room. She was slender and lovely, with a graceful neck and a pale, pretty face. She was a beautiful young woman who seemed oddly out of place in such a dark and dismal place, but Alasdair wasn't looking at her beauty. He was looking for confirmation.

He yelled to her.

"Ye!" he boomed. "Stop! Who is this woman?"

He was pointing at the Mother Abbess. The nun he had interrupted, now frozen fearfully where she had come to a halt, gazed apprehensively between the man who had yelled at her and the round woman in the fine robes. Annoyed at the delay, Alasdair boomed again.

"*Who* is this woman?" he demanded.

The interrupted nun jumped at the sound of his voice. "Our Gracious Mother!"

She fled. Alasdair turned back to the Mother Abbess, now satisfied that an independent source had confirmed the woman's identity. His annoyance in the situation in general seemed to ease.

"Ye will forgive me, yer ladyship," he said. "I bear a very important message. I did not want to give it to the wrong person."

The Mother Abbess wasn't so forgiving of his rude behavior. Her expression was unfriendly.

"What does thou have for me?" she asked. "And who has sent

thee?"

Alasdair didn't say a word. He simply presented her with a missive that he pulled out of his saddlebag, extending it to the enrobed woman. The Mother Abbess inspected the long, rolled parchment a moment before extending a hand, retrieving it. He held it very close to her eyes, for they were not very good these days, and inspected the dark red seal.

Recognition flickered.

Now, she was very interested in the man's appearance. Lifting her eyes from the missive, she hissed at the nuns standing around her, ordering them away. She even ordered the nun away who was just now starting the fire in the hearth. Smoke snaked into the room, filling the air with blue haze. As the infant blaze sparked and the nuns fled, the Mother Abbess took a step closer to Alasdair.

"The seal of the Holy Father is on this parchment," she said, her voice low.

Alasdair nodded. "I have just come from him," he replied. "He has sent me a very long way to bring you this missive."

The Mother Abbess' eyes narrowed suspiciously. "Why wouldst he send thee?" she asked. "The Holy Father has many men who serve him. Who art thee to him?"

"I am his servant," Alasdair said, sensing her distrust. "He sent me to England to deliver the missive because I know the country. I would know where to find ye."

"Thou art not English. Thou are clearly from Scotland."

Alasdair gave a weak smile. "I am," he confirmed, "but my mother is a *Sassenach*. I have spent my share of time here."

"Where?"

"In Lincoln."

The answer seemed to satisfy her for the moment. The Mother Abbess' gaze lingered on him before returning to the parchment in her hand. It was clear that she was curious, as well as concerned. Such suspicions made for an odd cast to her expression. After a slight hesitation, she broke the seal and unrolled the parchment, making her way over to the hearth as she did so in order that she might have some light to read by. Alasdair remained by the door.

The woman read quickly. She read it once and then read it again. Then, she simply stood there, seeming to read the missive in pieces. Mostly, her attention seemed to be focused on the latter part of it. She would read it over many times as Alasdair watched. Finally, she looked at him.

"Does thou know what this missive contains?" she asked, her voice sounding oddly strained.

Alasdair nodded. "Aye," he said honestly. "I am aware. The Holy Father and I have had many discussions about it."

The Mother Abbess smiled thinly, looking back to the parchment she held. "Prove this to me."

"It speaks of the death of the king."

The Mother Abbess grunted and lowered the parchment. "Thou speaks the truth," she said. "Does thou know what else it says?"

Alasdair came away from the door, his expression surprisingly pensive. "It speaks of the perfect weapon to create death."

"And you know what this perfect weapon is?"

Alasdair's dark eyes glimmered as he nodded faintly. "I do, indeed," he said. "Yer ladyship, William the Lion is my king. He has special favor with Rome. The Church of Scotland and Rome are allies. I was sent by William to Rome as an envoy and a gift of protection for the Holy Father. The Holy Father and Scotland have the same enemy in John, so we understand each other. Not only do I know the perfect weapon of death but I also know of the boy."

The Mother Abbess held up the parchment. "The boy spoken of here?"

"Aye."

"The son of *Coeur de Lion*?"

"Aye."

The Mother Abbess deliberated upon that information for a moment although it was difficult to know what she was thinking. The older woman had learned long ago to control her emotions and did so with skill. Reading her thoughts based upon her expression was nearly impossible.

"So he would supplant John with Richard's spawn," she finally murmured, turning back towards the fire. "He asks for my assistance in accomplishing this."

Alasdair nodded, again confirming what he already knew. "Indeed, Yer Ladyship," he said. "The Holy Father tried to hire *Sassenach* men to eliminate their king, but they refused. He knows that if he sends trained assassins, assassins from Rome or from France, that it will be difficult for them to get close to the king."

"Why?"

"Because the king is well-protected by English knights. English assassins would have made it much easier. If men of a different creed approach him, they will be immediately suspected for their difference. It will make their task far more difficult."

The Mother Abbess stood by the fire now, parchment in hand as she watched the building flame. "Then thou knows that I am that perfect weapon of death"

Alasdair nodded. "I do."

The Mother Abbess glanced side-long at him. "What he asks is an unsavory task."

Alasdair sensed her disapproval. "When he first told me of his plans, I was against it," he said. "Surely nuns canna be assassins. But the more I thought on it, the more brilliant the plan became. Ye will be the last person suspected as being an assassin. Yer ladyship, surely ye cannot have loyalty to the English king. Ye're not even English."

"I do not and I am not."

"But ye object to his death?"

The Mother Abbess returned her attention to the smoking hearth, clearly in conflict. She put a hand, plump, against the stone of the mantle as she gazed into the snapping flames. When the smoke would blow her way, moving in unseen drafts, she would move aside and wipe at her watering eyes.

"It is not a matter of objecting or agreeing," she said quietly. "It is simply a matter of doing what one is told to do. I came to St. Blitha many years ago. I was sent by the previous pontiff, as I was his younger sister, and when I came to St. Blitha, I became the Mother Abbess Seaxburga. I love my post. The Holy Father knows this; that is why he hast sent me such a missive. He will take all of this away from me if I do not do his bidding. He will ruin me, and I have worked too hard for what I have. All of this; it is mine. He has threatened to ruin me before, thou will understand. This is not the first time I have received such a directive from him."

Alasdair cocked his head; she spoke of her post as if it was a personal possession, something that had always and forever belonged only to her. But her last sentence had his particular attention.

"I dinna think so," he said. "It seemed tae me, when he spoke of ye, that he's used ye before."

The Mother Abbess nodded, unable to look at him. She was being reminded once again of her great sins of duty, sins that would never be fully cleansed.

"He has," she murmured.

"But... why you?"

Even if Alasdair was not shocked by killer nuns, there was curiosity there. Natural curiosity. She smiled thinly.

"Suffice it to say that he condemned my brother, the man who assumed the post before him," she said. "Any works my brother has done, the Holy Father has ruined them. To him, Celestine and the Orsini family, *my* family, are his greatest enemy. That includes me. What I do, I do to save myself and all that I have. I have built an empire here and I will not lose it. I *cannot* lose it."

Alasdair watched her closely. "So he gives ye orders and expects ye tae carry them out."

"He does."

"No matter how dirty the deed."

"No matter."

Alasdair was coming to understands the dynamics now, of this powerful Mother Abbess and her relationship with the pope. It was, truthfully, fascinating, and his curiosity was fed.

"Tell me," he said, his tone nearly pleading. "What has he asked of ye in the past? Something as grand as what is in the missive ye hold?"

The Mother Abbess lifted her slender shoulders. "Some would think so," she said. "The Bishop of Leeds spoke out against the Holy Father, many times, and went to Rome years ago on pilgrimage. He and the Holy Father evidently exchanged harsh words, enough so that the Holy Father could no longer tolerate his contentious presence. When the Bishop of Leeds traveled home again, the Holy Father instructed the man to seek respite during his travels at St. Blitha. The bishop arrived and when he came, he presented me with a missive from the Holy Father. Contained within the sealed parchment was the request from the Holy Father that I was to ensure the man did not make it home alive. When the bishop returned home, it was to his funeral."

Alasdair could sense great sorrow in the woman's words as well as resignation. "He asks and ye comply," he said. "Now he asks ye tae complete an even larger task."

The Mother Abbess nodded her head, wearily. Then, she tossed the parchment into the hearth and watched it catch fire. She could not leave such a missive intact, for obvious reasons.

"There is no choice in the matter," she said. "The Holy Father wishes for my sisters and I to rid England of its king and that is what we shall do. To supplant this boy upon the throne will mayhap be for the best. A young lad who will be pious and loyal to the church will be best for us all."

Alasdair could see that she was trying to rationalize the terrible directive, as a woman with no choice at all. "No one will ever suspect nuns as a danger to John," he said. "Ye will be able to get close to him, to serve him, and carry out your task."

The Mother Abbess watched as the parchment burned brightly,

going up in flames much as she felt her soul was going up in flames. "Simple enough, I suppose," she said. "The king comes to St. Blitha for her feast day. He has come the past three years, in fact, because St. Blitha is the patron saint of hunters and wine, among other things, and the king considers himself quite the hunter. There is a great feast and it would be a small thing to poison the man's wine as he takes his confessional. Ironic, really."

Alasdair watched the woman closely as if to make sure she was indeed planning on carrying out the Holy Father' orders. There was still something in her manner that was hesitant, as if divulging a great weakness, causing him to distrust her intentions.

"Ye will see to it?" he pressed. "I will send a messenger back to Rome with the news that the Holy Father' missive was received. He will know that you read and understood his directive."

The Mother Abbess turned to look at him, her dark eyes somehow darker and more hollow. It was the evil she was assuming that created the hollowness within her, hollowness reflected in her gaze.

The evil within.

"Tell him what you will," she said. "I will not fail."

Alasdair simply nodded even though he had his doubts. Would she be strong enough to do it? Would he be forced to step in and force her hand? He wondered. Alasdair suspected it would be a good idea to remain in London, close to the Mother Abbess, to ensure the Holy Father' orders were carried out. Women were weak, after all, especially when it came to matters of death.

Alasdair would ensure that the Mother Abbess didn't fail.

Silently begging his leave, Alasdair left the convent and headed towards the city proper where he could find lodgings for the night. Come the next day, he intended to hire a messenger that would return to Rome with a missive meant for the Holy Father, one that assured the man this his directives for the King of England would come to fruition.

If Alasdair had anything to say about it, they certainly would.

CHAPTER TWO

London
The Crowned Lion Inn
South of the Thames in Southwark

THE FIST CAME flying at Gart but, with his cat-like agility, he was able to dodge it. Instead, it hit the man behind him, who went sailing back onto the railing of the staircase. Rickety old wood that had seen far too much use and not enough maintenance creaked, groaned, and finally gave way under the weight. Everything splintered and the hapless tavern patron fell back in a heap of rotted wood and embarrassment.

Gart didn't stop to help the man because fists, and weapons, were now coming forth at his expense. They were after him and his three companions, one of which had the propensity of getting fights like this started. Battles were never far off when Achilles de Dere was around because, inevitably, the sometimes tactless and always bold knight would say or do something that triggered an explosion of aggression.

Like now.

Now, they were in the thick of it.

"Behind you!" Gart shouted to Achilles.

The enormous knight was wise enough to throw himself forward, down and away from whatever Forbes was warning him about. It turned out to be a man with a broadsword who sliced it over Achilles's head, barely missing the man.

Infuriated, Achilles regained his footing and lashed out a big boot, catching his attacker in the belly. With a grunt, the man fell backwards and Achilles went after him, all fists and fury. Gart shoved away another accoster by the face, nearly breaking the man's neck, as a big blond knight ended up beside him.

"Now what?" Kress de Rhydian asked, elbowing a man in the nose who came too close to him. "How in the hell did this get started? My back was turned on a game of chance and suddenly Achilles is standing up, throwing a man across the room."

Gart grunted, unhappy, as he watched Achilles pound a big, well-dressed merchant in the face. "He was speaking with that man's daughter," he said, pointing to Achilles and his victim.

Kress scowled at the pair. "The man currently being beaten with in an inch of his life?"

"Aye, the same."

Kress shook his head, exasperated. "Was he foolish enough to throw a punch at Achilles?"

Gart sighed. "He ordered one of his men to do it," he replied, "and the rest is as you see. Utter chaos."

Kress' jaw ticked as he watched Achilles kick the half-conscious merchant aside when one of the man's guards hit him across the shoulders with a chair. The chair splintered but Achilles did not; it simply made him madder. It was like pulling the tail of the bull.

"Christ," Kress hissed. "We must remove him from this place before the entire tavern is turned on-end. You know how he can be."

"Aye, I know how he can be."

"He will destroy everything in his path."

"He will, indeed."

Kress began looking around for the fourth man in their party, spying him over near the hearth in what appeared to be an oddly peaceful conversation with an older man, perhaps a traveler or merchant of some kind. In the midst of the chaotic room, the quiet conversation seemed out of place.

"Look at Max," Kress said, pointing to their companion at the other end of the rumbling room. "He does not have a care in this world."

Gart spied their companion as well. "He certainly is not afraid of conversation," he replied. "He has done this ever since we left Baux, speaking with strangers in taverns, on the road, in churches… I have never known Maxton of Loxbeare to be so interested in the rabble of the world. Now, instead of helping Achilles, he is casually conversing."

Kress's blue-eyed gaze lingered on Maxton as the man lifted his hands to emphasize a point, chatting away. Kress opened his mouth to reply but another victim of Achilles's rage stumbled past him, almost bashing into him, and Kress angrily pushed the man away, right back into Achilles's orbit, where he was subsequently pummeled to the ground. Kress then continued his conversation with Forbes as if nothing out of the ordinary had just happened.

"Max was oddly quiet during our time in captivity," he told Gart. "Do you recall that I mentioned this to you? He rarely spoke and when he did, it was oddly philosophical, as if the man was reliving his life and trying to figure out where he had gone wrong. Do you see these people he speaks with? Merchants, holy men, anyone who seems intelligent or well-read. Somehow, someway, Max is re-thinking the sins of his life. It is my opinion that now that we are freed, he believes he has a second chance to right the wrongs he has committed."

Gart's focus was also lingering on Maxton off in the corner of the smelly, smoky, and noisy room. "He cannot change his life," he said. "He cannot erase the past and the man is known for the strength of his sins as well as the strength of his accomplishments. The Marshal has a task for the three of you and Max is an important part of that equation. Has he mentioned to you that he does not wish to agree to The Marshal's terms?"

Kress shook his head. "He has not mentioned anything to me," he replied. "But, then again, we do not know all of it. Mayhap when we do, he shall voice his resistance."

"If he does, then William Marshal will send him back to the Lords of Baux, not to mention what Eleanor will do to him when she discovers her money has been wasted."

"I would fear Eleanor more than William."

"As would I."

Achilles, now bored with his fight because every man involved in it was now either unconscious or fleeing, rubbed at his bruised knuckles as he made his way back over to Kress and Gart. There were at least a dozen men picking themselves off of the tavern's dirt floor but when Achilles de Dere was involved in a fight, that was the normal aftermath. Achilles had no problem single-handedly taking on more men than he could count on his fingers and toes, or at least he boasted that fact. He was mostly right and no one had the courage to argue with him. A fight with Achilles de Dere was a difficult fight to win.

"Foolish whelp," Achilles muttered as he came to stand with Kress and Gart. "No man will accuse me of sullying his daughter when all I was doing was talking to the girl. And she was not all that attractive to begin with."

Kress simply shook his head, resigned, as Gart spoke. "You have made a mess out of the place," he observed, watching as the merchant was being helped to his feet by his plain-featured daughter. "Mayhap it would be wiser for us to wait outside for The Marshal. I do not want him to see the state of this room and think we are men without control."

Achilles looked puzzled as Gart and Kress turned away from him, heading back to their table to collect their possessions. "What do you mean without control?" the big knight wanted to know, trailing behind them through the up-turned tables. "I have perfect control. Moreover, we have not eaten yet and I am starving. I am not leaving before I have been fed."

Gart was collecting his saddlebags. "We will eat somewhere else," he said. "The tavern keeper will more than likely poison our food and wait until we are dead to steal from us to pay back the damage you have done to his tavern. I will not be robbed by a vengeful innkeeper."

Achilles was frowning greatly, but in a way, he understood. He, too, began to collect his bags.

"I would not die easily," he insisted. "It would take a lot of poison to kill me."

Kress snorted. "Do you care to test that theory?"

"I do not."

"Then pick up your bags and let us move on."

"But what about Marshal?"

"I shall have to send word to him that we have moved to another tavern. He can find us there."

Achilles slung his saddlebags over his broad shoulder, well-used and repaired bags that had been purchased second-hand from an old French smithy when they had left Baux-de-Provence. He didn't like them, but he didn't have the money, as of yet, to purchase finer. All of his possessions, including his fine horses and weapons, had been confiscated by forces loyal to the pope when they had been arrested last year. Achilles, much like Kress and Maxton, hoped to one day be outfitted to reflect their quality and status once again. Right now, all three of them looked like paupers.

"Max," Kress hissed to his friend in the corner. "Let us depart."

Maxton of Loxbeare was what most women would call deliciously formed. With dark hair and deep blue eyes, he was square-jawed and handsome. He was also aloof for the most part, at least towards women, and could be aloof towards men as well, which was why his sudden change in nature over the past several months had seemed so strange to his friends. Maxton was a complex man at best, but he was also extremely brilliant and an infallible commander, which made him something of an odd character. When the man heard Kress' call, he turned to look at him with a complete lack of concern.

"Why?" he asked. "My business is not yet complete here."

Kress grunted, displeased with the denial, as he looked to Gart for support. Forbes fixed on of Loxbeare.

"Your business is our business, and our business is outside of this tavern," he told the man in a tone that was not meant to be contested. "Gather your things, Loxbeare. We must depart."

Maxton eyed Gart a moment, simply to convey that he was not so easily ordered about, before finally rising from his chair and moving back to their table where his worn saddle bags lay across the wooden surface. Gart and Kress were already moving for the tavern door, a warped panel that was barely able to close. They were nearly to the door when it abruptly pushed back and blinding white light from late afternoon filtered in. Gart actually staggered back, momentarily blinded, as a well-armed man entered the tavern.

For the Executioner Knights, their moment of destiny had finally arrived.

CHAPTER THREE

"FORBES," WILLIAM MARSHALL greeted, amused when Gart stumbled back and tripped down a step, down onto the dirt floor of the tavern. "You looked quite staggered to see me. I was unaware my presence had such an impact on you."

Grinning, Gart blinked his eyes, as the light from the open door was still bright. "Always, my lord," he said seriously. "You cause me to stumble every time I see you."

William chuckled, noticing that Gart was with three other very large men. Knights, he assumed, although they weren't wearing any protection and a quick perusal of their weaponry showed it sorely lacking. He pointed to Kress, who was the closest man next to Gart.

"Introduce me to your companions, Gart," he said, inspecting Kress from the top of the man's blond head to the bottom of his enormous feet. "I would assume this is either of Loxbeare or de Dere or de Rhydian."

Gart nodded, turning to indicate Kress. "My lord, meet Sir Kress De Rhydian," he said. "You have never met a man more deadly with a sword."

William cocked an eyebrow at the knight. "We shall see," he said vaguely, throwing a finger in the direction of an empty table over near the front windows of the tavern. "Let us retreat away from the entry so our business is not heard by the entire world."

So much for them leaving the tavern to find another, less-hostile place. Gart simply followed William as the man headed for an empty table over near the front window.

"As you wish, my lord," he said. "But truthfully, we were not expecting to see you until tonight."

William waved him off. "We made excellent time with our travel," he said, glancing over his shoulder at the men following him. "If the big blond man is de Rhydian, then the other two must be Loxbeare and de Dere."

They had reached the table, which was empty except for a small man sleeping at one end of it. As The Marshal's men roused the man and chased him away, the group began to collect their seats. Gart indicated Maxton, who was closest to him.

"This is Sir Maxton of Loxbeare," he said, "and the tall brute is Sir Achilles de Dere."

As Maxton and Achilles acknowledged William with a nod of the head, Gart made a point of not introducing The Marshal by name because he didn't want anyone else in the room to hear the introduction. Already, they were conducting their business out in the open and he was uncomfortable, but William didn't seem to be particularly concerned. He'd brought about twenty heavily armed men with him inside, men who fanned out through the room, so that William on the inside was well protected.

As they settled around the old, worn table, William wasn't thinking about his men, or the tavern, or anything else for that matter. His attention was entirely upon the three knights he had just been introduced to.

He'd been waiting a long time for this moment.

"Loxbeare," he said to the bearded knight with the dark eyes. "I know your father well. He is quite thrilled to have you home."

Maxton nodded faintly. "That seems strange, my lord, considering I have not spoken with my father in almost fifteen years."

William could immediately sense a serious, if not somewhat morose, man beneath the hulking exterior. He wasn't quite sure how to respond to what seemed to be a family issue so he simply overlooked it. "Your father is a fine man," he said politely, turning his attention to the big blond knight who had been more congenial. "De Rhydian, is it? You must be an excellent knight if you are keeping company with Loxbeare and de Dere."

Kress smiled, lop-sided. "I have allowed them to keep company with *me*, my lord," he said arrogantly. "I would have hoped they have learned something from me by now."

William grinned; he liked a man with confidence. His attention finally came to rest on Achilles, the tallest of the group. He also looked to be the youngest with his smooth face and bright eyes, but from his weathered neck and hands, it was clear that he was much older than he appeared. Then William noticed the bloodied knuckles on the man and he couldn't help but notice that the common room of the tavern had seen some serious upheaval. He motioned to the room before them.

"Was there some trouble here?" he asked.

Gart, trying to appear entirely ignorant, lifted his eyebrows questioningly. "Why would you ask?"

William gave Gart a rather wry expression. "I entered the tavern as you four were fleeing," he said. "The room has been wrecked. What did you do?"

Gart held a serious expression for a few moments longer before being unable to do so. He cracked a smile, looking at Kress and Achilles, who were also grinning. Kress was shaking his head in exasperation. No one seemed willing to answer so Maxton was the one to finally speak.

"Achilles created a ruckus as only Achilles is capable of doing," he said calmly. "But surely you do not wish to speak about a brawl in a tavern, my lord. Your presence here represents something far more important than a knight's fight, so we would appreciate it if you would simply get on with it."

William turned to the serious, even blunt, knight. "Indeed, I will," he agreed. His attention was drawn to the man; he couldn't quite put his finger on what was wrong, but there was something behind Maxton's stormy eyes that made him appear quite edgy. Unstable, even. It was something William would have to watch. "I have come to see the three men who were ransomed with a good deal of money. I have come to ensure that you understand *why* you were ransomed."

Gart, seeing that William was having some difficulty with Maxton's seemingly hard attitude, cleared his throat softly. "I have informed them why they were ransomed, my lord," he said quietly. "They know that they have been returned to England to do a job."

"But you have not told them *what* job."

"Nay, my lord. That should come from you. We have been two months upon the road home, so you will forgive us is tempers are short and we are weary in general. Proceed as you will. They are ready to hear it."

He sounded as if he was making excuses for Maxton's behavior, which he was. William didn't like that and especially not coming from Gart. Forbes was not a man given to apologies. His gaze, intense and appraising, looked over the three knights seated at his table. The room around them was starting to show signs of life again as the tables were righted and patrons settled down again, but William didn't notice. He was only focused on the men before him.

"You know that you have been ransomed for a purpose," he said. "But hear me now; I will inform you of your purpose from my own lips and you will understand the situation as it stands. Firstly, let me be plain – you three now belong to me. I have ransomed you and you are therefore in my service. Is this in any way unclear?"

Kress and Achilles shook their heads, with Maxton responding a split second later. William continued. "Excellent," he said. "Now, I wish to discuss your reputation in The Levant. It is my understanding that the three of you carried out, shall we say, unsavory tasks for the Christian commanders. Is this true?"

Again, Maxton was the one to nod. When dealing with the three of them, it was always Maxton who spoke for the group. "We did as we were told, my lord," he said. "There was nothing more to it."

William cocked an eyebrow at the man. "I would hope there is a great deal more to it," he said. "I was also told that once you left The Levant, you found lords in France and Saxony and beyond who would also pay you for those particular skills."

"A man must make money the best way he can, my lord."

"Forbes tells me that you three are known as the Executioner Knights for your skill as assassins and spies."

The three men looked at Gart who gazed steadily back at them. It was clear he wasn't going to elaborate on what he'd already told William; he expected the men in question to do it. After a moment, Kress pursed his lips and looked at his lap whilst Achilles stretched his long arms over his head and leaned back in his chair, unwilling to answer. Only Maxton was left to respond, once again.

They would leave the explaining to him.

"All men have their strengths and weaknesses, my lord," Maxton said, his voice somewhat quieter. "Ours happens to be stealth, strength, and utter fearlessness. We work well as a team. We did as we were told and we accomplished our mission."

"No matter how unpleasant?"

"No matter, my lord."

"Your feelings do not come to bear?"

"Not in any case, my lord. They never have."

William could see that. He was coming to understand something else, too – when Loxbeare spoke, there was no boastfulness. Either he was being modest, or he was simply unwilling to elaborate on their reputation. William suspected it was the latter; assassins usually did not live long if they bragged over their accomplishments. He understood their position all too well.

Therefore, he sat forward on the old table, motioning the knights nearer. For what he was about to say, he didn't want to shout. As the three men leaned forward to listen, William eyed Gart, unspoken words passing between them; Gart would keep an eye out for anyone trying to listen to their conversation. As Gart sat back in his chair, far enough to keep on the alert but still close enough to hear the conversation, William began.

"You will answer me truthfully, in all things, or I shall send you back to the Lords of Baux without hesitation," he said in a tone that suggested utter, complete compliance. "I've no time for foolishness or lies. Do you understand?"

The three men nodded.

"Swear upon your honor," William said.

They did, in unison, and William continued. "I understand that you had an encounter with Lothar on your return from The Levant. Confirm this to me."

Lothar. Sitting on the right hand of The Marshal, the mere mention of the name caused Maxton to stiffen somewhat. He knew that William was referring to the pope by his birth name – *Lothario*. Rather than address the man by his proper title, he was using a casual reference and Maxton knew it was because of the ongoing war between the pope and the king of England. There was little to no respect there, long gone to dust in the constant embattlement between John and the Catholic Church.

Even so, now that the name of the Holy Father had been brought forth, the light of why he and Achilles and Kress had been ransomed by William and Eleanor of Aquitaine was beginning to flicker in Maxton's mind, and not in a good way. In truth, perhaps he'd always suspected, but now, he was receiving confirmation of it.

There was only one explanation – that they knew of the offer made from the Holy Father to the Executioner Knights. Maxton didn't know how they knew, but they did. He found his eyes flicking to Gart as the man sat there, alert and silent. But Gart wasn't looking at him and Maxton began to grow suspicious; perhaps Gart had told The Marshal, but how did Gart find out about the offer? Maxton had never told him and on their trip home from Baux, the subject of The Lateran Palace, or the pope, or anything else religious had never really come up. Perhaps that was because Gart had already known, and he'd been leading the three knights home to face an interrogation about it.

That had to be it.

Maxton was instantly on his guard.

"I will confirm it," he said after a moment. "But if you know that, then you also know that the very encounter was the reason we were prisoners of the Lords of Baux."

"I want to hear it from you."

Maxton wasn't comfortable speaking about a situation that had impacted him and his friends intensely, but he had little choice. His suspicions were growing, and he was coming to wonder if there weren't a hundred crown troops outside of the tavern, all of them awaiting a signal from The Marshal to come charging in and puncture him to death. If William knew he'd met with the pope, then he probably knew why. Even though the offer had been made in the strictest confidence, something like that wouldn't remain a secret forever. Men talked.

With that thought lingering on his mind, Maxton proceeded carefully, trying not to look like a man who was pleading his case.

But he was.

"Much as you have heard of our reputation, so had the Holy Father," he said, his voice so low that it was coming out as a growling whisper. "When we reached Rome on our journey back to England, an Italian knight we had become acquainted with during our time in The Levant spoke of a papal directive of a most secretive kind. It would seem that the knight had a cousin in The Lateran Palace, and the Holy Father had been looking for good English knights for a special mission. Our friend, the Italian knight, had mentioned what he knew of us to his cousin, who in turn told the Holy Father. We were evidently what the Holy Father was looking for, and we were brought to The Lateran Palace. When were deemed trustworthy, we met with the Holy Father himself."

William was listening intently. "Just like that? Was it so easy, then, to have an audience with Lothar?"

Maxton's lips twitched with an ironic smile. "Nay, it was not so easy as all that," he said. "We spent months in Rome, being seduced by those in The Lateran Palace and all they could provide us. Wine and woman, and even money. We lived like kings. When it was determined we were loyal enough to the Holy Father, we were summoned to speak with him. But it took time."

William sighed faintly, digesting the situation. "Why did you remain, then? Purely for the fact that you were being spoiled with food and comfort?"

Maxton lifted his big shoulders. "Nay," he said, "although I will admit that after the hell of The Levant, it was a welcome change. We remained because we were intrigued by whispers of large sums of money and property that the Holy Father was willing to pay for a most important task. Call it a mercenary intention if you must, but we had a purpose in remaining. It wasn't simply hedonism."

William's eyes glittered as he looked at him. "All men have a mercenary heart," he said. "It is the one thing every man has in common, if nothing else. So… you remained where you were pampered and spoiled, waiting for an offer of a task with great rewards. When you finally met with Lothar, what did he ask of you?"

Maxton didn't hesitate. "To kill the king."

"John?"

"Aye."

"And you refused?"

Maxton snorted. "That was why you found us in the possession of the Lords of Baux," he said. "We refused to assassinate our own king and the Holy Father took exception to that. So that his offer to us would not become public knowledge, he threw us into the vault and then sold us off to the Lords of Baux, who had never made it clear what they intended to do with us. The garrison commander at Baux-les-Provence, who became friendly with us because he hated his lord with a passion, told us that we were to be ransomed back to our families, but that never materialized."

William absorbed what he was being told. It was everything Gart had told him and more. "Did Lothar tell you *why* he wanted John removed?"

Maxton shook his head. "He did not," he said flatly. "But he offered us enough riches to buy our own army if we took to the task. My lord, it is well-known that John and the Holy Father are in contention with each other. That has never been a secret, so if I am made an offer to remove my king, I do not question it. But no reason given could be worthy enough for such a task. He may be a weak king, but he is the only one England has. He has his mother's powerful backing, and I would rather see him on the throne than one of his brother's children. A child upon England's throne would be an invitation for disaster."

They were astonishing and astute words. William stared at him a moment before finally shaking his head in a wry, and even foreboding, gesture.

"More than you know," he muttered. "But that is exactly why Lothar wanted you to remove John. To put a child upon the throne."

Maxton's eyebrows lifted as Kress and Achilles sat closer, now completely wrapped upon in the conversation. "A child?" Maxton repeated. "Who? Arthur? God, don't tell me he wants that lad for the throne. He is controlled by Phillip, the French king. Why would the Holy Father want a French-controlled king on the throne?"

William shook his head quickly. "He does not," he said. Then, he lowered his voice, his yellowed eyes fixed on Maxton. "There is another."

An expression of confusion washed over Maxton's face. He glanced at Kress and Achilles, who appeared equally perplexed. Seeing their reactions, Maxton returned his focus to William.

"Of whom do you speak?" he asked. "Who else is there?"

Their confusion was evident, telling William that everything Maxton had told him was the truth. They truly didn't know the motive behind the pope's request. With that realization, William sighed heavily before proceeding.

"Richard wintered in Sicily ten years ago in route to The Levant," he said grimly. "Whilst there, he had a liaison with a nobleman's daughter and a son was born. That child is now in the possession of Lothar and he plans to eliminate John and place Richard's own son upon the throne. He is prepared to swear that the child's mother was married to Richard, thereby rendering his marriage to Berengaria null. He will make the boy Richard's legal heir and the hereditary king of England."

Maxton stared at him. In fact, they were all staring at him, every man at the table other than Gart, who was still being alert for anyone else listening to the conversation. But the lull became extended enough that Gart finally looked to the table, seeing the shock on the faces of Maxton, Kress, and Achilles.

"This news you hear comes from me," Gart said quietly, watching three sets of astonished eyes turn to him. "I received the information from a man very close to the Holy Father."

Maxton wasn't over his shock. "Who?"

"Abramo."

That brought a reaction from Maxton. "I know this man," he said. "He is the right hand to the Holy Father. In fact, I would say that he controls those in the church even more than the Holy Father does. He is a sinister man who wields great power."

"And this information comes from him," Gart emphasized. "They wanted English knights to assassinate John because it was felt that Englishmen could get closer to the king than a foreign warrior. *That* is what they wanted of you, Max. They wanted you to remove John from the throne so they could put Richard's bastard upon it."

Maxton didn't think he could be any more astonished than he already was, but he was wrong. It was a massive plot and the more he pondered it, the more astounded he became.

"And I refused," he muttered. Then, his sharp gaze moved quickly between Gart and William. "But I would wager to say that was not the end of it. They would simply make the offer to someone else."

William nodded, seeing that Maxton was coming to fully understand the situation now. "And they have," he said, "but we do not know who it is. That is where you come in, why we have ransomed you. It will take men of your particular talents to prevent the assassins from reaching the king. In fact, I would suspect whomever has been charged with that task is already here, in England."

Maxton frowned. "But surely the king has enough guards of the body," he said. "You do not need us to protect the king."

"Nay, not protect," William said. "But you think like assassins because you are assassins. It will take men like you to find whoever Lothar managed to send and prevent them from completing their mission. Every dirty act you've ever committed, and every brutal thought you've ever entertained, has created a skill set in you that no one else has. Do you understand me, Loxbeare? You must find these men before they can get to the king. *That* is why you have been ransomed – this is a job that only you can do."

Now, Maxton did indeed understand everything and the entire situation made perfect sense. All of it. He looked at Kress and Achilles, seeing the same understanding in their eyes. Their purpose was made clear now and, not strangely, Maxton felt some relief. When he'd thought he'd been brought here to be interrogated about the popes' offer, the meeting turned out to be something altogether different. In fact, now that the truth was known, he felt some enthusiasm for the task. This was different from what he was usually called upon to do and there was some relish in that challenge.

Assassins finding assassins...

"You are correct," he said after a moment. "This is a job that only we can do. And you are also correct in that whomever the Holy Father managed to coerce into this task is probably already in England. I am surprised they have not yet made an attempt on the king, in fact. Have you made John's commanders aware of this threat?"

William shook his head. "Nay," he said, "but after this meeting, Windsor is my destination. John has just arrived from Winchester and he is expecting to see me, so before this night is out, John and his men shall know of this threat. And they shall also know that we have the best men for the job to prevent it."

Maxton agreed with him with a slight nod of his head; he could feel his confidence surging, the taste of a deadly game upon his tongue. It was a familiar flavor. But he knew a great deal of this game and it was important he speak of it to William. The man had to understand, too, that this was no ordinary task.

The stakes were too high.

"I must stress that John must do nothing differently," he said. "If he does anything out of the ordinary, or goes into hiding, whomever the Holy Father has sent will know that something is amiss – he will realize that John knows of the plot. Therefore, in order to catch these men, we need to draw them out, and we can only do that if John maintains his usual schedule."

William was nodding before Maxton finished speaking. "I am aware," he said. "I will ensure that the king does nothing differently, but you must come up with some manner of plan to catch these assassins, Loxbeare. You simply cannot prowl London hoping to run into them at some point."

Maxton smiled thinly. "Unfortunately, that is part of the job," he said. "We will indeed be combing London for information, but it will be for the purpose of formulating a plan. And we will need a base in London, somewhere to stay whilst we work."

William waved a hand. "Not to worry," he said. "You may stay at Farringdon House, near Aldersgate. It is a home that belonged to my mother, and my wife hates it because it is more fortress than home, so my men and my allies stay there when they are in London. It is place of knights and everyone knows it. You have use of it and whatever else you need."

Maxton glanced at his clothing. "I fear we need decent weapons and clothing," he said. "We cannot go on a hunt looking as paupers."

William nodded sharply. "Gart shall get you everything you need," he said. Then, he pointed a finger at Maxton. "But there is no time to waste. Get what you need and be quick about it. John is in London because he has called a meeting of his marcher lords, and I intend to be part of that meeting."

"Marcher lords?" Maxton repeated. "Is there trouble in Wales, then? Is that what has been happening since we have been in The Levant?"

William shook his head. "Nothing so dramatic," he said. "John has a surprisingly good relationship with the Welsh, but there are the usual things to discuss. It is a country always on the brink of rebellion, so he has called for his marcher lords. Christopher and David de Lohr shall be there, as well as the Lords of the Trilaterals, the de Laras. They should be all converging on London as we speak."

A flicker of recognition crossed Maxton's features. "The de Lohr brothers will be here?"

"I take it you know them?"

Maxton thought on the two men he'd known for twenty years or more, men who were essential for the control of the country. He'd fought with them, and killed for them, and had been allied with them for a very long time. But their relationship hadn't always been a good one; Maxton had a love/hate relationship with Christopher even in the best of times, and when the men had all served in The Levant together, Christopher and David had taken the path of glory at Richard's side while Maxton and Kress and Achilles had found themselves embroiled in the dirty dealings of the Christian commanders.

Perhaps there was a part of Maxton that had resented the de Lohr brothers and their righteous path to glory, and there had been contention between them because of it, but the truth was that Maxton's contention with Christopher in particular had old roots, indeed. The noble and honorable Christopher compared to the sly and ruthless Maxton. Maxton had watched Christopher soak up the adulation at times while Maxton remained in the shadows, doing the dirty work.

He was still doing the dirty work.

"Aye, I know them," he finally said. "Do Christopher and David know of this plot against John?"

William shook his head. "No one does," he said. "But I intend to tell them. They are trustworthy. And we may need their assistance, so it is better if they know."

Maxton couldn't disagree with him, but he had a point to make. "Tell them if you must, but I will not tolerate any interference from them. Chris was Richard's champion and he may feel as if his greatness is needed in this situation as well. You will tell him that is not. For what I must do, I do not need a de Lohr."

There was some animosity as he spoke, cluing William in on the fact that although Maxton knew Christopher, there was evidently no love lost there. But he wouldn't ask about it; he didn't care, anyway. He was more focused on Loxbeare and ensuring the man had his full confidence to do the job tasked to him.

"De Lohr will not interfere," he assured him. "In any case, I shall return to Farringdon in a day or two, and I shall expect to hear of your plan for the king. Is this clear?"

Maxton took him at his word when it came to de Lohr, making it easier for him to return his focus to the task ahead of him. "It is, my lord."

There was respect in his tone, not missed by William. "Excellent," he said. "Now that you have your duty, you will excuse me to go about mine."

Without another word, he excused himself and headed out of the tavern with his men in tow, leaving Maxton, Gart, Kress, and Achilles still seated at the table. It was true that a hint of shock still lingered among them, and perhaps the slightest bit of intimidation of the job ahead of them. It was an extremely important one, perhaps more important than anything they'd ever done. But they would not fail.

They *could* not.

"Well?" Maxton said, breaking the silence. "It seems we have a task to complete."

Gart, who had remained largely silent and observant throughout the conversation with William, could hear the confidence in Maxton's tone and it was both surprising and pleasing. The man he'd just spent the past few months with had lacked that tone in his voice; even Kress had commented about it. *Max was quiet during our months in captivity, and when he did speak, he was oddly philosophical.* If Gart hadn't known any better, he would think that Maxton was beginning to question everything he'd ever known, his very existence, in fact. Gart had witnessed the change in the man, but in just a short conversation with William Marshal, Gart didn't sense that change from Maxton any longer.

That confidence was much more like the man he knew.

Perhaps it was because the man had a purpose now, or perhaps it was because he was feeling useful again. Months in captivity could damage a man's soul, but Maxton was strong. Perhaps all of the quietness had been his way of dealing with the situation and nothing more. It didn't seem to matter now, whatever the reason, because Gart could see glimmers of the Maxton he knew before him.

A man who would get the job done or die trying.

He hoped it didn't come to that.

CHAPTER FOUR

London
Inside the city walls, near Bishopsgate

SHE WAS STARVING.

It was just before dawn on the dark, cold, and dangerous streets of London as she kept to the shadows, looking out for any threat, and then stumbling along the gutter in her quest for something to eat. It didn't even matter what it was; she hadn't eaten in two days and her insides were starting to gnaw themselves out. Her entire body was quaking, suffering from the lack of sustenance, but unfortunately it was an all-too-common state for her.

She starved on a regular basis.

The woman wasn't particularly young; perhaps she'd seen twenty-two or even twenty-three years. She wasn't a child. She was clad in simple woolen garments, undyed, and without shape. They were garments the poor would wear because they could afford nothing else, but in this case, the garments were worn by a pledge of St. Blitha.

The only clothes she had.

The gutters were pools of water mixed with urine and feces, and she slipped into the puddles more than once, soaking her simple leather shoes. They were worn, and had holes in them that had been repeatedly sewn and mended, because much like her woolen clothing, they were all she had. They were usually clean but at this moment, she didn't care about clean. She only cared about food.

It wasn't the first time the woman had escaped St. Blitha in search of sustenance. St. Blitha was a poor order, the order of St. Dominica, and they gardened and traded for food to keep them alive, only the food they kept in stores somehow rarely made it to those it was intended for – the nuns. More often than not, the Mother Abbess sold the food and pocketed the money to purchase fine food for her own table, leaving her charges to starve.

It was the nasty truth.

Therefore, ventures like this were the norm and the starving young woman wasn't the only one who ventured from the walls of St. Blitha in search of food. Others did, too, and the Mother Abbess was aware. She didn't care. As long as chores were done, and prayers were fulfilled, she turned a blind eye to her starving charges as they wandered the streets looking for something to eat. Some residents and merchants took pity on the charges, but most slammed their doors, ignoring their extreme poverty.

The wandering nuns of St. Blitha.

Two days. This would be her third day of not eating if she didn't find something soon. Desperate, she began to wander the alleys, looking for any scrap. Cooking smells assaulted her, reminding her of just how weak she really was, and more than once she had to grab on to a door jamb or a wall to keep from falling.

In this part of the city, towards the town walls, the homes were a little more spread out and there were plots of land where gardens could be kept. She knew of just such a garden, with branches of apple trees that hung over the garden wall. It wasn't even close to harvest time, and the apples would be small and unripe, but it didn't matter. It would be something in her stomach. Making her way to the corner of an alley and a street they called The Cripple, she could see the branches of the tree hanging over the brick wall, but as she hustled over to it, there were no apples to be found.

Her stomach tightened, cramping with emptiness. In desperation, the woman tried to climb onto the wall, but she was too weak. She stumbled over to the garden gate, assuming it was locked and shocked to discover that it wasn't. She could hear people in the house next to the garden, awakening as the sun began to rise, so she quickly slipped in and stayed close to the wall, scoping out the garden and spying carrots poking out of the ground. With trembling legs, she rushed to the carrots and yanked three of them out of the earth along with a rather large bunch of radishes. Afraid she'd be caught, whe ran from the garden with her stolen booty as fast as her legs would carry her.

There was rainwater in troughs from the storm they'd had the night before and she quickly washed the dirt from her vegetables, cramming them into her mouth and chewing quickly, so hungry that she couldn't stop herself. She was in danger of choking as she shoved them into her mouth, chewing and chewing until they all went down into her rumbling belly.

Although there was something in her stomach now, she wasn't satisfied in the least. She had to find more, something that would fill her until the next time she slipped from St. Blitha and engaged in this horrific dance of the hungry. She could smell bread coming from the street of the bakers, which was to the south, and the breeze blowing off the Thames carried that fragrant scent. Lured by it, she began to head south.

There were more people here in the merchant district, people beginning their business for the day. Merchants were setting out their wares, and that included food vendors. At this time in the morning, the big ovens that the bakers used to bake bread – sometimes several bakers would use the same oven – were burning full-bore. The smell of yeasty bread and pies filled the air, drawing her ever-closer to the source.

Rounding a corner, a large baker's stall came into view and the man already had bread loaves cooling on stones in front of his stall in a move meant to lure in shoppers. But they were also luring in the starving, and the woman had her eye on a small loaf of bread that was at the end of a line of loaves. She knew she could get to it. But she wasn't entirely sure she could run fast enough once she took it.

She would have to eat what she could of it before she was caught.

She was taking a terrible chance. Being a postulate, she knew she wouldn't be severely punished, not like a normal thief would be, but there was always the chance of being apprehended by someone who didn't believe those associated with the church deserved special consideration. She would offer to work it off; aye, that is what she would do. She could work off the bread and still return to St. Blitha in time to finish her chores.

It's not as if she had a choice.

With her hands shaking and her stomach now upset by the raw vegetables she'd consumed, the woman moved closer to the cooling loaves, keeping an eye out for the baker. He was back in his stall, tending to his product, so she waited until he turned his back completely before snatching the loaf. She broke it in two, taking a massive bite, when the baker's wife suddenly screeched.

After that, the chase was on.

WHAT A NIGHT.

It was dawn as Maxton emerged from one of the bathhouses that dotted the north end of London. This particular bathhouse backed up to the street of the bakers and used their massive ovens to heat the water. It was a smaller bathhouse, one that catered to noblemen, and it also had the dual distinction of serving food as well.

Maxton had just spent a couple of glorious hours sitting in a hot tub and eating bread and cheese, boiled eggs and boiled beef, as a burly male attendant with a missing eye scrubbed him down, shaved him, and cut his hair. Years of dirt and filth and incivility had been cleaned off of him in the early hours of the morning, and he'd dressed in clean clothes that William and Gart had provided for him – fine leather breeches, a soft woolen tunic, boots that Gart had loaned him until he could get some made, and a heavy leather coat that went all the way to the ground. Lined with fur, it was an exquisite piece of clothing, something that had been hanging in the wardrobe of Farringdon House until Maxton had confiscated it. He didn't know who it belonged to, but now, it belonged to him.

In fact, as Maxton exited the bathhouse on at dawn after a night of rain, he felt whole again. Human, even. Bathed, shaved, dressed, and fed, he felt better than he had in years, even if this moment had followed a night of no sleep after too much drinking. Now that he was back in civilization as a free man for the most part, he intended to do some living when he wasn't seeking out papal assassins.

Perhaps that's why he hadn't slept very much. There was a great deal on his mind. After the meeting with William Marshal the day before, Maxton realized that the mission assigned to him and his colleagues was perhaps greater than any mission he'd ever undertaken. And there had been many – slitting the throat of a rival Muslim commander, hunting down a rogue Christian knight who had defected to Saladin, and on and on. There was an entire list of assignments that he and Kress and Achilles had undertaken on behalf of Richard and the righteous way of Christiandom, and all of them successful for the most part. The Executioner Knights had a hard-earned reputation that wasn't built on failure. But this latest task was the most important they'd ever taken on.

And perhaps the least bit intimidating.

But he was up to it.

The sun was beginning to rise in the east and the city was coming alive with people going about their business. Maxton looked around, thinking that perhaps he should head back to Farringdon House since he was fed and bathed and relaxed, and still even slightly drunk, to sleep a little. In fact, that's where Kress and Achilles were; they had elected not to go to the bathhouse after their drinking binge, but rather sleep it off. It had been Maxton who had prowled the night. But at this moment, a soft bed was sounding good to him. Turning west along the avenue, he was thinking thoughts of a warm bed and very well minding his own business when a figure shot around the corner of an alley and straight into him

He was hit full-force in the groin.

It was a painful, heavy, and shocking blow right into his privates and he doubled-over, but not before he grabbed the person who had hit him with both hands. As Maxton was sinking to one knee in pain, he had visions of a woman in his grasp, shoving bread into her mouth in between shrieks of fear. He was going down, she was cramming bread into her face, and the whole thing seemed surreal and slightly ludicrous.

More yelling now. Someone was grabbing at the woman in his grip, trying to pull her away from him, but he roared, loudly enough to send everyone scattering. He had captured the offender and he wasn't about to let anyone take her away from him. His groin throbbing, he lurched to his feet, trying to shake off the stabbing pain in his family jewels.

"Enough!" he bellowed, blinking his eyes to clear his vision. The first thing he saw was a heavy-set man and a woman with a club in her hands, standing a few feet away and looking at him with a mixture of fury and fear. "What in the hell are you two doing? What goes on here?"

The woman with the club inched towards him. "That girl," she huffed, poised with the club. "She stole from us!"

Maxton blinked again, the pain in his crotch fading to a dull throb, as he finally looked to the woman in his grip. As his vision cleared, he found himself looking into terrified green eyes. But they were very pretty eyes. He found himself looking closer; she was very pale, with ashen lips and a sweet shape to her face. The woman was blonde, but it was a darker blonde with a hint of copper to it, and her hair was all over the place, hanging in dirty waves down to her knees.

When their eyes met and the woman gasped with terror and tried to pull away, Maxton could see that she had a long, swan-like neck, something that was so inherently elegant. Beautiful, even. She was tall, too. In fact, everything about her reeked of elegance and breeding were it not for the fact that she was as filthy and smelly as a pig. The woman looked as if she'd been rolling in the gutter. He frowned.

"Did you steal bread?" he asked, sounding unhappy. "Answer me truthfully and I may show mercy. It seems that I am all that stands between you and a sound thrashing. Well?"

The woman hesitated a moment and he saw her swallow, perhaps the last of the bread that she'd been trying so desperately to eat. Then he saw her swallow again, this time to perhaps show her courage.

"I… I was hungry," she said, her voice quivering. "I've not eaten in two days. I would offer to work off the bread, but they tried to beat me before I could speak. I swear that I will work it off. I have no money, my lord."

He eyed her; she was well-spoken, something he did not expect from one so slovenly. "I can see that," he said. "Where do you come from, woman?"

"St. Blitha."

His eyebrows lifted. "St. Blitha?" he repeated. "Are you a nun?"

"A pledge, my lord."

Now, he was becoming confused. "And they do not feed their pledges?"

"It is a poor order, my lord."

"You did not answer me. Do they not feed you?"

She shook her head, once, and tears filled her eyes, tears that she quickly blinked away. She turned to the baker and his wife, standing a few feet away.

"I swear I will work for the bread," she said, her voice trembling with shame. "Please show mercy. I've not eaten in two days, but you did not let me explain."

The baker's expression was dark; he'd heard what she'd told the very big knight. "St. Blitha," he muttered. "I should have known. I won't punish ye this time, but stay away from my stall, girl. If I see ye again, I'll take a switch to ye."

With that, he pulled his wife away, who wasn't so happy about not being able to club the girl. She was so unhappy, in fact, that she took a swing at her husband with the club, who yanked it our of her hands and slapped her. Now, they were fighting amongst themselves and the sounds of slaps and scolding faded as they headed back to their stall, leaving Maxton standing with the quivering girl still in his grip.

Once the pair was gone, it was oddly and uncomfortably silent between them. Maxton's gaze drifted over the long-limbed, slender creature in his grasp. His initial shock at their painful and chaotic introduction was turning into curiosity.

"What did he mean by that?" he asked her. "When he mentioned St. Blitha, it seemed as if he knew something about it."

The girl's quivering was growing worse. "It is of little matter, my lord," she muttered. "As I said, St. Blitha is a poor order and..."

He cut her off because he was starting to understand the situation. "So the merchants around here are used to the starving nuns that wander about, stealing food. Is that it?"

It wasn't as if she could deny it. All signs pointed to it and, clearly, she'd silently admitted it not a few moments earlier. But she didn't want the man's pity.

"The Mother Abbess sets a fine table," she said, trying not sound as ashamed as she felt. "The senior nuns eat well, but the unfortunate truth is that the rest of us must fend for ourselves most of the time. You are correct; clearly, you could see by the baker's reaction that this is not the first time someone from St. Blitha has been discovered taking his food. Ask any merchant in London and they will tell you the same thing – it happens all the time. My lord, if I could work for my food, I would, but there are those who feel it would be improper to employ a pledge or postulate, or even a nun. They would rather give charity, but unfortunately, very few do, and when the do, it is not enough for all of us."

Maxton could hardly believe what he was hearing. "And your bishop allows this?" he asked, aghast. "Who is your bishop?"

"Essex, my lord."

That stopped Maxton's building rage. He rolled his eyes and looked away. "That makes sense now," he mumbled. "I may have been away from England for a few years, but some things never change. Essex is a man who is only concerned for his own coffers and leaves the rest of his parishes to govern on their own."

"It seems so, my lord."

His eyes narrowed at her. "*Seems* so? Of course it is true. It has always been truth with Essex. You are a living example of that."

She opened her mouth to reply but abruptly seemed to catch sight of something behind Maxton and he turned to see what had her attention. It was another woman in the same shapeless woolen clothing stumbling along the street, but when she saw that she had been sighted, she suddenly disappeared into a side alley.

Jaw ticking, Maxton returned his focus to the woman in his hands.

"How many of your fellow pledges are out looking for food?" he asked, though not unkindly.

"At least twelve, my lord."

Maxton shook his head in disgust. There were things he could stomach, and things he couldn't. A woman, in poverty by dire circumstances, had his pity. Maxton was many things – brutal, deadly, and at times, cruel – but he wasn't heartless. That was a little fact he kept deeply buried, but in this case, that compassion he kept so tightly guarded was coming forth. He couldn't help it. He finally released one of her arms but held tight to the other.

"Come with me," he rumbled.

She looked at him, fear in her eyes as she dug in her heels. "Where?"

"You wish to eat, don't you?"

She hesitated a split second before nodding, and Maxton pulled the woman along, heading back into the merchant district.

He had a nun to feed, but he realized as they walked through the streets that it wasn't completely altruistic. Aye, he felt sorry for her, but there was more to it than that. Perhaps when he stood before St. Peter to recount the deeds of his life, feeding a starving pledge might off-set some of the horrible things he'd done. A holy man he'd spoken to on his trip home from Les Baux de Provence told him that God weighed a man's good deeds against his bad deeds. Some were weighed more heavily than others, and Lord only knew, Maxton had very little good deeds to outweigh the bad.

He didn't want to pass up this opportunity to give himself a few good marks. He could have just left her on the street, and probably should have, but instead, he wanted to do something good for a change.

Altruistic, indeed.

CHAPTER FIVE

The King's Gout Tavern
London

MAXTON HAD NEVER seen anyone so hungry in his entire life. He'd picked this tavern because it seemed to be relatively busy, and the smells of food coming forth were delicious, so he'd procured a table and a meal for the lady, and watered ale for himself. Now, he sat and watched her eat.

It was an experience.

Maxton had seen plenty of poverty whilst traveling to and from The Levant, and although he thought himself hardened to it, the truth was that he wasn't. For years, he'd pretended not to care, and his actions had proven that, but ever since departing The Levant and his bout with The Lateran Palace that caused him to question everything, he was starting to feel emotion more than he wanted to. He was starting to question things more than he should, and perhaps the starving pledge before him was an excellent example of that.

He had come to see that the Church was nothing he'd been taught. Perhaps somewhere buried deep, there were still good men there, men who truly upheld the code of Christ. But the realities of the evil that infected it was evident at the highest levels. Was selfishness and wickedness really the base of the religion? Was that what he had been fighting for all of these years?

The woman before him only fed those questions and doubts.

"When was the last time you've eaten a decent meal?" he asked her quietly.

The woman's mouth was so full she could barely speak. "I cannot recall, my lord," she said. "Martinmas, mayhap?"

He watched her carefully. "That was some time ago."

"Aye, my lord."

"What did you have to eat?"

She swallowed the enormous bite in her mouth as she thought seriously on his question. "There was goose," she said. "And we had bread that had been made sweet with honey. It was delicious."

He nodded faintly, watching her spoon more peas into her mouth. His thoughts moved from her situation to her appearance once again; his initial observations of her were not incorrect, for she was quite lovely beneath all of that dirt, but she was as skinny as a child from what he could see. Her wrists and hands were gaunt, her fingers slender but elegant.

"I do not even know your name," he said after a moment.

She swallowed the bite and took a very big gulp of watered ale. "Andressa du Bose, my lord," she said. Then, she paused, a flicker of sorrow crossing her face. "At least, that is who I used to be. Lady Andressa du Bose. Now… I do not know who I am not. It is not who I thought I would be."

His brow furrowed. "Explain."

Andressa shrugged, scooping more peas into her mouth. "It is nothing, my lord," she said, averting her gaze to focus on her food. "Pay no attention to me. I suppose all girls believe they will be a great lady when they grow up. That is all I meant."

He eyed her; he didn't believe her, that was clear. There was something quite wistful in the way she'd spoken. He took a thoughtful drink of his watered ale.

"Lady Andressa du Bose," he repeated softly. "You were born into nobility."

"Aye, my lord."

"Where are you from?"

"Culverhay," she said. "I was also known, once, as Andressa of Culverhay. My family home is Chalford Hill Castle, south of Gloucester."

"Does your father know what goes on at St. Blitha?"

She shook her head. "My father is dead, my lord, as is my mother," she said quietly. "Four years ago, in fact, this past winter."

"I see," he said, sensing her sorrow. "Who assumed your guardianship, then? Surely the man has checked on your welfare."

With the peas gone, she was starting in on the juicy boiled beef. "My father's sister assumed my guardianship upon the death of my parents," she said. "It is she who sent me to St. Blitha."

"Does *she* know of the conditions at St. Blitha?"

Andressa looked at him, then, and he could see the tears pooling. That told him everything he needed to know, even before she said a word. But she quickly blinked her eyes, dashing them away, not stopping to wipe anything away because that would have taken time away from eating.

"In truth, I do not know," she said, subdued. "Even if she did, I am sure that she would not care. Shall I be plain, my lord? I was my father's heiress. When my aunt assumed my guardianship, she quickly sent me away, as far away as she could, and now she lives at Chalford Hill whilst I am confined to St. Blitha. If you think to write her for reimbursement for this meal, do not waste your time. If it pertains to me, she will not pay."

"Why do you say that?"

"Because it has happened before."

Maxton stared at her a moment before leaning back in his chair, frowning greatly. "You are her niece. If she assumed your guardianship, then she is responsible for you."

Andressa swallowed the bite in her mouth, looking up at him with a dignity that wasn't taught. It was inherent; one either had it or they did not. It was a steely strength, perhaps a steely strength that had kept the lady from losing all hope these past years. But he could see in her eyes that her hope in life was beginning to dim.

"I did not tell you of my situation to complain," she said. "I told you because you asked, and because I wanted to impress upon you not to seek recompense for the money you have spent on this meal. If you wish for me to work this off, my lord, I am happy to do so. I am strong. I can sew and scrub. I can clean your clothes if you wish. I am more than willing to do almost any work you wish."

Maxton believed her implicitly. This was not a wilting flower; he could see that. Strong, well-bred, well-spoken… his curiosity about her grew.

"That is not necessary," he said. "It has been a long time since I have shared company with an intelligent woman. That is repayment enough."

Now, it was Andressa's turn to be curious. "But we've hardly spoken, my lord."

"We've spoken enough."

She returned to her food, hesitantly, but her attention drawn to him. For the first time, she permitted herself to be curious about him, this savior of starving pledges. He was very handsome; in fact, she'd never seen finer. He had dark eyes, a dark shade of hazel that flickered in the weak light of the inn, and thick dark hair, cropped short, that had bits of gray in it around the temples. But his face… that's what mostly had her attention. His lips were shaped like a bow, and he had a square jaw with a big dimple in his chin.

All of that male beauty was wrapped up in a man who was easily twice her size, and more than twice her weight, with fists that were nearly the size of her head. He was as powerful as he was beautiful, but there was something unsettled behind those glittering eyes. Something that suggested that man's soul was not at all at ease.

There was an air of mystery about him.

"May… may I ask your name, my lord?" she finally asked.

"Sir Maxton of Loxbeare," he said without hesitation. "My family home is Loxbeare Cross in Devon."

She smiled faintly, revealing surprisingly lovely teeth. "I fostered at Oakhampton Castle," she said. "It is also in Devon. Do you know where it is?"

He lifted his eyebrows. "Of course I do," he said. Then, he peered at her as if genuinely surprised. "*You* fostered at Oakhampton?"

"Aye."

"When did you foster?"

She shrugged, putting more food in her mouth. "I was there from the time I was eight years of age until I had seen sixteen years," she said. "I was called home because of the death of my parents, of a fever. It was my aunt who greeted me at Chalford Hill to inform me of their passing and the very same day, I was sent to St. Blitha. I have been there ever since."

He pondered that information. "Oakhampton is a fine castle," he said. "It is commanded by de Courtney, or so it was the last I heard."

"It is, still."

"And being that it is a fine castle, there are many fine knights there. The wards would also be from fine families. Not just anyone would be accepted as a ward."

"My father knew Hugh de Courtney," she said simply. "They were friends and allies."

For Maxton, that was a surprising bit of knowledge. The de Courtney family was extremely powerful, and they were also allies of Maxton's father, Magnus. They would not be allied with anyone other than a powerful family, and Maxton was starting to sense something quite tragic about the young woman's situation. *An heiress who has been sent to live in poverty by her guardian.* He sat forward, collecting his cup again, thinking on the circumstances as he saw them.

"So you fostered in a fine home and you were the heiress to your father's fortune," he said pensively. "Your father died and your aunt assumed your wardship, recalling you from Okehampton and sending you to a convent where you would never have a chance to find a good husband. She essentially threw you in the rubbish pile."

Andressa looked up at him sharply. "My lord?"

He held up a hand, begging her patience while he clarified. "The woman assumed your guardianship, yet sent you to an order she knew you would never return from," he said. "Women are not sent to convents to return from them unless there is an offer of marriage, but it seems to me your aunt knew you would never receive a marriage offer at St. Blitha. No marriage, no husband to inherit your father's legacy. That way, it all belongs to her, and will forever. She has stolen your inheritance. Am I wrong?"

Andressa lowered her gaze. Her chewing slowed and when she finally swallowed the bite, she didn't put more food in her mouth. She simply sat there, looking at her lap.

"I cannot know her motives, my lord," she said. "But I do know I am of age now, yet she does not recall me home. I assume she wants me to become a nun. It is her right to do with me as she wishes, given she is my guardian."

Oh, but he could sense such sorrow in her words. In the months or even years past, Maxton would have never given thought to such a tone, nor would have he even indulged in such a conversation, but at this moment, he was doing both. He was starting to feel things again, that newly awakened compassion wreaking havoc with his thought processes. He simply wasn't any good at gauging it or controlling it.

He didn't like what he was hearing.

It didn't seem right, this woman who had clearly had her inheritance stolen by a greedy aunt. At least, that was her story. As a seasoned knight, perhaps he should have been more suspicious of her than he was. The truth was that his background with women was spotty; those who weren't liars usually had some other issue – selfishness, perhaps greed. He'd never met one he fully trusted and as a rule, he stayed clear of them. But this pale, slender woman had him believing her story. All signs pointed to it being the truth.

He hoped he wasn't being made a fool of.

"Finish your meal," he said after a moment, scratching at his neck and looking around the room, wondering if this wasn't the first time she'd coerced a meal out of someone with her sad story. "If this inheritance is rightly yours, why do you not stand up for yourself? Why starve away at St. Blitha?"

He seemed dubious and the least bit irritated. Andressa could sense a sudden change in his mood; he'd been very interested in speaking with her at first, but suddenly, he seemed oddly distracted. Perhaps he was even nervous. She was coming to think that he was sorry he'd bought her a meal if he knew now that her aunt wouldn't pay for it. That seemed to be when things changed with him. With that in mind, she daintily wiped her mouth with the cloth that had come with the food.

"I fear I have taken too much of your time and money already, my lord," she said, quickly standing up. "God bless you for what you have done for me. I shall not forget it. If you do not wish for me to work off the meal, then I shall pray for you every morning for the rest of my life. God appreciates those who are generous and compassionate, and you have been both."

He looked at her, sharply. *Compassionate.* There was that word again. How could she know he'd brought her here hoping that the good deed of feeding the woman might take some of the sting out of his life of sin? It was his own fault for feeling sorry for her, for wanting to show God he wasn't just a murder. A killer.

An assassin.

It wasn't her fault that he'd forced her here.

"Sit down," he said, reaching out and pulling her back into her chair. "Finish your food."

His manner still seemed edgy. "Truly… it is not necessary," she said. "I have eaten enough. I should return to St. Blitha soon."

He shook his head at her firmly. "*Eat*," he said. "If you leave now, then you will have wasted my money, and that will displease me. Do you wish to displease me?"

She shook her head quickly. "Nay, my lord."

He gestured to her plate and she complied, plowing into the boiled beef. From the way she was pushing it into her mouth, he knew she was still very hungry. He was coming to think that his momentary suspicion at her had been misplaced. It was the natural doubt he carried with him, always, knowing that all men were not what they seemed. It was doubt that had kept him alive for many years, instincts that were better than most. As Andressa ate, he waved over one of the wenches who was working the common room, serving the tables.

"Something more, m'lord?" she asked.

It was a clearly suggestive question, but Maxton ignored it. "What more do you have in the kitchens to eat?"

The girl, round and pale with curly dark hair and rouged cheeks, was disappointed he didn't respond to her leering smile and purring question. Still, she dutifully answered him.

"The beef and peas," she said, gesturing to Andressa's half-empty plate. "Bread and cheese, which I already brought you. But I think there is barley pudding, too."

Maxton was interested. "What is in it?"

"Barley, eggs, milk, and honey. I think there are currants also."

"Bring it," he commanded quietly. "And listen closely; I want you to find a sack and stuff it full of all of the bread and cheese you can find. I wish to take it with me. Is that clear?"

"It is, m'lord."

"Off with you, now."

The girl scampered away to do his bidding and by the time he returned his attention to the table, he could see that Andressa was looking at him with some curiosity.

"If the barley pudding is for me, truly, I do not need such extravagance," she said hesitantly. "I am very satisfied with what I have. It is more than enough, my lord."

He knew that. He also knew she probably would have been happy with a simple crust of bread. But there was some satisfaction in giving the woman more food than she could eat.

"I know," he said. "But you may as well try it since we are here. You mentioned your love of bread sweetened with honey, so sample their pudding. It could be very delicious."

She nodded, a bit unsteadily, and returned to the beef, now pulling the remaining bits from the bone. Maxton's gaze lingered on her.

"What great lady did you wish to become?" he asked.

Andressa stopped sucking the beef from her fingers. "My lord?" she asked, confused.

"You said that all young girls wish to grow up to be great ladies. What did you wish to become?"

She put her hand down, wiping it off on the cloth at her fingertips. It seemed to be a question she didn't want to answer, but out of courtesy, she did.

"My family has raised beeves for generations," she said. "Cattle with red and white hides. I had an older brother when I was born, but he died at a very young age, so my father used to take me with him as he went about managing his lands. I learned about the cattle and I learned how to take them to market and to sell them for a fair price. I always believed I would retire to Chalford Hill and administer my family's legacy as I'd been taught. I hoped I would marry well and pass the empire to my children."

Maxton nodded as he thought on red and white cattle, and the gentle hills of Gloucestershire. "You still can," he said. "Send a missive to the king. Tell him that your aunt has stolen your lands. Ask for his good justice."

She lifted her eyebrows. "It is not such a simple thing," she said. "There is no way for me to send a missive. There is nothing to write with at St. Blitha; I do not have access to quill or parchment. I would have to see the king personally in order to deliver any message and I am quite certain he would not see me. I am no one of consequence. In fact, I would probably be in for a good deal of trouble if I did so. It would make me look ungrateful not only to St. Blitha, but also to my aunt. And do not forget that Essex is a confidant of the king. How would it make him look if a charge from St. Blitha told the king a tale of woe, of a Mother Abbess who sells our food to set her own fine table?"

He could see her point, but he wasn't one to surrender so easily. "Then I shall tell him," he said with firm quietness. "I have business with him, anyway. I will tell him your story and ask that he look into your aunt's dealings. What is her name?"

"Hildeth du Bose," she said hesitantly. "But..."

He cut her off. "Then it is settled," he said. "I shall speak to the king of this... this travesty and insist he investigate Hildeth du Bose and the entire Culverhay situation."

Andressa was shaking her head even as he spoke. "But you cannot," she insisted softly. "My lord, it is very chivalrous for you to want to help me, but if you do this, the king will know that I have told you everything. That information will make it back to the Mother Abbess, and I do not wish to cross the woman. She can be quite... brutal."

He cocked an eyebrow. "Brutal? Explain."

Andressa sighed heavily, clearly reluctant to say anymore but knowing he probably wouldn't let the subject rest. She could just tell; he had that aggressive manner about him. "I will explain, but only on the condition that you not speak to the king," she said with surprising firmness. "I must have your oath, my lord, or I will not tell you. I should not speak of such things. I could risk my own life in doing so."

Now, he scowled. "Risk your own life? What in the hell goes on at St. Blitha that you should fear for your life if you speak the truth?"

She was starting to tremble; he could see it in her hands. "I will not tell you unless I have your oath not to repeat it."

"You have it. Tell me."

Andressa sat back in her chair, hanging her head. "I should not have said what I did," she whispered tightly. "I should not have..."

"But you did," he said, cutting her off. Sitting forward so he could hear her better, he could see how frightened she was. He was genuinely, and deeply, curious. "My lady, please tell me."

She swallowed hard; he could see it. "When I first came to St. Blitha, I was warned by another pledge about the Mother Abbess," she murmured, blinking away tears of pure fright. "I was told not to cross her. I was told that she could make women in her charge… disappear."

Maxton was listening very carefully. "Disappear how?" he asked. "Send them away?"

Andressa shook her head. When she looked at him, it was with the greatest reluctance. "Nay," she said, taking a deep breath. "There is a vault below the abbey, a place that the Mother Abbess calls The Chaos. When I first came to St. Blitha, there were eighteen pledges. One girl, named Lora, came just before me. She was vivacious and kind, and she truly wanted to serve God. But she also had a bold tongue, and she was warned of her behavior several times. Then, she was caught singing as she swept the floor of the church and the Mother Abbess ordered her into The Chaos. I never saw her again after that. Lora was the first of seven women who have been sent to The Chaos since I have been at St. Blitha. They go into The Chaos but they never return. Ever."

Maxton had to admit that he was rather shocked to hear that. "They stay down there forever?" he said. "Or, it is equally possible that they are sent away, only you do not see it."

"They are not sent away, my lord."

"You know this for certain?"

"Aye."

"Then what happens to them?"

Andressa closed her eyes as if to ward off the question, but she was too deep into her ghastly tale to refrain from answering. "I… I have seen the Mother Abbess take the stairs down to The Chaos," she whispered. "When she goes, she always takes her staff with her. It is a big, heavy cross, taller than a man, and she calls it the Staff of Truth, but it is not as it seems. When she has come up from The Chaos, one of the nuns is always waiting for her with a piece of linen. The bottom of the staff, you see, is a dagger. A long dagger that is set within a wooden sheath made to look as if it is part of the staff. I have seen the nun remove that wooden sheath to reveal a bloodied blade. She uses the linen to wipe off the blade before replacing it into the wooden sheath. Do you not understand, my lord? The Mother Abbess kills those who go into The Chaos with her Staff of Truth and believes she is doing it with God's blessing."

Maxton sat back, hand to his mouth in astonishment as he pondered what he'd just been told. "Are you serious?" he gasped. "She *kills* them?"

Andressa nodded her head quickly, wiping at her eyes, at the tears of fright. "I swear upon our Holy Father that it is the truth," she said. "And you swore upon your oath that you would not repeat it. If you do, I will end up in The Chaos, and I do not wish to go there."

Maxton was horrified. "But why in God's name should she kill those she sends to the vaults?"

She shook her head. "I do not know," she said. "I have been asking myself the same question, except I heard the nuns over speak one day. They said that they had received the regular donation from Lora's family because they were able to purchase fine meat for the Mother Abbess' table."

"Then her family does not know she is missing? Or dead?"

"If they did, they would no longer send the donation."

That information hit Maxton like a punch to the chest; the family had not been informed so the Mother Abbess could continue collecting the family's donations. That was greed on an entirely new level. "God's Bones," he muttered. "The woman kills the charges who displease her, but doesn't tell the families? She continues to take their money?"

"Aye, my lord."

He threw up his hands, agitated and outraged. "Someday, the families are going to know that something is amiss."

Andressa remained calm; she had lived with this terrible secret for years and it was something that no longer outraged her, only terrified her. "We are not allowed visitors at St. Blitha," she said. "They would not know the truth, and if they did, I am sure they would be told that their daughters died of an illness or an accident. Anything but the truth."

"But you have seen the bloodied staff."

She appeared pale and sickened. "I have seen everything but the actual killing, my lord."

"God help us," he muttered in disbelief. Then, he pointed in the direction of the street outside. "And this is the same woman who lets her charges run loose in the streets of London, begging for food?"

She nodded again, swiftly. "As long as we do not speak against her and as long as our chores and prayers are completed on time, she has no conscience about it," she said. "As long as we do not disrupt her life, she cares not what occurs. It has been like that since I have been there."

It was a truly ghastly story. Maxton could hardly believe it, but in the same breath, he knew what the pope himself was capable of. He had experienced it first-hand. Therefore, it didn't surprise him that this Mother Abbess was capable of the same, vipers in a church that was full of men and women hiding behind the veil of religion. Therefore, it took very little thought for him to be utterly convinced that Andressa was telling the truth, as dreadful as it was.

"I will not repeat this," he assured her. "But you cannot go back there."

Andressa looked at him with some surprise. "I must," she said. "I have nowhere else to go."

He was starting to think quickly, thinking of a place where he could take her. The poor woman couldn't return to the hell of St. Blitha.

"I will think of something," he said. "You said you had an older brother once? I will assume his role. I will not let you suffer any longer than necessary, my lady. Yours is a horrible story. I am sure I can find a place for you, somewhere. St. Blitha is not a fit place for you, or for anyone."

She bolted to her feet. "Nay," she said, moving away from the table so she was out of his arm's length. "I *must* return, my lord. You do not understand. She would find me no matter where you take me because I have seen it happen before. Pledges have tried to leave her, but she always brings them back. I... I cannot leave!"

With that, she dashed away from the table, knocking into men and even knocking over a chair. Maxton stood up, rushing after her, but she was moving faster than he was. She raced from the entry and by the time he got out to the street, he saw her down the avenue, running as fast as her slender legs would carry her.

Very quickly, she was out of sight, but he didn't go after her. To do so would surely cause a scene and she'd made her wishes known. Something in that God-forsaken abbey had her terrified, so terrified that she couldn't leave it. But from the story she told, he didn't blame her for her fear – a Mother Abbess who murdered her charges, and a woman who was apparently all-knowing and all-seeing.

It was the most appalling thing he'd ever heard.

As he turned back to the tavern to pay for the meal they'd so abruptly left, thoughts of Andressa du Bose were lingering in his mind. That lovely, pale-faced woman with the tragic life had his attention. He wasn't sure why, but she did. He was interested in her, but no longer in an altruistic way. He'd mentioned assuming the role as her older brother, to protect her, but that wasn't why he did it. He did it because if he simply announced he wanted to protect her, it would have been improper considering they were not betrothed or even courting. Moreover, she was meant for the church. A relationship with a man wouldn't be part of that plan.

Still...

Maxton suspected that in the days to come, he would find her out on the streets again, looking for food.

And he would be waiting.

CHAPTER SIX

Farringdon House

It was a chamber filled with knights.

In fact, the very walls reeked of power... swords... and blood. They had absorbed such things over the years, walls that seen much of the politics of England.

The first floor solar of Farringdon House was a meeting place, one that William Marshal used to summon the great and powerful of England. It covered nearly half of the floor, and it was a very big floor, so there was easily room for fifty or more men in the solar with its great stone hearth, exposed beams overhead, and painted walls. The floor was made from wide slats of wood, heavy, but pocked from men who had walked upon it with their spurs and heavy boots. It was a spectacular room, meant for men of greatness.

This morning was no exception.

After his encounter with Andressa, Maxton had returned to Farringdon House, entering through an arched and secured gate built into the house itself and protected by several guards. Once inside, he passed through a tunnel that led into a damp, enclosed courtyard. To his right were stalls for the horses and a small corral, but stretching above that were four stories of a great stone house.

Windows faced into the interior courtyard and he could hear voices coming from the open panels – servants, people moving around, and the smells of baking bread. To his left was another arched doorway, heavily fortified, and there was another guard standing at it. He passed through with ease, entering the ground floor of the house, which was mostly servants' quarters, a big armory, and the kitchens. It was low-ceilinged and dark. A stone walkway through the ground floor led to a large mural staircase, and he took the stairs two at a time as he made his way to the first floor above.

This floor was bigger, with higher ceilings, and bright with windows. It was also the floor with the enormous solar. Maxton could hear men in the solar and as he entered the room, which was lit by the morning sun because the windows facing west were all wide open and the sun was filling up the sky, he could hear Kress' voice.

"Finally!" Kress declared. "We were about to send a search party out for you, Max. Where have you been all night?"

Maxton quickly realized there were several powerful knights in the chamber, all of them turning to look at him as he sauntered in. In fact, his reply to Kress caught in his throat as he looked at the familiar faces, some men he'd known for years, and men he'd served with in The Levant and even before.

He was, in truth, shocked to see such a collection, and it looked as if they were all waiting for him. Every eye was on him, including The Marshal, who was sitting near the window with a cup of something steaming in his hand.

"Well?" William said, gesturing with his cup. "Answer de Rhydian. Where have you been all night? We have been waiting for you."

Maxton's attention was drawn to The Marshal, but he was distracted by several grinning faces of men he considered his friends, for the most part. "I was not tired last night," he said evenly. "I sought to enjoy all that London has to offer."

"To indulge?"

"To think."

William came away from the window and approached him; he didn't appear genuinely perturbed at Maxton's disappearing act, merely curious. "Good," he said. "I hope you have been thinking a good deal. That is why I have brought these men with me. Some are friends of yours, I believe."

Maxton nodded, now looking at some of the men who were starting to crowd around him. "You said you had a meeting with the king and the marcher lords," he said. "I did not realize that you meant they were gathering here, at Farringdon House."

William was rather humored by the man's surprise. "They weren't until last night," he said. "I sent word to them and asked them to join me here this morning. And not all of these men serve marcher lords, either, but are simply men loyal to England. I will come to the point, Maxton – I have told them of the threat against the king. They know of your mission. That is why they are here. They want to hear of your plan to keep the king alive and they want to know how they can help."

Looking at the group, Maxton respected those he knew a great deal, but he really didn't want or need their help. Moreover, there were a few men he didn't know and he wasn't pleased that they were in on his mission. Too many men with that knowledge and he might not have the edge he hoped because men, even trustworthy ones, had been known to talk. That was the truth. Nay, he wasn't pleased at all. But that irritation was pushed aside when he focused on Christopher de Lohr, the very same knight he had told William he wanted no interference from.

Odd how the usual resentment and even annoyance he usually felt for the man wasn't there at the moment. All he saw was a fellow knight, someone he'd been allied with for years, for better of for worse.

In truth, he was actually glad to see him.

"Chris," he said evenly. "I see you made it home from The Levant in one piece."

Christopher de Lohr, a blond god of a man, smiled at Maxton but didn't go so far as to offer a hand in greeting; that wasn't the kind of relationship he and Maxton shared. They were critical of each other, perhaps far too competitive with each other, and there had always been the threat of a very nasty fight breaking out between them. However, they were also men who would defend one another to the death. Christopher was the light to Maxton's darkness and they both knew it.

Even the night must have a day.

"I did," Christopher replied after a moment. "And I see that you did as well, although it seems to have taken you a very long time to come home. I was told of your troubles, Max, and I suppose I should say that I am glad to see you made it back to England at all."

Maxton shook his head. "Do not say that," he said. "It would make me feel all warm and giddy, and I could not stomach it, not from you. Remember how much I detest the sight of you."

"And I, you."

Maxton held the man's gaze a moment longer but couldn't keep a straight face. With a smirk, he turned to the man standing next to Christopher, with somewhat similar features, but shorter and smaller. Given the size of Christopher, and he was a very big man, that wasn't saying much. Maxton's eyes narrowed at David de Lohr, Christopher's younger brother and perhaps an even bigger nemesis to Maxton than Christopher was.

"And you," he said. "Those men I paid to make sure you did not make it home alive took my money and failed to do their job. I am displeased."

David was the more hot-headed brother, quick to temper, but a hell of a fighter. Still, he knew Maxton was joking for the most part, but was quick to dish out as much as he was given. He wasn't about to let Maxton get the upper hand with him, not even this early into the conversation.

"Be careful," he said, holding up a finger. "You should not say such things. You are in the presence of powerful men now."

Maxton snorted. "Who?" he said. "You? Chris?"

David's blue eyes glimmered with mirth; he was relishing the expression on Maxton's face when he told him the truth. "Both of us," he said. "When you address Chris, you are now addressing the Earl of

Hereford and Worcester. Show due respect."

Maxton looked sharply at Christopher in an expression that satisfied David a great deal. It was one of surprise and perhaps even disbelief. Maxton hadn't heard about Christopher's titles since his return, something Gart hadn't bothered to tell him. Gart was deeply entrenched with the de Lohrs, as he served David, but Maxton knew why he hadn't mentioned it – it was best that he hear it directly from Christopher and David, given his contentious relationship with them. Still, Maxton couldn't help but feel a stab of jealously at the news, his contemporary who had been given a glorious title.

"My congratulations," he said to Christopher, wondering if he sounded as if he meant it. "When did this happen?"

"Shortly after my return to England," Christopher replied. "Remember that I came home several years ago, so it has been about seven years ago. And David was made Earl of Canterbury very recently, after the death of his wife's father."

Another de Lohr with a title. The knowledge compounded the resentment Maxton was trying to fight down and he struggled with his reaction.

"Congratulations to you, also, my lord," he said to David as neutrally as he could manage. "It seems that while I was off fighting other men's wars, you and your brother were making good for yourselves here at home."

David simply shook his head. "It hasn't been that simple, Max," he said as he turned away. "We've had a mess on our hands for the most part."

Maxton could have questioned him, but he didn't have the will to. Whatever David meant, he would find out soon enough. Instead, Maxton turned to the other men in the chamber, men who were waiting to greet him, and he found himself shaking the hand Cullen de Nerra, a mountain of a man who was the son of the High Sheriff of Hampshire, probably the highest law-position in all of southern England.

Cullen was a knight's knight, a powerful young man with great talent, so great, in fact, that he'd been knighted before he'd seen his twentieth year. Maxton had fought beside the skilled young knight many times, but he hadn't seen him in ten years, since before he went to The Levant. As he shook the man's hand, he looked him over carefully.

"Bloody Christ, Cullen," he said. "You've grown into a behemoth since the last I saw you. What happened to that giddy young knight with the big dimples?"

Cullen grinned, displaying the dimples that Maxton had referenced. With his sandy-blond hair and dark eyes, the man didn't want for female attention. If there were women around, they would gravitate to Cullen before anyone else, making him something of a hindrance to his friends at times. Maxton remembered being rather envious of that particular trait.

"He is still here," Cullen said. "I had to gain muscle and size to compete with the likes of you. You always were my idol, Max."

"Shut your silly mouth or you'll have me weeping like a woman."

Cullen's grin widened. "'Tis good to see you home, but I am sorry to hear you've had such troubles."

Maxton waved him off. "It was nothing," he lied. "Thanks to The Marshal and Eleanor, Kress and Achilles and I have made it home in one piece. That is all that matters."

"Indeed, it is."

Cullen slapped him on the shoulder in an affectionate gesture, but further conversation was cleaved as William pulled Maxton away from Cullen and towards the rest of the men in the chamber. They didn't have all the time in the world for pleasantries with old friends and it was time to finish up the introductions so they could get down to the business at hand.

"Or course, you already know Forbes," William said, flicking a wrist at Gart, who was standing over by the open windows overlooking London. "But I do not think you know the others. Allow me to introduce you to the fine young knights who have come into service since you have been away from England. Remember the names of these men, Loxbeare; these will be knights with great legacies."

Maxton came face to face with four big and well-armed knights, as deadly as he had ever seen. The first two looked similar in features, while the third one had pale blond hair and the bluest eyes he'd ever seen. He thought he recognized the fourth knight, as a cousin to the de Lohr brothers, a rather muscular man with auburn hair and an auburn mustache. William began introducing them, from left to right.

"This enormous fellow is Sir Sean de Lara," he said. "Sean is young, but he has been in my service for four years and there is no finer knight in the land. Since we have total trust in this chamber, and what is said here will not be spoken of outside of these walls, know that Sean has recently entered the service of the king as part of the man's personal guard. You will come to know de Lara, Maxton; he will be close to the king at all times and you will have to work closely with him."

Maxton nodded as he eyed the young knight; he was handsome, square-jawed, and powerfully built. But the eyes… they were a shade of dark blue, but the intensity radiating from them was palpable. He nodded his head briefly.

"De Lara," he greeted. "You and I will converse privately at some point very soon."

Sean nodded firmly. "Aye, my lord. A pleasure."

Maxton didn't linger on Sean because William was pulling him to the knight standing next in line.

"And this is Kevin de Lara, Sean's younger brother. He has the strength of a bull, so do not let his shorter stature fool you. He will take you off your feet before you know what has hit you." He came to the last two men in the line of knights. "And these final two warriors are particularly important – the man with the blue eyes is the premier knight for the House of de Winter. He's also Irish to the bone and he'll rip your head off before you know what hit you, so beware. I've never met a meaner man next to you, Loxbeare."

Maxton lifted his eyebrows at the large knight with the piercing blue eyes, so blue that they were silver. "Is that so?" he said, a hint of doubt in his tone. "Forgive me, my lord, but if this is a gathering of marcher lords, then I am not sure why de Winter need be present. De Winter is not a marcher lordship, the last I heard."

William answered. "De Winter has a small outpost near Gloucester, so there is some vested interest in the marches," he said. "Bric MacRohan leads the de Winter war machine, and that is something we cannot do without."

Maxton nodded in understanding. "I see," he said. Then, he addressed the silver-eyed knight. "Where are you from, Irish?"

A blond eyebrow lifted. "The name is MacRohan," he reminded him in an Irish accent so thick that it was barely understandable. "My family hails from Dungarvan Castle, but I was born in Ardmore."

"I see," Maxton said. His gaze was intense on the man. "No offense intended, but you are not English. The situation we are to discuss requires men who are loyal to England to the core. I have never heard of such loyalty from an Irish knight."

That comment only seemed to bring color to MacRohan's pale cheeks, and William took the hint. He quickly pulled Maxton away from the Irish knight with the flaring nostrils.

"Don't look at him any longer," he muttered. "I've seen him throttle men for less than what you have just said. Every word out of your mouth from this point on will be a challenge to him."

"It is a legitimate concern."

"MacRohan is related to de Winter by marriage. His loyalty to England is beyond contestation. One more comment like that from you and we may have real trouble from him, so look away, lad, look away. Don't look a mad dog in the eye."

Maxton wasn't sure if he was joking or not, but to tempt fate, he looked over his shoulder at Bric MacRohan to see that the man was indeed glaring at him as if waiting for him to say the wrong word.

In truth, Maxton thought it was rather humorous, although he appreciated a man with such a commanding presence and a quick temper. Men with little control fascinated him, which was probably why he had made a companion of Achilles. He was the same way. As Maxton fought off a smile, thinking that he already liked MacRohan for some strange reason, the last knight in the chamber was introduced.

"Finally, this is Dashiell du Reims," William said. "He is a cousin to the de Lohr brothers, as his father is the Earl of East Anglia. Dash is his heir and holds the title of Viscount Winterton. Currently, he serves the Duke of Savernake and helps command the great Savernake armies."

Maxton greeted Dashiell with a nod of his head, noting the powerfully built man with the auburn hair. He didn't look much like the de Lohrs, who were both blond-haired and blue-eyed, but he had the same build as David, and as a commander of the massive Savernake army, he was a man of considerable power.

"Du Reims," he said. "Your family legacy is a great one."

Dashiell had a rather gruff manner. "It is, my lord," he said. "Thank you."

Maxton cocked an eyebrow. "But that greatness is tempered by your relationship to the de Lohr brothers. You could have picked better relatives."

A smile played on Dashiell's mustache-covered lips. "Next time I will be more careful."

"See that you are."

The grin broke through. Dashiell was the last introduction in a meeting that had already been full of them, but Maxton's mind was very sharp. He had the ability to completely recall every detail from nearly every moment in his life, and that included introductions. Once he met a man, he never forgot him, or anything about him, so as he absorbed the considerable power that was filling the chamber, William spoke to him.

"These are the men who will be at your disposal as you make plans for what is to come," he said. "I realize you said that you and your companions work best as a team, but know these men are ready and willing to assist you, whatever your need may be, and in particular, you must establish a working relationship with Sean since he is going to be so close to John. You will need that communication."

Maxton nodded. "I imagine so," he said, glancing over at Sean, who had turned to speak quietly with his brother. "Does the king know that Sean reports to you?"

William shook his head. "Although I gifted Sean to the king as a token of trust, and Sean has sworn his fealty to John, the truth is that Sean is there to watch John's every move. It may not be entirely possible because John surrounds himself with his hand-chosen advisors, but Sean will at least know of the man's movements. He will report them to me as he can."

Maxton pondered that directive. "Then he is your spy."

"He is."

Maxton understood. "Does anyone else know?"

William shook his head. "Nay," he mumbled. "Not even his brother. Kevin adores Sean and if he knew, he might try to help him, and we do not need young Kevin involved. He is an excellent knight, but I am afraid his willingness and emotion would give Sean away. And nothing must give the man away."

"Agreed," Maxton said. "But Sean's position with John will be invaluable."

William nodded, holding up a hand to Maxton to prevent him from further conversation at this point. William, in fact, had an agenda and he needed to complete it quickly. He had plans for the day that were already set and they did not include lingering overly at Farringdon House. Therefore, he motioned the men in the room closer so they could all hear the conversation.

"Now that I have made the appropriate introductions, you are all allies on a first-name basis," he said seriously, looking to every man around him. "Total trust and total loyalty are imperative from this point on, with all of you. I have explained the situation with Lothar and John; you know that Lothar offered Maxton and Kress and Achilles great rewards in exchange for the assassination of John, an offer they refused. We know that Lothar is in possession of Richard's bastard son and that he is prepared to remove John and supplant him with the boy. And we know that Maxton, Kress, and Achilles are here to stop the assassins that Lothar has undoubtedly already sent. They could be in England as we speak. It is up to the Executioner Knights to find them and eliminate them. That is the gist of the situation, gentlemen, but make no mistake; we need John. As difficult as he is, he guarantees an England free of papal rule. To place the illegitimate son of Richard upon the throne would assure the destruction of everything we hold dear."

A heady mood settled about the room, the situation as serious as these seasoned men had ever seen it. Now, this horrible plot was out in the open, something that William had only whispered about to each of them until now. Speaking of it in something other than hissed tones somehow made it more real, and far more powerful than they could imagine. Every man there realized that they were the last line of defense between the England they knew and an England ruled by The Lateran Palace.

It was a devastating thought.

"What do you have planned?" Christopher broke the silence as he spoke to Maxton. "And what do you need from us?"

Maxton looked at the serious faces around him; he could see that they were all sincere in assisting him, but as he'd told William, he didn't need the interference. It would have been easier to tell them all to go away, but he couldn't. They had a genuine desire to help against this heinous threat because it was something that affected every one of them. Not wanting to insult anyone, he tried to be tactful in his response.

"I will need intelligence," he said. "You good lords have a wide scope in England; I need information on anyone unusual. Men you do not recognize, men who seem out of place. It is my guess that the Holy Father sought out other seasoned knights when my comrades and I refused his offer, and it is further my suspicion that those knights are

English. The Holy Father was concerned that foreign knights would not be able to get close enough to John to carry out their mission, so we would be looking for English knights, newly return from the continent and beyond. If you hear of such men, I must know."

Heads were nodding as Maxton turned his attention towards Kress and Achilles and continued. "In between pitchers of ale last night, my comrades and I spoke of the correct approach to this," he said. "We have decided that the best approach, at this point, would be to remain in London near the docks. Anyone entering the country would most likely come from there, so we will be infiltrating the taverns and gangs that are near the docks. We will make friends with the trollops and the street urchins. Often, they see and hear things that would prove valuable to our cause, so that is where we are headed. If anyone slips past our net, then that is where you good men come in. Remain vigilant. Look for anything strange."

"What about sending word to our allies in France and beyond?" David wanted to know. "Mayhap they will have heard something – *anything* – to aid our cause."

But Maxton shook his head. "The more men know of this, the more chance there is of word reaching the very men we seek," he said. "We do not know who they are, or where they are, but if they know we are aware of their existence, it will make our task far more difficult."

That drew a few nods from men who agreed, mostly Sean de Lara. Given that he had been tasked with spying on the king himself, he well understood that the less men who knew of the issue, the better. Considering the nature of the situation, Maxton's plan seemed to be a strong one, and a logical one. In truth, there was nothing more they could do. As the men began to turn to each other, speaking softly, Maxton made his way to Cullen.

"And you," he said, putting a strong hand on the young knight's arm. "Your role in this will be most important. The king's favorite castle of Winchester is not far from your father's fortress. You would do well to frequent the village of Winchester on the hunt for men who do not belong there."

Cullen nodded grimly. "And my father?" he asked. "He is the High Sheriff, Max. I know you wish to keep this situation quiet, but he is trustworthy. He should know what is happening."

Maxton glanced at William, who had heard the request and nodded his head in response. "Then tell him," Maxton said with William's approval. "Tell your older brothers, too. Gabriel and Gavin de Nerra are excellent knights and very trustworthy. They will be able to assist you and your father in making sure Winchester is covered. Since it is no secret that John is in residence there often, it could be that the assassins will try to strike there."

Cullen had his orders, eager to get on with it. This was the most important thing he'd ever been involved in and he understood that. Seeing the knight's confidence, Maxton knew that Winchester would be in good hands, but that also brought about the subject to of the king's movements in general. The man liked to move around. He turned to Sean, standing with his brother.

"Unfortunately, this will be a burden for you to bear, Sean," he said. "If the assassins slip past us in London, then you will be the last line of defense. The king does not know of this threat for good reason; he will panic and go into hiding, and it will lessen the chance that we will be able to catch these men. If they think the king is oblivious, and that no one knows there is a threat against him, they will move more freely and we will have a better chance of finding them. Therefore, do not share this information with any of the king's guard. These are men we do not know or trust, and we cannot take the chance that someone will inform the king of the threat. Do I make myself clear?"

Sean nodded. "You do, my lord," he said, "but if the assassins make it past you, then they shall not make it past me. This, I swear."

Maxton didn't know the knight, but he believed him. There was something in his tone that suggested nothing other than complete certainty.

"Good," he said. "But you must let me know any time the king moves from location to location. Even if he simply wants to go on a walkabout in the city, I must know. You must send word to Farringdon House, as we will check in daily for such missives. If John moves, we will shadow him. Mayhap his movements will draw the moths to the flame."

"Or the assassins to a king."

"Exactly."

Sean understood the seriousness of it. "I will do my very best to send you such information."

With that, plans were finally cast. At least they had a directive now, a scheme that would hopefully prevent the country from being thrown into turmoil. But there wasn't one man there who didn't believe they were in for a battle – a battle of locating just a few men who had been directed to kill a king in a city, and a country, of thousands and thousands of people. The proverbial needle in a haystack. But it was a battle with no real lines drawn, no definitive enemy, simply phantoms.

They were looking for phantoms.

"You have your directives, good men," William finally said, breaking the silence that had settled. "I will see you later today when we meet with John and his issues with Wales, and even then, we will be on the look out for those sent by Lothar. Your vigilance, and Maxton's sense of danger, is the only thing standing between England and ruin. Remember that."

No one had to be reminded. The seriousness of the situation had been hammered in to them.

It was do or die.

Christopher and David were the first to leave the chamber, bidding Maxton and Kress and Achilles a polite farewell as they departed. Having been involved in the politics of England for many years, a mission of great importance was nothing new to them, and they took it very seriously. Dashiell and Bric were next, with Bric casting Maxton a final glare as they followed the de Lohr brothers from the paneled room.

Maxton saw the expression the Irish knight had thrown him but he ignored it, instead, focusing on Cullen as the man bid him a warm farewell. Cullen also shook the hands of Kress and Achilles as he went because he was the amiable sort. He liked to hug and shake hands, as least of men he was fond of. Kevin de Lara followed after him, a silent knight who was deeply introspective and made no real move to be polite in his departure, but his brother, Sean, lingered behind. He hadn't followed Kevin, not yet; he had something more to say.

"I will head to Westminster now to join the king and his entourage," Sean said quietly, his gaze moving between Maxton and William. "I can tell you that John has been toying with the idea of hunting tomorrow in the forests outside of Windsor Castle, which will make it difficult to protect the man. I cannot prevent a well-placed arrow from the trees."

William grunted unhappily. "Nay," he said. "But you can watch the trees. Send men into them to keep them clear. That would be a normal procedure for the protection of the king, in any case, so there should not be anything unusual about that directive."

Sean didn't say what he was thinking – it wasn't as simple as that. John didn't like men in his forests, even if it was to protect him. He felt that it scared away the game. But he didn't argue the point with William; there was little reason to because William would tell him to do it anyway. And he would.

He would do as he was told.

Resigned, he simply nodded his head. "If John does decide to hunt tomorrow, I will send you word later tonight."

"See that you do," William replied. "And, Sean... know that we are depending on you a great deal for any information you can provide. Know that I have complete and utter faith in you."

Sean's gaze lingered on William a moment, perhaps surprised by a statement that sounded suspiciously like praise, before departing the chamber, his boot falls fading as he took the stairs down to the ground floor. When the sounds of his footsteps were gone and the world around them was silent, Maxton turned to William.

"He has a very difficult job ahead of him," he said. "How good is he, my lord?"

William lifted an eyebrow. "As good as I have ever seen," he assured him. "Have no fear, Maxton – I know how to judge a man. Sean de Lara is destined for greatness, mark my words. As are you. Now, I also intend to head to the Palace at Westminster, as that is where we shall be meeting with the king. Keep me informed."

He put a hand on Maxton's shoulders as he walked away, followed by Gart, who had remained silent during the entire meeting. He had been lurking on the outskirts, watching everything, absorbing. It was an important moment for him because he was the one who had recommended Maxton and Kress and Achilles for this task, so more than anything, his reputation was on the line as well.

He could see that he hadn't been wrong.

"I will be shadowing The Marshal, but send word if you need me," Gart said as he moved past Maxton and headed for the door. But he paused just shy of it, turning to look at the three men still remaining in the chamber. "This is your moment, gentle knights. If ever the fate of a country rested with only three men, this is time. You were sprung from the bowels of Les Baux de Provence for a reason, and that reason is upon you now. *Bonne chance*, my friends. You will need it."

With that, he departed, leaving Maxton and Kress and Achilles in the vast solar with his words hanging in the air. Maxton's gaze was on the vacated doorway but when he turned to his friends, he found that they were looking at him rather intensely.

"We never spoke of the approach to this situation in between pitchers of ale last night," Kress muttered. "But I am impressed with what you told them, Max. If that was a scheme without any true thought given to it, then it was a good one. Is that what you really want to do?"

Maxton ran a hand through his dark hair, letting his guard down for the first time. All of the alcohol he'd ingested from the night before had worn off completely and his head was beginning to throb.

"Aye," he said. "I think it is as good a plan as any. Did you two sleep last night?"

Kress nodded, glancing to Achilles. "A little," he said. "Did you?"

"Nay."

"Then what would you have us do today while you get some sleep?"

Maxton put his fingers to his temple, feeling the pain coming on. "Get out into the city by the docks," he said. "I want you to study every street, every hovel. Find the taverns. Watch the people along the docks; we may need eyes on that dock at all times and mayhap there is a man who would keep track of the comings and goings of ships, and their place of origin, for a few coins."

Kress nodded. "We shall," he said. "You will meet us there later?"

Maxton closed his eyes, feeling very weary all of a sudden. "I shall," he said. "I plan to sleep for an hour or two and then join you, because I will admit that I am starting to second-guess my brilliant idea of remaining awake all night. At this moment, it does not seem quite so brilliant."

Kress smirked. "There are quiet chambers on the top floor," he said. "Find a bed up there."

Maxton nodded, but his attention moved to Achilles. "No fights," he said to the man. "And leave the women alone. I realize that fist-fights and wenches are your natural inclination, but you do not need the distraction. And in speaking of women, remind me to tell you of the pledge from St. Blitha I came into contact with this morning. A rather harrowing tale."

Achilles, who had been rather incensed with the directive to stay away from women and anything violent involving his fists, appeared puzzled by the mention of a postulate.

"A pledge?" he repeated. "What were you doing at St. Blitha?"

But Maxton shook his head. "I was no where near St. Blitha," he said. "I came across her in the street, stealing food. But I will tell you of it later; at the moment, I must find a bed before I collapse, and you two must head out to the docks. I'll join you there in a couple of hours."

That was the cue to depart for Kress and Achilles, and depart they did. Maxton watched them head out of the solar, leaving him standing alone. Instead of seeking a bed, however, he found himself lingering on the meeting that had just taken place and thinking of everything that had been discussed. He'd been surprisingly pleased to see the de Lohr brothers, definitely pleased to see Cullen, and amused by the rabid-dog Irish knight. He was also intrigued by Sean de Lara, the plant by William Marshal in the king's entourage.

But all of that seemed to pale by comparison to thoughts of the lovely, starving pledge from St. Blitha. He'd essentially forgotten about her once he'd reached Farringdon House, and during the course of the meeting, but now that he mentioned her to Kress and Achilles, she was filling his mind like a fog.

Now that he was alone, with no men or conversation distracting him, thoughts of the woman were heavy upon him. That lovely, pale face and swan-like neck that was so very elegant. He just couldn't dispel the images of her flitting through his brain and something told him that even if he tried to sleep, he wouldn't be able to. Not with thoughts of her dancing in his head. But he would have to force himself, knowing that after some sleep, he might see things a bit more clearly.

He was a man with much on his mind.

Maxton was about to head from the chamber when he caught sight of a hulking figure coming up the darkened stairwell. The shape looked oddly familiar and as he watched, the face of someone he knew very well came into view, but it wasn't just any face. It was a face he hadn't seen in years, perhaps a man he thought he would never see again.

His eyes widened.

"Sherry...?" he gasped. "Bloody Christ... Sherry is that *you*?"

Sir Alexander de Sherrington gave a rather cocky grin as he came off the stairs and entered the chamber, his arms wide open as he sucked Maxton into a powerful embrace. Alexander, or Sherry as he was known to his friends, was an enigma, a man unto himself, and an elite knight that was squarely in the same league as Maxton, Kress, Achilles,

Gart, and the de Lohr brothers, to name a few. They didn't come any greater or any smarter. And he was utterly, completely delighted to see Maxton.

"Max," he breathed as he hugged the man tightly. Releasing him, he stood back so he could take a good look at him. "I saw everyone downstairs and they told me you were up here. It is good to see you, my friend. Thank God you and Kress and Achilles survived the Lords of Baux. I will admit that I had my doubts."

Maxton drank in the sight of the man who could be considered the fourth Executioner Knight. Alexander had worked with he and Kress and Achilles, many times, in The Levant. They'd accomplished some harrowing missions together, and after leaving The Levant, they spent time at The Lateran Palace together, as well. The four of them had been as thick as thieves.

Alexander was dark, with dark eyes and dark hair, and a beard covering his jaw. He was also enormously built and had the brightest smile Maxton had ever seen. When he grinned, framed by that black beard, Maxton swore he could see every tooth in the man's head. It was an infectious grin, in truth, and completely deceptive. When he looked friendly, even jolly, the truth was that Alexander de Sherrington was a killer beyond the talent of most mortal men.

He was Death personified.

"So did I," Maxton admitted after a moment. "But we survived purely on the grace of Eleanor and William. Had they not ransomed us, we would still be there. My God, Sherry, I still can't believe it. What are you doing here? No one ever mentioned you were in London."

Alexander nodded, patting the man on the shoulder. "That is because I only just arrived," he said. Then, he quickly sobered. "I heard about your tribulations after leaving Rome, Max. It is a shame, really, to have ended your time in Rome with such a terrible happening. Personally, I have fond memories of the place"

Maxton wasn't hard pressed to agree. "I do, also. It may have ended badly, but while we were there, it was a debaucherously good time.

Stories I will never be able to tell my children, anyway."

Alexander grinned as he recalled those decadent months of wine, food, and women. For a moment, he warmed to the memory. "Nor I," he said. "We all lived like kings for the time we spent at The Lateran Palace, until those sworn to serve God made us questionable offers that went against His teachings. In truth… it seems like another lifetime ago."

Maxton found himself reflecting on those very same things. "It does," he said. "But our lives, Sherry… they have never been comfortable nor pleasant for any length of time. That is not the nature of our business."

Alexander's good humor faded. "That is true," he said. "But what we received at The Lateran Palace went beyond comfort, at least for the time we were there. But after the depravity and self-indulgence, when were offered missions for a great sum of money, that was when everything changed. The offer that came to me was the pursuit of a double-agent, a man who was discovered to spy for both the Holy Father and the Scottish king. And the offer that came to you and Kress and Achilles… your offer was far worse than mine. They wanted you to kill your own king, an offer that turned against you when you refused, and the Holy Father sold you to the Lords of Baux in punishment."

Maxton's voice was soft. "He wanted us to kill John to supplant him with Richard's bastard son," he said. "Did you know that? Richard had an affair before marrying Berengaria and the boy was the result. A boy currently in the possession of the Holy Father."

Alexander sighed heavily. "I'd hear rumor," he said. "Nothing definitive, but now the mission to assassinate John makes sense. It wasn't simply a random directive."

"It was not."

"Max… forgive me for not helping you and Kress and Achilles in all of this. I should have tried to free you from the Lords of Baux. I should have…"

Maxton shook him gently, cutting him off. "Nay," he said firmly.

"You had agreed to your offer and you were already on your way by the time everything happened to us. If you had gone back on your word simply to help your friends, your fate would have been the same as ours. Never second-guess your decision, Sherry. You did the right thing. Have you found your man, by the way?"

Alexander shook his head. "He is in London, somewhere," he said. "I have tracked him all across the continent, up to the land of the Northmen, and back across the sea. He came ashore in Berwick and then found his way back down to London. It has been a long year of following him, but I am confident I will find him now."

"Why do you say that?"

Alexander dropped his hand from Maxton's shoulder. "Because it seems that my target is where he wants to be – here, in London," he said. "Alasdair Baird Douglas, as he calls himself, has been an agent for the Holy Father for some time, a gift from the King of Scotland, so I'm told. But it was discovered that the man is also feeding secretive information to the Scots, information about the Holy Father, and that is why they want him stopped. They paid me a king's ransom to do it."

"I never did ask you who made you your offer. Did the Holy Father send you after him?"

Alexander shook his head. "He did not," he said. "Abramo did. You know the man."

That drew a reaction from Maxton; he rolled his eyes unhappily. "I know him," he muttered. "So does Gart. All of us who spent time at The Lateran Palace know him. He's a deceitful, ambitious beast hiding behind the guise of a priest."

Alexander cocked an eyebrow. "Was he the one who told you about Richard's bastard, then? Because the rumors I heard were that Abramo was the one speaking of the boy."

"He did not tell me," Maxton said. "I knew nothing of it until the Marshal told us of the boy after we were freed from Baux. All Kress and Achilles and I knew was that the Holy Father wanted our king dead, and that came directly from the Holy Father himself. He never once mentioned the lad."

Now things were a bit clearer. When they'd last seen each other, the situation for all of them had been a bit chaotic. Alexander had been forced to leave on his mission before Maxton had agreed to his offer, and it had only been later on, through another knight, that he'd heard of Maxton's imprisonment.

Still, he'd never forgiven himself for not helping his friends, for not being there when they needed him. But Maxton had been correct – he'd agreed to an offer and his word was his bond. It was the way men such as them worked; they were only as good as their word. Were they to break it, then the respect they'd worked for, and their reputation, would have suffered. It seemed harsh to choose a mission over friendship, but they all understood the risks of their vocation.

Honor was everything, even among assassins.

"I saw Gart yesterday, right after he left a meeting with you and William Marshall," Alexander said after a moment. "We spoke briefly, but he told me that The Marshal has tasked you and your Unholy brethren with finding the papal assassin meant for the king. Do we know for certain the Holy Father has sent others?"

"We do not know for certain, but we can surmise. We refused to do the job, so they would simply find another."

"That is my thought, as well," Alexander said. Then, he paused. "I have a thought about that, Max."

"What?"

"I wonder if the assassin is Douglas?"

Now, Maxton was very interested. "The man you are chasing? What makes you think so?"

Alexander stroked his bearded chin, turning towards the windows overlooking London, a glorious sight now that the sun had risen. He'd missed this sight in the years he'd spent away from England. The ribbon of the Thames was to the south, glittering in the early morning light, and the land to the west spread out to the horizon like a vast green jewel. Green, beautiful England.

He was glad to be back, no matter what the circumstances.

"I say that because I have been chasing the man for a year and we have ended up in London," he said. "Coincidentally, when John happens to be here. Douglas has led me on a merry chase, but he has never stayed more than a night or two in any given location – we have been to more cities and villages than I can count, and I have never been more than a few days behind him. But now that we are in London, we are going on the third night here and I've seen no movement from the man. He is dug in like vermin on a dog."

"Do you know where he is?"

Alexander nodded. "I do," he said. "He is down by the docks."

Maxton cocked his curiously. "Then if you know where he is, why not fulfill your task and do away with him? Why wait?"

Alexander glanced at him, something lurking on those dark eyes. "Because the man has my curiosity," he said. "I could have killed him many times during the course of my travels, but his movements intrigue me. He has left his share of used women and death in his wake, but once we reached Berwick, he sent a messenger north into Scotland, but I managed to catch up to the messenger and kill him, so the Scottish king will not be receiving any intelligence from Douglas. I am sure he does not know that, and now he is here in London, lingering. But what is most strange about his movement is this – I tracked him to St. Blitha, a Poor Dominica order outside of the city walls to the north. I have no idea why he was there, but he stayed for more than an hour before departing and fleeing into the city."

Maxton's eyebrows lifted. *St. Blitha!* That was where his starving angel resided, the woman who had occupied his mind since nearly the moment he'd met her. Confusion swept him.

"Why in the hell would he be going to St. Blitha?" he said. "There are only women there. What message could he possibly have for them?"

Alexander shook his head. "I cannot tell you," he said. "It is possible he has a sister there, I suppose. Mayhap he went to visit her. Or, more than likely, he has a message from The Lateran Palace for one of the nuns."

"A message from whom?"

Alexander lifted his shoulders. "According to Abramo, Douglas had many audiences with the Holy Father before he left," he said. "Mayhap it is a message from the Holy Father himself, although I have no idea why the man would be sending a message to a tiny, poor order like St. Blitha."

"But it was Abramo who sent you to kill the man?"

"Aye."

"Did he do it on the order of the Holy Father?"

Alexander shook his head. "He made it clear that there was no such order," he said quietly. "It is Abramo who wants him dead, not the Holy Father."

All of that made absolutely no sense to Maxton. "Baffling," he muttered. "What concerns me, however, is your thought that he could be the very assassin I am looking for. Could it be possible he went to St. Blitha asking for sanctuary after he completes his task against John? If you think about it, killing the king and then hiding in an obscure abbey until he can escape London is a rather brilliant plan."

"A plan that could have come from the Holy Father in one of those many meetings with him that he has had with the man."

The light went on in Maxton's eyes. "Indeed," he growled. "Now, this is starting to make some sense. Your assignment to kill Douglas could solve both our problems."

Alexander nodded knowingly, tapping the side of his head as if to congratulate them both on figuring out a most complex and confusing scheme. *If* it was true. At this moment, they had no reason to believe it wasn't.

"What next?" Alexander asked him.

Maxton thought on that question quite seriously. "I believe you should go to the docks," he said. "Kress and Achilles are already there, scouting out the area. Find them and tell them what we have discussed. As for me… I have business at St. Blitha."

"What are you going to do?"

Maxton wasn't sure, but thoughts of Andressa were weighing more heavily on his mind than they ever had before. He was coming to think that meeting the starving woman that morning hadn't been a coincidence… perhaps it had been a sign from God, sent to help him prevent the murder of a king.

He couldn't think of it any other way.

"I am not certain as of yet," he said, "but I will meet you at the docks when I am done. Wait for me there."

Alexander nodded, giving him yet another slap on the shoulder as he departed the chamber, heading down the stairwell. Maxton wasn't far behind him; suddenly, he wasn't sleepy any longer. His mind was working furiously on what he'd been told, and what he needed to do.

An eventful morning was about to turn into an eventful day.

CHAPTER SEVEN

SHE WAS WASHING laundry for other people.

Andressa's main duty at St. Blitha was the laundry – she washed clothes for the nuns as well as religious cloths and other things that belonged to the abbey. Anything that was washable, she took charge of. But three years ago, the Mother Abbess began to take in laundry and charged a hefty price for it, telling the rich of London that the clothing was washed in holy water and, therefore, cost more to wash. It was Godliness on a whole new level, and being that there were many pious people in London and the surrounding areas near the Bishopsgate area, there was often a good deal of laundry to wash.

Of course, the clothes were only washed in ordinary water from the small creek that ran alongside the abbey and the Mother Abbess pocketed the money that was paid for the privilege of having a starving, over-worked woman pound out the dirt on the clothing. Sometimes, Andressa even delivered the laundry back to the rich clients, taxing her already-strained body. But at St. Blitha, hard work and laundry were all Andressa had ever known, because when she had first come to the abbey, she'd been put where she was needed, and that was in the laundry helping an old nun who was clearly dying.

The woman could hardly breathe, and hard labor was difficult, but she gamely did her best. She had been kind to Andressa and had taught her what she needed to know about doing the laundry and pleasing the

Mother Abbess. She taught her how to boil the water for washing and use the wood ash from the fire to make the tallow soap for the laundry.

Andressa had become quite adept at making the soap from wood ash and tallow that was gathered from any fat source – beef was preferable, but she had also used mutton. Goose fat was frowned upon because it smelled so badly, and Andressa made new soap about once a month. Lumpy, slimy bars of yellowish soap, but it was a good product because it cleaned well.

Sometimes, she even added lavender to it from the wild bunches of lavender that grew in the herb garden of the abbey, and the nuns throughout St. Blitha used her soap on hands and dishes and even bodies from time to time. Her soap, along with the starch she made from flour and water, made her quite a skilled laundress thanks to the old nun who had taught her.

But the old nun had soon passed away after teaching Andressa what she knew, so for the past four years, Andressa had been the laundress of St. Blitha. The skin on her once-soft, pale hands had long turned red and chapped. Sometimes it even bled. She would rub oil on it, oil from the lamps inside the abbey when no one was looking, and that provided her with some relief, but even now, she'd been scrubbing most of the morning and her knuckles were already raw and chaffed. She was down to her last few items to wash for the day and thankful for it. Most of it was hanging to dry, kept off of the ground by hemp rope strung up in the yard. The Mother Abbess didn't give care to many things around the abbey, but she cared about the laundry, so Andressa had everything she needed for quality work.

St. Blitha was located outside of the city walls of London, but built with sturdy walls of its own. It had a neighbor in St. Mary's Hospital to the south, but for the most part, the order kept to itself. The chapel and dormitories were clustered together on one end of the rectangular-shaped compound, while the kitchens, stable yard, and vegetable garden were on the other.

Because the Mother Abbess didn't like the smell of the barnyard, a large and strangely out of place flower garden was between the stables and the chapel and dorms, including the Mother Abbess' fine quarters. It was out of place because it looked so luxurious in the midst of a poor order, and no one was allowed in the flower garden but the Mother Abbess and Sister Petronilla. Carefully tended rose bushes filled the area, as well as foxglove, nightshade, hemlock, a variety of lavender, and other things.

The laundry was lodged by the kitchens, as they shared many of the same big fires for water boiling, but Andressa had an area all to her own. There were several large willow trees on the other side of the wall, hanging partially over her area and creating pleasant shade on warm days. The postern gate was here, a heavy iron gate with an enormous lock on it, through which a small stream was accessed.

Andressa passed through the gate several times a day, hauling water from the stream to boil, so much so that the gate was only locked at night. They didn't worry about anyone invading their sanctuary; no one ever had, so they moved rather freely even outside the massive walls.

On this particular day, Andressa had moved better and faster than she had in some time because of the meal she'd had that morning. Her belly had been full for the most part, and she'd returned to St. Blitha feeling satisfied, which was a rare occurrence in her world. She began her chores immediately, hauling water from the stream and putting it on to boil. It was so much easier to work with food in her belly, but all the while she kept thinking of the enormous knight with the deep blue eyes who had made the food possible.

A man who had been as handsome as he had been generous.

It was strange, really… Andressa had spent the last four years living with women, essentially isolated from men, which had been a drastic change from her days at Okehampton Castle. Not that Lady de Courtney allowed her charges to interact with the men at the castle without restraint, but she had been around them constantly. There had even been one man she'd been fond of but she didn't think of him any longer, a young warrior who had lied his way into her heart and the had ripped every last shred of dignity she had from her.

A relationship that had been as tragic as it had been disappointing.

As Andressa went to the stream for more water for the last of her afternoon washing, she found herself entertaining thoughts of Rhyne de Leybourne. After that fateful June day when he'd seduced her, she'd fought to put him out of her mind. Her humiliation ran bone-deep, humiliation in her own foolishness for having believed him in the first place. She'd known him the entire time she'd been at Okehampton Castle, a vain but handsome knight, someone she's been very attracted to, and he towards her.

For the first year at St. Blitha, she'd thought of him quite often, wondering where he was and if he was well. Secretly, she hoped he'd come for her at St. Blitha, but the truth was that he probably had no idea where she was and she was sure her aunt would never tell him. He'd been away when her aunt had summoned her from Okehampton, and then she'd been sent straight on to St. Blitha.

But Rhyne had been clever. She saw that in hindsight now. In Andressa, he saw the opportunity to marry well and inherit a substantial fortune, and he wouldn't let her get away so easily. She remembered when he finally came to St. Blitha and had laid in wait for her to tend to her washing, as she did every day. It had been in this very spot by the stream when he'd found her and coerced her into the barn of a neighboring farm, where he'd told her how much he loved her before stealing her innocence away.

Oh, he'd promised to return for her, but that promise wasn't as important as a marriage to a French heiress. In truth, Andressa didn't even really know why he'd come to St. Blitha that day; it was clear she had nothing to give him. Her aunt had seen to that. Perhaps Rhyne thought he could fight for her inheritance and steal it back from the aunt, but it must have been too hard for him to work for it. The French heiress he married must have been an easier catch. Or, at least he probably hadn't had to fight for her. It had been wealth for the taking, leaving Andressa at St. Blitha with nothing but a memory she had all but pushed from her mind.

She wouldn't think of him.

She couldn't.

Kneeling down beside the stream for the twentieth time that day, she fought off thoughts of Rhyne. Any fondness she'd ever felt for him had turned into bitter hatred those months ago. Lost in thoughts of the brash young liar, she was startled from her thoughts when a deep voice came from behind.

"I've never been to St. Blitha before. And when I do, I see that you are drawing water? Have you no well?"

Stumbling forward and nearly falling into the stream, Andressa was able to catch her balance in time, looking over to see Maxton approaching beneath the willow branches.

For a moment, her breath caught in her throat; it was a surreal experience to watch the powerful knight as he moved beneath the trees with the gait of a hunter stalking prey. There was something so magical about the way he walked, powerful strides from a powerful man. He was clad in the same clothing she'd seen him in earlier in the day, leather breeches and a tunic and heavy, fur-lined coat, but as he came closer, she noticed that there was something in his eyes that hadn't been there before. There was... warmth.

Was that even possible?

Her stomach began to twist in knots.

"Considering this is a female order, I am not surprised that you have not visited before, my lord," she said, standing up with the bucket in her hand. "And, aye, I am drawing water because I am the laundress. We do have a well, but the water has a tint to it, making it no good for the laundry."

"The laundress, eh? An honorable duty."

"What are you doing here?"

Maxton didn't quite smile at her, but his lips twitched as if he was entertaining the thought.

What *was* he doing here?

It was a question with more than one answer. The first answer was, of course, a fact-finding mission. After his conversation with Alexander at Farringdon House, he had to come to the focus of their discussion – this mysterious, treacherous place called St. Blitha. An order of poor nuns, and a Mother Abbess who apparently had no trouble committing murder. It was a distorted and complex place, indeed, if all of that was true, and if Douglas had indeed been here, it only added to that chaotic concept. Maxton wanted to scout the place out, because Reconnaissance was the smart thing to do.

Perhaps St. Blitha was not all it seemed.

But the second answer, of course, was a certain a certain young woman who lived here. That was perhaps the more prevalent answer, especially now that Maxton had lain eyes on her. Pale, graceful, with the face of an angel, Maxton had never been smitten with anyone in his life, but oddly enough, he suspected he might quickly be approaching that state with Andressa. He couldn't explain his curiosity towards her, and his interest, any other way.

"I had business outside of town and happened to be passing by," he lied. "I could see you from the road."

That part was true; the angle of the road made it so the area beneath the trees and the stream was visible from it, but only briefly. Briefly enough that Maxton had seen the movement and spied her, making his story believable.

But Andressa didn't question him, even if she did look past his shoulder, to the distant road beyond, just to make sure she could really see the road. "I see," she said, fixing him in the eye. "Then I am glad to see you again to apologize for my behavior this morning. I ran from you rudely when I should not have. You were simply being kind and trying to help me from my... well, my predicament here."

He shook his head, cutting her off, though it was gently done. "I should not have been so bold as to suggest finding a place for you away from St. Blitha," he said. "It is your home, right or wrong, and it was improper of me to suggest you leave. Forgive me."

Her face brightened as she realized he wasn't upset with her. "There is nothing to forgive, my lord. Please allow me to thank you once more for the meal this morning. It was most generous of you, my lord. You must be a very kind and generous man to all those in need."

He lifted his eyebrows, averting his gaze as he looked for a place to sit down. Now that he'd finally found her, he had no intention of leaving. "There are many, many people who would dispute that."

Andressa watched him meander around until he found a stump from a long-dead willow tree worth sitting on. "But I cannot believe that," she said. "Clearly, you are a pious man who gives greatly of himself. I am sure God will reward you."

Maxton snorted as he planted his buttocks on the stump. "Lady, I cannot permit you to entertain the thought that I am anything other than what I am," he said, looking up at her. "I am a knight of the highest order. I have just returned from The Levant after many years away. You cannot possibly imagine how un-kind and un-generous I am."

Her brow furrowed curiously. "The Levant," she repeated. "You went on Richard's Crusade?"

"I did."

She gasped softly, suddenly quite interested in his presence whereas only moments before, she'd been seemingly wary of it.

"I have never met anyone who went on his Crusade," she said. "Will you tell me of it? If you have the time, of course. I can only imagine how glorious it must have been, wielding the word of God against the savages. What a great and fearsome sight that must have been."

It was a dreamy and misguided opinion; he could see it in her face. The woman was naïve, living sequestered as she did. "Do you truly wish to know what kind of a sight it was?" he asked. "I do not think you will like the answer."

She nodded eagerly, sinking to her knees in the grass with her bucket still in her hand. "I very much want to know," she said. "Will you please tell me?"

Maxton looked at her; he wasn't a man with tact, nor did he couch harsh realities. In fact, his blunt honesty was one of his traits. But in this case, he was considering softening that particular talent because, somehow, Andressa seemed like a delicate flower, idealistic and innocent, and he didn't want to crush that spirit in her. He found it intriguing because in his line of work, he didn't often meet people with such an ingenuous view of the world.

He cleared his throat softly.

"The Levant is a land with golden sand as far as the eye can see," he said. "Everything is golden for the most part. And it is very hot."

She was already hanging on his description. "Hot? It is never cold?"

"Hardly ever. And they have amazing creatures there called camels. They look like a very large horse with big lips, big eyes, and big feet. They also have a hump on their back that stores their water for times when they cannot drink."

Her eyes widened. "Camels," she repeated in awe. "They sound like monsters."

He grinned, lop-sided. "They are most assuredly not, though they are ugly enough," he said. "Many of the Muslims travel with them instead of horses. They have more endurance than a horse."

She was fascinated with the idea of a camel. "It seems incredible to imagine such a beast, truly. Are there any in England?"

He shrugged. "I have not seen any," he said. "I think they prefer the hotter climate. They would not do well in our cold and wet seasons."

He suddenly stood up from the stump, making his way over to where she was sitting. Andressa watched him curiously, perhaps a bit fearfully, preparing to leap to her feet if he came too close. When she saw him pick up a stick, she was very close to scrambling away from him, but he came to a pause by a strip of mud near the stream, something that didn't have any growth or grass on it. He began to draw in the mud with the stick.

"This is what they look like," he said as he sketched out a shape. "Very tall, very big. They have also been known to spit when displeased."

Very interested, Andressa moved so that she could see what he was drawing. It looked like a horse with a big, flat head and a hump on its back.

"Fascinating," she said, grinning. Then, she sat back, looking up at him. "What else did you see? Were the savages truly dressed in skin and speaking the language of Satan?"

He shook his head. "Nay, they were not dressed in skins," he said. He thought carefully on his answer because his reply was something that was not conventional thought amongst the Christian armies. "If you want to know the truth, many were men of intelligence and education. Their families are thousands of years old. They have strange customs, that is true, but there were some I came to know and I found them inoffensive."

Andressa listened seriously. "But they worship their own god."

"They worship one god, as we do, and it is the same god. They simply call him a different name."

It was clear she had never heard such a thing. "What do they call him?"

"Allah."

She thought on that. "What a strange name," she said. "Why do they not simply call him God, as we do?"

"Allah means God in their language."

"Mother Abbess has said it is Satan's language."

He finished with the camel drawing, standing back to take a look at his handiwork. "It is *not* Satan's language," he said. "It is an ancient language, and quite beautiful if you listen closely. *Ladayk jamal alshams almushriqa.*"

Her eyes widened. "Is that their language?" she gasped. "What did you say?"

A smile played on his lips. "I said that you have the beauty of the rising sun," he said. "The Muslim poets are great flatterers. That is part of a song I heard once. I was riding down an alley in the city of

Caesarea, north of Jerusalem, and I heard a young man singing as he played a harp he had made himself. The words went something like this – *In a world of darkness, you are my only light, with the beauty of the rising sun.* It was a lovely song."

Andressa was enchanted with the entire conversation, swept up by his deep, rumbling voice and stories of the great and mysterious Levant. But it also brought her back to the days of Okehampton Castle, when she was exposed to the beauty and excitement of life. Minstrels, plays, book reading… they had been everyday occurrences and as Maxton spoke of far away lands, she began to realize just how much she was missing tucked away in St. Blitha.

The loneliness and isolation were something she'd long struggled with, even as memories of her former world were shoved aside. She was so very lonely in this cold, terrible place, and she missed the beauty of the world outside the walls of St. Blitha. Hearing Maxton's words were like a stab to her tender heart because she could see just how isolated she had become from things that used to bring her joy.

"It is very lovely," she said, feeling sad. "Thank you for telling me of it. But I am sure I have kept you long enough; surely you must be on your way now."

She stood up, taking her bucket with her, and Maxton tossed the stick in his hand aside. "I have men waiting for me near the docks, but they can continue to wait," he said. "I thought to spend some time speaking to a former charge of Okehampton. It is not often I come across someone who is from Devon, from places that I know."

She smiled weakly, glancing over to the old walls of the abbey and the open postern gate as if looking for those who would see her speaking with a man, which would be greatly frowned upon. There weren't many nuns in the kitchen area or stables, but there were a few. She truly didn't want to be seen because such information would undoubtedly make its way back to the Mother Abbess.

She didn't want to enrage the woman.

"I would like to speak of such things, truly, but I have work to do," she said, moving away from him. "I... I will thank you once more for your generosity today, not just with your money, but with your time. I cannot remember when I have spent such a pleasant time."

"It does not have to end."

Andressa wasn't sure what to say to that. It made her want to run away from him, but it also made her want to stay. In fact, his words made her feel very strange inside; her stomach was quivering and every time she looked at the man, she seemed to forget how to breathe. It occurred to her that the last time she trusted a man, it hadn't gone well in her favor. She wasn't sure she was ready to trust again, but Maxton made it so easy to believe that she could. Perhaps she really was a fool, because she wanted to trust him.

She wanted nothing more.

"I must go," she said, feeling uncomfortable and the least bit afraid. "Good day to you, my lord."

"Do I frighten you, Lady Andressa?"

She hadn't taken three steps when she came to a stop and turned around, eyeing him. "Nay," she said, though it was a lie. "You have been very kind."

He smiled, a rather lazy gesture. "Then do not leave," he said. "Let us speak more on The Levant and Okehampton. At the very least, I can help you draw water as we speak."

She frowned. "Are you mad?" she said. "That is woman's work. Moreover, you cannot help me. I must complete my chores alone."

"But..."

"Remember what I told you about the Mother Abbess. I do not wish to be punished by her."

That brought an instant change in Maxton's over-eager demeanor. In fact, he did remember what she'd said. *No one returns from The Chaos*, she had said. He couldn't believe he hadn't thought of that threat before, but it honestly hadn't occurred to him. He'd been so pleased to see her, and so selfishly eager to talk to her, that he hadn't really thought of anything else, including her safety. His gaze darted to the wall, the postern gate, to see if anyone was watching them.

"Bloody Christ," he muttered. "I did not even think about that. Will she punish you if she knows you have been speaking with me?"

Andressa lifted her shoulders, turning to the gate and the wall as well to see if anyone was spying on her. The longer she stood there, the greater chance there was. She thought she saw the nun who ran the kitchens through the gate, but she couldn't be sure.

"I do not know," she said honestly. "I have never spoken to anyone like this before, so it is best if you leave now and I return to my duties."

Maxton wasn't going to try to coerce her into remaining. It was a selfish want and something that could very well get her into a good deal of trouble. He wanted to speak with her more, perhaps even ask her in a roundabout way about Douglas' appearance at the abbey, but he wouldn't, at least not now. But he hoped there would be time for that later. He took a few steps towards her, now within arm's length of her.

"One more question and I will go," he said quietly. "Will you be searching for food again tomorrow?"

Her cheeks flushed with embarrassment and she lowered her gaze. "I… I do not think so."

"Then when?"

She sighed heavily. "It is difficult to say," she said. "I would like to say that I shall never venture out again, but that is not the truth."

Maxton could see that she was ashamed over what she had to do in order to put food in her belly and he felt like a cad for pushing her, for wanting to know when she would be starving again so that he could see her and speak with her. It was rude of him and he knew it. Therefore, he tried another tactic.

"If you come out tomorrow, I will be waiting for you at the same tavern where you ate today," he said, his deep voice coming out as something of a purr. "I shall buy you another meal and we can continue our conversation."

Oh, but it was tempting. And that voice! Like the caress of angels! Andressa couldn't decide if the lure of eating another full meal was more than the lure of conversation with the man, who had so far proven to be a window back into the world she'd forgotten about. She knew that she should retreat into the abbey yard this very moment, but she couldn't seem to do it. His presence was starting to confuse her – why should the man want to speak with her again? Why should he want anything to do with her? He knew her story. She had nothing to offer by way of charm or even intelligence, and as a pledge to a poor order, she had nothing to offer, *period*. She was dressed in rags and the lovely, long hair she'd been so proud of all her life was surely a dirty sight to see.

She was ashamed.

There was nothing she could offer this handsome knight and she surely wasn't going to allow herself to be lured into anything clandestine. If he was looking for a companion, or more, then he would have to look elsewhere.

His intentions were most confusing.

"I cannot, my lord," she said, turning for the postern gate again. "Although I am grateful for your generosity, I will not accept your offer. Good day to you."

She was nearly at the gate, moving swiftly, with her water bucket sloshing. Maxton was a step or two behind her, following her when he knew very well he should not be.

"I did not mean to offend you," he said quickly. "I simply meant… if you ever need me, my lady, leave word at The King's Gout Tavern. Leave it there and I shall answer. Meanwhile, I will tell the tavernkeep that you are to be fed anything you wish, at any time, and I will pay for it. You do not even have to see me or speak with me; simply go to the tavern and they will feed you. It is the least I can do for someone from Okehampton who listened to my stories of camels without laughing at me."

Andressa's hand was on the postern gate as she turned to look at him, the expression on her face of surprise and distress and gratitude all rolled into one. God, how she wanted to believe this man and his kindness, but she simply didn't understand why he should pay her such attention.

Why he should be so kind to her.

Impulsively, she sought to make her position clear.

"Again, your generosity knows no limit," she said, "but I cannot accept or expect such charity. Surely you can understand that."

"Then stealing is better?"

Her cheeks flushed again. "Nay," she said after a moment. "I am more than willing to work off the price of a meal. I cannot simply accept food from you without providing you with some manner of payment or reciprocation."

He shrugged. "Then look at the food as a loan," he said. "Someday, I will expect you to pay me in return, in money or in trade. Would that make you feel better if we had that understanding?"

Did it? She wasn't sure. But the prospect of a regular meal was almost more than she could bear. To know that she would be fed regularly, as much as she wanted, was the greatest blessing she could think of. But she still didn't understand his motivation.

"Why?" she finally hissed. "Why should you do this for me? I am no one to you."

He smiled, dimples carving into his cheeks. "I told you," he said. "It is not often I have a chance to speak to someone who knows Devon as I do, and as I also told you, I have just returned from The Levant. It has been a very long time since I have spoken to an Englishwoman who was worth knowing. Is that not reason enough?"

"And I am worth knowing?"

He dared to reach out, drifting his fingers over hers. It was a reckless and inappropriate action, but one that sent Andressa's heart racing with shock and excitement. She very nearly dropped the bucket. As her mind reeled, she could only thing of one thing to think, of only one thing to say -

Do it again!

But the words, thankfully, didn't come. Before she could reply in any manner, she caught movement out of the corner of her eye. It was the nun who tended the kitchens and she was peering from across the yard, an expression of condemnation on her face. It was enough to cause Andressa to forget Maxton's touch and bolt through the postern gate, pulling it shut and bolting it from the inside.

But she could still see Maxton standing outside the gate through the big iron slats. He hadn't moved. Terrified that the kitchen nun might say something to the Mother Abbess about the laundress and the strange man, she hissed at him.

"Please leave," she said. "Every moment you remain brings me one step closer to trouble."

Maxton knew she was correct, so he backed away from the gate. He, too, had seen the nun near the kitchen, so he quickly moved away from the gate, losing himself in the trees that were next to the enormous wall and hoping he would not be seen by anyone else. But he was prevented from running off completely by the fact that he knew Andressa was on the other side of the wall. He just couldn't seem to leave her, even if he couldn't see her, and he couldn't help the smile that played on his lips as thoughts of the pale young woman lingered.

That lovely, graceful lass...

Still, it wouldn't do any good to hang around, so he began to move towards his horse, the old charger that Gart had purchased for him in France so that he would have something to ride home from Baux. But he hadn't taken two steps when he began to hear voices – raised voices. One voice was clearly Andressa's; he could tell because she had a rather deep speaking voice for a woman. It was sultry and smooth.

There was an argument going on.

Curious, he made his way back towards the wall, listening to what was being said. He couldn't really hear the words, but he could hear the tone. It was strained. Whoever Andressa was talking to had a shrill voice that was saying something about sin. *You are wicked*, the woman said. Andressa replied steadily, but try as he might, Maxton couldn't really hear what she was saying because she was keeping her voice quiet. Yet, there was nothing quiet about the loud slapping sound he heard next.

After that, it was grunts and shrieks and more slapping noises.

Maxton did what he shouldn't have done; he bolted for the postern gate. It didn't even occur to him to stay out of sight because he was more than likely the very reason for the fight, so he rushed up to the gate, pressing his face between the iron slats only to see Andressa sitting on top of the kitchen nun, pinning the woman's arms.

The woman on the ground was screaming and trying to kick, but Andressa held the woman down firmly. It was rather impressive, in truth. Maxton watched with great concern, his natural instincts wanting to help Andressa, but those thoughts were curbed as shouts began to come from the dormitories. Women in woolens and veils over their heads began to pour from the building and he let go of the postern gate, moving away from it and sinking back against the wall to watch where he could not be seen.

Unfortunately, it wasn't a good vantage point because there were vines in the way and even a tree trunk inside the compound, preventing him from seeing very much. He could see several nuns rushing out to break up the fight and he could hear stern words being passed around, tones that seemed to him like scolding. He strained a little, trying to see what he could see and increasingly concerned for Andressa when, abruptly, he saw her being led away by two nuns, back in the direction of the dormitory and chapel.

The nuns had her by both arms, one on each side, holding on to her to make sure she wouldn't try to escape them. Maxton realized that his heart was pounding against his ribs as he remembered once more what Andressa had said about the Mother Abbess and what happened to charges that displeased her. God, that horrible thought came pouring over him as he watched the nuns leading her away.

Leading her away because he had been stupid enough to seek her out and have a conversation with her like a giddy squire. This was all his fault.

He'd gotten the woman into trouble.

At a loss as to what to do about it, his first instinct was to make his way inside the abbey and save her. He could move with stealth; that was part of his skill set. He knew he could make it into the abbey and find her, and kill anyone and everyone who got in his way, but then he would be violating the sanctity of a holy order. Not that it really mattered to him; after his bout with the Holy Father and all that entailed, he had no respect for the church at all. Not one bit. But there was the real fear that he would only make things worse for Andressa with his actions. It wasn't as if she'd ever given him an indication that she, in fact, *wanted* to be saved.

He couldn't save a woman who didn't want his help – and had clearly refused it.

There were voices near the wall now, catching him off guard, so he bolted away, moving swiftly through the trees and across the streaming, circling around to come to his horse, who was tied off in a copse of trees a fair distance away from the abbey. He didn't want to be caught lingering around the abbey. Perhaps the best thing for him was to simply leave.

It wasn't as if he had a choice.

Even as he mounted his steed and charged off southward along the road, paralleling the abbey and her old walls, all he could think of was Andressa and how to help her. Kress and Achilles and Alexander were waiting for him at the docks along the Thames, but here he was, thinking of a pledge. In fact, after leaving St. Blitha, he spent an hour lingering by Bishopgate, a massive opening in the London wall, thinking on what to do, but he kept coming up with the same answer – *stay away.*

Wait.

Perhaps that was all he could really do.

But he did know one thing – he was going to be at The King's Gout tavern tomorrow morning before dawn, waiting to see if Andressa showed up. If she did, all well and good. But if she didn't…

Then he would add breaching an abbey to his list of sins.

One way or the other, he wasn't going to let her fall victim to The Chaos.

CHAPTER EIGHT

"He called himself Alasdair Baird Douglas and he brought a message from our Holy Father," the Mother Abbess was speaking in hushed tones in her native Italian language. "He has made his wishes known to us."

She was addressing three small women bound up tightly in the woolens of their order, older women with non-descript faces set within the confines of their non-descript habits. One woman had a hook nose and small, brown eyes, while the woman next to her was a little rounder, with a round face and strangely dark eyebrows. The third woman was taller, far more slender, and had a nervous tick. She kept scratching her eyes, leading to no eyebrows or eyelashes.

"Did we have a visitor?" the eye-scratcher asked, also in the Italian language. "I did not see anyone. Did anyone else? Did anyone see him?"

It was nervous chatter, but that was normal coming from her. Sister Dymphna portrayed a woman who was frightened of her own shadow, and a constant worrier, always the one to speak out with questions or concerns. It didn't matter the subject; Sister Dymphna had been known to worry herself into vomiting on more than one occasion, and sometimes she vomited blood, which the Mother Abbess told her followers was a sign that the Holy Spirit was upon her. Sister Dymphna's nervous stomach worked well to strike fear into the hearts of those at St. Blitha on several occasions.

But she was always the one with questions, now about the appearance of the mysterious Alastair Baird Douglas. The Mother Abbess answered patiently, but as always, her patience was limited.

"Sister Vera saw him," she said. "She admitted him into the chapel. Then, the du Bose girl was passing through the chapel at that time and he spoke to her, asking her to confirm my identity. She saw him as well."

Sister Dymphna was still twitching, itching at her eyes, but she didn't ask any further questions because she knew that tone in the Mother Abbess' voice. It hinted at silence and obedience. Therefore, she looked to the other two women in the room, waiting for them to voice their own questions, but no one did. They remained silent. Therefore, Sister Dymphna fell silent as well.

It was the usual dynamic between the four of them. The Mother Abbess would speak and the three of them, her most trusted companions, would listen, mostly with unbridled adoration, but sometimes, Sister. Dymphna had questions. Like now. Questions that would die one her lips because asking them, to the Mother Abbess, signaled a lack of faith. And no one wanted to project that.

The four of them had been together for a very long time, since they had been very young and had all been orphans in the Santa Giulia convent in northern Italy where the Mother Abbess had been a nun at the time. She took the three orphans under her wing, teaching them how to survive and thrive under the strict rule of the Church.

But the Mother Abbess lived by her own rules, even back then, as they soon discovered.

The Mother Abbess' name was, in fact, Giulia. Her parents had been wealthy land owners, the Orsini family, and Giulia and her brother, Celestine, had both been given over to the church at a very young age. Whilst Celestine begged, borrowed, and schemed his way to the top, Giulia did much of the same, only her actions were darker and more sinister than her brother's behavior.

Guilia had the heart of a killer.

If she had felt threatened, a pillow over the face of her sleeping rival would take care of the issue. She had never been beyond such things. She didn't view life as most people did; to her, it was disposable. There was no value to it. The three orphans, Dymphna included, had watched Giulia kill and lie and scheme, and once, she'd even surrendered her virginity to a particularly lustful priest who had then, in turn, given her a glowing recommendation when it came to assuming a post at a wealthy convent. A post that had been a stepping stone to becoming the Mother Abbess of her own convent – St. Blitha.

The woman had clawed her way to the top.

Therefore, Dymphna and her two comrades were shadows of the Mother Abbess, Seaxburga as she was now known, and they catered to her every whim, her every need. They were mere shadows themselves now, wraiths of what they'd once been, women who no longer possessed minds or wills of their own. Everything they did, and everything they thought, came from the Mother Abbess, and that included the directive they were now facing.

There was no remorse, no sense of morality.

Just death.

The Mother Abbess knew all of this, of course. She knew how much control she had over these women and it pleased her deeply. Seeing that Dymphna's questions had been silenced for the moment, her gaze drifted to the other two women in the chamber. The woman with the hook nose was known by her chosen name of Sister Agnes, while the round woman with the dark brows was Sister Petronilla. All names they'd chosen at their consecration, names of Christian martyrs, leaving their birth names behind as one would shed a skin.

The innocence they'd once had, as children, was long since vanished. What was left in its place was nothing short of mindless obedience, women who had convinced themselves that ambition and servitude on behalf of Christ and the Mother Abbess knew no boundaries or no limits. Much as Christ had disciples to do his bidding, she had hers, and in this case, they would understand the significance of this particular undertaking.

It was perhaps the most important they'd ever faced.

"As I was saying, Alasdair Douglas brought a message from our Holy Father," she said, lowering her voice. Even though they were in her private chamber, and she was speaking in Italian, she did not want her words over heard. "He serves the Holy Father as we do, a great and pious servant of God. It seems that the Holy Father has a task for us, a task of the utmost importance. We have never had such an important calling, sisters. We have been asked to change England's destiny."

As Sister Dymphna scratched, Sister Agnes looked at the Mother Abbess most curiously. "But how are we to do such a thing?" she asked. "Surely we cannot change the destiny of an entire country."

The Mother Abbess lifted a thin eyebrow. "We can," she insisted quietly. "I shall be plain – we have been asked to remove the king."

Now, all three of the nuns were looking at her with great confusion, shocked by the words coming out of her mouth.

"Remove the king?" Sister Agnes repeated. "But… how? We have no great weapons, no great armies. The king is surrounded by knights, men we cannot fight. How are we supposed to remove a man who surrounds himself with men who could easily kill us?"

The Mother Abbess shook her head sadly. "Have you learned nothing, Sister?" she asked. "When have we ever used force to accomplish that which has been asked of us?"

That brought Sister Agnes some pause, but she wasn't sure how to proceed at that point. Sister Petronilla spoke instead.

"We would not know how to use force, Gracious Mother," she said calmly. "But making way to the king is much different from any of the other tasks we have accomplished. What is expected of us, then? How are we do accomplish that which has been asked of us?"

Sister Petronilla tended to be the more rational one of the three. The Mother Abbess turned to her.

"Remember the Bishop of Leeds?" she said. "And you will recall the priests from Kent who sided with the king against our Holy Father. Do you recall what we did for them? We have used ingredients from our garden. Why do you think we grow this great garden of deadly flowers and herbs? It is because they are our weapons in fighting for the rights of the Church. It will simply be a matter of using those weapons again, this time against our king. He will die a death that looks to be from the heart or from the brain. Nothing sinister will be expected, and it will truly be the Will of God. He has provided us with the necessary tools, as evidenced by our great and beautiful garden. He allows it to grow by giving us the sun and the rain. All we need do is use what God has provided."

She made it sound so very simple, as if it was merely another task in a long line of tasks the four of them had undertaken under the years. Anything that displeased the Holy Father, or his minions in Essex or Ely. In fact, the nuns had accomplished several tasks for the Bishop of Essex, and both bishops that had been known to give a command to remove a rival or enemy. In any case, no one ever suspected the method of delivery – when they were looking for armed men, they failed to overlook the unarmed women.

And it was their downfall.

Who would suspect a nun?

"It *is* the Will of God," Sister Petronilla agreed without reserve. She tended to be the first one to follow Mother Abbess in all things. "When are we to complete this glorious mission?"

There was no reserve with any of them. It was simply another request from the Holy Father in a long line of them. As far as they were concerned, they were doing God's work; that was how they rationalized it. The Mother Abbess moved to the window of her solar, the one that overlooked her lovely garden. She was looking to at the tall stalks of foxgloves in particular.

"The Feast of St. Blitha is next week," she said. "The missive from the Holy Father was a great coincidence to this feast because the king has come every year for three years. I have been told that he will be in attendance this year again, eager to pray to the patron saint of hunters.

He will take Communion and it will be a simple thing to poison the man's wine."

Sister Petronilla stood up, making her way over to the windows where the Mother Abbess was. "But the king surely has tasters," she said. "They will taste the wine before it goes to the king."

The Mother Abbess looked at her. "Let them," she said. Then, she returned her focus to the garden, pointing to the tall, purple foxgloves stalks. "Some of those plants are just preparing to blossom. Cut the leaves from them, dry them, and crush them into fine powder. We shall mix the powder with the king's wine. Even if he has someone taste it first, there will be no evidence of the poison and the taster will not become ill right away. It will take time, and by then, the king will have ingested enough to kill him."

It seemed like a logical enough plan, and it was something they'd done once before with the Bishop of Leeds. The man had died in his sleep after a fine meal at the Mother Abbess' table.

"I shall prepare the wine myself," Sister Petronilla said quietly. "I will all ensure it is the only wine the king drinks."

The Mother Abbess nodded but she seemed to be distracted by what she was seeing out the window, beyond the garden. Sister Petronilla looked to see a few nuns milling about, including the nun who managed the kitchen and the pledge who tended to the laundry. It was difficult manual labor, given to the young and the strong. As Sister Petronilla tried to figure out what had the Mother Abbess' attention, the older woman pointed from the window.

"The du Bose girl was there when Alasdair arrived, as I mentioned," she said, gesturing to the woman who had just come in from the postern gate and seemed to be engaged in an animated conversation with the kitchen nun. "I have been watching her, you know. She is an orphan and her aunt, the woman who gave her over to us, paid me a mighty sum to keep the girl here for always. She says that the woman is head-strong and rebellious, but I have never seen that in her. She is an excellent worker and she is obedient."

By this time, Sister Dymphna and Sister Agnes were moving to the window, straining to see what the Mother Abbess was pointing to.

"I have been thinking, sisters," the Mother Abbess continued. "The truth is that we are not growing any younger. If St. Blitha is to remain loyal to the Holy Father, then we must bring in new blood to serve him, as we do. We must bring in young women who understand the importance of fulfilling his wishes, in any circumstance. Women with no ties to family, no ties to the outside world. Women who could disappear from this earth and no one would mourn them. Women who have nothing else to live for."

Now, all four nuns were looking from the windows at the laundry yard, where the tall and pale du Bose girl was in what seemed to be an increasingly heated conversation with the kitchen nun, Sister Blanche.

"I know Andressa," Sister Agnes said, her gaze on the girl in the distance. "She is joyful and she never complains. She does as she is told."

The Mother Abbess nodded. "She pleases me," she said. "Her wash commands a fine price and she is quite valuable to me. I have been thinking of rewarding her for her work by asking her to serve as one of us. She would never have to want, and never have to worry. She would know my care and protection. She is young and strong and bright, and she could carry on our work and traditions long after we are gone."

Sister Dymphna looked at her. "Do you wish her to replace you when the time comes, then?"

"Mayhap."

"But what if she refuses? What we do is only for the most faithful, Mother. What if her faith is not strong enough?"

The Mother Abbess' dark eyes flickered, a ripple of evil in the black depths. "Then she shall belong to The Chaos," she said simply. "No family will miss her when she disappears, and I'll not have her out in the world where she can tell others of our business. If she does not agree to my offer, she will die. And I am sure she will choose life and dedication to the Holy Father over anything else. As I said, she is a bright woman. She will understand and she will be grateful."

The woman said it without any remorse or grief whatsoever, as if discussing something as benign as the weather. She'd lived with her evil so long that, to her, it was normal. It was the way of things.

And they needed new blood to continue their way.

Before anyone could speak again, the object of their attention was slapped by a very angry kitchen nun, and as they watched in shock, Andressa struck back and sent the kitchen nun to her arse. Then, she jumped on top of her and they lost sight of the fight behind the vast garden that was between them and the kitchen yard. The Mother Abbess snapped her fingers.

"Go," she instructed her followers quickly. "See what has happened. Bring Andressa to me and confine Sister Blanche to her room. I will decide what is to be done with her."

The three nuns scattered, fleeing the fine chamber, rushing out to do the Mother Abbess' bidding. As they fled, the Mother Abbess returned her attention to the yard where more nuns were now rushing to break up the fight. She saw clearly when two of them pulled Andressa to her feet and began pulling her away while the kitchen nun, Sister Blanche, continued to scream angrily.

It was a chaotic scene, but one thing was for certain – Sister Blanche struck first. The Mother Abbess didn't know why the woman had lashed out and it didn't matter. All that mattered was that the woman had struck out at someone the Mother Abbess had her eye on, and that kind of thing could not be tolerated. There was no fighting or violence at a convent, as Sister Blanche was about to find out. No matter the reasons, Andressa was about to discover that the Mother Abbess would protect her from a nun out to do her harm. Perhaps it would make the offer to join their exclusive little group that much sweeter, knowing the Mother Abbess would protect her and keep her in all things.

If not, then she, too, would eventually find herself buried deep in The Chaos along with Sister Blanche, never to see the light of day again.

CHAPTER NINE

The Saucy Pigsy tavern
The wharf along the Thames (also known as the docks)

"IT'S ABOUT TIME you came," Kress said. "Where have you been?"

Maxton had come around the corner of an alley, heading onto the main thoroughfare along the river's edge, when a hand shot out from the shadows and grabbed him around the collar. His dirk was unsheathed faster than the blink of an eye and Kress very narrowly missed being shanked. When Maxton saw who it was, he rolled his eyes and sheathed his blade.

"You idiot," he growled. "You know better than to do that."

Kress cast him a long look, a smile playing on his lips. "We've been waiting for you," he said. "Sherry is down here, you know."

"I know."

"He told us about the man he's been trailing and we found him."

"Where?"

Kress threw his thumb in the direction of the tavern behind him. "In there," he said. "Sherry is scouting the exterior of the place to see if there are any escape routes."

"And Achilles?"

"He's already inside."

That caused Maxton to roll his eyes again. "Are you mad? Achilles, alone, in a tavern?"

Kress put up a hand. "Easy," he admonished. "He simply secured a table and some drink. We have a plan."

"What *kind* of a plan?"

About that time, Alexander appeared down the alley that skirted the east side of the tavern. Kress lifted a hand to the man, who noticed both Kress and Maxton, and began making his way towards them swiftly.

Around them, there was the usual hustle and bustle of the docks, with dozens of cogs lined up on the shore. Men were hanging from the riggings, offloading supplies and material, as those on the shore busied themselves around the ships like bees in a hive. There was quite a bit going on, and Maxton glanced at the activity as he waited for Alexander. He also noticed a very strong, very foul smell of fish and sewage, one of the more unpleasant things about being down at the river's edge.

"Nice of you to join us, Max," Alexander said as he came near. "I'd nearly given up on you."

Maxton turned his attention to the man. "My business at St. Blitha took me longer than I thought," he said, quickly changing the subject because he didn't much want to elaborate on what had kept him several hours, including a stop at The King's Gout to make arrangements with the tavernkeep about Andressa. "What's this I hear about a plan?"

Alexander nodded. "I found Douglas," he said, successfully diverted from the subject of St. Blitha. "He's inside this tavern and was fairly drunk when I found him. He's still in there and I have sent Achilles in to watch him to ensure he doesn't slip away."

"What is the plan to capture him?"

Alexander crooked a finger, pulling both Maxton and Kress out of the main street where people were bustling about. He didn't want to be heard with what he was about to say.

"I have been thinking about our conversation earlier, Max, when I mentioned that Douglas might be our papal assassin," he muttered as they stood beneath the shadows of the tavern's upper floor. "I have told Kress and Achilles my theory, too, but now I want to discuss this with you. If I go in there and capture him, there is a great chance that he will never confess to anything and we will never know if he is the assassin you are seeking. I have a feeling the man is a wealth of information, and he's quite drunk now. As we know, drink loosens the tongue, so it might be worth trying to press him for information. I am fairly certain he knows me on sight, but he does not know you or Kress or Achilles. Mayhap if you go in there and drink with him…"

Maxton caught on right away. "Then mayhap we can find out about him and any papal directives."

"Exactly."

Maxton nodded, glancing at Kress as he did so. "I am willing to give it a try if it will help in find our assassin," he said. "I still have not recovered from my drinking binge last night, but I suppose I'll have to push that aside and forge ahead for king and country."

Alexander grinned. "I'll wait out here and watch the doors in case he tries to flee," he said. "There is this front door and then a kitchen door into a yard behind the tavern. I can watch them both while you're inside."

"And if the man confesses?"

"Get your confession and then bring him out to me. I still have a task to complete."

"You'll kill him?"

"That was my order. But in this case, I think we shall take him to The Marshal. The man may wish to interrogate him more. It is not often we have a double agent in our possession."

Maxton couldn't disagree. With the plans laid out, he ventured into the tavern with Kress in tow, entering the low-ceilinged structure. He was immediately hit in the face with the warmth and stench of it; it smelled like dozens of unwashed sailors straight off the cogs on the river who had been at sea for months or even years on end. They had seawater in their blood and they reeked of it.

Kress tugged on him, pointing to the corner near the front window of the tavern where Achilles was sitting. Pushing through the crowds of smelly, laughing men and women, they made their way over to Achilles, who had a cup of ale in his hand, half-full. He greeted them both amiably.

"No fights and no women, Max," he announced as if proud of himself. "See? I am behaving myself."

Maxton snorted. "For once in your life, you dolt," he said. Then, he looked around the common room of the tavern. "Where is our man?"

Achilles lifted the cup to his mouth, using one of the fingers wrapped around the cup to discreetly point. "Over there by the hearth," he said. "The man with the shaggy dark hair. He's wearing a long tunic like the Scots do, hose, and a very big sword. I can see it beneath his cloak."

Maxton didn't turn to look at the man right away. He poured himself some ale first before casually looking in that direction. "I see him," he said. "Is he alone?"

Achilles nodded. "For the most part," he said. "There has been a wench at his table from time to time, but she hasn't been back in a several minutes."

"Then it is time for us to move," Maxton said quietly. "He's a Scotsman, correct?"

"Correct."

"Then we all suddenly have family in Scotland, too. Follow my lead."

They did. Cup in hand, Maxton stood up and began to meander his way over to the table with the lone Scotsman as Kress and Achilles followed. As they crossed the room, they passed by a table of drunken men, singing one of the typically bawdy songs that could be heard in any of the taverns in England. Every squire to old man knew the song.

There once was an old whore named Rose
with a wart on the end of her nose,
She'd give you her best,
With the swell of her breast,

And lick you from your bung to your toes!

One of the singers grabbed at Kress, demanding he sing along, but the blond knight politely refused. He continued on with Maxton and Kress as they headed to the Scotsman's table. They had the pitcher of ale with them and the first thing Kress did was slam the pitcher on to the table to catch the man's attention.

"*Do dhia agus Alba,*" Maxton said happily, in Gaelic. *To God and Scotland.* It was a traditional Scottish toast. "I see that you are from the land of my mother's people, lad. Have a drink with us to celebrate the greatness of Scotland and to William, our very own lion."

The Scotsman looked up at them in shock. All he knew was that drunken men were suddenly toasting Scotland, and the king, and generally creating a ruckus as they commandeered his quiet little table in the corner of the dirty tavern. As the three men overwhelmed the table, cheering the toast as they took up seats, the Scotsman pushed himself away from the table, mostly for self-protection.

"I dinna invite ye tae sit wi' me," he hissed, snatching his cup from the table because he was afraid one of the men might confiscate it and drink it up. He wasn't finished with it. "Go away from me. I want tae be alone!"

Maxton looked at the man, puzzled, before looking to his companions. "He's unfriendly," he said, slurping drunkenly from his cup. "You would think the fact that he is in an enemy country, surrounded by Sassenachs, that he would be a little more friendly to someone who is trying to be friendly to him."

Kress and Achilles nodded firmly, eyeing the Scotsman with disapproval as they, too, drank noisily from their cups.

"I'll drink to Scotland and to William," Achilles said, slurring his words. "I will drink to the man's king even if he won't. I wonder if his king knows that he has a kinsman who will not drink to him?"

"No respect!" Maxton declared.

"No honor!" Kress put in.

"Wait!" The Scotsman sat forward, perhaps a little closer to the table. "I'll kill ye if ye say I have no respect or honor for my king. He's *my* king!"

"Then drink to him!" Maxton boomed.

All four of them down healthy swallows of ale, but in the case of Maxton and Kress and Achilles, it was a very small swallow made to look like a big one. They wanted to get the Scotsman drunker than he was, but they didn't want to follow suit. At least, not at the moment. Maxton smacked his lips and reached out, yanking the Scotsman back to the table by the collar of his cloak.

"You remind me of my mum," Maxton said, pretending to get weepy. "Every time I see a Scotsman, it reminds me of her. She was from Edinburgh. Where are you from, lady?"

The Scotsman was too drunk to pull away from Maxton as the man threw a massive arm over his shoulders in a brotherly gesture. "Dumfries," he said. "A beautiful place."

"Not more beautiful than Edinburgh!"

Now, the Scotsman pulled away from Maxton and scowled at him. "Are ye mad?" he asked, incredulous. "Are ye blind, man?"

Maxton geared up to argue with him but then he backed down, pretending to be too drunk to really care. "Edinburgh," he insisted calmly and feigned another big drink of ale. "What's your name, Scotsman? I cannot keep calling you Scotsman, you know."

The Scotsman's gaze lingered on him a moment before replying. "Ye dunna need tae know."

"Ah," Maxton looked to Kress and Achilles. "He does not have a name. His mother hated him so much that she did not give him one."

That brought a reaction from the man. "I'll have ye know she gave me a great name," he said, drinking from his cup and draining it. Achilles quickly filled it up. "I am Alasdair Baird Douglas. I am a Douglas of Clan Douglas and William Douglas is my liege. Do ye know the man?"

The name confirmed that he was indeed the double agent Alexander had been trailing. Now, they definitely had their man, and Maxton shook his head in response to his question.

"I do not," he said. "But I have heard he is a great man. Let us drink to him, Alasdair."

The cups were lifted again and when they came down, Alasdair pointed to Maxton. "What's yer name, Sassenach?" he demanded, his pointing finger moving around the table. "All of ye; I would know who I'm drinking with."

Maxton threw a thumb into his chest. "Magnus," he lied, giving his father's name. "Hugh and Archie."

He pointed to Kress and then Achilles, giving their father's names as well. Alasdair lifted a cup to them. "Now we are good friends."

The cup was back at his lips, but this time, Maxton and the others didn't drink. They were pretending to, but they had backed off of any more liquor because they needed their wits about them. Alasdair was far gone into his drink, more so now, so Maxton decided to start his interrogation before Alasdair grew too drunk to make sense.

"Aye, we are," Maxton said, waving over the serving wench to bring them more ale. "Tell me of yourself, Alasdair. Why are you in London? Surely you'd rather be in Scotland."

Alasdair nodded, bobbing his head up and down until he became dizzy with it and he had to stop. "Aye, lad," he agreed quietly. "I wish I was."

"Then you must be here because of a woman," Maxton said, snorting. That caused Kress and Achilles to snort as well. "The only reason you would be away from your beautiful Scotland is because of a woman. Well? Is she beautiful?"

Alasdair shook his head, his good humor seeming to fade somewhat. "No beautiful woman," he said. "I wish it was true, but it 'tis not."

"Then you must have business for your laird," Maxton said, snatching the pitcher away from the wench when she came to the table and pouring it into Alasdair's cup. "We are on business for our lord, you know. De Longley out of Northwood Castle. He's right on the border of

Scotland, far to the north. Maybe you have heard of him?"

Alasdair's expression suggested that he was a million miles away, his mind wandering to perhaps the real answer to Maxton's question. But he shook it off when Maxton grabbed at his shoulder, shaking him good-naturedly.

"De Longley?" Alasdair repeated. "Nay, lad. I've not heard of the man. Do ye fight Scots, then?"

"Only if they fight me first."

Alasdair looked at him a moment before breaking into snorts of laughter. "Scots and Sassenach," he muttered. "That's not where the real battle lies, don't ye know. There are battles greater than we can imagine."

"What do you mean?"

Alasdair pointed at him. "I mean the battles we fight against each other are meaningless," he said, taking another huge gulp of ale and then smacking his lips. "'Tis all for naught, Magnus. There are higher powers controlling our destinies."

He said it with certainty and Maxton thought it might be a very good way to lead in to what they all wanted to know – what Alasdair was really doing in London. Maxton topped off Kress and Achilles' cups, which didn't need much refilling considering they had barely been touched. Alasdair was growing more inebriated by the moment.

"Is that so?" Maxton said. "Do you know that for a fact?"

Alasdair nodded, nearly throwing himself off-balance as he did. "No man controls his destiny," he said. "Do ye know who controls it?"

"Who?"

Alasdair winked at him. "God," he said. "God and the church."

"What about the king?" Kress asked, entering the conversation. "Every man is sworn to his king. He creates your destiny."

Alasdair waved him off as if he was spouting nonsense. "The king," he scoffed. "The king? Laddie, the king has nothing to do with a man's destiny. Kings come and go. They are frail men, easily removed. Don't ye know that ye never fight for a king? Ye fight for yer country, no matter who the king is."

Maxton was extremely interested in the path of the conversation at this point. He looked at Kress, silently instructing the man to continue. Kress took the hint; they'd played this game before. He or Achilles would engage someone in conversation while Maxton would sit back and observe, noting weaknesses or discovering truths.

This was a time to discover truth."

"Then you don't fight for William?" Kress asked Alasdair. "He's your king, man."

Alasdair took another sloppy drink of ale before pointing to the ceiling. "But there is a greater king," he insisted. "God is our king above all."

"That is true, but He's not here to give you orders. Your earthly king is."

Alasdair shook his head. "Nay," he insisted. "God gives his command through the church, through our Holy Father. It is the Holy Father who truly controls a man's destiny, even the destiny of a king."

He was pointing to his head as if he'd truly come up with the greatest philosophy of all time. Kress had done well in directing the conversation, but Maxton jumped back into it. He was deeply interested in what the man was saying, considering they all knew he'd been to Rome recently and had contact with the Holy Father according to Alexander.

Now, it was getting interesting.

"Then you are a man of great faith," Maxton said, making it sound like a compliment. "I admire a man of strong faith. You listen to your priest and you do as he says. You lead a good life."

Alasdair looked at Maxton, his head bobbing unsteadily. "Do ye know where I have been?" he said. "The Lateran Palace. I dunna listen tae just any priest, lad. I listen tae the Holy Father himself. He speaks tae me and I listen. And I obey!"

Maxton patted him on the shoulder. "You are a good man, Alasdair," he said, lifting his cup. "To Alasdair. He is a devout man of good faith."

Kress and Achilles lifted their cups, feigning a long drink, followed by Maxton and, finally, Alasdair. As they set their cups back to the table and Kress picked up the pitcher to refill Alasdair's cup, Maxton continued.

"Did the Holy Father shape your destiny, then?" he asked. "You said he speaks to you. Did he tell you to lead a good life and stay out of taverns like this one?"

He grinned, making a joke of it, praying that Alasdair, in his drunken state, didn't realize how much he was probing him. He breathed a sigh of relief when Alasdair responded to his attempted joke.

"He did not shape my destiny," he said, winking at Maxton. "But he uses me to shape another's. How much do ye like yer king, Magnus? Is he a good king tae ye? Because he and the Holy Father dunna like one another."

Maxton glanced at Kress and Achilles, seeing they had the same reaction to that that he did – *how much do ye like yer king, Magnus?* God, that sounded leading. It sounded as if Alasdair had a reason for asking, as if he knew something they did not. The expression on his face only compounded that suspicion. Maxton knew what he said next would matter a great deal if Alasdair had information they were looking for.

It was an effort to look disinterested.

"John is worthless," he muttered, looking around to make sure no one had heard him. "I pray every night that the man falls dead and we are given a better king. I think most Englishmen have the same prayer."

Alasdair's dark eyes glimmered at him. "Prayers are meant tae be answered, Magnus."

"And you know this for a fact?"

Alasdair grinned, a knowing grin, and turned back to his drink. "I do," he said. "Prayers are answered when ye least expect it, in ways ye canna possibly imagine."

Maxton leaned forward, giving the man a doubtful look. "Does God intend to come down from the sky and pluck John off his throne? Is that what is to happen? Be serious, Alasdair. Like it or not, we are stuck with our king. There is naught any man can do about it."

Alasdair shook his head. "Ye're right," he said. "But yer prayers are not tae be answered by a man. Just ye wait, Magnus. Yer prayers will be answered and ye'll get yer knew king."

"Who says so?"

"The Holy Father says so."

With that, he drained his cup, tossing his head back as he did so, and toppled right over onto the floor. As Maxton, Kress, and Achilles looked down at the man, he lay there unconscious, having hit his head on the floor when he fell. Although it wasn't a hard hit, he was so drunk that he instantly knocked himself out, which was frustrating for Maxton. No more answers to his questions.

In fact, if anything, the mystery had deepened.

CHAPTER TEN

St. Blitha

"GRACIOUS MOTHER, I am very sorry about what happened in the kitchen yard." Andressa was speaking quickly and her voice was quivering with fear. "I did not mean to knock Sister Blanche down, but I did not want her to hit me again. I am very sorry for creating such a scene. Please forgive me."

In the lavish solar that belonged to the Mother Abbess, Andressa stood just inside the door, speaking to the Mother Abbess and three other nuns, women she'd known in her four years of servitude at St. Blitha. They were the Mother Abbess' personal servants, nuns who shadowed the Mother Abbess, catered to her, and fulfilled her every whim. Andressa had seen more than one of those women take victims to The Chaos, so she feared them as much as she feared the Mother Abbess. To have all four of those deadly women looking at her, she was feeling cornered and terrified.

But the Mother Abbess, oddly enough, didn't seem too angry. In fact, there was no hint of rage on her face as she stood over by the elaborate oriel windows of the chamber, the same windows that Andressa assumed provided the woman a clear view of what had happened with Sister Blanche.

She knew why she was here.

It must be bad, indeed. After the fight, she had been escorted back to the dormitory by two nuns when Sister Dymphna and Sister Petronilla came to take her to the Mother Abbess. That told Andressa that the situation was dire, indeed, so as she stood just inside the entry door and awaited her punishment, her knees were knocking so badly that it surely must have been clear in her manner. She was certain that the Mother Abbess' rather calm expression was only a ruse, for she was in arm's length of the Staff of Truth as it leaned up against the stone wall.

Andressa was certain that The Chaos awaited her.

God help me!

"You needn't be frightened, Andressa," the Mother Abbess said in her heavy Italian accent. "We saw the entire happening from here. We saw Sister Blanche strike you first. Why did she strike you, child?"

It was not the reaction Andressa had expected, which threw her off-balance. More than that, it was a question she didn't want to answer. She knew it would only make things worse and she wasn't a liar by nature, so the truth of the matter would come out. That was her problem; she had never been able to deliver a bold-faced lie and make it believable, not even to save her own neck. But perhaps she could soften it a bit with some half-truths. Those were a little easier. Swallowing hard, she prayed her explanation wouldn't turn the Mother Abbess' manner from calm to furious.

Please, God!

"She was angry because she saw me speaking with a man outside of the postern gate when I was collecting water, Gracious Mother," she said nervously. "He... he saw me from the road and came to ask if he could draw water for me. I told him to go away, but he insisted on staying. He said that he had gone on the Crusade with King Richard and he spoke of a beastly animal called a camel. He would not leave so I took my water and entered the gate, and that is where Sister Blanche confronted me. She told me I was wicked for speaking to him and slapped me."

That was as close to a lie as Andressa could come and she prayed it sounded believable. She honestly didn't know. She watched the Mother Abbess' face as the woman digested the information. Her only outward reaction was a slight lift of the eyebrows.

"I see," the woman said. "Thank you for telling me the truth. And you do not know this man, Andressa?"

She shook her head. "Nay, Gracious Mother."

"Did he give his name?"

"Maxton, Gracious Mother."

"That is all he gave?"

Andressa nodded. "Aye, Gracious Mother."

The woman's dark gaze lingered on her for a moment before turning to glance at her minions, standing behind her. They were all looking at the Mother Abbess to see what her reaction would be to the situation so that they could react in kind. If she was angry, they would be angry. But if she wasn't angry, then they wouldn't be, either. In this case, the Mother Abbess seemed strangely thoughtful about the situation.

"It is true that the world outside our walls is exposed," she said, to the sisters as well as to Andressa. "And the road from the city is not far off. Clearly, our stream and postern gate can be seen from the road. You did nothing to encourage this man, Andressa?"

Andressa shook her head firmly. "Nay, Gracious Mother. I begged him to leave me alone."

That was the truth, for the most part, but she'd only asked him to leave when she was afraid they would be seen. But the Mother Abbess couldn't know that. Andressa watched the woman pace over to the oriel windows, looking out over the cloister with its vast garden, and feeling a great deal of angst.

Was she angry?

Was she not?

"Did... did I do wrong, Gracious Mother?" Andressa asked, unable to keep silent. "I did not mean to. I was drawing my water and he came upon me."

The Mother Abbess shook her head. "You did not do wrong," she said. "But next time, do not linger on a conversation. Simply come in to the cloister and close the gate. It is best not to speak to a man who was bold enough to approach you from the road. He could have meant you harm."

Andressa nodded quickly. "He did not seem threatening, Gracious Mother, but next time, I will not speak. I will simply come back to the cloister."

The Mother Abbess looked at her. "Did he say there would be a next time?"

"He did not say, Mother Abbess."

The Mother Abbess drew in a long, thoughtful breath. "I hope he will not," she said. "If he does, you will send for me. I will tell him to stay away."

Andressa nodded again, firmly. "I will, Gracious Mother," she said. "Thank you for your protection."

The Mother Abbess turned away from the window, giving Andressa her full attention. "I am here to protect you, child," she said. "In fact, I wish for you to know that you are special to me. You work hard at your task and your work has fine results. I am pleased."

Andressa smiled timidly. "Thank you, Gracious Mother."

A flicker of a smile crossed the Mother Abbess' lips. "You have proven yourself an intelligent, hard-working, and obedient girl, Andressa," she said. "So much so, in fact, that I would very much like for you to truly become one of us at St. Blitha. I wish for you to become one of my personal attendants. Would you like that, child?"

Andressa was deeply surprised by her question. The Mother Abbess didn't pay much attention to her other than her laundry duties, so she thought, so the woman's desire that she should become a nun at St. Blitha was something of a great surprise. It had never even been discussed, but as she thought on it, she knew there was only one answer she could give. Refusal might find her in The Chaos because she was quite certain the Mother Abbess wouldn't take kindly to it.

What the Mother Abbess wanted, the Mother Abbess received.

"I... I would, Gracious Mother," she said. "I suppose I always thought I would take the veil at some point. My aunt has given me over to St. Blitha so I assume she wishes for me to remain here and serve God."

The Mother Abbess came away from the window. "And you shall," she said. "You shall serve him as I serve him. I shall not ask you to do anything I have not done or would not do when it comes to fulfilling God's Will. That is what Sister Dymphna and Sister Agnes and Sister Petronilla and I have been doing, lo, these many years. We have dedicated our lives to serving the Will of God through our Holy Father. Our Holy Father has a very special need for St. Blitha."

Andressa cocked her head curiously. "I did not realize that, Gracious Mother."

The Mother Abbess came nearer, pulling out one of the elaborate chairs from the elaborate table she dined upon. It was a table bought with ill-gotten gains, with food and supplies stolen from the nuns, but it was a source of pride for the Mother Abbess. She didn't see the sorrow on that table, only the luxury of it. The woman sat down, wearily, but her focus remained on Andressa.

"There is more you may not realize," she said. "My brother, Celestine, was the pope before our current Holy Father came into power. As I was the servant to my brother, I am also the servant to *Innocente*. His name, long ago, was Lothario, or Lothar. But now he is the Holy Father known as *Innocente*, a very great and powerful man. He is also a man that the king of England hates and disputes. Are you aware of this?"

Andressa nodded. "When I fostered at Okehampton Castle, Lady de Courtney, my patroness, demanded that her ladies kept with current events," she said. "As of four years ago, I know that King John had disputes with our Holy Father, but since then, I have not kept up with their relationship."

The Mother Abbess nodded faintly. "It has not improved," she said. "The king continues to mock and dispute a man who represents God upon this earth. I fear it is a travesty that the king continues to perpetuate. Surely his subjects see his lack of respect for our Holy Father and that diminishes their faith in him and in the church. That diminishes their respect and faith in us, here at St. Blitha. Mayhap that was even why that man approached you today – because he has little respect for the church you represent."

Andressa knew that wasn't why Maxton had come to St. Blitha, but she didn't want to explain that away, so she simply remained silent. Still, there was something to what the Mother Abbess was saying – there was great contention between the king and the Holy Father, though she really wasn't sure why the woman was bringing it up. Almost as if she was confiding in her, which was starting to throw confused Andressa even more than she already was. She thought she had been brought in to the Mother Abbess' solar for punishment, but now it was turning into something else.

"I am sure anything is possible, Gracious Mother," she said. "And it saddens me to think that our king's behavior towards the Holy Father could turn his subjects against the church. Without the church, there is no civilization. We would all be animals. Lady de Courtney said so."

The Mother Abbess smiled faintly. "It pleases me to hear you say that," she said. "It warms my heart to know that I am making the right decision about you."

"What decision is that, Gracious Mother?"

"The decision to bring you into my fold."

There it was again; that declaration of possession. It wasn't simply that Andressa was to become a nun at St. Blitha, but more than that – a personal attendant, as the Mother Abbess has phrased it. Frankly, Andressa was repulsed by the idea, terrified that this evil woman wanted to bring her closer but knowing there was no way for her to prevent it.

She had no choice.

The expression on her face must have been interpreted as confusion because the Mother Abbess continued quietly.

"For many years, I have served the Holy Father, as have the Sisters

Dymphna, Agnes, and Petronilla," she said. "We have all known each other since we were children. We are all orphans, like you, and we also have a strong desire to serve God, much as you do. But we are not getting any younger, Andressa. There are things we do for the Holy Father and those most loyal to him that we must pass to younger women. It is a great honor to become part of our sisterhood because we carry out work for God that no one knows of, nor will they ever. What we do is secretive and vital. You must become part of what we do and learn our ways, and how important our service to God is, so that you can assume our mantle when we have gone to our heavenly reward."

It seemed to her that the Mother Abbess was talking in riddles. Andressa still wasn't entirely clear on what was expected of her but she tried to sound cooperative. "I am will to do whatever you wish for me to do, Gracious Mother," she said. "Teach me and I shall learn."

The Mother Abbess leaned forward, placing her elbows on the table and folding her hands, as one would whilst praying.

"I shall, child," she said. "I shall teach you everything. From this moment onward, you are part of us. You will become one of us, meaning our secrets, our knowledge, will become yours. Do you agree to this?"

Andressa nodded. "I do, Gracious Mother."

"You will vow before God that you shall never go back on your word to me, Andressa, and that you shall keep to yourself everything I teach you. Will you do this?"

"I swear it, Gracious Mother."

"Good. Because if you do, you shall know the pain of The Chaos first-hand."

Andressa's belly lurched, sinking straight down into her ankles. She'd gone from frightened, to confused, and back to frightened again during the course of the conversation. A deadly threat had just been delivered in a kind voice, as kind as any tone she'd ever heard. Such vile words, so softly spoken – that were pure evil, and there was no doubt in her mind that the Mother Abbess meant them sincerely.

Her knees began to quiver again.

Oh, God...

"I will not go back on my word, Gracious Mother," she said steadily. "I only wish to serve God and be obedient to you."

The Mother Abbess' smile turned into a grimace. In truth, it was still a polite smile, but to Andressa, it was a gesture of wickedness and horror. "You are a good girl," the Mother Abbess said. "Sit down and listen to me. We have much to discuss."

Andressa quickly sat down in one of the fine chairs around the table. Across from her, Sisters Dymphna, Agnes, and Petronilla also sat, their focus solely on her. Andressa felt as if she was being scrutinized down to her very bones. She further wondered if those three nuns ever felt the same fear and horror of the Mother Abbess that she did.

She doubted it.

"It is important that you understand we have been given a great mission by the Holy Father," the Mother Abbess said. "Do you recall two days ago when a man was in our chapel and he shouted at you? He wanted to know who I was. Do you recall this event?"

Andressa nodded unsteadily as she remembered that day and that moment. A dirty man had been standing before the Mother Abbess and he had screamed at her across the room, a Scottish accent demanding identification of the Mother Abbess. She recalled it clearly.

"I do, Gracious Mother."

"He was a messenger from the Holy Father," the Mother Abbess said seriously. "He had come to deliver a message to me personally. It is a message that will change the destiny of England, Andressa. Since you are to be part of us, you must know what has been asked of us. *God* has asked it of us, child. A directive from the Holy Father *is* a directive from God. Do you understand?"

Andressa bobbed her head. "I do."

"And we are servants of God. We do what he asks us to do."

"Aye, Gracious Mother. Always."

That was the response that the Mother Abbess evidently wanted to hear. "As we carry out the Holy Father's wishes, you will help us," she said. "You will see what we do and how we do it, and we shall teach you what you need to know because you will carry on our work after we are gone. Do you understand?"

Andressa was afraid to say that she didn't, but the truth was that she *didn't*. She was so terrified of the consequences of failure that she needed to be clear.

"I do not completely, Gracious Mother," she said honestly. "What am I to learn?"

The Mother Abbess' gaze was intense. "You are to learn true service to God," she said. "You are to learn what it means to accomplish a great and important task."

"What *is* the task, Gracious Mother?"

"To kill the king."

Andressa thought she hadn't heard correctly. She sat there a moment and stared at the woman before her face flickered with confusion.

"To kill…?"

"John. Our directive from the Holy Father, and from God, is to kill King John."

Andressa simply stared at her as the reality of what she was being told sank in. Much to her credit, she didn't react outwardly, but inside, she was screaming. She wanted to run as far and as fast as she could, for now she understood why the Mother Abbess had sworn her to secrecy. A directive had come down from the Holy Father to murder a monarch and the nuns believed they were doing God's work because of it.

She could see it in their faces.

Andressa was very bright; she understood what it would mean should she refuse to participate. Death awaited her, and God knew, she didn't want to die. But she also didn't want to be party to regicide, which was what these nuns were plotting. Andressa knew the Mother Abbess was capable of murder; God help her, she knew it. But to kill the king? Andressa knew her reaction to what she had been told would determine whether or not she lived or died.

She wanted to live.

Bracing herself, she spoke.

"If God has demanded it, then we must obey the holy command," she said, praying she didn't sound as shaken as she felt. "I am anxious to serve our Holy Father."

Oh, but it was a lie coming out of her mouth. She didn't want to help. She didn't want any part of it. But self-preservation was flowing fast and heavy through her veins. She had to make it out of this alive. She watched the Mother Abbess for her reaction, praying it would be one of approval.

Praying she was believed.

Her prayers were answered. The Mother Abbess was evidently pleased, or at least encouraged by it, because she sat back in her chair with an expression of approval on her face. The dark eyes glittered.

"Is that all you have to say to this?" she asked. "You are English, Andressa. Our command is to kill your king. And you have nothing more to say to that?"

She does not believe me, Andressa thought with panic. Quickly, she struggled for a believable response. "Should I?" she said. "My father supported Richard, not John. In fact, he fought for Richard in his wars against his own father. My family has no love for John. But if he is removed, then who shall take his place?"

The Mother Abbess waved a dismissive hand. "Our Holy Father has already made that determination," she said. "Suffice it to say he shall be better than what England has with John. We are *saving* England, Andressa. There is great honor in this."

There was no honor in it. It was murder, but the Mother Abbess was trying very hard to convince her otherwise. She also alluded to the fact that there was already a replacement for the king, ready and waiting, someone clearly chosen by the Holy Father. It was already planned, all of it. Now, it was simply a matter of executing the plot. Andressa was so frightened that she simply went along with it.

"There is great honor in serving God," she said, "and I… I am honored that you would trust me into your sisterhood. I shall not disappoint you, Gracious Mother."

The Mother Abbess studied her a moment longer before looking away, rising from her chair. As she did so, the three sisters also rose, and Andressa took the cue and also bolted to her feet. The four of them watched as the Mother Abbess wandered over to the oriel windows overlooking the cloister.

"It will happen thusly," the Mother Abbess said. "The king will come to us on the feast day of St. Blitha and it is then that we shall carry out our command. You, dear Andressa, are an excellent servant of God and I urge you to continue to be so. We want no failings in our sisterhood."

"I shall not fail, Gracious Mother."

The Mother Abbess turned to look at her. "I believe you," she said. "And as a reward for your obedience, I shall expand your duties. After you complete your usual laundry duties, you shall help Sister Petronilla in the garden and she shall show you what we must do in order to carry out our mission. She will take you under her wing and ensure you know all she knows. Won't you, Sister Petronilla?"

Andressa found herself looking at a round woman with heavy, dark brows. She knew Sister Petronilla by name only, because in the time she'd been at St. Blitha, she'd never had any closer interaction with her. But Sister Petronilla was looking her over now, perhaps even haughtily.

"I will, Gracious Mother," Sister Petronilla said. "I will work closely with her to ensure she understands everything."

"Excellent," the Mother Abbess said. "Then the matter is settled. Andressa, finish your duties in the laundry today and tomorrow, once they are completed again, you will join Sister Petronilla in the garden."

"Aye, Gracious Mother," Andressa agreed. She hesitated a moment before speaking. "The last of my duties today includes Lady Hickley's fine dress. She wanted it for this evening. May I take it to her?"

"Of course," the Mother Abbess said. "She is a fine customer. Collect any additional washing from her while you are there."

"I will, Gracious Mother."

"And I know that Lady Hinkley likes to entertain. If she asks you to remain and eat with her, you may do so. We must keep Lady Hinkley happy so that she will send us all of her washing."

"Aye, Gracious Mother."

With that, Andressa sensed they were at the end of their clandestine gathering and she was nearly frantic to get out of that room. That hellish room where the evil of the Mother Abbess coated the very walls. She'd always known the woman to be wicked, but after the conversation they just had, even Andressa couldn't have imagined how deep that malevolence ran. But she didn't dare leave before she was dismissed, so she stood there until the Mother Abbess decided the subject at hand was concluded. It was a painfully long wait.

"Be on your way," she finally told Andressa. "There is much to do. God is on our side, Andressa. Remember that."

"I do, Gracious Mother."

"You may go."

Andressa did. She went to the Mother Abbess, kissing the woman's hand as a sign of respect, before making her way from the chamber at a calm and leisurely pace. It wasn't until she made it into the corridor outside, the one with the stairs that led down to The Chaos, that she collapsed against a wall, fighting off tears that were threatening to explode. It took her a moment to regain her composure but when she did, she hastily made her way back out to the laundry yard, resuming her duties in case the Mother Abbess was watching from her windows.

Something told Andressa that she was.

Even as she went through the motions of removing the dried laundry from the hemp ropes, her mind was working furiously. No matter how the Mother Abbess had phased it, to kill King John was not God's work. The God Andressa worshipped was not a wicked deity, demanding the death of a monarch. The very rationale was ludicrous, but Andressa seemed to be the only one who saw it that way. To think that God was demanding the death of a king through the Holy Father was delusional. God didn't demand death, and if He did, then He had the power to make the man drop dead. He didn't send mortal man to do his bidding.

It was the pope who wanted the king dead.

Andressa was having a difficult time realizing just how vast this plot was. The pope himself wanted his enemy removed and had finally ordered John's death, and the Mother Abbess would carry it out. The king would be coming to St. Blitha on her feast day, in just a few days in fact, and the Mother Abbess would be waiting for him like a spider waiting for a fly. The king would be oblivious to the danger awaiting him at the Abbey of St. Blitha, and there wasn't a thing Andressa could do to prevent it. If she tried, then her life would be forfeit.

But Andressa knew one thing – she couldn't stand by and watch the King of England murdered by women who professed to love God. They were beyond reproach, and beyond suspect, and in that sense, it made them the perfect assassins. Even Andressa understood the beauty of that.

God, help me. What do I do?

Those words rolled over and over in her mind as she continued to remove the dried laundry, separating it into batches that would be collected by the servants who had brought them to the abbey in the first place. Servants from the fine families who thought their clothes were being washed in holy water.

They were being washed in lies.

God, help me!

As Andressa began to remove the fine undergarments of Lady Hinkley's that she would soon deliver to the woman in her townhome in London, her gaze fell on the postern gate. That reminded her of Maxton and the very reason she'd ended up before the Mother Abbess in the first place.

A knight...

Then, it began to occur to her. She'd told Maxton of the Mother Abbess, of her Staff of Truth, and of The Chaos. She'd told a man she didn't even know about things that could kill her, but she'd trusted him right away. Perhaps it was only because he'd bought her a meal, but she knew it was more than that. There was something about the enormous knight that told her he was trustworthy. She didn't know what it was beyond a feeling or an instinct, but she knew there was something in him that was honorable. He'd already tried to help her escape St. Blitha once, but she'd refused. Perhaps he would know what to do in this terrible situation. Perhaps he could even warn the king off of coming to St. Blitha for the feast day. In any case, she had to try.

She had to find him.

If you ever need me, my lady, leave word at The King's Gout Tavern.

Gathering Lady Hinkley's fine things, she left via the postern gate, quickly heading out to the road that lead into the city of London.

CHAPTER ELEVEN

Farringdon House

"Has he awoken yet?" William asked.

Maxton shook his head at The Marshal. "Nay, my lord," he replied. "We plied him with much alcohol after he was already drunk, so it may take time to sleep this off."

William sighed heavily. He was standing on the top floor of Farringdon House with Maxton, Kress, Achilles, and Alexander. The four men had just brought in an unconscious man who stank to the heavens of alcohol and body odor, tossing him into a bed to sleep off his binge before telling William who, exactly, the man was and why he was there.

It had been the catch of a lifetime.

William, who happened to be at Farringdon House because his meeting with the king and the marcher lords had dispersed early, stood in the doorway of the chamber that held the snoring drunkard, hoping that they'd found the key to the papal assassins in that smelly, slobbering Scotsman.

"Then I suppose we'll have to wait until he decides to awaken," William said. "There is nothing more we can do."

"Nay, my lord," Maxton agreed. "We will send a guard up to keep an eye on him."

Alexander, who was still by the door, shook his head. "Nay, Max," he said. "I will remain here. He is my quarry, after all. Moreover, I feel as if he is an old friend now. I must stay and greet him when he awakens."

Maxton agreed with the wave of a hand and the men moved away from the chamber door to go about their separate ways. Before they could get too far, however, William stopped them.

"Max," he said. "I saw Sean at Westminster Palace earlier. It seems that John is indeed hunting tomorrow in the woods of Windsor, so you and your men may wish to shadow the hunting party for John's sake. But he mentioned something else, too, because you asked to be apprised of his movements – John is going to St. Blitha in two days to take part in the feast day. St. Blitha is the patroness of hunters, as you know, and he intends to offer prayers so she will bless his hunting bloodlust. It might be wise to appear at St. Blitha as well."

St. Blitha. There was that name again, that abbey that kept popping up. It wasn't as if St. Blitha was the only abbey in or around London; there were several, but on this day, St. Blitha was the only one he'd heard of today. First with Andressa, then with the drunkard Douglas, and now the king. Rather fortuitous, he thought. He would happily shadow the man to St. Blitha – he was only sorry it was two days away.

"Aye, my lord," he said. "In fact, I was already at St. Blitha today. It is a very long story, but I shall do my best to make it concise – this morning, as I was returning to Farringdon House after my night of food and drink, I came across a young woman stealing bread. As it turned out, she was a pledge from St. Blitha."

"So *that's* what happened," Kress said. "You mentioned St. Blitha this morning, but you did not say why. What in the world was a pledge from St. Blitha doing stealing bread?"

Maxton held up a hand, asking for patience as he continued. "Feeling pity for the woman, I fed her," he said. "But what she told me... God help me, St. Blitha's is a place of sin and sorrow. She said that the Mother Abbess sells the food meant for the nuns and pledges of St. Blitha to fill her own table with fine food, leaving her charges to starve. That is why she was stealing bread. The pledge further told me that the

Mother Abbess murders women who displease her."

That drew a reaction from all four of the men; eyebrows lifted in surprise. "A Mother Abbess who murders?" William repeated, shocked. "Are you certain? I have never heard such madness."

"Nor I," Maxton assured him. "The pledge, whose name is Andressa du Bose, told me that the Mother Abbess carries a staff with her that she calls the Staff of Truth, but the bottom half of the staff is really a sharp blade sheathed in wood to make it look like it's part of the staff. She sends those who displease her into the dungeons of St. Blitha, a place she calls The Chaos. No one returns from The Chaos alive because the Mother Abbess evidently murders them with the blade from her Staff of Truth."

More shocking information. "My God," William breathed. "A horrific tale, if true."

Maxton shook his head. "I did not sense the pledge was lying. If you'd only seen the woman, my lord, you would believe her, too. It was a terrible story she told."

"St. Blitha belongs to Essex, doesn't it?" Achilles spoke up; surprisingly, he was the most pious of the Executioner Knights, and often wrestled with that faith when carrying out his dark missions. "It is part of the Bishopric of Essex, and I am sorry to say that it is well-known that Essex is a man of questionable honor."

"Exactly," Maxton pointed a finger at him to emphasize his point. "He also has questionable morals. Remember the nun that was executed in Chelmsford the year we left for The Levant? She told everyone she was pregnant by Essex and was executed for her blasphemy."

William pinched the bridge of his nose as if struggling with the dark and dirty deeds from people who were supposed to uphold the morality of the church. He'd had his own troubles with them, which made the story Maxton was telling more than believable in his mind.

"I remember," he muttered. "I'd also heard through reliable sources that it wasn't the first bastard of the Bishop of Essex. It was simply the one that became public knowledge."

Maxton shook his head. "Given that quagmire of sex and lies, I tend to believe the pledge," he said grimly. "She lives behind walls that hide that hell from the world, but more than that, remember that St. Blitha's was the abbey that Sherry tracked Douglas to. He knows that Douglas spent some time there for an unknown reason."

William nodded, remembering what he'd been told of the entire situation with Alexander and Alasdair Baird Douglas. He'd also been told of the ensuing conversation in the tavern when Maxton, Kress, and Achilles plied the man with drink and tried to interrogate him, a conversation that still had his head swimming. So much of it was leading, with very little answers. He felt as if they were no better off than they were before.

"We need to find out why Douglas was there," he said. "If the man is our assassin, then we must find out all he knows. Your conversation with him in the tavern has brought us more questions than answers, unfortunately."

Maxton leaned against the wall behind him, lost in thought. It was a conversation he'd been stewing over since it happened. "When we spoke to Douglas earlier, he said something that caught my attention," he said. "He said that our prayers will be answered and we shall have a new king, so clearly, he knows about the assassination order. That was increasingly evident as we spoke."

"But he also said that no man will answer our prayers," Achilles put in. "He was very clear about no *man* answering our prayers."

Maxton looked at him, his eyebrows lifted. "So we shall have divine intervention?" he said. "A saint is supposed to answer our prayers for the death of a king?"

"He *was* at St. Blitha," Alexander entered into the conversation. When the men looked at him curiously, he continued. "You just finished telling us of the terrible darkness of the abbey, of a Mother Abbess who murders and pledges who starve. Mayhap Douglas went to St. Blitha to pray for a successful assassination, knowing of the evil of those who control St. Blitha. Think of it; the Holy Father has a devout servant in the Bishop of Essex, and Essex controls St. Blitha. There must be a connection there that we are not seeing."

Maxton held up a finger as a thought formed. "Or...," he said, paused, and started again. "Or given the fact that the Mother Abbess is a murderer, mayhap he sought her advice on how to proceed. Mayhap she is part of the assassination plot, too."

"Or mayhap she *is* the assassin," Achilles said quietly. "Douglas said that no *man* would answer our prayers. The Mother Abbess is not a man."

Maxton's eyes widened as the logic of that statement made complete and utter sense. "The nun," he hissed. "And John is due to St. Blitha in two days."

The hammer had fallen. Now, the pieces of the puzzle were falling in line and the astonishment was clear on their faces. An assassin nun? It seemed far too outlandish, but given the clues, it made sense.

No man shall answer yer prayers, Douglas had said.

But a woman could.

"God's Bones," William hissed. "Is it true? Do we have to protect John from a nun?"

No one had a definitive answer for him because they were all swept up in the shocking possibilities. As Maxton opened his mouth to speak, a guard from the manor gate appeared on the stairs, distracting them.

"My lord?"

William responded. "What is it?"

The guard shook his head. "Nay, my lord," he said. "I meant Sir Maxton."

Maxton looked over his shoulder. "What do you want?"

The guard gestured with a thumb down the stairs. "There is someone asking for you at the gatehouse," he said. "He says he's from The King's Gout. He wants to talk to you."

Maxton didn't react for a moment, but then his eyes opened wide and he flew down the stairs without another word. As the guard ran after him, William, Kress, Achilles, and Alexander looked to each other with some concern.

"The King's Gout?" Kress repeated. "That's the tavern over by the Street of the Bakers, isn't it?"

Alexander's brow furrowed, as if a thought had suddenly occurred to him. "Didn't Max say that the pledge this morning was stealing bread?"

The light went on in Kress' eyes. "And then he fed the woman a meal. It must have been at the nearest tavern."

"The King's Gout," they all said in unison.

Soon, they were all moving down the stairs, thinking there must be a connection between The King's Gout and the pledge from St. Blitha. So many pieces to a puzzle that was pulling together, but all of them were thinking the same thing – there had to be a connection between the pledge and the tavern, and now someone from the tavern had come to give Maxton a message.

There wasn't one of them that didn't want to know the details of that message.

The mystery deepened.

MAXTON RECOGNIZED THE messenger.

It was the son of the tavernkeep at The King's Gout, a tall and pale young man who was half the size of his blobish father. Maxton remembered the young man because he was evidently somewhat of a loaf and when Maxton had been at the tavern earlier, the father had been yelling at the lad because he hadn't moved fast enough for his liking. There was also a swat with a shovel involved.

But the young man appeared healthy enough, with no imprints of shovels on him. Unless he'd been hit in the head, of course, which was a possibility because had crossed eyes, making it difficult to know where, exactly, the young man was looking. Maxton had the gate guards usher him into the shadowed courtyard.

"Well?" Maxton demanded. "Why has your father sent you?"

The young man looked at him; or, at least, *one* of his eyes looked at him. "Are ye Loxbeare, m'lord?"

Maxton nodded sharply. "Do you have a message for me?"

The young man looked him up and down. "I do, m'lord," he said. "From a lady. She wants to know if you'll see her."

"What lady?"

"She gives her name as Andra... Andra..."

"Andressa?"

"Aye, m'lord."

The mere mention of the name seemed to set Maxton on fire. He reached out, grasping the young man by the arm. "Is she at the tavern?" he demanded forcefully. But just as swiftly, he let go of the young man's arm. "I shall go with you. Let me collect my things."

But the young man put his hands up to slow Maxton down. "She's not at the tavern, m'lord," he said. "Wait here. I'll bring her."

Maxton's eyebrows drew together. "Bring her *here*?" he said. "Where is she?"

The young man kept his hands up as if to beg patience from the enormous knight who seemed quite fired up by mention of the lady. He dashed away, heading for the fortified door where the guards were, and at Maxton's urging, the guards opened the door and the young man ran through it.

Puzzled, Maxton was heading for the door himself to see what was going on when the young man suddenly reappeared with a figure in tow. It took Maxton less than a brief second to realize it was Andressa.

She looked frightened and a little dazed, wrapped up in her dirty woolens like a shield from the world at large. The young man had her by the arm, urging her forward, but when she saw Maxton, she needed no urging. Their eyes met and she scurried through the open door.

"My lady?" Shocked, Maxton moved quickly to her. "Are you well?"

Andressa gazed up at him with an expression that told him all he needed to know. No, she wasn't well. Something was very wrong, and he immediately noticed that she was trembling. As she struggled for an answer to his question, he dug into the purse at his belt and gave the young man a coin. When the young man dashed off, Maxton took Andressa by the arm and gently pulling her into the courtyard.

"I... I am sorry to have come uninvited," Andressa finally said. "You said that I could leave word for you at The King's Gout, but... it could not wait for you to receive it. I asked the tavernkeep if he would tell me where you lived and he had his son bring me here. I am very sorry to be such trouble, but..."

Maxton interrupted her. "It is no trouble at all," he said. "I am glad you found me. How may I be of service?"

Andressa looked around; they were in the interior courtyard of a very big manor house and there were people all around, people she didn't know. People who could tell the Mother Abbess that she'd come to this place. Suddenly, her fear had the better of her and she began to back away.

"I should not have come," she whispered tightly, tears filling her eyes as she tried to pull her arm from his grip. "I should go. Forgive me, please."

There was something desperate and almost incoherent about her manner, concerning Maxton a great deal. As much as she tried to pull away from him, he would not let her.

"Do not be troubled," he assured her calmly. "No one will hurt you, I promise. What is so important that you had to come and find me?"

Andressa was coming to realize he wasn't about to let her go so she stopped pulling. But she didn't want to speak in front of all of these people even though they appeared not to be paying any attention to her. She couldn't be sure they wouldn't overhear what she had to say. She was trying very hard not to cry.

"May we... may we speak privately, please?" she whispered. "I do not have much time, my lord. Quickly, please."

His reply was cut off as men suddenly surrounded them. Kress, Achilles, Alexander, and William were suddenly there, all around them, and Andressa panicked at the sight of so many armed men. She shrunk back from the big knights, struggling to pull away from Maxton again, so much so that he grabbed her with both hands and pulled her against him, trying to give her some comfort.

"Have no fear, lady," he assured her quickly, backing away from his friends to put distance between the frantic lady and the strange knights. "They will not hurt you, I swear it. They are simply clumsy, but they mean you no harm. Please meet my close and good friends Sir Kress de Rydian, Sir Achilles de Dere, Sir Alexander de Sherrington, and William Marshal, Earl of Pembroke. Surely you have heard of Lord William? He is a very great and important man."

Andressa was looking at all of them with big eyes, caught up in a web of men that had her re-thinking her idea to seek out Maxton. It didn't seem like a good idea any longer, but she felt as if she was trapped now. She couldn't even respond to his introductions. She looked at him, her big eyes pooling with tears.

"Please," she begged again. "I must speak to you privately."

Maxton simply nodded, holding a hand out to the four men hovering around them, silently pleading with them not to follow. They obeyed, but it was clear they didn't want to. Seeing the very poorly dressed woman in Maxton's grip suggested this was the very pledge Maxton had been speaking of throughout the day, something that had their curiosity sharpened. She was from St. Blitha, and they all knew that St. Blitha was the key to this entire mystery.

Maxton knew that, all too well. He knew exactly what they were thinking as he put a big arm around Andressa's shoulders and led her back into the house, into the darkened ground level. The only thing down here were armories and kitchens and servants' rooms, so he took her up the great mural stairs and into the first chamber they came to, a smaller receiving room that was next to the massive solar.

The receiving room was generally meant for retainers of the great men who would attend The Marshal in his solar, so it was comfortable and well-appointed. It was also private, with only one door and one window that faced out over the inner courtyard. Maxton escorted Andressa inside and turned to close the door, but the moment he released her, she drifted over to the other side of the chamber and collapsed in the corner.

Distressed, Maxton watched Andressa roll herself up into a ball and sob. She had her hands over her head in a protective gesture, as if hiding from something quite horrible. With a sigh, one of great concern, Maxton made his way over to her.

"My lady," he said gently. "What has happened? All you need do is speak the word and I will do all in my power to help you. Please tell me what has happened."

It took Andressa a moment to respond. In fact, her only response was to lift her head and wipe off her face with her dirty sleeves. It was all she had. She was a quivering, weeping mess and Maxton sat carefully in the chair nearest her, not wanting to startle her.

"My lady?" Maxton said again. "Please tell me – what has happened?"

She wiped at her face, furiously, before daring to look at him. When she did, he could see the tears starting all over again.

"I do not know what to do," she murmured, her lower lip quivering. "I do not know who to ask for help. You have been kind to me and I thought mayhap…"

"Mayhap… *what*?"

"Mayhap you could tell me what to do."

"About what?"

Her face threatened to crumple again but she fought it. She had little time to speak and didn't want to spend the entire time weeping like a fool, but God, she needed to cry, just a little. It had been building up since her meeting with the Mother Abbess, an explosion waiting to happen. But the explosion was over now.

She needed to tell someone.

She took a deep breath.

"You must swear to me that you will not repeat what I tell you," she said.

He nodded. "Of course," he said. "What is it?"

Andressa took another deep breath. "I need your help."

"Tell me what I can do to help you."

"I am so frightened. I have never been so frightened in my entire life."

"Why? Won't you please tell me why?"

Her gaze grew intense. "You must tell the king not to go to St. Blitha for the feast day."

Maxton never knew that one little statement could electrify him so much. His entire body began to tingle, tensing up as if he'd been wound up as tightly as he could go.

"Why is that?"

Andressa wiped at her eyes that continued to leak. "Because if he goes to St. Blitha, he will be murdered. They will murder him!"

"*Who* will murder him, Andressa?"

"The Mother Abbess and her attendants."

Maxton couldn't help his reaction; he slid out of the chair and onto the floor beside her, reaching out to pull her towards him. His big hands trapped her as his dark eyes drilled into her with white-hot intensity.

"You will tell me everything," he said as calmly as he could manage. "From the beginning, please. How do you know this?"

Andressa felt as if she wanted to vomit as he asked that question. She'd been wanting to vomit since the moment the Mother Abbess clued her in on a plot as dark and deadly as anything she was capable of comprehending.

She'd come to Maxton because she didn't know where else to turn, and as Andressa looked at the man, she realized one thing – there was something immensely comforting about him. He was so close to her that she could feel the heat from his body, and the fists gripping her arms were the size of a man's head. He was big, and he was powerful, and it occurred to her that never in her life had she known such safety or comfort.

Amidst all of the terror she was experiencing, the man made her feel as if nothing in the world could touch her, not even the darkness of the Mother Abbess. It was something she'd never experienced before, and in that realization, some of her terror fled. She could think more clearly now.

She had come this far. He needed to know everything.

"After you left today, I was brought before the Mother Abbess," she said.

He grunted. "I thought so," he said, sighing with regret. "I heard the fight. I am very sorry to have caused you trouble, Andressa. That was never my intent."

She shook her head, calmer now. "I thought you had caused me trouble, too," she said, a weak glimmer of mirth in her eye. "But in truth, you did not. When I was brought before the Mother Abbess, I was certain she was going to punish me for speaking to you, but instead, she said some very strange things."

"Like what?"

Andressa thought back to the conversation, organizing her thoughts against the fear that the very subject provoked. "She told me that she had been watching me," she said. "She told me that she wanted me to take the veil and become her personal attendant. She spoke of things I did not understand at first; she said that she and her attendants, nuns she has known since childhood, have been called upon to do the bidding of our Holy Father. She said that he had entrusted them with missions, many times. I did not know what she meant until she started speaking of men who were dead. One man, in particular, was the Bishop of Leeds. He died at St. Blitha following a feast the year after I came to the order. The Mother Abbess said that our Holy Father asked her to kill him and she did. Now, she says that our Holy Father has asked her to do the same thing with King John and she wants me to participate in it so that I can learn her ways."

Now, it was Maxton's turn to feel sick to his stomach. He had experienced many things in life. He'd seen more than his share of sorrow, and death, and of betrayal, but never in his life had he heard about nuns who killed on command. Even though he and the others had been speculating about a deadly Mother Abbess only minutes earlier, he wasn't sure he really believed that. His money had been on Douglas, the double-agent. But at the moment, a baby could have knocked him over, so stunned was he. One good push and down he'd go.

He was still trying to drink it all in.

"You are sure of this?" he managed to ask. "She told you that the Holy Father wishes for her to assassinate the king?"

Andressa nodded. "That is what she said," she assured him. "A messenger from the Holy Father came to tell her of this command. In fact, I saw the messenger; he was at St. Blitha two days ago. I remember because he bellowed to me, wanting to know if the woman he was speaking to was indeed the Mother Abbess. I was afraid to answer because I could hardly understand him. I did not wish to give him the wrong answer."

"Why was it difficult to understand him?"

"Because he was Scottish."

Another revelation. Now, he knew what Alasdair Baird Douglas had been doing at St. Blitha – he hadn't been praying about an assassination or asking the Mother Abbess' advice on it. He'd been there to tell the woman is was her duty to kill the King of England, straight from the mouth of the Holy Father.

Maxton was deeply astonished with what he was hearing; it was confirmation and clarification of the great mystery they'd all been dealing with. The Holy Father had indeed sent more assassins to fulfill the mission that he and his Unholy brethren had refused, only the assassins were something Maxton would have never considered –

Nuns.

He never saw that coming.

As he became increasingly lost to his own thoughts, he could see Andressa looking at him anxiously. He loosened his grip on her arms and began to caress her slender limbs, comfortingly. He could see how utterly terrified she was.

In truth, he didn't blame her in the least.

"She wants you to assist her, does she?" he said calmly. "What did you tell her?"

Andressa drew in a long breath; she was calming a great deal, but the mere mention of the Mother Abbess made her tense up again.

"I agreed," she said. "I did not know what else to do. She told me if I spoke to anyone about this, then I would end up in The Chaos."

Now, it was all coming together and Maxton was starting to understand why she was so terrified; she'd been burdened with a huge weight, knowledge that would create stress and havoc with even the most seasoned man, and then her life was threatened if she spoke about it. This poor woman had been forced to endure hell over the past four years, cast off by a greedy aunt and left to the mercy of the soulless sisters of St. Blitha.

"You will not end up in The Chaos," he said quietly, rubbing her arms in a soothing gesture without really realizing he was doing it. "I would not let them do that to you."

Andressa was looking at his face as he spoke. In fact, the moment he started caressing her arms, discreetly but unmistakably, she found herself looking at him with increasing interest. The way he made her feel – safe and warm and comforted – was pushing aside the abject terror she'd been suffering since leaving St. Blitha, taking her back to the days at Okehampton when she was safe and warm and comfortable, living the life of a respected ward for Lady de Courtney.

Her mind drifted back to the days of feasts and knights and chivalry, days that were only distant memories to her now. Thoughts of Rhyne popped into her head again, but as she looked at Maxton, she could see that Rhyne had been a foolish boy compared to the man who now held her in his grip. She remembered seeing knights of Maxton's caliber at Okehampton, great men with great legacies, but they were unattainable to her. At least, that's what she believed. As she continued to gaze at Maxton, she wished with all her heart that he could see her as something other than what she was – a dirty, poor pledge.

She wished it could be otherwise.

"Will you please tell the king not to come to St. Blitha?" she asked again. "He must know of the danger should he go there. I do not know how they are planning to kill him, but they promised to teach me."

Maxton's dark eyes lingered on her for a moment. "They gave no indication?"

She shook her head. "Nay," she said. "Except… except I am to assume new duties in the garden tomorrow with Sister Petronilla."

"Who is that?"

"One of the Mother Abbess' personal attendants," she said. "The Mother Abbess said that Sister Petronilla would teach me what I needed to know."

"She is one of the assassins?"

"Aye."

Maxton considered that for a few moments, but not for long. He was still lingering on what he'd been told as a whole. He needed to speak with William, desperately, but he wanted to make sure Andressa was calm before he left her. He had much to do and more than likely little time to do it, and the pale pledge in his hands had been the key to everything. Without her, he'd still be hunting phantoms.

That poor, sweet, frightened little rabbit.

"Surely you must be hungry," he said to her. "I would like you to remain in this chamber and rest, and I shall have food brought up to you."

She started to get that panicked look again. "Where are you going?"

He smiled at her, giving her arms a squeeze before rising to his feet and pulling her along with him. "I must speak to The Marshal about preventing John from going to St. Blitha."

"Nay!" she cried, grabbing him with her boney fingers. "You must not tell him what I have told you! You swore that you would not!"

Maxton understood her panic. Carefully, he sat her down in the nearest chair, taking a knee in front of her hand holding both of her cold hands in his big, warm mitts. He looked her directly in the eye as he spoke to her.

"What you have told me will not go any further, I assure you," he said. "But it is also a task that cannot be handled by one man. We are speaking of the king, Andressa, and if I am to tell him he cannot go to St. Blitha, he will want to know why. Do you understand that? There are others I must trust to help me."

Her eyes were filling with tears again. "But... but if the Mother Abbess discovers I have told you..."

He shook his head and squeezed her hands. "She will not know," he said. "She will never know. In fact, now that we know of her plan, we will remove her from St. Blitha so that she can never harm anyone ever again, including you."

The tears stopped and her eyes widened. "Remove her?" she gasped. "How... why...?"

Maxton lifted her hands to his lips, kissing her fingers sweetly. "Trust me," he murmured. "Please, Andressa. You have asked for my help and I am so glad you did. I swear to you that I will protect you with my life. You have come to me with trust and now I ask you for the same as I help you solve your problem. Will you do this?"

She was still lingering on the kiss; it had been so sweet, so subtle, that her heart was racing because of it. It was a struggle to focus on his question.

"I... have been without anyone close to me for such a long time," she said, her voice trembling. "I had friends at Okehampton, and my parents and I were also close, but since I have been at St. Blitha, I have learned that every day is a fight for survival and that there is no one I can trust because every woman at St. Blitha is also fighting for her survival. I do not even know you, yet your kindness this morning was endearing. It has been so long since I have known any kindness."

It was a confession of sorts, a glimpse into the protected, confused, and frightened world of Andressa. Maxton could see how vulnerable she was and it touched him; he was fortunate. He had close friends he could trust. But when it came to an emotional and personal level, much like her, he had no one at all. He had seen forty years and three; he was an old man to some, but to others, he was seasoned and wise and strong. But there was one thing in all of those years that had escaped him –

Someone to love.

Did he see that in Andressa? All he knew was that in the short time he'd known her, he had feelings towards her that he'd never had for anyone, at least that strongly. The woman was terrified and cold, and hungry, and all he wanted to was shield and protect and feed her. He wanted to take care of her. He didn't know why other than his gut told him that he should.

His instincts had never been wrong.

"I am coming to think that our unexpected meeting this morning was not a mistake," he said quietly. "Although I have never given much stock in God because, surely, I destroyed my chances of ascending to heaven long ago, I think that he brought you to me."

She had wiped her tears away, listening to him intently. "Why?"

He forced a smile. "Because you need someone to trust. Clearly, you need me."

Andressa wasn't sure if he was joking; something in his eyes told her that he was for the most part. But not entirely. There was a glimmer there, something warm and kind, that made her racing heart flutter yet again.

"I will admit it looks that way," she said. "I suppose I could have gone straight to the king with this and try to tell him, but I thought you might be of more assistance."

He shook his head. "I did not mean that, entirely," he said. "I mean with everything. You needed food this morning and I was happy to provide it. You need help now, and I am also happy to provide it. You see? God knew you needed me, although I am not entirely sure why he would send you to someone who has one foot in hell. That has me puzzled."

Andressa cocked her head, thinking of the conversation they'd had earlier whilst by the stream. *You cannot possibly imagine how un-kind and un-generous I am*, he had said. She was deeply curious about that statement, as she was about the rest of him.

"In the short while we have been acquainted, you have alluded to things you have done in this life," she said. "Although I cannot imagine you being anything other than what you are to me – a strong, honorable knight – tell me why you think you have one foot in hell."

"Think?" he snorted. "I know."

"What have you done?"

He let go of her hands, rocking back on his heels and averting his gaze. "That is a question with many answers."

"Don't you trust me?"

He cast her a long look suggesting he was displeased with the fact that she'd ably trapped him. She'd shown such trust in him and now she was expecting the same. *Clever girl.* When she smiled timidly, he simply shook his head with feigned frustration.

"Of course I trust you," he said. "But why do you wish to know about an old knight like me? I am nothing in the grand scheme of things except that I have sinned more than most."

"What have you done?"

He grumbled softly, with displeasure, but answered. "I have always been a man of great talent and little remorse," he said. "Lords and kings have used that combination for, shall we say, unsavory tasks."

"Like what?"

"You truly wish for an example?"

She nodded, firmly, and he frowned at her. Still, he dutifully continued. "Very well," he said. "You have asked for it. Whilst in The Levant, my cohorts and I were tasked with the abduction of a Muslim general. You met the men I speak of outside, though you probably cannot recall their faces – Kress de Rhydian and Achilles de Dere. The Christian armies called us the Executioner Knights and the Unholy

Trinity, among other things, but if there was an impossible task to accomplish, it was given to us. Like the abduction of this general; the Christian commanders believed he was responsible for an ambush of Christian knights outside of the city of Nahala, so my colleagues and I were charged with abducting him and bringing him back alive. You do not want to hear more than that, my lady. Trust me when I tell you it was an unpleasant task."

But Andressa was listening closely, very interested, indeed. "But I do want to hear more," she insisted. "At this moment, I still see you as a great and noble knight. I do not think there is anything you could do, so terrible, to shatter than opinion."

He looked at her, then. "What if I want you to continue believing that," he said, his suddenly tone hoarse with emotion. As if he was pleading. "No one has thought such things about me before."

Andressa felt silent a moment, but it was a thoughtful silence. "No man is perfect unless his name is Christ," she said. "There are only degrees of mortal perfection, and to many, that is in the eye of the beholder. Did you kill this Muslim general, then?"

"I did, but only when he tried to ambush me. He knew we were coming."

"Then you did it in self-defense."

"I also killed his seven-year old son who stabbed me in the leg with a dagger. Am I still great and honorable to you now?"

She didn't hesitate. "The boy tried to kill you. Did you have a choice?"

He shook his head, slowly. "Nay," he said. "I did not because the child had clearly been trained to kill. I told the boy's mother that right before I slit her throat – I told her that she had raised a killer. Now… do you still think I am great and honorable?"

That gave Andressa pause. "Why did you kill her?"

"So there would be no witnesses to the death of her husband and son."

It was a blunt, brutal, but truthful answer. Andressa sat back in the chair, pondering what she'd been told. It had been more than she's bargained for, but oddly enough, it didn't change her mind about him. She had a rational quality not easily found.

"You were at war," she said quietly. "I am sure the woman would have killed you if she'd had the chance. She was your enemy and there is no shame in killing an enemy in times of war."

Maxton shook his head slowly. "That is not why I did it," he said. "I did it because I wanted to. Because I did not want to leave her alive. My lady, you do not seem to realize what I am telling you – I am a killer. I am paid to kill men and women, and children if I must. When I tell you that I will remove the Mother Abbess from St. Blitha so she can never again harm anyone, know that I have no such reservations about the fact that she is a woman. It matters not to me. I will do what is necessary, and I mean every word I say."

Andressa believed him. His confession about the Muslim general and the man's family opened her eyes to him a little, but the truth was that all she could see was a man fighting to survive. Perhaps it was foolish of her, but that was her opinion.

No one would ever change it.

"I believe you," she said quietly.

"And you do not think differently about me?"

"Nay."

Maxton wasn't surprised to hear that, but he thought she was still a little idealistic about him. But as he'd said… perhaps he wanted her to think that way of him. He wanted her to think that he was noble and kind, because God only knew, no one else did. More and more, the little pledge was breaking down something in him, walls he kept up, great things that protected everything about him. He'd spent years building those walls. But with her, those walls were cracking.

He could feel it.

"As you wish," he muttered. "Now, I have things to attend to. While I am away, I wish for you to rest and I shall send you food. I must go speak with The Marshal and ask him what he thinks we should do given this situation. Will you wait here whilst I speak with him?"

Andressa glanced to the window; the sun was starting to set, sending pink ribbons across the sky. "It will be dark soon," she said. "I... I told the Mother Abbess that I had to deliver laundry to Lady Hinkley, but even she said that Lady Hinkley often likes to talk and invite the less fortunate to a meal. But Lady Hinkley was very busy with her party tonight and she did not invite me in."

Maxton was on to her line of thinking. "Then if you stay here a little while and feast with me, the Mother Abbess will think you are with Lady Hinkley."

Andressa nodded and there seemed to be some relief in her expression. Even a few hours away from that hellish place was a God-send.

"Aye," she said after a moment. "She will think that."

"Then you will stay a little while? I am sure the cook has a very good supper planned."

That seemed to close the deal for Andressa. Two good meals in one day was nearly unheard of in her world.

"I will stay."

That pleased Maxton immensely. He stood up, gazing down at her as she sat in the chair. To him, she looked so forlorn and vulnerable. He could only imagine what the woman looked like in all her glory; if she was beautiful now, scrubbed and fed and dressed, she must have been a sight to see.

And that gave him an idea.

"Wait here," he said. "Do not leave this chamber. Promise?"

She nodded. "I do."

"I'll be back."

With that, he quit the small chamber and she could hear him outside, barking to the servants. *Hot water. Food. And build a fire in the retainer's chamber!* Andressa heard him snapping orders, fading away as he went down the stairs, until she could only hear a dull rumble.

Alone and worried, she remained in the chair he'd left her in until there was a knock at the door. The latch lifted and a servant with wood and peat entered, swiftly moving to the hearth and starting a lovely, warm blaze. The room filled with a golden glow and when the servant left, Andressa went to the hearth, sitting next to it and warming her frozen body. The Mother Abbess wouldn't allow for fires at St. Blitha unless it was snowing, so more often than not, Andressa had to warm herself by the fire she used to heat the water for her laundry. There was no other opportunity.

But now, she was in a warm chamber with a warm fire, basking in a luxury she hadn't had in four years. It was heavenly. But not heavenly enough that she forgot about her situation, or the fact that she needed to return to St. Blitha soon.

Back into the heart of the Devil.

She prayed she'd done the right thing by seeking Maxton. God only knew what tomorrow would bring.

CHAPTER TWELVE

"NAY," MAXTON SNARLED. "She is not going back."

There was a battle brewing in William's solar. A half-hour after Maxton relayed Andressa's revelation to The Marshal, the productive and interesting discourse had turned into something else, and William had brought about the statement that Maxton had been dreading from the moment the news had been revealed. Somehow, he knew it would all come down to this.

Now, it was Maxton against William, perhaps the most talented assassin ever known against the greatest knight England had ever seen. And all of it over… a woman.

But in the face of Maxton's fury, William stood firm.

"Think, Maxton, *think*," he implored. "It is the perfect situation. If we send her back to St. Blitha, then she can report on everything that is taking place. We will have a spy right in the center of the viper's nest."

But Maxton was having none of William's bigger-picture rational. He was looking at the woman in the middle of it, not the king she would be saving as she spied upon a very deadly mother abbess. To him, the very suggestion was ludicrous.

There had to be another way.

"She is *not* a spy," Maxton snapped. "She is a pledge, a simple woman. She does not have the skills for this, nor the experience. She will get herself killed spying for you."

There was an accusation there, slung at William at full velocity, but the man didn't flinch. There wasn't much he flinched at these days. It was just past sunset, and Farringdon House was lit up with candles and fires, projecting light into the darkness of night that had settled. The smells of the evening's meal wafted on the breeze, tantalizing those who were ready to eat. Mostly, that meant William, his retainers, and the knights who were in residence that night, but at the moment, the feast would have to wait.

Everything would have to wait.

Kress, Achilles, Alexander, and Gart as witness to the brewing storm. Gart had been out most of the day with the de Lohrs, as he served David these days, but he'd returned to Farringdon House to see how Maxton's plans were coming along only to run head-long into what seemed to be a very angry confrontation between William and Maxton. Kress had filled him in on the reasons behind it, through swift whispers, and now Gart stood on the fringes of the chamber like the rest of them, watching Maxton and William hash out the situation, hoping they weren't going to have to pull Maxton off of the old earl at some point.

It was a tense circumstance to say the least.

"What you do not seem to realize is that she is already in danger," William said. "Sending her back where she belongs is safer for her in the end because they will not suspect that anything is amiss. They will not know she has told you of their plans, but if she stays away any longer, I am sure they will become suspicious. You told me that she left the abbey to deliver laundry to a noblewoman here in town?"

Maxton nodded his head, his jaw ticking. "Aye," he grumbled. "She delivered garments to Lady Hinkley. Andressa is the laundress at St. Blitha."

"Then send her back," William said sternly. He wasn't used to meeting with opposition from a man who served him, so his patience was thin. "Maxton, you do not seem to realize that this is not your decision to make. The pledge has given us a great gift. What we were expecting you to solve in weeks, or months at most, she has solved for us in one day. Do you not understand that? Therefore, she will return to St. Blitha where she shall continue to administer her duties and watch the happenings. If there is a new development, she will let us know immediately."

Maxton looked at William; he knew the man was legendary. That was an indisputable fact. But he was also ruthless, manipulative, and controlled those around him as a man would control his pieces in a chess game. To William, life itself was a great game of skill, plotting, and chance, and he used those under his command accordingly. In this case, Andressa was to become a pawn, and there was nothing more to it than that. She was a means to an end.

No heart.

No emotion.

Normally, Maxton would have agreed with the man, especially where it pertained to a woman, but he couldn't quite reach that state of apathy when it came to this particular woman. He didn't want to see Andressa caught up in a game that would more than likely kill her.

"So you would throw her to the wolves," he snarled, turning away because he was sincerely afraid of losing control if he didn't. "She did not have to come to me, Pembroke. She could have easily kept it to herself, but she didn't. She came to me because of her concern for John and for no other reason than that. She did the right thing and now you would punish her for it by making her return to that pit of vipers."

William could have risen to his anger, but instead, he found himself truly baffled. "What does it matter?" he asked. "Maxton, what is this girl to you that you would defend her so rabidly?"

Maxton turned to look at him, a frowned on his face. "That should be obvious," he said. "She has just saved the king's life. Does she not deserve our protection for it?"

William sighed sharply, his patience gone with Maxton's compassionate reply. "Where is this pity coming from?" he said with disgust. "This is not the assassin I was told was the best in the world. What I am hearing is an old woman, bleeding sorrow and mercy all over the place. Where is your courage, Loxbeare?"

Now, the insults were becoming personal and Maxton stiffened. "Would you really like to find out?"

It was a threat and they all knew it. This was no longer just a tense discourse but threatening to turn into something violent. But William simply displayed a humorless smile.

"Mayhap. It would prove to me that you are not the fool I take you for." Suddenly, he slammed his fist on the table before him. "The only thing that matters is the king. Not you, not I, and certainly not some inconsequential pledge. Send that girl back to St. Blitha and tell her to inform us if anything changes. But if it will make you happy, should she perform well in this instance, I will reward her greatly. Will that satisfy you?"

It was nearly a sarcastic question; had anyone else spoken to Maxton in that tone, he would have ripped their head off. In fact, Kress and Achilles, who were standing nearby, each took a step in Maxton's direction. He was bigger, taller, heavier, and stronger than William, so physically, he could have very much overpowered the old man.

But no one wanted to see that, probably not even Maxton. William was heaping insults on him that were more than likely justified, given the fact he was sparing some concern for a woman he didn't even know. But the fact remained that Maxton had little control once he was pushed over the brink, so when Kress and Achilles moved towards him, Gart began casually moving for William, preparing to put himself between an enraged Maxton and the old earl. It wasn't an ideal spot to find himself in, but he was prepared nonetheless.

Fortunately, Maxton didn't move in William's direction, though it was clear he wanted to. He held his ground, clenching and unclenching his fists.

"Define reward," he rumbled.

William realized he had probably pushed Maxton to the breaking point in this situation, but he didn't much care. "Nay," he said. "I will let you define it. Whatever you want to reward her with, I shall grant, so let her reward come from you. For now, I want her taken back to St. Blitha before they wonder why she had been gone overly long. The longer she remains here, the more she jeopardizes her position there. Is this in any way unclear?"

Maxton was grinding his teeth so hard that he was certain he'd chipped a tooth. "It is clear."

With that, William eyed the man as if to emphasize his position in the situation. The truth was that he didn't know Maxton well; everything he knew, he knew from Gart and the de Lohr brothers. They had painted a picture of a stalwart, obedient knight who had a dark streak in him. William could believe the part about the dark streak, but the part about obedience had him questioning whether it was true or not.

Time would tell.

"Good," William said. "Now, I intend to send word to Sean so he is aware of this latest development. It seems that mayhap assassins will not be stalking the king when he goes on his hunt outside of Windsor tomorrow, but I would suggest you still tail the man, just in case."

"Aye, my lord."

"Meanwhile, return that girl to St. Blitha. I want her out of this house within the hour."

Maxton simply nodded, once, because he had to give him some kind of acknowledgement. But his heart certainly wasn't in it.

Without another word, William quit the solar, heading for the hall on the other side of the house where supper would soon be served. His boot falls faded away, taking some of the tension with them. Once he was gone, Gart moved in Maxton's direction.

"What is the matter with you?" Gart hissed. "Do you dare argue with the Earl of Pembroke?"

Maxton wouldn't let Gart scold him. "What he is demanding is not right and you know it," he said pointedly. "That woman risked her life to solve our problem, and now he wants to send her back into the belly of the beast, to spy for him no less? Since when does The Marshal use untrained women for that kind of work?"

Gart sighed heavily. "I do not disagree with some of your concerns, but it is not as if we are asking the woman to do anything differently," he said. "All William wants is for her to return to her usual tasks and behave in her usual way. He's not asking her to save the king, for God's sake. Stop acting like he's sending the woman to her death."

Maxton didn't say anything. He'd already said enough, and the truth was that he was confused about his passionate defense of Andressa. He'd never felt so protective over anything, or anyone, in his entire life. He felt as if he wanted to wrap his arms around her and shield her from the world, this fragile blossom that was so broken and bruised.

Now, he was becoming embarrassed, trying to think of a way to explain his behavior.

The trouble was, he couldn't. Not even to himself.

"I told her I would send her back and I will," he rumbled. "I am expected to be obedient and I shall be. But do not expect me to like it."

Gart didn't have anything more to say to that. He passed a glance at Kress and Achilles and Alexander before he left the chamber, silently suggesting they talk some sense into stubborn Maxton. As Gart followed William's path from the chamber, the trio of comrades surrounded Maxton as the man stood there and fumed.

"Max, what is going on?" Alexander asked. "Why defend this girl so passionately? What is she to you?"

Maxton's guard came down a little now that he was surrounded by his close friends. Running his hand through his dark hair, he simply shook his head.

"I do not know," he said. "Mayhap I feel some pity for the woman. She's had a difficult life, yet there is a spark of strength in her eyes that I can see every time I speak with her. She is an heiress, you know. Her inheritance was stolen from her by a greedy aunt, her guardian upon her parents' death, who proceeded to throw her into the rubbish heap of St. Blitha. She has existed at St. Blitha for the past four years and she seems so helpless. As if she needs a friend."

"And you wish to be that friend?" Alexander asked quietly.

Maxton hesitated a moment before nodding. "It sounds odd, I know," he said. "I have spent my whole life ignoring women like her, so why is she any different from the rest? Because I know her name. Because she endeared herself to me. She gave me a glimpse into this terrible world she lives in and she trusts me. And she has absolutely no one she can talk to; no family, no friends. No one at all. I am fortunate in that I have you three and although I cannot get rid of you, at least I have you. And I love you all for it."

He'd meant the last few sentences with some humor, so there were smiles all around. But there was also a distinct sense of surprise because Maxton wasn't one to show emotion. He was as hard as they come, or at least he had been until their experience in the dungeons Les Baux de Provence. That's when those close to him had noticed a change, as they'd mentioned several times. Maxton had become more philosophical, more introspective. It had been an odd change for one with a stone where his heart should have been.

Maxton was changing.

"Max," Kress said, his gaze lingering on the man, perhaps seeing him through new eyes. "It is no secret that we thought you'd lost your mind during the time we spent at Les Baux de Provence, and even afterwards. You became far more thoughtful, speaking to priests and old men, philosophers – anyone you could that could give you a perspective on life. You are no longer the man with the soul of the mindless killer."

Maxton knew what Kress was talking about, although it really wasn't something he'd ever acknowledged. But here, at this moment, he found it necessary to speak on such things.

"Nay," he agreed. "I am a killer with an awareness, which makes me even more dangerous. Do you want to know why I spoke with holy men and apothecaries and physics? Because I want to understand more than I have ever understood before. There is more to this life than what we have lived – there is joy and happiness and innocence, something that is very rare in our world. And mayhap that is why Andressa fascinates me so much – she has that innocence, but the joy and happiness has been taken from her. It would be so easy to bring it back. I have the power of death; I prove that every day. But the power of peace and joy? That, so far, has been something that has eluded me."

"And you see a chance for that with Andressa?" Kress pressed gently.

Maxton shook his head, emitting a heavy sigh. "I do not know," he admitted. "I have been asking myself that over the course of the day. I have literally only known the woman for a day, but something about her has gotten under my skin. I cannot explain it any better than that."

Kress looked at Achilles and Alexander, who had much the same expression as he did on their faces. It was genuine surprise. Achilles, the most introspective of the four of them, spoke softly.

"God works in mysterious ways, Max," he said. "But remember that the woman is a pledge, meaning her guardian has consigned her to God. If you want to change that, then you must speak to her guardian."

Maxton held up a hand. "I did not say I wanted to change her status," he said. "I do not even know if I want to change mine. But I am… curious. I am in the grip of something I do not understand, but it is not something I can explore at the moment. My oath to my profession above all and, at the moment, we have a task on our hands. I must finish it before I can, and will, consider anything else."

That was the Maxton they knew and they were pleased to hear that his devotion to his knighthood was still intact no matter what confusion over a woman that he may have been feeling. Kress patted him in the shoulder.

"That is good to hear," he said. "Because, certainly, we have a task on our hands and I believe you have a pledge to return to St. Blitha now, and we shall leave you to that task."

Maxton simply nodded, watching the three of them file out of the solar, leaving it cold and still in their wake. The sun was completely down now and there were a few tapers lit in the chamber, but the hearth was dark. It was only when a servant entered the room, thinking it was empty of the knights, that Maxton went to seek Andressa.

In truth, he was dreading it.

He didn't want to let her return to that horrific place, but he had little choice. Deep down, he understood why William wanted her back at St. Blitha and it made sense to him. The trick would be asking Andressa to do the unthinkable when she returned.

To spy.

The door to the retainer's chamber loomed before him. Gathering his courage, he would do what needed to be done.

THE GARMENT WAS the color of wine.

Andressa couldn't take her eyes off it as an older serving woman brought it in and laid it upon the chair next to the hearth. The woman smiled kindly at Andressa and told her that Sir Maxton had ordered clean clothes and a bath for her, something that greatly confused Andressa. Why should she need clean clothing and a bath? She had to return to St. Blitha, and she certainly couldn't do it in clothing that did not belong to her.

But then, she started to think about it... *a bath*. Something clean to wear. God only knew how long it had been since she'd had either. Whilst at Okehampton, Lady de Courtney had insisted on cleanliness, so her charges bathed regularly and their clothing was always clean.

In fact, Andressa had never even experienced vermin during that time – no vermin on the body or in the hair, no vermin in the beds or linens, but at St. Blitha, vermin was the norm. It was in the clothing, in the bedding, but Andressa had spent a great deal of time boiling her own bedding and clothing, trying to stay away from the other nuns who suspiciously itched. Vermin traveled, but she kept things that touched her body as clean as she could, and although she'd seen other nuns and pledges with the red rash that foretold of vermin, Andressa had been careful enough to avoid it for the most part.

But it had been a struggle.

Therefore, when the old serving woman came into the chamber with clean clothing and talk of a bath, Andressa didn't hesitate for long. She almost wanted the bath more than the food. She wasn't as dedicated to her to the cloister enough to refuse the clean comfort of the material world, so she stood in the corner as several servants entered the chamber with a big copper basin. She didn't utter a word of protest when they filled it, sending steam into the chamber. She was ready, willing, and able to wash herself when the servants left.

"I'll take your clothing and have it washed, m'lady," the old serving woman was the only one left, holding out her arms to Andressa. "Let me take your garments and while they are being cleaned, you can wear the clothing I brought you."

The lure of worldly comforts was almost too much for Andressa to take. Her gaze was on the steaming water. "There is no time to clean my clothing properly," she said. "It will take time to dry out and I do not have such time."

The servant didn't give up. "Then let me take it and clean what I can," she said. "Clean the spots off of it, as it were."

Andressa looked down at herself. She wore what was essentially a long tunic, all the way to the ground, tied about her waist with a loose leather belt. Beneath that, she wore a shift, but it was made from rough material and that, too, had been given to her. Cast downs from other nuns who had moved on to finer habits. On her feet were leather shoes, with a hole in the sole of the right one, and that was all she wore. No hose, nothing to protect her skin.

Gone were the days of the fine garments she used to wear, the lovely dresses made from silks. Her hair, which had been a source of pride for her, had always been elaborately dressed. She looked like an heiress, which she was, but all of that finery had ended the day she entered St. Blitha. The lovely dress she wore had been taken from her and in its place she'd been given the monstrosity she currently wore. She had a second shift, for sleeping or the rare bathing, but she was basically wearing everything she owned, and she knew it was a sight.

Not a good sight, either.

Her resistance to the call of comfort wasn't very strong. She hadn't much willpower where that was concerned. Therefore, with a sharp nod, she began to untie her belt, removing it and pulling the heavy woolen garment over her head to hand to the servant. As the woman moved to the door, presumably to go clean the wool, Andressa removed her shoes and made her way over to the basin to peer at the clean, warm water.

Heavenly!

But she jumped away from the basin, startled, when the old servant opened the door and was met by another servant outside. The old woman handed off the woolen garment to the servant and took something from her in return, something she carried with her as she closed the door, bolted it, and headed over to the table near the hearth, where she sat everything down. She then picked up a three-legged stool from a corner and headed for the big, steaming basin on the ground.

"Remove your shift, m'lady," she said as she placed the stool inside the basin. "Get in, sit down, and I shall wash you down."

It was almost too good to be true, but Andressa refused to remove the thin linen shift. She simply wasn't comfortable doing so. The serving woman encouraged her to get into the basin, anyway, easing her down onto the stool. The water was several inches deep, deep enough so that when she sat down, her bottom was right at the water level. Once she settled down, the old servant went to work.

Such a simple comfort as a washing had never felt so good. It wasn't a full bath, as Andressa wasn't immersed, but the serving woman used a large pitcher to pour water over her, drenching her, before scrubbing what skin she could get to, from her head to her toes, with a bristly brush and a cake of hard soap that had seeds in it, and smelled of honey and pine.

It was a glorious smell, and Andressa reveled in the pleasure of being scrubbed down. Her ankles, filthy above the edges of her shoe, were scrubbed clean, as where her elbows, knees, hands, and any other piece of flesh the serving woman could get to.

More water rinsed over her and the serving woman took her hair out of its thick braid, the one that went all the way to her knees, and began pouring water through it. Andressa wasn't exactly sure how she was going to explain wet hair when she returned to St. Blitha, but at the moment, she didn't much care. It was a heavenly bath and she was savoring the moment.

She'd worry about the consequences later.

"I have soap meant for your hair, m'lady," the serving woman said. "It's meant to kill any vermin and make your hair very fresh."

With the warm water and the scrubbing, Andressa was quite relaxed at that point. She was game for anything the woman wanted to do to her. "How is it that you have so many things for a bath?" she asked. "Is there a lady of the house?"

The old woman began to pour something over Andressa's hair, something that smelled strongly of vinegar. "Lord William has five daughters," the servant told her. "When they visit London, this is where they stay."

Andressa looked to the dress hanging over the chair. "Then the gown belongs to his daughters?"

"Aye, m'lady."

That made sense to Andressa. She said a silent prayer of thanks to the daughters of William Marshal, loaning her their bathing things and something to wear. Perhaps a bath and clean clothes was the simplest thing in the world to them, but to her, it was everything. It reminded her of the outside world she was coming to miss, so very much.

God, she wanted to live in a fine house like this, with all of the food and comfort she could tolerate, and it deeply saddened her that it simply wasn't meant to be. Therefore, she was determined to enjoy the moment, as short as it would be, because God only knew when she'd ever known such comforts again.

The old woman washed her hair once with bar soap that smelled strongly of Sulphur, and then rinsed it clear with vinegar again. Seated on the stool, Andressa's hair was so long that it went all the way to the floor and then some, and the old servant spent a good deal of time combing out her tresses while Andressa sat in the cooling water. Cooling or not, it was still as blissful as she could imagine and she would stretch it out as long as she could.

Bless Maxton and his requests for her comfort.

When the water became too cold, the old woman urged her out of the basin by holding up a large piece of drying cloth. Andressa did as she was told, stepping onto the cold floor while the woman vigorously dried her and her sopping shift. As the old woman came around to the front of her and began drying her arms and torso, as least as much as she could, she suddenly came to a halt.

Andressa had been enjoying the attention until that moment, but when it abruptly stopped, she peered at the old servant only to see that the woman was looking at her midsection with some alarm.

"What is it?" Andressa asked curiously.

The old woman opened her mouth to speak, then quickly shut it. She shook her head, swiftly, and returned to her drying duties.

"I… I do not believe that dress shall fit you, m'lady," she said hesitantly. "I will go and see if I can find something else that is suitable."

Andressa wasn't able to reply before the woman was hastily bundling her up in the drying cloth and pushing her towards the hearth.

"Stay here," she told her firmly. "The heat from the fire will dry you and your hair, but careful you don't get too close. We wouldn't want to see your hair go up in flame."

Andressa nodded, thinking the woman was acting rather strangely all of a suddenly. As she watched, the woman grabbed the wine-colored garment and fled the chamber, shutting the door behind her.

CHAPTER THIRTEEN

MAXTON WAS IN no mood for a nervous servant.

He'd met the woman rushing out of the chamber where he'd left Andressa, nearly running into her because she was moving so fast. When she saw him, she gasped, and Maxton received the distinct impression that she wasn't happy to see him. She looked frightened. His brow furrowed as he peered at her.

"What is wrong?" he demanded. "Is Lady Andressa still in that room?"

He was pointing to the closed door and the old woman nodded vigorously. "Aye, m'lord," he said. "You asked for clean clothing and a bath and food for her, and she has just finished her bath. But… but the clothing I brought for her will not fit her."

"Why not?"

The old woman seemed to pale. "Because…," she started, swallowed, and tried again. "M'lord, is the lass a nun? She wears the clothing of someone meant for the cloister."

Maxton nodded. "She is a pledge," he said. "What about her clothing? What is this about?"

The old woman struggled past her nervousness; she had to. She didn't know of the knight's relationship to the young woman, so she wasn't sure how to answer him. She didn't even really know the knight, only that he was one of William Marshal's men. But he was looking at her, expecting an answer, so she proceeded as discreetly as she could.

"I brought her a dress belonging to one of the lord's daughters," she said quietly. "It will not fit her because of her belly, m'lord. I must find her a bigger garment."

"What do you mean 'because of her belly'?"

"She is with child, m'lord."

Maxton stared at her for a moment. He wasn't sure he'd heard correctly. He simply stared at her as her words flitted about in his muddled mind, trying to find some sense in them.

"She's *what*?" he finally said. "That is impossible. You are mistaken."

The old woman could see a flash of something in his eyes, of untold madness that could rip her limb from limb should he be displeased enough. But she knew what she saw.

"M'lord," she said quietly, firmly. "I have had seven children myself. I know what a woman looks like who is with child, and the lass in that you had me bring clothing and a bath for is clearly with child. I would not have known it, either, for the shapeless clothing she wears, but believe me when I tell you – she *is* with child."

Maxton couldn't help his jaw from hanging open. He wasn't sure what he felt at the moment, but astonishment was certainly among the possibilities. Shock, dismay, even sadness... was she really carrying a *child*?

What horrible secret had she been hiding from him?

Stunned, he struggled to think clearly.

"Then find her something suitable to wear," he said. "Is she still in the room where I left her?"

"Aye, m'lord."

Sending the woman on her way, Maxton headed straight for the chamber. The door was closed, and in hindsight, he should have knocked, but he was so determined to get to the truth of the situation that he barged in without thinking.

The chamber was lit by firelight and a few fat tapers, and almost cloyingly warm from the steam of the bath. He heard a gasp and caught sight of Andressa sitting next to the fire on a small stool, a comb in her hand and an expression of surprise upon her face. She had a drying towel wrapped around her, a big one, so he couldn't see anything other than her bare feet and hands, and her head.

"My lord?" Andressa said, fear in her voice. "What is it? Has something happened?"

He looked at her. *Has something happened?* Clearly, something had, but not to him. Looking at the woman, all of the shock and dismay he'd felt had turned into something else, and now all he could manage to feel was sorrow. Pure, black sorrow, as black as a moonless night.

Hurt…

Bleeding Christ, why was he feeling hurt?

Because he was feeling something for *her*.

The thought struck him like a hammer to an anvil. He hadn't been sure what he was feeling for her until this moment, but now, he knew. He'd known the woman all of one day and somehow, someway, they had connected on a level he'd never known before. Perhaps it was her dire circumstances, or perhaps it was simply the way she looked at him – with utter, complete trust. She knew of his background, but she didn't care. He'd said it best when he told her that he wanted her to think he was indeed noble and generous. He wanted her to think well of him.

But why did he feel hurt? Because as much as she assured him that she trusted him, she hadn't trusted him enough to tell him of her condition.

Perhaps there wasn't complete trust, after all.

"Are you with child?" he asked bluntly.

He was a man with no tact, and that was evident when Andressa's eyes widened at his question. Even in the dim light, he could see the color drain from her face.

"My lord," she breathed. "Why would you ask such a…?"

He cut her off. "Answer me," he said. "Do you carry a child?"

Her breathing grew quicker; he could see her nostrils flaring as she looked at him with such horror that it was spilling out all over the place. The comb fell from her hand and she suddenly stood up, clutching the drying cloth tightly around her.

"I do not have to answer you," she whispered tightly, verging on tears. "Tell the woman to bring my clothing."

"You are not going anywhere until you answer me."

"Let me out of here or I shall scream!"

She was quickly growing panicked. But Maxton backed up, standing by the door as if to block it. He wasn't going to let her leave.

He wanted the truth.

"Nay," he said, his head wagging back and forth slowly. "You are not leaving. You are going to tell me the truth, Andressa. You said you trusted me. You came here *because* you trusted me. Did you lie to me?"

"Nay," she shook her head quickly, unable to look at him. "I did not lie."

"Then if you trust me, tell me the truth."

The tears were right on the surface, but she fought them. In fact, she looked a little lost, seemingly pondering his question, perhaps even the situation in general. All intentions ot leave the chamber seem to fade, and slowly, she lowered herself back to the stool, slumping over.

Defeated.

It was several long, painful moments before she dared speak.

"Why do you ask such a thing?" she murmured.

"I can easily discover the answer to my question myself, so I am asking you to tell me the truth."

"And how would you discover it?"

"Do you truly think you can hide your condition beneath a thin drying towel and a shift?"

That brought her pause. Every emotion, every horror and every fragment of despair, rippled across her face as she tried to form the words that would give him a suitable answer.

She was trapped and she knew it.

"It is not as it sounds," she finally said.

"*What* is not as it sounds?"

She looked away from him completely, so he could not see her face, but he could see her shoulders heaving as she silently wept. There was a long pause before she replied.

"He... he told me he loved me," she whispered. "I believed him. He said he would return for me, but he did not."

It was confirmation as far as Maxton was concerned and he felt as if he'd been punched in the gut. He felt sick. Moving in her direction, he spoke softly.

"Tell me all of it," he said softly. "Please."

She was looking at the wall. "I cannot speak of it," she whispered. "To speak of it makes it real, and I do not want this to be real."

Maxton sighed faintly, lowering himself to the nearest chair. He was so despondent he found it difficult to stand. It was as if all of the energy had drained right out of him.

"It is real whether or not you speak of it," he said. "Please tell me what happened."

She sat there and struggled. Maxton could see that she was wiping her face. When she finally began to speak, he could hardly hear her.

"He said he loved me," she repeated. "We knew each other at Okehampton. I thought we would marry someday, or at least I thought so before I was sent to St. Blitha. Last summer, he finally found me at St. Blitha and he told me he loved me. He said he would return for me, but he never did."

Maxton could see how ashamed she was. "And he left you with child?"

She wiped at her face, struggling for the last vestiges of her dignity. "I did not want to admit it," she said. "I have pretended nothing is wrong."

"Did he force himself upon you? Did he rape you?"

She shook her head. "Nay," she said. "But he seduced me and I did not resist as much as I should have. He told me he loved me and he wanted to demonstrate that love. I was so happy to see him that I believed him."

"And he lied to you."

Sobs caught in her throat as she nodded. "I will end up in The Chaos for this," she said, finally turning to look at him. "I shall end up in The Chaos and so will the child. It will be dead before it ever has a chance to live. I will have killed it!"

Her voice was lifting in panic. Sighing heavily, Maxton stood up from the chair and made his way over to her.

"You will not end up in The Chaos," he murmured. "Stand up."

Andressa looked up at him, terror in her eyes, but as she gazed at him, the trust they'd established took hold. She had no one else in the world to turn to, but she had Maxton. He'd proven that.

Slowly, she obeyed him, clutching the damp drying towel around her body. The moment she rose to her feet, Maxton pushed the towel out of the way so that he could get a look at her torso. When the damp shift concealed too much, he put his hands onto her swollen belly to feel it for himself.

It was a bold move, and an intimate one. He heard her gasp, but she didn't pull away. The moment his hands collided with her rounded belly, Andressa burst into quiet tears, turning her head away as he ran his fingers over the perfectly rounded bump. If there had been any question about the trust between the two of them before, his intimate action sealed their complete trust.

Now, it was set in stone.

"Don't cry," he whispered. "When did this happen?"

She put her hand to her mouth, trying to stifle the sobs. "Last summer."

"Then you should be delivering this child in the next month or two."

That only made her weep harder, as if she had no answer for him. "Did you truly not know you were with child, Andressa?" Maxton asked. "Did you truly think that the swelling of your belly meant something else?"

She lifted her slender shoulders. "I was praying it was not true," she whispered. "I was praying it was all a great mistake. If I ignored it, I hoped it would go away. I... I worked very hard, hoping the seed would die, but it did not. Then, when the child began to move..."

"He moves?"

She nodded. "It moves quite a lot, especially when I am trying to sleep."

He couldn't help but notice she addressed the child as 'it'. Not he, or she, but 'it'. Beneath his hands, her belly was warm and firm. Not huge, but definitely rounded, about the size of a large melon and easily concealed by the loose clothing she wore. He removed his hands and pulled the damp drying towel tightly around her, covering her up.

Now, Maxton had a dilemma. A massive one. William Marshal wanted Andressa to return to St. Blitha, but if Maxton had been uncertain before, now he was doubly so. He couldn't send a pregnant woman back there and a wild sense of protection swept him. This wasn't even his child, but it didn't seem to matter. Andressa was vulnerable and needed protecting. Wasn't that what he was sworn to do, as a knight? God, he's spent so much time killing men on command, or fighting other men's battles – right or wrong- that the chivalry had left him long ago.

But now, it was back.

It didn't matter that some foolish knight had seduced Andressa and left her with his child to deal with. Nay, that didn't matter in the least. Maxton was the last one to judge when it came to sinning.

He told me he loved me...

It was one more horrific situation for this poor woman to deal with.

"I am sorry, my lord," Andressa suddenly spoke, breaking the silence between them. "I am so very sorry for my failings and my weakness. It would seem that all you have known from me since the moment we met is failings and weakness, but I assure you, I was not always like this. Once, I was a strong, noble woman. I was excellent in my studies. I had many friends. Believe it or not, I was pretty once, too. Or, so I am told. But you have discovered me at my lowest and for that, I am very sorry. I wish you knew me before… before all of this."

He looked at her. "You *are* beautiful," he said as if she was mad to believe otherwise. "As for discovering you at your lowest, I am in no position to condemn you. My sins far outweigh your own."

She looked at him in astonishment. "Then… then you are not… you do not think I am a horrible, failing creature for what I have done?"

He cocked an eyebrow. "I am going to tell you something, Andressa," he said pointedly. "I, too, have indulged in pleasures of the flesh outside of marriage, so if that is a sin, then I have sinned many times over. You are not alone."

One might have thought it to be a tasteless confession, but to Andressa, it was possibly the best thing he could have said. When he could have turned his nose up at her, he proudly told her that she wasn't alone in her failings. Not every man would have done that.

"Then… you are not disgusted?" She was still incredulous.

"Nay," he said. "We all have our moments of weakness. You are not to blame."

Andressa could hardly believe his reaction. For something she'd been trying to ignore, to pretend wasn't real, his attitude made her feel as if there was hope… hope for her, hope for everything. Hope that perhaps this wasn't the end for her, after all.

"You are very understanding," she said. "Most anyone would judge my actions harshly."

He snorted softly. "As I said, I have sinned in such a way many times over, with many women who were not my wife."

"Then you are not married, my lord?"

He shook his head. "Stop addressing me formally," he said. "It seems ridiculous under these circumstances. You will call me Maxton. Or Max. Call me what you wish, Andressa. I will answer. But to answer your question, I am not married."

"But why not?"

"Who would have me?"

She blinked, as if the question was ridiculous. "Any woman would be very fortunate to have you as a husband," she said. "You are a skilled, kind, and generous knight, and surely you have much to offer any woman. Has someone been foolish enough to deny your suit? Is that it?"

He looked at her, a flicker of a smile on his lips. "I've not been brave enough or stupid enough to actually pursue a woman," he said. "But your words are appreciated. I am not sure if they are true, but they are appreciated."

Andressa eyed him. "You have told me of things from your past, things you are not proud of," she said. "Will… will you tell me where you come from, my lo… I mean, Sir Maxton? You know much about me, but I know very little about you."

"Why do you want to know?"

"Because I do. Will you please tell me?"

He thought on that. It seemed an odd subject shift, from the subject of her illicit pregnancy to speaking of his background, but the truth was that he was glad to be off the subject of the child, at least for the moment. Perhaps speaking of himself might distract her enough to cause her to relax.

"If you call me Sir Maxton again, I am going to pinch you," he said, watching a timid smile spread across her face. He couldn't help but grin in return, a light moment in the midst of a heady situation. "It is simply Maxton, or Max. As for my background, you already know I am from Devon. Though my family name is de Long, we are known for our castle of Loxbeare Cross. An ancestor of mine built it one hundred and fifty years ago, and simply used it to refer to his family instead of our family name. That is what we are known as – Loxbeare."

Andressa understood. "So you are Maxton de Long of Loxbeare Cross," she clarified, watching him nod. "I have heard of men using the names of their homes as identification. One such family that comes to mind is Pembury. There was a Lady Pembury, a friend of my patroness,

Lady de Courtney, and she was from the town of Pembury. But her family name was Culpepper."

Maxton nodded. "Exactly," he said. "And I have two younger brothers and a younger sister, all three of whom I've not seen in almost twenty years."

"Why not?"

Maxton lifted his shoulders, averting his gaze. "I left home at a young age," he said. "My father, Magnus, and I do not get on well. Magnus wanted me to remain at Loxbeare Cross, as his heir, and be his shadow. He did not want me to leave, but I... I wanted to see the world. I wanted to find my own way in life and do what I wanted to do, and not what my father told me to do. My father is quite overbearing."

"Did your brothers and sister remain with him, then?"

Maxton turned away from her at that point, returning to the chair he'd been sitting in as he settled into a conversation that, under normal circumstances, was uncomfortable for him.

"My brother, Emmett, is more like my father," he said. "He is content to remain at home and rule with my father, while my brother, Jasper, has devoted his life to the church. The last I heard, he had taken his vows as a Benedictine priest somewhere in York. And my little sister, Lucy... I do not know what has become of her. She and I were quite close and when I left, she was around eight years of age. That would be at least twenty or more years ago. She was a light in my world. I miss her."

Cracks in his façade were starting to show, emotions from the usually emotionless man. Andressa sensed that. "Surely you can write to your father and discover what has become of her?" she asked. "Mayhap she is married now, with many children to call you uncle."

Maxton thought back to the little girl with the red curls, and how much she had wept when he'd left home. "I *have* written to my father," he said quietly. "I never receive a reply."

"Oh," Andressa said as if sorry she had even suggested such a thing. "Is your father angry with you for leaving Loxbeare Cross, then?"

Maxton considered that question. "Angry? Aye," he said. "But mostly disappointed. He did not want me to see the world and seek my own way in life. He wanted me to take after him, to be exactly like him. I could not do it. I had to follow my own path."

"But you do not regret doing such a thing?"

"Never," he said resolutely. "But I am sure my father has caught wind of my unsavory reputation as an Executioner Knight, among other things. Most everyone in England has. I am sure that is why he does not answer my missives. He is ashamed of me."

Andressa was silent for a moment as she turned for the stool next to the hearth, lowering herself down to it. "You are still his son," she said. "He has not stopped loving you."

"I would not be too sure."

"Mayhap you should go home and find out for yourself? At least, you would know for certain."

Had anyone else made that suggestion, he would have scoffed, but coming from Andressa, he couldn't seem to refute her. Her tone was gentle, her words reasonable. She had a great sense of wisdom about her, something he'd seen from the start. Therefore, he simply nodded his head.

"Mayhap," he replied quietly. "But not today. Mayhap someday. In any case, now you know something of me. I am unspectacular."

"You are fascinating," she countered. "You are a man of great experience and I am sure your father will realize that someday. He raised a son who is not a follower, but a leader. Even I can see that."

Maxton looked at her. Everything out of her mouth about him sounded like praise. He was quite unused to that, but it didn't sound forced. In fact, he heard great respect in her tone when she spoke of him, and to him, and it was something that made him feel strong and alive. Perhaps that was why he was so attracted to her; unknowingly, she fed something in him that needed to be fed, filling a hole he never knew he had.

She made him feel like a man in ways he couldn't begin to comprehend.

But that brought him around to the reason why they were in this room and why Andressa was even here. He couldn't send her back to St. Blitha, not now. They would have to figure out how to stop the assassin nuns without her, because surely, he wasn't about to put her and the life she carried into harm's way again. He didn't relish telling William of the latest development, but it had to be done.

There had to be another way.

"I am sure there are many who would disagree with you, but I thank you for the confidence," he said, rising wearily to his feet. "Now, if you are finished interrogating me, I have duties to attend to. You may remain here and rest for the time being. Have you eaten yet?"

There was a lightness to his mood that hadn't been there before, an undercurrent of humor that was appealing. Andressa liked it. But to his question, she shook her head. "Nay," she said. "Truthfully, the bath was so wonderful, I have not missed it."

He waved her off. "You must eat," he said firmly. "I shall ensure food is sent up to you immediately. God only knows how the child you carry has been starved, so you must eat well if only for the child's sake."

He started to turn away but she stopped him. "Maxton?" she said, using his name for the first time and watching him turn to her immediately. "You have not mentioned... what I told you about King John... did you discuss this with William Marshal?"

It was exactly what he didn't want to discuss with her, but looking into her anxious face, he reckoned that she had a right to know what was going on. It wouldn't be fair to keep it from her since she was involved in it, as much as he was.

"I have," he said. "We have been honest with each other from the start, so I will be honest with you now. The Marshal wants you to return to St. Blitha and keep an eye on the situation. If something unusual happens, then he wants you to tell us."

Surprisingly, she didn't seem distress by that directive. "But he is going to tell the king not to come to St. Blitha, is he not?"

Maxton shook his head. "Nay," he said. "The king is not to know. Andressa, you must understand something – we knew of this threat to the king. We knew because last year, I was offered money to do what your Mother Abbess has been instructed to do. I refused and was jailed for it. We suspected that more assassins would be sent to complete the task, but we never dreamed the assassins would be killer nuns. When you told us of this happening, you unknowingly solved a mystery we had been trying to figure out. You, my little friend, have been the key to all of this. You have helped save your king."

He watched her eyes widen at the news. "The Holy Father asked you to kill the king?" she gasped.

Maxton nodded. "I spent a long time at The Lateran Palace, at the Holy Father's invitation, and was offered the task," he said. "When I refused, he imprisoned me and simply gave the task to the nuns who, from what you have told me, have done this kind of work before."

She nodded solemnly. "Aye," she said. "They have. And they show no remorse for it."

"That is why I do not want you to go back," he said. When she looked at him with surprise, he continued. "I did not want you to go back before I knew you were with child, but now… now, you cannot possibly go back into that den of demons. That is no place for you or your child."

The last time he had suggested she not return to St. Blitha, she'd become panicky and ran from him. But this time, she didn't run. She could sense his concern, and she was flattered, but it didn't change facts.

"I have no choice," she said. "I told you that others have tried to flee the Mother Abbess and she has found them and brought them back. The woman will find me no matter where I go, and frankly, I do not have the means to go anywhere. It is not as if I can return home."

Maxton sighed heavily, scratching his neck as he thought of his reply. "You will let me worry about that," he said. "I told you I would protect you, like a big brother should. I will not go back on that promise."

Andressa stood up, pulling the now-dry towel around her as she moved towards him, timid steps. "But I am not your responsibility," she murmured firmly. "While I greatly appreciate your offer, the truth is that I am not your responsibility. You have made the offer out of pity and it will soon become a burden if I permit it."

She had come within arm's length of him and Maxton's dark gaze moved to her. Her hair was dry now, curling around her face, long and silky down to her knees. He could see such beauty in her, such grace and wisdom. Something about her swept him off his feet and made him feel giddy, a feeling that not even her pregnancy could dissolve. He didn't care that she carried another man's child. It was a mistake; he understood that.

All he cared about, at the moment, was *her*.

"You would never become a burden to me," he said. "And… and mayhap I have not been completely honest with you about my intentions."

"What do you mean?"

What *did* he mean? He fumbled for the right words. "It is not as a big brother that I look upon you," he said. "I do not look at you and see a sisterly relation. I look at you and see a woman of grace and beauty, and I have since I first met you. There is something so haunting about you, yet so strong. I am not sure I can explain it better than that. Let me take care of you, Andressa. Let me take care of you and the baby, and let us find a corner of this world where two sinners can find happiness with each other."

Andressa was looking at him in astonishment. Her eyes widened and she simply stared at him as if he'd just said the most shocking thing she'd ever heard.

"You… you want to take care of… of…?"

"Aye, I want to take care of you."

She swallowed hard, taking a step back as his words impacted her. She'd only just met the man; that was her first thought. How could he know that he wanted to take care of her? It was his pity talking. She knew that. He had a great deal of pity for her, more so now that he knew she was with child, and it was that kind and generous man acting on impulse. As much as she was flattered, and deeply touched, the offer terrified her immensely.

I am not your responsibility.

But, God, she wished that she was.

Maxton was a powerful, seasoned, handsome knight of the highest order. She remembered thinking that she wished she was good enough for him, because a man like Maxton deserved a fine, elegant wife, not a lowly pledge who was pregnant with another man's child. She was certain he'd not thought extensively on the offer he just made, because if he had, he probably would not have made it. The mere thought of what he was suggesting was ludicrous.

For his sake, she could not agree to it.

"Your offer is as beautiful as your soul, Maxton," she said quietly. "I know you have a past that suggests your soul is as black as soot, but my experience with you has been much different. You are a man that every girl dreams of. But you said that William Marshal wishes for me to return to St. Blitha?"

Her response made him hopeful. "He does."

"Then that is where I should go."

He grunted unhappily. "Andressa…"

"Please, Maxton," she said, reaching out to put a slender hand on his arm. "I know you are trying to help me, but you must let me think on what you have said. I will not make a decision of this importance in only a few moments. Will you send food to me now? I am rather hungry."

She was changing the subject and he was aware of it. He was also grossly unhappy that she wasn't jumping on his offer, but he understood for the most part. It had been a turbulent day and a turbulent situation, and he was certain that she wasn't thinking clearly. He thought that once she'd filled her belly and she'd had time to consider everything, that perhaps she would be more agreeable to his offer. If she was, then he would have to find a place to put her until the situation blew over. When the king went to St. Blitha in two days, he didn't want her anywhere near the place.

He wanted her safe.

Collecting her hand as it rested on his arm, he held her cold digits in his big, rough palm. "I will get it for you," he said. "But you will think on my offer. Swear it?"

She nodded steadily. "I am deeply grateful for it. And you."

Maxton thought he sensed something in her tone, something that gave him great hope that perhaps she was feeling for him what he was feeling for her. He couldn't even put it into words; all he knew was that he could see it in her eyes.

Impulsively, he put his arms around her and pulled her against him, his mouth slanting over hers to deliver a kiss that was warm and curious, tender and titillating. She stiffened at first, but only momentarily – quickly, he could feel her relaxing, surrendering to his power, and that only made him kiss her more deeply. She was warm and soft in his embrace, if not a bit boney, but it didn't take away from his excitement or his enjoyment. He could also feel her hard belly pressing against his torso and strangely enough, it excited him. Her fertility excited him. He found it alluring and womanly, all strange thoughts from a very unconventional man.

He could get used to the feel of her in his arms quite easily.

A knock on the door startled him and he quickly let her go, moving a few feet away as the door opened and the old servant woman appeared. When she saw Maxton in the chamber, she gasped.

"I'm sorry, m'lord," she said. "I didn't know you were here."

Maxton took a couple of long strides and was at the door. "I was just leaving," he said, pulling the panel open wide. "I will have food sent up to the lady."

With that, he was gone, leaving the room unnaturally fast. Andressa stood there a moment, glancing at the old serving woman and wondering if the woman was thinking that he had behaved strangely. Did she know they'd been in a passionate embrace only moments before? Andressa's cheeks felt hot and she put a hand to them, feeling the heat, knowing Maxton had put it there.

It had been a moment she never thought she'd experience, but it only served to confirm what she was already thinking – Maxton was a man of impulse, and that was exactly what his offer had been – impulsive. But he was also sweet, passionate, and wildly handsome.

And that kiss… she was still reeling from it.

Still, she couldn't let him make such a mistake, and the truth was that she didn't want to make a mistake, either. She'd already had one foolish moment in her life. She couldn't stand to have another and possibly ruin Maxton's life in the process.

"Come along, m'lady," the old serving woman cut into her thoughts. "I've brought something that you can wear."

As the old woman went to pull away the drying towel, Andressa balked. "Nay," she said. "Not that clothing. Where is the garment you took from me?"

"The spots are being cleaned from it, m'lady."

Andressa pushed aside the garment that the old woman was extending to her. "Bring it back to me," she said. "Hurry, now. I do not wish to wear anything else."

"But –!"

"Now, please. Bring it in a hurry. I do not wish to catch a chill."

Begrudgingly, the old woman left the chamber with the garment she had brought with her, a fine robe that belonged to William Marshal's wife, and went down to the kitchens where a maid was scrubbing out the dirt from the rough woolen tunic. Collecting the half-cleaned garment, she took it back up to the stubborn lady, who took the garment from her and then asked for a blanket to cover herself with.

As the old serving women left Andressa alone to dress as she went on the blanket suitable for the young lady, Andressa very quickly pulled on her woolen garment and yanked on her shoes. The leather belt she wore was draped over a chair and she collected it quickly, rushing for the door as she tied it on.

Very quietly, she opened the chamber door, sticking her head out to see if anyone was around and, seeing that it was mostly vacant, she dashed from the door and down the stairs that led to the interior courtyard outside.

It was dark now, with dozens of torches lighting up the night, as she scurried through the courtyard and to the front gate. The gate guards were surprisingly willing to let her leave without so much as a word, and once the gate was opened for her, she slipped out into the night, braiding her freshly-washed hair as she rushed through the darkness, disappearing down the street on her way back to St. Blitha.

It wasn't until nearly a half-hour later when Maxton returned that he discovered her missing.

No one had to tell him anything. He knew where she had gone.

CHAPTER FOURTEEN

"I WAS TOLD you were awake," Alexander said. "How do you feel?"

While the men of Farringdon House were feasting in the hall and Maxton was off dealing with the St. Blitha pledge who had unknowingly solved all of their problems, Alexander had been informed that his prisoner had awoken from his drunken stupor. He'd left William and the other men supping on boiled beef to tend to Alasdair, who looked as if he'd been hit by an ale wagon and then some. The man groaned as he rubbed at his head.

"I feel as bad as ye smell, Sassenach," he muttered. Then, he looked up at Alexander and seemed to have some clarity. The light of recognition went on in his eyes. "'Tis ye. I should have known. Are ye behind all of this, then?"

Alexander leaned against the door jamb, feeling rather smug. After the months he took to follow this man, he had every right to feel victorious.

"Do you recognize me?" he asked. "I thought you might. There is no way you could have avoided me as much as you did without knowing me on sight."

Alasdair sighed heavily as he blinked, trying to clear his vision. "*An leanabh*," he said. "You are The Follower. Ye've been following me since I left Italia."

Alexander nodded, feeling some sense of satisfaction now that they had acknowledged each other. Not that he had any doubt, but the truth was that he'd followed Alasdair around for so long he felt as if he was seeing an old friend.

"I have," he said. "Do you know why I have been following you?"

Alasdair shrugged. "Someone put ye up to it, I imagine," he said. "Who paid ye? Was it Abramo? Or Idiamo? I can only guess it would be one of those two, shadows of the Holy Father and suspicious of all who come near him. Well? Which bastard was it?'"

Alexander wasn't going to tell him who had paid him, so he simply shrugged his shoulders. "Does it matter?" he said. "I was paid to hunt you down and kill you, but you proved quite a challenge. I will congratulate you for evading me until now. I did not know that a Scotsman could be so clever."

Alasdair smiled thinly. "There's much ye dunna know about a Scotsman," he said. "Now that ye know who I am, tell me yer name."

"De Sherrington."

That made Alasdair peer more closely at him, this time in surprise. "De Sherrington," he repeated. "God's Bones, it *is* ye. I dinna recognize without the hair on yer face and yer clothes on. The last I saw ye, 'twas during a summer feast at The Lateran Palace. 'Twas as hot as Hades, as I recall, and ye had women in yer arms. Yer part of the *Sassenach* contingent that the Holy Father invited tae The Lateran Palace."

"I am."

"I heard that ye and yer friends are called the *Cavalieri de Boia*. The Executioner Knights." He suddenly grinned. "I was more clever than a bunch of Sassenachs. Admit it."

Alexander smirked. "For a time, mayhap," he said. "But I have you know."

"Do ye intend tae kill me?"

"I've not yet decided. You are a very interesting man and it would be a shame to kill one so clever. In fact, I am very curious about you."

"Why?"

Alexander shrugged. "You are a double agent," he said. "I find that fascinating. And, by the way, the messenger you sent north to Scotland whilst you were in Berwick shall not make it to the king. He's dead."

Some of the smile faded from Alasdair's face. "I see," he said, rather calmly. "A pity."

"He would not tell me the message he carried. Mayhap you will."

Alasdair sighed heavily and scratched at his bushy head. "I hardly remember it," he said. "It seems like it was so long ago."

"Did you send him with word of the Holy Father's directive to kill King John?"

Much to Alasdair's credit, he didn't overly react to the question, but that was the training in him. Years and years of training, of spying and lying, had given him excellent control over his moods and emotions. He continued scratching his head, casually, glancing up at the enormous English knight.

"I wouldna know, lad."

"I think you do." Alexander came away from the door jamb, wandering into the chamber. "In fact, I know you do. I have it on good authority that you delivered a message to the Mother Abbess of St. Blitha and instructed her to kill the king when he comes to the abbey for St. Blitha's feast day. Did you think you were the only double agent around? Think again, Douglas. There is a mole at St. Blitha and we know everything you told them. You may as well confess the truth."

Alasdair sighed heavily and dropped his hand. "Ye seem tae already know it," he said. "What more could I say that ye dunna already know?"

"You can tell me that this is the message you carried all the way from The Lateran Palace," he said. "Douglas, think of it this way – you carried a message from the Holy Father and I was paid to kill you, presumably before you delivered it. Someone at The Lateran Palace didn't want that message to make it to St. Blitha. Someone there either hates the Holy Father enough, or loves King John enough, that they did not want you to succeed."

Alasdair had been in the game along time, enough to know that defeat was sometimes part of that game. He simply shook his head.

"Someone will succeed," he said, a grin returning to his pale lips as he looked up at Alexander. "The hatred against John... it goes deeper than ye know, de Sherrington. 'Tis not only the Holy Father who wants yer king dead."

Alexander thought about that for a moment before an idea occurred to him. His eyebrows lifted. "Of course," he muttered. "I should have guessed. The Scottish king is in on the plot, also. That is why you were sending a message north to him."

Alasdair lifted his hand in a way that was both vague and confirming at the same time. "Then ye know if ye stop the nuns at St. Blitha, someone else will come forward," he said. "They always do. Ye cannot cut all of the threads of the spider's web. Where one is snipped away, others remain strong."

"True enough," Alexander said. "But we can hunt down Richard's bastard son and kill him. With the boy out of the way, neither the Holy Father or William the Lion, or any other enemies, will have a legitimate issue to place upon the throne."

The fact that Alexander knew about Richard's bastard son drew some reaction from Alasdair, however weak. His dark eyes flickered as he realized that, indeed, de Sherrington knew the extent of their plans. Whoever the mole was inside of St. Blitha had done a thorough job, which was rather disappointing.

"Ye'll never find the lad," he finally said. "The Holy Father sent him away. I dunna even know where he is."

Alexander waved him off. "It is of little matter," he said. "If enough money is presented, I am sure whoever guards the boy will happily turn him over to us. No man is more loyal to the Holy Father than he is to his own purse."

Alasdair conceded the point. "Money is the most persuasive language in the world," he agreed. "I wish ye luck, *Sassenach*. Ye'll need it."

Alexander dipped his head as if thanking the man. "Your confidence in me is overwhelming," he said. "But have no fear; in the end, we shall do what needs to be done, for the good of England."

Alasdair's dark eyes littered. "Would ye care tae wager on that, lad?"

Alexander couldn't help the grin on his lips. "I may keep you alive just long enough to see who would win that wager."

"If I win, then ye'll set me free. If I lose, ye can slit my throat."

"I do not need anything as frivolous as a wager to do that."

"Then ye still intend tae kill me, in any case?"

"That is what I've been paid to do. And I am loyal to my own purse."

Alasdair laughed softly, thinking of the words on the value of money presented only moments earlier. "If I pay ye more, will ye spare me?"

Alexander appeared intrigued by the offer. "Can you?"

"My king can."

Alexander rather liked that. It was the mercenary in him. He had no great loyalty to Abramo or the money the man had paid him, but if he could make even more money by sparing Alasdair's life, he would consider it.

"Then mayhap I shall send word to William the Lion and ask him what your life is worth to him," he said. "Meanwhile, you will be my guest for a time. You may as well get comfortable. You are going to be here a while."

Alasdair simply nodded, torn between showing de Sherrington just how clever he was and making the man think he had surrendered to his fate. He didn't want to tip off the big knight with suggestions of a future escape, but from the moment he'd awoken in this unfamiliar chamber, that was exactly what he'd been thinking. As he sat there, rubbing at his head again and waiting for de Sherrington to say something more, another muscular knight came to the doorway.

"Max has more information," the warrior muttered to de Sherrington, who turned to look at him. "The Marshal wants you down in the hall to hear it."

Alexander grunted in acknowledgment. "Very well," he responded, returning his attention to Alasdair. "I'll send some food to you, ye madman. Behave yourself while I am gone."

He said *ye madman* with a perfect Scots accent, using a Scottish insult for a drunkard. But Alasdair waved him off.

"Nay," he said, falling back down on the bed. "No food now. Let me sleep, lad. That's what I need most. I'll see yer ugly face on the morrow."

"You can stake your life on it."

Alasdair put an arm over his eyes, indicating the great pain in his head, as de Sherrington was pulled away by the other knight and the door was closed behind him. The sound of the bolt being thrown was unmistakable.

The moment the door was shut, however, Alasdair sat up and rushed to the panel with movements that suggested he was much more sober, and far less hungover, than he had let on. Putting his ear to the door, he listened carefully for any sound that de Sherrington might be returning. When he was certain the coast was clear and the man wasn't about to make a return, he bolted straight away to the window.

It was a square window with shutters that Alasdair easily unlocked and threw open. Night had fallen, so all he could see below were houses, lit from the inside by weak fires, and a vacant alley below. There were no walls around the fortified manor because the first floor had no windows, so the alley ran right up to the house itself. There was a gutter down there that he could smell more than he could see it, and better still, no activity.

But it was a good drop from where he was, which is why they hadn't barred the windows on him. Only an insane man would leap from the window with that kind of drop to the ground below, but Alasdair had never been accused of being sane. His mission to London had been discovered, and there was a mole in St. Blitha, and now the nobles of England knew that the Holy Father had ordered the nuns of St. Blitha to assassinate the king.

Like any good spy, Alasdair wasn't going to give up easily. He wasn't going to sit back and nurse an aching head while the entire objective of him being in England was at stake. The Holy Father himself had entrusted this mission to him, and even though he hadn't been the one ordered to eliminate the king, it would still be on his shoulders if the nuns failed.

He had to get word to them.

He had to get out of there.

The chamber he was in hadn't been stripped; there were curtains around the bed for warmth and linens on the mattress, and he immediately went about constructing a rope from the fabric. With the three pieces of linen on the bed followed by all four brocaded curtains tied end to end, he peered from the open window again to ensure no one was watching before securing the linen rope to the heavy bedframe and throwing the rest of it from the window. With hardly a back glance, he leapt onto the windowsill and began lowering himself down the rope.

Reaching the bottom, he still had about ten feet to go, so he released the rope and fell the rest of the way to the alleyway. He landed awkwardly on his ankle, twisting it, but he didn't stop to examine it. He was on the run, so he hurried down the alley as fast as his injured ankle would take him and having no idea that at this time, the very mole he was seeking was also fleeing from Farringdon House down a different avenue, returning to St. Blitha before her over-long absence was discovered.

The mole, and the spy, would soon cross paths.

CHAPTER FIFTEEN

"WHERE HAVE YOU been, Andressa?"

Having barely just returned to St. Blitha under the cover of darkness, Andressa was in the dim corridor leading to her tiny cell, and her uncomfortable bed, when Sister Petronilla had come out of the shadows. Andressa hadn't even heard the woman, and now suddenly, she was standing face to face with her.

For a moment, Andressa simply stared at the woman. She'd barely had five words with the old nun in the four years she'd been at St. Blitha, but now it seemed as if they were to have their first real conversation.

And not a comfortable one.

"I delivered garments to Lady Hinkley," Andressa answered after a moment. "You heard the Mother Abbess give me permission to do so. Lady Hinkley then asked me to remain for a time."

Sister Petronilla's gaze lingered on her for a moment as if debating whether or not to believe her. In fact, she was sizing up the woman altogether; it was clear that she didn't like the idea of someone new joining the Mother Abbess' band of attendants, so her scrutiny was on the young woman that the Mother Abbess seemed to favor.

Everyone at the abbey knew that Andressa had turned their laundry into a business, a business that the Mother Abbess was profiting greatly from, but Sister Petronilla didn't see anything quite so remarkable in the young woman. She didn't appear all that special to her.

Her jealousy was rising.

"Why did you stay so long?" she asked. "Did she feed you?"

"She did not," Andressa replied. "I remained in her servant's kitchen and warmed myself until she told me to go."

Sister Petronilla's gaze remained on her for a few more moments before deciding that interrogating the woman any further would be fruitless. It wasn't as if Andressa didn't already spend a good deal of time going back and forth between noble households, collecting laundry when the household servants were too busy to deliver it. It was part of her job. Therefore, Sister Petronilla let the subject drop.

For now.

"Our Gracious Mother has plans for you," she finally said. "As she told you, she feels that our work must be carried on. Unfortunately, we will not live forever."

Andressa breathed a sigh of relief that Sister Petronilla didn't press her further about her absence. Still, she received the distinct sense that the older nun was suspicious of her. There was something in the woman's dark eyes that suggested doubt.

Her guard was up.

"I am honored to carry out God's work," she replied steadily. "I am not worthy, but I shall endeavor to do my best. And I am honored to work in the garden with you. You have great skill with the herbs and flowers."

Sister Petronilla turned away from her, heading back down the corridor and towards the doors that led to the courtyard outside.

"Walk with me," she said.

"Where are we going?"

"Into the garden."

"Now? But it is dark outside."

"Much of what we do is in the shadows, Andressa. Come with me."

Andressa did. She scooted after the woman, wondering why they were doing out to the garden and just the least bit apprehensive about it. They headed back to a main reception chamber where the front door to the church was located and a second set of doors that led to the courtyard beyond. It had been those doors that Andressa had just come through as she'd come in from the yard.

The main reception chamber of St. Blitha was a cavernous room, stripped of all furnishing except for a shrine dedicated to St. Blitha. There was a tapestry of her on the stone wall, the ancient Roman saint who had been martyred by Roman soldiers. Sister Petronilla collected a bank of yellow tallow tapers from the shrine, candles that were always there lighting the tapestry of the saint, and moved to the doors that led to the courtyard.

Andressa followed.

Once outside again, the temperature was brisk and cold, with moisture heavy in the air. Sister Petronilla headed straight into the garden, turning once to ensure that Andressa was still behind her.

"My father was an apothecary," she said as they walked. "He knew what to grow and how to grow it. He knew the properties of everything that grew on this earth. What I learned, I learned from him. He was a great man."

Andressa suspected the best way to deal with Sister Petronilla was to make it seem as if she admired the woman greatly. Perhaps flattery would cause whatever suspicion there might be to fade.

"I am sure he was," Andressa said. "You must miss him, being so far away from him."

But Sister Petronilla simply shook her head. "He was a great and knowledgeable man, but he was also quite wicked," she said. "I was beaten every day when I was young, which fed my hatred against him. When I was nine years of age, I put a potion in his soup, a potion he himself had made, and it killed both him and my mother. That is why I was sent to the convent of Santa Giulia."

It was a shocking confession, but in truth, it wasn't surprising. After what Andressa had been told yesterday, it seemed that murder wasn't something outlandish or new to these women.

It was a way of life.

"And now you find yourself here, in London," Andressa said, truly having no idea what to say after that horrific confession. "I have no parents, either, as you know. Only an aunt who stole my fortune."

Sister Petronilla glanced at her. "Then mayhap I can teach you something useful," she said. "I am sure you have been wondering how we are to accomplish our task for our Holy Father. Our Gracious Mother has asked me to instruct you on our process, and I shall. The king shall be here for the Feast Day of St. Blitha and we intend to have a great feast set out for him, something prepared by our own hands. You, Andressa, shall be in charge of the kitchen that prepares his feast."

Andressa looked at her with surprise. "But what of Sister Blanche?"

"Sister Blanche has been lost to The Chaos."

Andressa was horrified by the news but, for her own sake, she knew she had to keep her composure. Guilt swept her; she knew why the woman had ended up there.

"Because… because she struck me yesterday?"

Sister Petronilla glanced at her. "She should not have struck you," she said. "The Mother Abbess said she would protect you, especially from those who would attack you. Sister Blanche has been published for her sin. Now, the kitchen shall be your domain and you shall oversee the feast for the king."

Andressa knew something of the kitchens only because they were right next to her laundry area, so she had seen a good deal of what went on there. There were other nuns who cooked and prepared the food. The truth was that Sister Blanche had only ordered them about. She had been an older nun and she had a sense of self-importance.

But no longer.

Shocked at the cold demise of Sister Blanche, Andressa knew that the only thing she could do was go along with whatever the Mother Abbess and her minions wanted her to do. Any hint of resistance, or doubt, and she knew they would toss her into The Chaos, too. It was the ever-present threat hanging over her head.

She was starting to feel sick to her stomach.

"I will do whatever you wish me to do," she said. "I do not know a great deal about managing the kitchen, but I shall learn quickly. Will you tell me what to prepare for the feast day?"

Sister Petronilla had led her into the heart of the garden by this time, the forbidden garden where no one but the Mother Abbess and those close to her were allowed to walk. It was damp and dark, only lit by the bank of tapers in Sister Petronilla's hand, and most of the plants were dormant because of the season. Still, some things were growing in spite of the cold. There were shades of green amongst the brown.

"St. Blitha is the patron saint of hunters and wine, so the feast will be simple, as it is every year," Sister Petronilla said as she came to a halt. "We will only have meat and wine and bread. There are sisters who will cook these things. All you need do is ensure it makes it to the Mother Abbess' table and to the king. But for the king, we shall have a very special wine meant only for him."

With that, she began to pull at the dried leaves of the very tall foxglove stalks. She pulled off several, then had Andressa hold out her hands. Into her open palms, Sister Petronilla began to pile more leaves and using the tapers as light, she located even more to strip from the stalks. The leaves were shriveled up and ready to fall to the ground. As Andressa looked at the leaves curiously, Sister Petronilla spoke.

"My father taught me that there is great poison in the dying leaves of the Foxglove," she said quietly. "You will take these leaves and you shall crush them into a powder, and that powder shall be put into the king's wine pitcher. Make sure to grind the leaves up terribly fine so that he will not see them nor taste them. Mull the wine a little with cloves and cinnamon to ensure he does not taste any hint of the poison. You will also make sure that the rest of the wine, that not meant for the king, is mulled with cloves and cinnamon so that it all tastes the same. He must not be suspicious."

Andressa was looking at the leaves in her hand, feeling the familiar taste of fear upon her tongue. "How... how will I know how much powder to use?" she asked.

Sister Petronilla moved to a second stalk and stripped more dead leaves from the base of it. "Crush all of these leaves and that shall be sufficient." She moved on from the foxgloves, to another patch of scrub-looking plants, and pointed to one that was bushy, with fibrous stalks and purple berries. "This is *Dwale*. All parts of this plant are poisonous. Take care not to touch it with open cuts on your fingers, and after you have handled it, you must wash your hands thoroughly with soap and vinegar. It is so deadly that it can be absorbed through your skin."

Andressa looked at the plant, wide-eyed. "What would you have me do with it?"

Sister Petronilla studied the plant for a moment. "Tear two or three plants out of the ground," she said. "Mash the roots and put them in an oilcloth to steep in the king's wine. Remove the oilcloth before you serve it. There are also berries on the plant, though at this time of year, there are few. Pick them and squeeze the juice into the wine as well. The more, the better."

"And do this in addition to the crushed leaves from the other plant?"

"We want to ensure that the job is done."

It seemed like a good deal of poison for just one man. "Are you certain that you would not like to do this yourself?" Andressa asked, thinking that something like this was too big for her to manage. "This is a very important task. I do not want to fail."

Sister Petronilla shook her head. "You shall not fail," she said patiently. "Andressa, this must be your task. The Mother Abbess cannot do it; she is expected to escort the king. I cannot do it, nor can Sister Dymphna or Sister Agnes because they will have other duties. You must ensure the powder of the leaves, and the juice of the roots, make it into the king's wine. Be sure to seal the pitcher so we know which one is meant for the king. Seal it tightly with oil cloth that is tied to the mouth of the pitcher."

Andressa was feeling sicker and sicker with the realization that they expected *her* to be the one to poison the king. "Then… then you wish for me to do this?" she asked, looking at the woman. "The Mother Abbess said I was to learn, but I did not know she meant that I would be carrying this out alone. It is such an important mission, Sister Petronilla. I fear that I cannot do this all by myself."

Sister Petronilla didn't seem overly concerned. "All you need do is follow my instructions and make sure that the king is the only one who is served that particular pitcher of wine," she said, sounding oddly reassuring. "You *must* accomplish this, Andressa. This is your test to see if you are truly worthy to follow in our footsteps."

So it was a test! Andressa was stunned to hear that such an important task would be placed squarely in her hands. It was like a nightmare, something she wanted no part of, but she had no way to decline. If she didn't accept the task, the pain of The Chaos would indeed belong to her. She would suffer right alongside Sister Blanche and countless other women who had found themselves in that hellish place. It was a do-or-die situation.

They want me to kill the king!

It was becoming increasingly difficult for Andressa to keep her composure. The more she heard about the evil intentions of these women, now imposed upon her, the more she wanted to run away and never return.

Maxton had begged her to, in fact. He'd offered her his protection, asking her to find a corner of the world with him where two sinners could find happiness in each other. It was such a beautiful offer, but she was still deeply torn by it. She still didn't want to accept an offer on impulse, but she was terrified of remaining at St. Blitha. Was it possible Maxton would have made her the offer even if there hadn't been a deadly threat involved?

She wondered.

She felt as if she was going mad.

"I will do as you ask, Sister Petronilla," she said, but she was having trouble looking at the woman. "I will ensure the crushed leaves and the root juice make it into the king's wine."

"Be very careful, Andressa."

"I will, Sister."

Sister Petronilla was watching her closely, perhaps looking for cracks or hints of untrustworthiness. "Do you have any plans to leave St. Blitha tomorrow?"

Did she? Andressa hadn't really thought about it, but as Sister Petronilla asked, it was as if a light went on in her mind. She had promised Maxton she would return with any additional news, and certainly, she had additional news now. After a brief hesitation, she nodded to the woman's question.

"Not tomorrow," she said, daring to glance up at the woman. "But I intend to return to Lady Hinkley's tonight. When I was there earlier, she had nothing to give me at the time. That… well, that was why I had waited so long. She told me to go away and come back later, which I assumed meant later tonight. I thought to see her before I go to bed. She is such a valuable customer that I do not wish to disappoint her. I want to please her."

One of Sister Petronilla's bushy eyebrows lifted. "Tonight? But it is already well into the night, child."

"As I said, she said return later. I can only assume that meant when she retired so I could have her clothes cleaned in the morning. I would rather go tonight in case that is what she meant."

Sister Petronilla nodded faintly but didn't reply. Andressa thought that meant their conversation was ended, but just as she turned away, Sister Petronilla's hand shot out and grabbed her by the arm.

It was an abrupt move with a clear message. The woman's long, dirty nails dug into her skin as Andressa looked to the woman with a mixture of curiosity and disapproval. She didn't like to be grabbed. But Sister Petronilla's dark-eyed gaze was grim.

"Be sure that is the only place you go this night," she growled. "You are one of us now, Andressa. The eyes of the Mother Abbess are upon you. Remember that."

Andressa was no cowering flower; she never had been, and she didn't like being threatened by this woman, no matter how wicked she was. She feared her, aye, but not enough to shrink from her.

"I have been trustworthy since my arrival to St. Blitha," she said, taking a stand against the woman. "I do my work and I am obedient. You slander me to insinuate otherwise."

Something flashed in Sister Petronilla's eyes, perhaps even a flash of rage, but she quickly banked it. She wouldn't lash out at the girl like Sister Blanche had, although it was clear that Andressa had a defiant streak in her.

But no matter.

She'd been warned.

Sister Petronilla released her without a word and Andressa went to her laundry area, still carrying the dried leaves. She didn't want to take them inside because she shared a cell with two other pledges and she didn't want the women questioning the purpose of the dried leaves. Therefore, she put them very carefully into a cloth and tucked them into a cubby that contained the soap she used. She pretended to busy herself, all the while thinking about the encounter with Sister Petronilla and the clear threat that had been made to her.

The eyes of the Mother Abbess are upon you.

Andressa knew that. Even now, she could feel them, whether or not the woman was actually viewing her from the windows of her fine solar. All Andressa knew was that she had to get the most recent information to Maxton. Time was growing short and she had no idea if she would be able to get to him tomorrow, so she would take the chance to return to Farringdon House one last time tonight.

She might not have another opportunity.

She had made a fine excuse by mentioning Lady Hinkley again, but she didn't want to be overlong. Now that she knew they were watching, she didn't want to give them any cause for suspicion, and that meant actually stopping at Lady Hinkley's home to see if there was any laundry to collect. If the Mother Abbess actually had any reason to speak to Lady Hinkley, Andressa wanted to make sure that Lady Hinkley mentioned her presence there.

She had to cover her tracks.

With the half-moon overhead in a clear night sky, Andressa departed through the postern gate, heading towards Bishopsgate along the muddy road as her thoughts focused on what lay ahead.

Maxton.

He had to know.

But what she didn't know that the moment she left St. Blitha, she was followed.

CHAPTER SIXTEEN

FORTUNATELY, ST. BLITHA wasn't too far from Farringdon House. Alasdair had been running perhaps ten minutes, fifteen at most on his bad ankle, when he came to Bishopsgate, which remained open because of the two churches and the hospital on the road beyond. It was nighttime, with an icy chill to the air, as there had been snowfall in London the week before. But that snow had quickly turned to water, leaving the roads swimming in mud puddles.

In fact, the entire north side of the city seemed swampy and cold to the bone, with little warmth in sight. At Bishopsgate, the usual guards were nearby, sentries appointed by the Lord Mayor of London, and really no more than older men who had bells and horns to sound in times of trouble. The weapons they carried were clubs.

They didn't even look at Alasdair as he came near. In fact, they continued standing around their blazing fire as Alasdair passed beneath the big stone archway and headed straight for St. Blitha. The bright half-moon low in the sky gave little light to travel by, but Alasdair could see St. Blitha in the distance. Some of the windows had glowing light from within, signifying the life within.

He moved faster.

As Alasdair neared the front entrance, a figure in pale robes caught his attention, moving further down the road that paralleled the old walls of the church. As he watched, the figure went off the road, headed through the trees, and entered the abbey through the postern gate. A nun was returning, evidently, slipping in through the rear of the abbey. She'd moved quickly, a wraith that was soon gone from his sight.

But Alasdair didn't give the figure entering St. Blitha's yard much thought; he was in too much pain from his ankle, and there was too much to tell the Mother Abbess. In fact, by the time he banged on the front entry to the church, he'd forgotten all about the wandering nun. Now, he was becoming angry because they didn't open the door fast enough.

It was an old, warped door that finally creaked open on its rusted hinges. In truth, the response was very quick, but for Alasdair, it wasn't quick enough. He pushed his way into the shadowed, cavernous reception area just as a nun with bushy eyebrows approached him.

"What do you want?" she demanded in a heavy Italian accent. "We take no men for the night. You will have to sleep outside if it is lodgings you are looking for."

Alasdair's temper was short. "I'm not here tae sleep," he said. "Where is Seaxburga?"

The nun stood her ground. "Get out," she said. "You'll not violate the sanctity of this place."

"I'll not get out," Alasdair snarled. "I came to see Seaxburga and if ye'll not tell me where she is, I'll go find her myself."

Before the nun could reply, a woman's voice could be heard from the chamber off the entry. "Sister Petronilla, be on your way," the Mother Abbess said as she came into the light. "Douglas… why have you have returned?"

Alasdair pushed past the bushy-eyebrow nun and headed straight for the Mother Abbess. He marched into the chamber where she was standing, motioning the woman to follow him as he went. The Mother Abbess obeyed, curiously, shutting the door softly behind her.

"Well?" she said. "What is it? Why are you here?"

Alasdair turned to the woman. "They know," he said flatly. "They know of the plot tae kill John. Ye have a traitor in yer midst, woman."

The Mother Abbess looked at him as if rather confused by his statement. "*Who* knows?" she asked. "What are you talking about?"

Douglas was agitated. He waved his arms around as he found the nearest chair and planted himself. "I was followed when I returned tae England from our Holy Father," he said as he gingerly touched his swollen ankle. "For almost a year, I was followed. The assassin who was paid tae follow me, sent by someone in The Lateran Palace no less, caught up tae me today. He told me that the plot against John is known and he told me that the information came from St. Blitha. Had I not escaped the man, I'd still be taking insults from him."

The Mother Abbess listened to him carefully, surprisingly calm at the shocking news as Alasdair grunted and raged. When he was finished spewing forth his information, she turned away from him, making her way over to a sideboard table that contained expensive wine in a fine pewter pitcher. It was the very best wine, purchased with money she'd accumulated while everyone in her charge starved. She poured one cup, only for her, and took a sip as if it would help her think.

"He told you that the information came from St. Blitha?" she asked. "And he was sure of this?"

Alasdair groaned as he lifted up his muddy boot and put it on one of Mother Abbess' fine chairs. "He was gloating," he said, rather sarcastically. "Of course the man was sure. He had no reason tae lie. Which of yer nuns did ye tell, Seaxburga?"

The Mother Abbess knew who she had told, but who could have betrayed her? Sister Dymphna had been fearful when she'd first been told of the plan, vocal in her concern. She was in charge of the postulates, and she'd been known to gossip to them in the past, so it was possible she'd told one of her charges and word had spread. But that was unlikely, as Sister Dymphna had been known to smother charges that displeased her. The women under her were terrified of that particular inclination.

Then, there was Sister Agnes, who did the dirty work down in The

Chaos. She was the one who took the bodies of the dead from the vault and boiled them down to bones that were then ground up and mixed with oats and other rubbish to be fed to the pigs. However, before she boiled them down, she removed what fat she could from the bodies and mixed it with animal suet to make the tallow candles that they used at the abbey. Their candles had an odd smell because of it, and they were quite yellow in color, but it was simply the way they did things at St. Blitha. Fat, from any breathing creature, was too valuable to be wasted.

Lastly, there was Sister Petronilla, the master of the garden who could poison a man so cleanly that there would be no trace of it. The entire garden that the Mother Abbess was so proud of was peppered with poisonous plants amongst the roses, but no one every commented on that. They were simply awed by Sister Petronilla's green thumb, but it was a green thumb with a purpose – every one of those poisonous plants had served the means to an end from time to time.

Each sister with her particular gifts.

All three of the nuns had been with the Mother Abbess for such a long time that trust wasn't much of an issue. She did trust them, for the most part, but it wasn't a blind trust. There was always some suspicion to it. Complete trust was a foolish thing, so in truth, Alasdair's revelation didn't shock her much.

But she did want to know where the news had from.

"I have three women that I have known for years," she finally said. "We have worked together on many occasions."

"And ye're sure they've not told anyone else?"

The Mother Abbess shrugged. "I cannot be sure of that," she said, turning towards Alasdair. "Clearly, someone has spoken about this. Or mayhap the knight who captured you only told you such things so that you would betray your purpose. Mayhap he manipulated you into confessing. Did you think of that?"

Alasdair shook his head. "He knew everything," he said flatly. "I told him nothing, but he told *me* a great deal. He even spoke of Richard's bastard son, something no one is supposed tae know of. But someone at St. Blitha did know – and they've told John's men."

The Mother Abbess sipped at her wine. "That may be," she said casually. "But the king has not cancelled his visit to St. Blitha. I would have been informed by now. Until he does, we do not deviate from our plans."

Alasdair threw up his hands. "It is possible that the king simply willna come. Do ye think he'll tell ye if he finds out that ye plan tae kill him? Ye should be worrying about bolting yer doors and fighting off men who will be coming tae arrest ye!"

The Mother Abbess smiled, but it was without humor. "The allegations would have to be proven," she said, "and nothing can be proven unless you yourself confirm these rumors. You would do well to stay out of sight, Douglas. If they happen to catch you again and you talk, know that we can reach you anywhere. We can kill you as easily as we can kill a king."

Alasdair's eyes widened. "Ye'd be a fool tae try, witch," he said. "I'll not make an easy target. Better men than ye have tried."

"Then stay out of sight and we'll not have any issues."

Alasdair eyed the woman; she was so calm and collected as she threatened a man's life, which was a particularly eerie talent.

And he believed every word.

"Dunna worry about me," he said. "Worry about yerself. If the king comes tae the Feast Day, then ye'd better mind yerself. They'll be looking for ye tae move against him."

The Mother Abbess took another drink of wine before answering. "We have nothing to fear," she said. "God is on our side. He shall see that the Holy Father's plans are accomplished."

Alasdair sighed heavily; the woman didn't seem upset by the news in the least. She remained confident that all would work out as it should. As he looked back to his ankle, rubbing at it, there was a soft knock on the door. The Mother Abbess bade the caller to enter, and the door opened to produce Sister Petronilla.

"I am sorry, Gracious Mother," she said, pausing when she saw

Alasdair. "I did not realize you still had your guest."

She started to close the door, but the Mother Abbess waved her in. "Come in, Sister Petronilla," she said. "Come in and meet Alasdair Baird Douglas, a man who is close to our Holy Father. He is so close, in fact, that he is the one who delivered the Holy Father's instructions to us regarding the king."

Sister Petronilla entered the chamber, her dark gaze on Alasdair. "Welcome to St. Blitha, Brother," she said, looking him up and down. "I did not know who you were when you entered earlier. If I was rude, my apologies."

Alasdair barely glanced at the woman; he was more focused on his injured ankle. The Mother Abbess could see that he was working over the joint and she turned to Sister Petronilla.

"He seems to have injured himself," she said. "Mayhap there is something in the garden that can help his swelling."

Sister Petronilla peered at the ankle, but from a distance. "I was just in the garden with Andressa," she said. "I can return and gather a few things that may help the pain."

The Mother Abbess looked at her. "Andressa?" she said. "What was she doing outside in the darkness? Surely she wasn't washing clothing at this hour."

Sister Petronilla shook her head. "Nay," she said. "We were discussing the plants in the garden and their particular properties for our task with the king. She had just returned from Lady Hinkley's and she said that she must go to her again."

The Mother Abbess' brow furrowed. "Tonight?"

"Aye, Gracious Mother."

"But why?"

"Because she said Lady Hinkley was not ready with her washing the first time. She told Andressa to return, and that is what she is doing because you said it was important to keep Lady Hinkley happy."

It was true; Mother Abbess had said that. But as she realized that, she also realized that Andressa knew of the plot against John, too, and in the course of her duties as the laundress, she traveled in and out of St. Blitha quite freely. It was true that she was an obedient girl, and had proven herself, but trust on this level was not something the Mother Abbess had experienced with her. Though she'd never known the girl to gossip or even talk, there was always the possibility that, in this case, she had.

In truth, anything was possible.

Going to the big windows that overlooked the garden and the kitchens beyond, the Mother Abbess could see a figure in pale robes moving around in the moonlight over near the laundry area.

"Sister," she said to Sister Petronilla. "Is Andressa still in the yard?"

Sister Petronilla wandered over to the window, watching the ghostly figure across the yard as it moved around. "Aye," she said. "I gave her foxgloves leaves and instructions on how to crush them. I believe she is putting the leaves away until she can accomplish this."

The Mother Abbess's gaze lingered on Andressa as the woman continued to move around in the dark. Finally, she turned to Douglas, sitting over on one of her fine chairs with his dirty boot on another.

"Douglas," she said. "Come here."

Unhappily, Alasdair did as he was told. He limped his way over to the window, watching the Mother Abbess to something in the yard beyond. In the moonlight, he could barely see it.

"See the woman over towards the postern gate?" the Mother Abbess said.

Alasdair nodded. "Aye."

"Follow her," she said. "I cannot be sure that she is not our traitor. She will be leaving shortly; make sure you discover where she is going."

Alasdair lifted a dark eyebrow. "Does *she* know of the plot, too?"

"She will be the one putting the plan into action."

"And if she's the traitor?"

"Kill her."

It was a simple, unemotional command, one that peeled back the bones and revealed the true darkness of the Mother Abbess' soul.

Violated trust was a killing offense.

"But my leg," he complained. "Can't someone else follow the lass?"

"You are the only one capable of killing her with force should it come to that."

There was no arguing with her; Alasdair could see that. With a growl, he limped from the room, heading out of the front door to hide in the shadows until the woman in question emerged from the yard.

It didn't take long; in little time, a tall, slender woman in pale robes rushed along the road, looking over her shoulder constantly as she made her way to Bishopsgate and beyond. In fact, Alasdair realized that this was the same woman he'd seen come back to the abbey about the time he'd arrived himself. He could tell by the shape of her. Therefore, he waited until she was through before following her, like a hunter tracking prey.

If she was the traitor, he would discover it for himself.

CHAPTER SEVENTEEN

The King's Gout Tavern

Kress, Achilles, Gart, Alexander, and Cullen were seated around a leaning, warped table at the tavern that was favored by most fighting men on the north side of London. It was the biggest one and had the best wenches. They had invited Sean and Kevin, and the de Lohr brothers to join them, but so far, they had yet to make an appearance.

It was well after the supper at Farringdon House, the one that had been so tense because of the friction between William and Maxton. It had been obvious when Maxton had joined their table later in the meal, informing them of his extended conversation with the St. Blitha pledge.

It had been rough from the start because William had asked, straight away, if Maxton had sent the girl back to St. Blitha yet. The entire conversation prior to Maxton's arrival had been about the pledge and what a valuable spy she would make inside of St. Blitha, and when Maxton appeared, William went for the throat. When Maxton had explained that not only had he *not* sent the girl back, but that she was pregnant, it seemed to throw the entire situation into question.

To everyone but William Marshal, that was.

He saw no difference in the girl being pregnant. It wasn't his concern that a pledge had conceived a child. His only concern was in keeping the nuns from accomplishing their task of killing the king, a hard attitude that seemed to turn Maxton into stone. He sat silently for the most part while William discussed their loyalty to the king and listed the reasons as to why that was all they should be concerned with.

Maxton had listened to William pound home his loyalty to king and country before replying to the man's prattle by telling him that he would send her home as soon as she was rested. That evidently wasn't good enough for William, who pressed him further only for Maxton to tell him that any man who would save a monarchy by sacrificing the blood of an innocent woman was not a man he had much respect for.

At that point, Kress and Gart ushered Maxton out of the hall and sent him back up to his chamber to avoid any further confrontations with William, who was clearly annoyed with Maxton's behavior. It was concerning enough that Gart had sent word to Cullen, Sean, and Kevin, and the de Lohr brothers to meet them at The King's Gout because they had to discuss the situation before it got out of hand. Concerns were running high that Maxton was deviating from the course set for them and the circumstances needed to be clarified, because it was increasingly clear that Maxton, the man who had changed since leaving Les Baux de Provence, had changed even more than they had realized.

He was a different man.

Which was why they all found themselves here, inhaling the smoke of the common room, ignoring the tables that were screaming with laughter, drunk as the minutes of the night ticked away. Cullen de Nerra seemed to be more distressed by the situation than the rest of them as he hovered over his half-empty cup.

"This does not sound like the Max I know," he said quietly. "He actually argued with The Marshal? I've never known the man to argue with anyone other than the de Lohr brothers."

They were nursing two pitchers of dark, heavy wine imported from the Mediterranean region. Gart picked up one of the pitchers to fill Cullen's cup as he answered.

"The problem is that The Marshal has not worked with Maxton before," he said. "He does not know that Maxton is a man of his word.

He has been given a task and he will accomplish it regardless of his personal feelings, but Max was never one to hold back when expressing his thoughts on a matter. And he can be very moody, moodier still since his time at The Lateran Palace. I am not sure he is the Max that any of us knew any longer. He has… changed."

"Mayhap he has changed in personality, but the soul of the man is the same," Kress said quietly. As Maxton's closest friend, he was the one best suited to speak to the situation. "Those of us who have spent time with him over the past year have seen it – the introspection, the seeking of knowledge from wise men, holy men, or any man who might have an insight into the world at large. Now that I've seen him react to the pledge from St. Blitha, it is increasingly clear that he's growing a conscience. Something about that girl has stirred something in him, as if he's only noticing the injustices of the world for the very first time."

Gart grunted unhappily. "God's Bones, of all time for the man to develop a heart," he said. "What happened to the cold killer we all knew?"

"He is still there," Achilles said. When they all turned to look at him, he merely shrugged. "Make no mistake; the cold killer is still there, as deadly as ever. But Maxton has grown up. He is a man of flesh and blood, and I think that girl has stirred the man in him – the romantic."

The table looked at Achilles as if the man was crazy. "You must be drunk," Gart muttered. "The man has no romance in him."

Achilles was unrepentant. "All men have romance in them, Forbes," he said. "Some simply keep it buried deeper than others."

Cullen seized on the possibility. "Are you saying that Max actually has feelings for this… this *pledge*?" he asked, incredulous. "Not only is she pledged to the church, but she has clearly been with another man. The girl is pregnant. And *this* is the girl who is stirring Maxton's romantic feelings?"

Achilles simply lifted his shoulders. "We have seen the girl," he said. "She is not unattractive. In fact, she's rather beautiful in a pale sort of way. Whatever she is, and whoever she is, she has bewitched Max, but I do not believe William has figured that out yet. He simply thinks Max is being stubborn."

"Then he is risking his reputation for a woman he just met," Gart growled. "In fact, I..."

He was cut off when the tavern door slammed back on its hinges and four big knights entered the common room of the tavern, adding to the noise and chaos. Gart could immediately see that it was the men they'd invited, and he stood up, catching their attention and waving them over.

Kevin de Lara, Christopher and David de Lohr, and finally Sean de Lara approached the table, grabbing chairs as they moved through the crowded common room and sitting down at the table with their pilfered seats. Cups and wine were passed to them.

"My wife is furious because I answered Gart's summons in the midst of a family feast, so let this be brief," Christopher said as he poured his wine. "What is so important that I had to travel across London for this meeting? And why are we not converging at Farringdon House?"

It was Gart who answered, since he was the instigator of the meeting. "Because we do not want The Marshal to be part of this conversation," he said. "Much has happened since the meeting this morning, Chris. We now know the means by which the assassination against the king will be made."

Christopher was very interested. "What is it?"

"Nuns."

Christopher's cup of wine stopped halfway to his lips. "What?" he hissed. "Nuns? Who told you this madness?"

Gart shook his head. "It is not madness, I assure you," he said. Then, he looked to Alexander across the table. "Tell him, Sherry."

Alexander sat forward, lowering his voice as much as he could in a room full of loud, drunken people. "I have been trailing a double agent since leaving The Lateran Palace," he said. "In fact, a high-placed advisor to our Holy Father paid me to kill this man. There is far more to the story than I am going to tell you, but for the sake of time, I will tell you the gist of it. The man I was paid to kill is a Scotsman named Alasdair Baird Douglas. He delivered a message to the mother abbess of St. Blitha, a personal message from our Holy Father, that instructed the mother abbess to murder the king when he arrives at St. Blitha to celebrate her feast day."

Christopher's wine never made it to his mouth. Incredulous, he set his cup down and stared at Alexander as if the man had gone completely daft. "Christ," he finally muttered. "The feast is in two days. And you are certain of this?"

Alexander nodded. "Unfortunately," he said. "It was corroborated by a pledge from St. Blitha, quite by accident. In fact... the pledge is why we have called this meeting."

"Why?"

"Because Max seems to have developed an attachment to the woman."

As Christopher made a face suggesting complete confusion, David wasn't so subtle. "That is ridiculous," he said. "Max has no attachment to any woman."

"That is what we know of the Maxton from the past," Alexander countered. "But the Maxton who has returned from eight years away from England, including years of fighting with you two in The Levant, is a different man altogether. He is behaving in ways we never knew possible."

"What do you mean?" David asked.

"He has come close to throttling The Marshal at least twice because of the man's stance on the pledge," Alexander explained. "William wants to use her to spy on the nuns of St. Blitha since she lives there, but Maxton does not want the woman involved. He says she is not a spy and does not have the skills needed for what William wants her to do."

David didn't have a quick answer to that. He looked at his brother, baffled by what he was hearing. "Since when does Maxton of Loxbeare argue with his liege?" he finally asked. "Better still, since when does he even care about anyone other than himself and a few fellow knights? Max is blindly obedient in all things. I've never known him to be otherwise."

Alexander sat back in his chair. "He is still obedient," he said, but it was clear that he, too, was confused with the change in his friend. "He's not disobeyed any order from The Marshal, not yet, but he is not happy with the man's intentions when it comes to the pledge."

"Who *is* this pledge?" Christopher demanded softly.

Alexander looked at him. "A girl that Max met quite by chance this morning," he said. "Through her, we have come to hear some terrible things about St. Blitha, mostly that the Mother Abbess is a thief and a murderess, and that she allows her charges to go hungry. That is the least of it, truly, but Max met the girl this morning when she was stealing food because she was starving. He fed her a meal and came to know her, and later in the day when she came into trouble, she sought him out for help. I would say that she is as attracted to him as he is to her. In any case, it has been a trial with the girl throughout the day, and Max is bewitched by her."

The situation was coming clear somewhat and Christopher finally took a drink of his wine, pondering what he'd been told. "So it is the pledge who told him of the plans for the nuns of St. Blitha to assassinate the king?"

"Aye," Alexander said.

"And your double-agent told you the same thing?"

"Aye."

"Then is it possible she is setting him up?" Christopher continued. "What I mean to say is why would the girl tell him such a thing when that is exactly what he has been tasked to discover? Don't you think that is too great a coincidence?"

Alexander shook his head. "The way Max explains it, it was purely coincidental."

"Or it was fate."

Everyone looked at Achilles, who uttered the softly-spoken words.

When he saw all eyes upon him, he simply lifted his eyebrows as if it was the most simple explanation in the world.

"It was a chance meeting," he said. "You all speak as if Max would be a fool to fall for a woman who was trying to betray him, and he is not the kind of man. He is too sharp and too seasoned for such a thing. No woman in all the world can get the best of Maxton of Loxbeare, so the fact that he met a woman who has helped us solve the mystery of the assassins meant for the king is purely, and utterly, fate. God put that girl there at the right time so that she would find Max. It is as simple as that."

Devout Achilles had a way of looking at things that encouraged divine assistance, but some of the others weren't so devout. Christopher was one; he simply scratched his head.

"I suppose I can take some things on faith, but this seems terribly coincidental," he said. "In any case, we now know what form the assassin will take. Sean, did you know this?"

He turned to Sean, who had been sitting silent throughout the exchange. He was a man more involved than almost any of them since he was the one who shadowed the king. Everything they were saying was of great importance to him.

"I had received word about the nuns earlier today from The Marshal," he said. "He also said that I am not to discourage the king from attending St. Blitha for the Feast Day. It is clear he wants to catch the nuns in the act. He'll need proof if he is to arrest women of the cloth, and proof is not the hearsay of a pledge or a Scottish prisoner."

Alexander nodded. "That is another reason why we have called this meeting," he said. "We must have a plan for that day, Sean. I've not spoken to Max about it, so I do not know if he has come up with a scheme, but it is my thought that we must be within close proximity of the king if we are to prevent the nuns from moving against him. I believe Max would say the same thing."

Sean was listening. "What did you have in mind?"

Alexander was much like Maxton in that he had a tactician's mind.

He was able to see situations clearly and map out an end result. But as he geared up to explain, the door to the tavern opened again and in stepped a familiar figure.

Kress saw him first and it was the expression on his face that alerted the others; they all turned to see Maxton entering the tavern, shoving aside a drunkard who came to close. As the man slammed into the wall, Maxton caught sight of Kress and Achilles, sitting at a table with many other faces he recognized. Shoving his way through the crowd of bodies, he headed in their direction.

"Sherry," he said, his intense focus on Alexander. "Your prisoner has escaped."

That was not what they had expected to hear. Alexander bolted to his feet, followed by the rest of them.

"*Gone*?" he hissed, unbelieving, as he moved away from the table. "How long?"

Maxton shook his head. "I do not know," he said. "I went looking for Kress and Achilles, and finally you, and in finding no one, I went to the prisoner's chamber to see if you were all there. I found an empty chamber being guarded by a knight who had no idea that his prisoner had escaped and we found a rope of linens that hung from the window to the alley below. The gate guards said they saw you leave with Kress and Achilles, so I took a chance that you had come to this place."

Alexander growled. "I should have killed that bastard when I had a chance," he said. "Does The Marshal know?"

"He knows. He heard the shouts when we discovered the man missing."

Alexander was trying not to feel like a colossal failure when he suddenly came to a halt, his eyes widening with horror.

"Bloody Christ," he breathed. "Douglas knows that we are aware of the nuns of St. Blitha. I mentioned it to him, thinking he would tell me more about his message from the Holy Father, but he didn't. It never occurred to me that he would… oh, God…"

Maxton understood exactly what he meant; he could see the abject terror in the man's eyes. "Then he's gone back to St. Blitha to tell them that their plan has been exposed," he said. "Sherry, you did not tell the man *how* we knew, did you? You never mentioned the pledge?"

Alexander shook his head. "Nay, Max. Nothing like that."

Maxton's relief was visible. "Then he's gone back to tell the nuns that we know everything," he said. "Come on; we have work to do."

The ten of them pushed through bodies and chairs and tables of the common room, making their way back to the entry door, throwing it open and charging out into the icy air beyond.

Farringdon House was only a few blocks away, a relatively short walk, but at this moment, it seemed like an eternity. Christopher, David, Sean, Kevin, and Cullen had stabled their horses in the livery across from the tavern, and they ran to collect their animals as Maxton, Alexander, Kress, Achilles, and Gart began to race those few blocks back to Farringdon House, back to the scene of the crime so they could make plans for the fact that Douglas had probably already told the nuns of St. Blitha that their assassination plans for the king were already known.

And the nuns would undoubtedly wonder how those plans were known.

In truth, Maxton was muddled by the whole situation and trying to stay focused. After being hustled out of the Great Hall when the conversation between him and William had become too heated, and then discovering that Andressa had fled back to St. Blitha on her own, he'd spent some time alone in his borrowed chamber, wondering what he was going to do about all of this.

He'd never faced a situation like it.

Perhaps that was his problem. He knew it had been his kiss with Andressa that had chased her off, but he wasn't sorry about it. He'd been with many women, and he'd even been fond of a few, but the kiss with Andressa felt like the first real kiss that he'd ever experienced. Perhaps feeling that way was the reason he'd been so petulant with William when the man bullied him about sending Andressa back to St.

Blitha. As it turned out, he didn't have to send her back.

She went back on her own.

After that discovery, he'd gone in search of Kress and Achilles, only to discover that those two, along with everyone else it seemed, had gone missing. Now, he wanted to know what his friends were doing in a tavern, evidently talking when he hadn't been invited, but he couldn't dwell on that now. He was more concerned with what Douglas' escape meant to Andressa. Alexander said he never mentioned her name and he believed him, but still, the nuns would now know that their secret had been discovered. They would undoubtedly be looking for a traitor among them.

Perhaps a young woman who had been wandering in and out of the abbey for most of the day.

But he couldn't think about that now. They had to return to Farringdon House and make plans to track down Douglas. The man had information that was far too sensitive, on many levels. His mind was wrapped up in what the Scotsman's escape would now mean for all of them when he heard a distant scream coming from the direction of Farringdon House.

Something told him that he knew who it was.

CHAPTER EIGHTEEN

A NDRESSA THOUGHT SHE heard someone behind her, but when she would turn to look, there would be no one there.

It is my fear causing me to imagine things, she told herself. She had traveled in and out of Bishopsgate on numerous occasions and had never been followed, so there was no reason to believe she was being followed now. Besides… who would be following her?

A murderer? A robber?

It wasn't as if she had anything of value for anyone. Surely they could see that she was in the garb of a pledge or postulate, meaning the only thing of value she had were, literally, the clothes on her back. And no one wanted those rages.

Foolishness, she scolded herself silently.

Pulling her woolens more tightly about her slender body, she continued onward, staying to the shadows, hugging walls before darting across an alley to the safety of the shadows on the other side. More than once, she found herself slipping in the mud long the edges of the avenues, which was really more horse dung than it was mud, built up from years and years of horses defecating on the streets.

But that was the norm of these streets and not something Andressa paid much attention to other than to try and keep her tattered shoes out of it. There was a hole in the sole of the left one and she could feel the dirt and dung squeezing into her shoe, dirtying the foot she'd so lovingly cleaned in the bath.

But no matter.

She had to get to Maxton.

Farringdon House was over by the western city walls, near Newgate, its towering structure overlooking the walls and giving those on the upper floors a clear view in all directions. It was like a beacon for all to see, four stories of gray stone in a city that was littered with wattle and daub homes, looming over the cityscape in all its glory. The manor was on a smaller lane, all to itself, and Andressa was coming to think of it as a safe place. She'd already been there once today; by the second time, she was growing familiar with it.

More and more, she was thinking on Maxton and his offer to take care of her, and after her most recent encounter with Sister Petronilla, she was thinking that perhaps it wouldn't be such a terrible thing to accept Maxton's offer. She couldn't imagine he had meant marriage – for, who would want to marry a woman carrying another man's child? – but perhaps he meant for her to take care of his house, or to somehow be of service to him.

That was all she was good for these days – hard work and laundry. Her years at St. Blitha had stripped her of the dignity she'd once had as a lovely young woman. Now, she was subject to the Mother Abbess' wicked schemes.

God, she hated what her life had become.

She hated what *she* had become.

As Andressa slipped down an alley and on to a larger avenue that would take her to Farringdon House, she found her thoughts turning towards Maxton. Her heart swelled with joy at the thought of him, the only person since the death of her parents who had shown any concern for her and her welfare. But it was more than that… even if she'd been a normal woman, on any normal day, she would still think he was fine and brave and strong. He seemed to think he had sinned so terribly in the past that no woman would have him.

He was wrong.

She would.

Thoughts of the man were warm on her mind and a smile played on her lips as she neared the junction where the alley intersected with the main avenue. She was distracted, so much so that when a man suddenly appeared right at the corner of the two roads, she didn't even look at him. She simply tried to go around him. But he blocked her path.

"Andressa, is it?" he said in a heavy Scots accent.

Andressa came to a halt, startled. She stared at him, eyes wide with shock. "What... who are you?"

The man was bushy and hairy, and smelled heavily of alcohol. "A friend," he said as his eyes raked her body from head to toe. "Ye serve Seaxburga."

Andressa was starting to feel the slightest bit of fear. At first, she thought he might be a comrade of Maxton's since they were so close to Farringdon House, but it was clear in that statement that he was no friend of Maxton's.

He knew the Mother Abbess.

"I do," she said, taking a step back from him. "And since you know that, you also know that I am meant for the veil. Touch me and the Mother Abbess will punish you."

A smile flickered on his lips. "I dunna intend tae touch ye," he said. "I've no use for women, and especially lasses with no meat on their bones."

"Then move aside."

"Not until ye tell me where ye're going."

More fear clutched at her as it began to occur to her that she'd seen the man before, yesterday when he'd come to St. Blitha and demanded she identify the Mother Abbess. Aye, she remembered that snarling face well.

"I am on business for the abbey," she said, trying to move around him. "Get out of my way."

He reached out and grabbed her by the arm. "Tell me where ye're going, lass. I'll not ask again."

She slapped his hand away, backing away from him so she was out of arm's length. "And I'll not tell you, so you may as well stop asking," she said. "I told you I was on business for the abbey. Beyond that, it is none of your affair."

She continued to back away and managed to trip, stumbling. He was on her in an instant, grabbing her by the arms and dragging her back over to the shadows of the building they happened to be standing by. As Andressa twisted, trying to force him to release her, he dug his fingers into her soft flesh.

"Ye're going tae tell John's men what ye know, aren't ye?" he snarled. "'Tis ye who have told them of our Holy Father's command to be rid of the *Sassenach* king, isn't it? Admit it!"

Astonished, Andressa stopped fighting for a split second, staring at him in horror, before resuming her fighting with a vengeance. She knew exactly what he meant and terror flooded her veins.

Dear God... how did he know?

"Let go of me!" she beat on him. "Let me go or I shall scream!"

But the smelly Scotsman wouldn't let her go. He had her by both arms now, trying to shake her so that she would stop fighting him.

"Someone has told the king's men of our Holy Father's plan," he seethed. "Seaxburga told me tae follow ye when she saw ye leave the abbey tonight. She knows it's yer guilt. Well? Confess yer sins, lass, and I'll go easy. Resist me and I'll kill ye where ye stand."

In a panic, Andressa tried to pull away from him again and he stumbled, grunting when he took a bad step on his swollen ankle. Andressa seized on his bad ankle; could see that he was favoring the leg so she kicked out, striking him in the swollen shin. Howling, the man released her.

The chase was on.

Because of the mud and wet, the avenue was slippery, and given that Andressa's shoes were in a horrible state, she immediately slipped as she tried to gain traction to out-run him. She went down to one knee, screaming when he reached out and grabbed her woolens. Throwing out a hand, she managed to strike him on the face, scratching his right cheek and immediately drawing blood.

The shock of the blow was enough to cause him to release her and she managed to get away from him, but not for long. His shoes were better, and he had longer strides, and he caught her after only a few steps.

Andressa began to scream her lungs out.

Infuriated, the Scotsman grabbed her by the throat, squeezing the breath from her. "I'll kill ye," he breathed, watching her cheeks darken in the moonlight, knowing her face was turning red. "Ye treacherous bitch, I'll kill ye!"

Andressa was beginning to see stars. She couldn't breathe and her face felt hot and swollen, like it was about to pop. Her knees began to weaken and she tried to lash out and fight back, but the world was growing darker by the second. Just as she began to sink to the muddy road, thinking that the Scotsman's angry face would be the last thing she ever saw, a strange thing happened.

Suddenly, there were men all around them and someone was pulling her away from the Scotsman, who was swarmed by several men. She could hear the Scotsman cry out as someone told him that he should have killed him a long time ago. Then there were sounds of grunting and groaning, and sounds of blades being used. It sounded like metal slicing through a side of beef, a dull and deep sound.

And then, it was silent.

Andressa had no idea what had happened. Her heart was thumping and her head was swimming, and the next she realized, Maxton was standing in front of her. His hands reached out to steady her.

"Andressa?" he asked, sounding worried. "Are you well? Did he hurt you?"

She opened her mouth to answer but no sound would come forth. That blackness that had been threatening since the Scotsman had wrapped his hands around her throat finally claimed her and she pitched forward, right onto Maxton.

In the darkness, there was finally peace.

CHAPTER NINETEEN

THE NIGHT WAS deep and still outside of Farringdon House, but inside, it was full of men who were concerned with the turn of events. The latest drama had been the escaped spy trying to strangle the pledge within shouting distance of Farringdon House, and once the unconscious woman had been brought back to the house and put to bed, Christopher had summoned the remaining men in their tight little circle. Much had happened, and much needed to be discussed, and they had little time in which to do it.

Events were happening too quickly.

Gathered in William's great solar, it was the same group who had been there at daybreak – Gart, the de Lohr brothers, both de Lara brothers, Cullen, Kress, Achilles, Alexander, and Maxton. Bric MacRohan and Dashiell du Reims, who had still been in London, arrived within an hour of the attempted strangling to round out the group.

There was a sense of expectation now, knowing that the situation was quite fluid. Christopher filled Bric and Dashiell in on the information from Andressa's first visit to tell Maxton of the nuns' intentions, which was shocking in of itself. That made her second appearance at Farringdon House rather worrisome for all concerned. The first time she'd come, it had been with a great revelation to aid their cause, so this second visit had them somewhat anxious.

Why had she been traveling the streets in darkness?

Was there more evil on the horizon?

It was the exact questions lingering in Maxton's mind as he stood by the hearth, gazing into the yellow flames. He was reliving Douglas' death over and over, feeling great satisfaction in the man's ghastly demise. In truth, there had never been any possibility of a different outcome once Maxton saw the man with his hands wrapped around Andressa's throat, and although Maxton had been killing men in unsavory ways for a very long time, this specific death had been particularly brutal.

There had been something more behind it than simple duty or simple anger.

As Maxton stood there and stewed, the last person to enter the solar made an appearance. William had just come from an unrelated discussion with his advisors, the retinue of men that formed his inner circle. Oddly enough, they were not involved in these proceedings, mostly because William only wanted to deal with a hand-selected group of men and not a gang of followers. He needed knights for this task, not politicians, which most of his inner circle was.

For this, he needed killers.

"Maxton," he said as he entered the chamber. "I am informed that our guest has returned again."

"Aye, my lord."

"Where is she now?"

"In bed. After we saved her life, she fainted."

"And she said nothing to you before she collapsed? No hint of why she has come again?"

Maxton shook his head. "She said nothing," he said. "By the time we got to her, Douglas had thrashed fairly well. She was quite shaken."

"Did you have my physic look at her?"

"He said she is only sleeping now," Maxton said. "She suffered no lasting damage in the attack."

William seemed to look at him rather strangely. Then, he chuckled, though it was an ironic sound. "If she did not, the Scotsman certainly did," he said. "I saw your handiwork, Maxton. Very brutal. You sliced the man from his throat to his groin, then you dismembered him out on the street for all to see. For the first time, I am starting to see why you are called the Executioner Knight. That was an impressive execution."

Maxton wasn't thinking of it in those terms. He simply did what he had to do. In truth, he was still angry, still filled with rage at what he'd seen. What he did to Douglas wasn't half of what he wanted to do, and he'd only stopped because Alexander had prevented him from doing anything more. Alexander had merely slit the man's throat; Maxton had chopped him into mincemeat, and quite happily so.

He was unapologetic.

"I sent the pieces back to St. Blitha," he growled. "Kress and Achilles dumped them right on the street outside of the abbey. Mayhap they will think again before they send spies out into the world."

"You mean after the girl."

"Take it as you will."

William could hear the unrepentant tone. "I would be willing to agree with that," he said. "But the truth is that until we talk to the pledge, we do not even know if they sent him after her in the first place."

"Of course they sent him after her," Maxton said, irritated. "There is little doubt that when Douglas escaped from Farringdon House, he went straight to the sisters at St. Blitha and told them that we are aware of their plans. Where else would the man go?"

"So why was he following your pledge?"

Maxton threw his hands up. "Because he probably saw her leave the abbey," he said as if it was obvious. "The man was a spy, my lord. He thinks like a spy, meaning he believes everyone in the world is spying, too. You know this; you have been in the politics of England a very long time. You know how men of that vocation think. I am certain he saw Andressa leave and he followed her, thinking that mayhap she was the one who told us of the Holy Father's plans and St. Blitha's involvement."

William nodded faintly; it wasn't as if he disagreed with Maxton. In fact, Douglas' grisly death showed William what Maxton was truly capable of and that action, strangely enough, erased much of the doubt William was feeling about the man. Maxton was a man without hesitation when it came to killing, up to and including making a statement from how badly the body was desecrated, and that impressed William. It was beginning to lend credence to what Gart had been telling him all along – that Maxton of Loxbeare was born to kill.

And he was born to prevent the death of a king from assassins who, more than likely, thought just like he did.

"I will agree with you on that point," he finally said, turning to glance at the roomful of men who were standing around, listening to the conversation. "But I am further concerned that leaving Douglas' body at St. Blitha will cause the nuns to suspect he was killed on the pledge's behalf. I am concerned they will know we will do anything to protect our spy and she is not finished there, Maxton. Not until the feast is over and the king is safe. You could very well have jeopardized her by killing Douglas and returning the body to St. Blitha."

Maxton knew that. "There are a thousand murders running about on the streets of London," he said, though he didn't want to admit that William might have a point – the death, and dumping, of Douglas had been made in anger. "Anyone could have killed the man."

"And put the body on the doorstep of St. Blitha?"

Maxton's jaw ticked faintly. "There is still no way of knowing who did it, or why."

William wasn't going to argue with him because he suspected, deep down, Maxton knew what he'd done. He'd taken a risk. So, he let the subject drop because there was no going back now.

What was done, was done.

"I shall not debate it with you," he said, "for I have stated my concern. In any case, we should discuss what is to happen the day of the feast so that each man knows his role. Have you given thought to such things, Maxton?"

In fact, Maxton had, though very little. Much like the first time William asked him of his plan where it came to the king's protection, which had only been that morning, Maxton began to concoct a plan as he went. Shifting his focus away from the dismembered spy, he looked to Sean, the king's shadow, standing over with his brother by the windows.

"Sean, does the king still plan to hunt tomorrow?" he asked.

Sean nodded. "He does," he said. "But now that we know it is the nuns of St. Blitha that we should beware of, do you still intend to shadow the king through the forests?"

Maxton looked at William, who lifted his shoulders. "Let us decide that depending on what your pledge says," he said. "I cannot imagine that the nuns would venture into the woods to kill the king, but we cannot be certain. Make your determination after you speak with her."

Maxton nodded. "Agreed," he said, but he returned his attention to Sean. "Then let us speak of the day of the feast. Do you know when the king intends to arrive at St. Blitha?"

Sean stepped forward, closer to Maxton and William. "The feast is to take place at the nooning hour, the traditional time of a hunt," he said. "John still plans to arrive at that time."

Maxton thought on that. "How many in the king's personal guard?"

"Twelve, including me."

"And these are guards of the body?"

"Aye."

"What of regular men at arms?"

"He will take a small contingent. At least fifty men because they will block off the streets and surround the abbey, most likely. But that is usual with him. The king is cautious, if nothing else. Something I suppose he learned from a father and brothers who were constantly trying to kill one another."

Maxton lifted his eyebrows in utter agreement with that statement.

"Then it would be a simple matter to add extra men to the contingent of men at arms," he said. "A few more men would not matter. But we also need to place men inside the abbey; that is the most important factor. But we do not know the layout of the place."

"I do."

Everyone turned to see Andressa standing in the door to the solar. She looked a bit ashen, but alert. She was looking straight at Maxton and after the surprise of seeing her washed over him, he couldn't help but feel his heart lighten at the sight of her. It was an odd sensation, something he'd never experienced before, but a wholly welcome sensation. Something about it brought him contentment like he'd never experienced, this woman he couldn't seem to stop thinking about. She was well, and she was whole, and that was all he cared about at the moment. Leaving his position by the hearth, he made his way over to her.

"How are you feeling, my lady?" he asked.

She smiled timidly at him as he came near. "A bit tired, but thanks to you, I am unharmed," she said. "You have my deepest gratitude for coming to my aid."

Maxton smiled in return, his eyes glimmering warmly at her. "It was my honor," he said quietly. "Are you sure you feel well enough?"

"I do."

"Then I am glad we could be of assistance," he said. Taking her by the arm, he pulled her into the chamber and indicating the men who were now looking at her quite openly as the mysterious pledge came into full view. "Some of these men helped save you as well. May I introduce you?"

Andressa had been around knights and men of rank most of her life, from her many years at Okehampton, and she was not intimidated by them. She nodded politely as Maxton introduced every man... *the Earl of Hereford, the Earl of Canterbury, Viscount Winterton, Bric MacRohan, Sean de Lara, Kevin de Lara, Cullen de Nerra, Kress de Rhydian, Achilles de Dere, Alexander de Sherrington, and Gart Forbes.*

All great men of the highest order and Andressa politely greeted each man, showing her well-trained manners. She recognized a few of them from earlier in the day, when she'd come the first time, but the rest were new. She was formally introduced, once again, to William Marshal, and he stood up from his chair to greet her.

"My lady," he said, looking her over closely. "Now that we have formally met, I would like to thank you for the information you have provided to us. I do not know if you realize it, but you have provided key information to a dilemma was have been faced with."

Andressa nodded. "Sir Maxton told me," she said. "He said that you knew someone was going to try to assassinate King John."

"And you have provided us with the answer to that mystery."

Andressa drew in a deep breath. "But there is more now," she said, looking between William and Maxton. "That is why I came back. That man who tried to kill me... he is a friend of the Mother Abbess."

Maxton took her by the shoulders and guided her over to the fire, away from the chill of the room. "He is," he answered. "It is complicated to explain who he is, but..."

"I know who he is," she said, interrupting him. "He came from The Lateran Palace to deliver our Holy Father's command to the Mother Abbess personally. I saw him at St. Blitha the day he brought the message. I told you of seeing him. He is the Scotsman."

Maxton nodded. "His name is Alasdair Baird Douglas and he can no longer harm you. We saw to that."

Andressa looked at him with some relief. "Did you lock him away?"

"We killed him. Don't you remember?"

She really didn't. Andressa didn't remember much after the Scotsman grabbed her around the throat. Shaking her head, she looked to the men standing around her. "I am sorry that I do not," she said. "I remember that he grabbed me... and not much else. But I thank you for saving my life, all of you."

Christopher was standing the closest to her. As a man with a wife and several children, including two daughters who were verging on womanhood, he knew how to handle a woman. He could see how frightened and exhausted she was, so he had his brother grab a chair and he pulled it up for her, sitting her down next to the fire. He also asked his brother to send a servant for food for the lady, including a warmed drink. As David headed out of the solar, calling for a servant, Christopher smiled politely at Andressa.

"My lady, you have saved us more trial and trouble than you can possibly imagine," he said. "And it was Maxton who mostly did away with your attacker, so he is the one to thank. We simply cleaned up his mess when he was finished. Now, you said you had more to tell us. Would you please tell us what more there is?"

Andressa found herself looking up at the very big, very blond earl who sported a neatly trimmed beard over his jaw. Behind him, his brother was returning to the group and she could see the family resemblance. They all seemed to be crowding in around her, which made her a little nervous, but she knew they were of no threat. They had saved her life. Therefore, she wanted to be cooperative.

"I know how the nuns are going to kill the king," she said, looking between Christopher and Maxton at this point. "Sister Petronilla told me how to do it. She stripped leaves from a foxglove plant and told me to crush them and put them into the king's wine. She also told me to take the root from the *dwale* plant and mash it, and to put that in as well as juice from the berries. They intend to poison the king and I am in charge of the wine."

The men looked at each other. "Neat and uncomplicated," Maxton said as he looked at Christopher over Andressa's head. "And completely untraceable. The man would be dead before we could do anything about it."

Christopher nodded. "Indeed," he said, scratching thoughtfully at his beard. "Quite clever of them. What do you have planned, then?"

Maxton's attention returned to Andressa. "You said you know the layout of the abbey," he said. "Can you draw it out for us?"

Andressa nodded eagerly. "I can," she said. "If you bring me a pen and parchment, I can draw out where this will take place."

William sent one of his servants on the run for parchment and quill, which he kept in a smaller solar next to his bed chamber. While the man was gone, Andressa went to the hearth, where there was a solid layer of ashes on the stone, and picked up the fire poker. Kneeling down, she began to sketch out the footprint of the abbey.

"The abbey is laid out like so," she said, sketching out a rudimentary rectangle with a long, oblong shape at one end. "This is the chapel. That is where Communion will take place for the Feast Day. The Bishop of Essex will be conducting the mass."

She glanced up as she spoke, looking at a host of shaking heads. She continued. "He always performs the mass on Feast Day," she went on. "That was something that was ordained long ago, long before the command for the king's death ever came from our Holy Father."

"Essex," Maxton grunted as he looked at the others. "The vile beast himself will be giving Communion."

"He will," Andressa said as she sketched. "But he does not know of the plot against the king. I am sure the Mother Abbess would not tell him, given he is a confident of the king. He is simply there to give Communion and nothing more."

A floor plan was beginning to take shape in the ashes, one with chambers and buildings, and the men watched with interest.

"Is the king's Communion wine poisoned?" Maxton asked.

She nodded. "All of it," she said. "He will be given the same wine at Communion as he is at the feast. And this… this is where the feast will take place. This is the Mother Abbess' private solar."

She was indicating a large room that was next to the chapel. Maxton crouched down beside her, pointing to the drawing.

"So this is the chamber," he muttered. "Where are the entry points of this complex?"

Andressa pointed. "The main entry to the cloister, the postern gate, and then two doors leading from the church into the dormitories and cloister," she said. "Once Communion is completed, they will move from the church through one of the two doors into the cloister. My guess is that it will be the door that leads out to the gardens. The Mother Abbess is very proud of her garden and she will want to show it to the king."

"The garden where the plants grow that will kill him," William muttered. "She will be parading him past his fate."

It was the truth. Maxton continued to focus on her map. "Christopher," he said, indicating the all of the external access points. "We must have men on these entry points. I would suggest putting MacRohan on one of them. The man shouldn't be in a position where he has to speak with anyone, but we may very well need his sword. I fear that if they hear his Irish accent, they might be suspicious. John wouldn't have any Irish soldiers."

Christopher nodded, looking over at Bric, who understood their logic. "Come and look at this map," he said, having the man move up beside him. "See the main entry? You and du Reims take it. That way, you're both guarding the main entry and Dash can do any speaking if need be. If there is trouble, the entry has direct access to the Mother Abbess' solar – and you can come running."

Both Bric and Dashiell were looking at the map, nodding as they understood their position.

"Someone will have to unlock the entry door from the inside," Bric said. "I can only imagine it is heavily barred."

Christopher nodded. "I will make sure someone unlocks it," he said. "You and Dash make sure it *remains* unlocked."

The two young knights nodded, eager and ready to participate in this great plan. They were hungry and talented, eager to gain the experience, eager to serve their king. Once those two were set, Christopher looked at Maxton.

"You realize that David and I cannot join the ranks of John's men," he said. "John and I have a long history. The man knows me on sight. Forbes, too – he has seen Gart. We cannot pretend to be part of his guard. We can, however, show up for Communion, as worshippers."

Maxton saw his point. "Then you should," he said. "That will put you three inside with the king and fully prepared to defend and protect the man."

At that point, Sean moved up between Christopher and David. "I will be with the king and his personal guard," he said, pointing to the layout of the church. "I will take my brother, Cullen, and Alexander with me in the personal guard. We shall stay close to John."

Maxton nodded. "And that leaves me, Kress, and Achilles to dress as royal men-at-arms," he said. "We'll have more freedom to move about if we're part of the lesser contingent."

"My thoughts exactly."

There was some satisfaction to those plans, now knowing what their roles were and what the general plan was. But Maxton wasn't finished yet. He looked at Andressa.

"You mentioned that the Mother Abbess will have assistance with this assassination," he said.

She nodded. "Sister Dymphna, Sister Agnes, and Sister Petronilla."

Maxton sighed. "We will need help identifying them, Andressa. As much as I do not like the thought of you returning to St. Blitha to be part of this operation, the truth is that we need you. You will have to point the assassin nuns out to us so we can watch out for them and arrest them."

She looked a bit frightened by that, fearful that such an action might give her away to those deadly nuns, but she didn't say so. She knew that Maxton realized the danger and would not have asked her to do such a thing if it wasn't absolutely necessary; he'd said himself that he didn't like the thought of her returning to St. Blitha yet again, and she'd known his reluctance to let her return all along. From the beginning, he'd been trying to keep her from returning, as if she meant something to him. More and more, she was wondering…

… was it possible that the man really did care about her?

"I will do what you need me to do," she said after a pause. "I will be in the kitchens and also bringing the Communion wine, so I will be moving about with some freedom."

Maxton could see her nervousness. "We will have men posted all around the complex, as you heard," he said. "Look at these faces; know them well. You can tell any one of them who the sisters are and they will spread the word. We are all there to help you, Andressa. And we will not let anything happen to you, I swear it."

That was something of a relief to hear him say that, even though she had already known it. They'd proven it. This task, which could have been so utterly terrifying, was made far easier knowing that these men would protect her at all costs.

"I know," she said, smiling timidly. "It is just that this… I have never been involved in anything like this. It is quite frightening. How do you do this on a regular basis? You must have nerves of steel."

That brought laughter from the group. With a grin on his face and a twinkle in his eye, Maxton reached out and clasped her hand.

"It takes practice, believe me," he said. "You will do fine. Know that we are all there to help you and protect you, so simply complete your duties as normal and everything will work out as it should. In fact, we must discuss what will take place at the feast so we know when to act. What can you tell us about the schedule for the day?"

Andressa knew this; she'd been part of the Feast Day for the past four years. "In the past, the king has arrived later in the morning and the mass begins. The bells will call the faithful to *Sext*, the midday prayers, and the bishop will perform mass. At the conclusion, he will perform the act of Communion for the worshippers."

"And the king is to have his own special wine," Maxton clarified.

She nodded. "Aye," she said. "Of course, the king would demand his own wine as it is, so this is nothing new. It will be my task to ensure the king receives the poisoned wine, only I will make sure he does *not*. But the sisters will think otherwise."

Maxton was still holding on to her hand; he squeezed it. "Good girl," he murmured. "Then what?"

Andressa was having difficulty focusing on his question because his hand, so big and warm, was holding on to hers. Her heart was beating firmly against her rib cage, thrilled by his touch.

"Then the king, the bishop, and the Mother Abbess will retire to her private solar for the feast," she said. "It will only be for special guests, this feast. The Mother Abbess has never opened the feast to all those at St. Blitha, so they will dine in her solar."

"Maxton," William said; he'd been listening to everything and a thought had just occurred to him. "How do you intend to catch the nuns in the act? As it is, they are guiltless women until you can prove they tried to poison the king. How do you intend to do that?"

It was an excellent question and everyone looked to Maxton for the answer. He glanced up at his friends, seeing their curiosity, before finally looking at William.

"Simple," he said. "You will be attending this mass, will you not?"

William nodded. "Much like the de Lohr brothers and Gart, the king knows me on sight, also. I will be attending the mass along with them."

"And I will assume you will be attending the feast."

"I've not been invited, but I'm sure I can find my way to the table."

Maxton released Andressa's hand and stood up, facing William. "Then that final step will be up to you," he said. "It is you who will ask the Mother Abbess to drink from the king's wine. If she refuses, it will be because she does not want to drink poisoned wine. She will be the only one, along with her cohorts, who know it is poisoned and when she refuses to drink it, you will ask her why. Press her. As far as I am concerned, a refusal is as good as a confession."

William liked that answer. In the end, he would be the one arresting the king's assassins and look like a hero. Anything that brought him glory in the end was well received.

"Excellent," he said. "And Lothar shall know it is I who foiled his plot. *Perfect*. And you will be nearby to arrest the other nuns?"

"When Andressa points them out, we will move on them as soon as you move on the Mother Abbess."

"Wait," Andressa spoke up before they became too excited over the idea that the nuns wouldn't resist their arrest. "The Mother Abbess has a staff that she carries with her, always. As I told Maxton, it has a blade at the end of it, a very big blade, and she is not afraid to use it. You must treat her as you would treat any other killer – she would show no hesitation in using her blade against you."

William smiled faintly at her concern. "My lady, I have been a knight longer than both you have been alive," he said. "I believe I can defend myself against your Mother Abbess. Besides, Sean and Kevin and Cullen will be in the solar with me because they will be accompanying the king. They can assist me in apprehending the Mother Abbess. But where will her minions be?"

Andressa shook her head. "That is something I do not know," she said honestly. "I will have to locate them and point them out to your men. Last year, they joined the Mother Abbess for the feast, but the year before, they did not. Therefore, I do not know if they plan to join the feast this year."

William considered that. "Then we must have eyes on them at all times," he said. "But let me make this clear, young woman – you are to have no involvement in apprehending these women. I am perfectly happy to use you as a spy, but not as a martyr. You will go about your duties as usual, you will help my men identify the nuns involved in this plot, and nothing more. Is that clear?"

Andressa nodded solemnly. "It is, my lord," she said. "And I am grateful."

William grinned at her. "You are doing quite enough, and it is we who are grateful," he said. "In fact, I told Maxton that you would be rewarded when this is all over. Has he told you that?"

Andressa shook her head. "Nay, my lord," she said, looking to Maxton in surprise. "A reward?"

Maxton could see that she was puzzled by the thought. He ended up crouching down beside her again. "You are helping us save the country," he said softly. "Without you, we would still be fumbling around in the dark, trying to figure this all out. Don't you understand? You have made everything possible and you deserve as great a reward as we can give you."

A reward. Andressa had never even considered such a thing and even now, she simply couldn't comprehend what he was saying.

"I…I do not even know what I would ask for," she said. "I do not do this to be rewarded."

Maxton smiled. "That is why we are eager to reward you," he said. "You are doing this because it is the right thing to do, not because you will gain something from it. Is there anything you can think of? Anything at all."

She considered his question very carefully. "Would… would a new pair of shoes be too much?"

William chuckled and Maxton did, too, at her sweet and simple request. "You would not want something more?" he asked. "Say the word and I shall ride to Chalford Hill Castle, remove your aunt, and restore your inheritance. The Marshal shall supply the army and no man, or woman, can stand against it."

Her eyes widened. "You… you would do that?"

"Aye, I would do that. For what you have done, every man in this room would do that."

She stared at him a moment longer before tears began to fill her eyes. "It is too much," she whispered. "That is far too much to ask."

"Nonsense," William said firmly. "If that is what you wish, consider it done. When the Mother Abbess has been arrested, you will have seen your last day at that abbey. Won't she, Maxton?"

Maxton had a smile playing on his lips. "I would say so," he replied, feeling the least bit self-conscious because he suspected what most in the room were thinking – there was more than simple chivalry involved in his declaration. "The day after the feast, I will muster an army and ride to Gloucester. Your aunt will be arrested for stealing your inheritance and you may assume your rightful place as the heiress to the Culverhay fortune."

Andressa's hands flew to her mouth as tears popped from her eyes. She was so grateful that she could hardly express herself.

"Thank you," she murmured. "It all seems like a dream… I cannot believe you should help me so."

Maxton's expression was gentle, something completely out of character for him. But with her… it was easy. "You are unaccustomed to someone being kind to you," he said. Then, he winked at her. "You had better get used to it."

Before she could reply, several servants appeared at the solar door bearing food and drink. There was also a servant bearing parchment and quill, and with the situation more or less settled, the knights began to disburse as the food was brought into the chamber and placed upon a table near the hearth. The knights broke into small groups, quiet conversation among them, as Maxton pulled Andressa to her feet and, collecting her chair, took it over to the table so she could sit.

Now, it was just Maxton and Andressa at the table as the others wandered away. The servants had left behind boiled beef, boiled carrots and peas, a soft pottage of cheese and honey, bread, butter, and a steaming pitcher of hot milk with honey and cinnamon in it. Andressa picked up a spoon, her eyes big on everything in front of her, before she delved into the cheese pottage. Once she tasted it, she couldn't shovel it into her mouth fast enough.

"What do you plan to do once you are back at Chalford Hill?" Maxton asked, reaching over to pull the parchment and quill left on the table in his direction. "It has been four years since you have been there. Surely you have great plans."

Andressa's mouth was full of more soft cheese. "I do not know," she said honestly. "I never thought I would return, so I do not know what I will do."

"Well," he said casually as he began to sketch out Andressa's map in the ashes from memory. "The first thing to do is find someone to help you manage it."

"Why?"

"Because you are to deliver a child soon. The infant will take much of your time. What will you do with your empire?"

She hadn't thought of that and a hand moved to her belly, timidly touching it. She spent so much time avoiding touching it, avoiding acknowledging it, that it seemed strange to feel her belly, firm and rounded.

"Everyone will wonder about the father of the child," she said, swallowing the bite in her mouth. "How can they know the truth? I am sure they all know I have been at St. Blitha for the past four years. They will know that I have not married."

"Why not?" he asked, concentrating on drawing the chapel exactly the way she had. "Do you really think anyone at Chalford Hill has kept watch on you?"

Andressa thought about that as she pushed the cheese away and moved to the beef. "Probably not," she conceded. "In truth, I do not know anyone there any longer. I was gone for eight years and when my parents died… I am sure my aunt has brought in her own servants and maids. I am sure I do not know anyone there any longer."

"Then they would not know that you left St. Blitha, say, a year ago and married," he said, scratching out the old abbey walls. "They would not know that it was your husband laying siege to Chalford Hill to regain it for you."

She stopped chewing. "Husband? But I have no husband."

He looked up from the parchment. "You have me."

"You are not my husband."

"I would like to be."

Andressa almost choked with what was left in her mouth. She had to quickly grab at the cup of hot milk Maxton pushed in her direction and slurp it to push the beef down. When she was finished coughing and sputtering, she looked at him with utter shock.

"Maxton," she hissed. "Are you mad? Why should you want to marry me?"

He set the quill down, a smile tugging at his mouth. "Because you see me in a way no one else does," he said quietly. "You have called me kind and generous from the start of our association. You see me through the eyes of someone who does not know of my past, or of the things I've done. No one has ever looked at me that way before, Andressa. I never thought to marry, but if I did take a wife, I would want her to look at me the way you do. You only see the good in me and that makes me want to be the best man I can possibly be. If you have such faith in me, then mayhap I should have faith in myself."

It was, perhaps, the sweetest thing Andressa had ever heard. Not only that, it solved her question of whether or not she was good enough for Maxton, something she'd been wrestling with from nearly the start of their association. But she was still overwhelmed with it all; everything was happening so quickly.

"You are the kindest and most generous man I have ever met," she murmured. "Oh, Maxton... you cannot know how happy your words make me, but clearly, you are a blind man. Can you not see what I am? I surrendered myself to a man who was not my husband and now I am paying the price. I have been a laundress at an abbey for four years, working my hands until they bleed, eating crusts and berries and anything else I can steal in order to survive. I live like an animal. Are you sure that is the kind of wife you want?"

His smile broke through and he reached out, collecting her cold, slender hand. "If you are willing to see the best in me, then I am willing to see the best in you," he said. "I told you that you are not the only sinner between us, and as for the rest, you did what you had to do to survive. That tells me that you are stronger than you know. I would be proud to have such a woman by my side."

"Even though you have only just met me?"

"I do not need days or months or even years to tell me what my heart already knows."

Andressa stared at him a moment longer before tears of joy pooled in her eyes. "And you are certain of this?"

"More certain than I have ever been."

She blinked and the tears spilled down her cheeks, which she quickly wiped away. "Then if you are certain, I would be honored," she whispered. "More honored than you will ever know. But tell me one thing."

"Anything."

"You are not offering marriage simply because I am the rightful heiress to a rich fortress, are you?"

He laughed softly, flashing his big, white teeth. "I can promise you that I am not," he said. "In fact, I would take you with only the clothes on your back. Regaining Chalford Hill for you… it is yours, Andressa. It will always be yours."

She was enchanted by his smile, his words, feeling such hope and joy swell in her that she could hardly contain it. It seemed surreal, all of it, but in the same breath, nothing had ever seemed so right or so true. It was glory beyond imagination.

It was to be hers.

"And yours," she said, squeezing his hand. "I will share all that I have with you, for always. But… will you do something for me?"

"All you need do is ask."

She squeezed his hand again, that big and strong thing, trying to put her thoughts into words. "When I was young at Chalford Hill, and when I was fostering at Okehampton, no one called me Andressa," she said. "My parents only named me Andressa because they hoped I would be a boy. They wanted to name him Andrew."

"You are most definitely not a boy."

She giggled. "Nay," she agreed. "But because they wanted a boy, they called me Andie from birth. I was always known as Andie until I came to St. Blitha. It reminds me of better days. Days I never thought I'd see again."

He brought her hand to his lips, kissing it sweetly, and he didn't care who saw him. "I am happy to call you Andie if it pleases you," he said. "But know that I think your name is quite beautiful. Like you."

Andressa's cheeks flushed a dull red, the most color Maxton had ever seen in them. It gave her such a glow, a hint of the true beauty this woman possessed. He was still holding her hand when she lowered her head and continued eating.

All with one hand.

It was the best moment of his life.

CHAPTER TWENTY

St. Blitha

IT WAS A cold, misty morning, much colder and denser than the day before, but the Mother Abbess and her attendants were up before dawn, preparing for the day. With the Feast Day on the morrow, there was much for them to do.

They had a traitor in their midst.

"Is she awake yet, Sister Petronilla?" the Mother Abbess asked. "Is she at her duties?"

Sister Petronilla was over near the windows that overlooked the garden. She peered out, trying to see through the mist that had settled. The sun was just rising, turning everything a lighter shade of gray, like a mystical land the color of silver.

"Aye," she said after a moment. "I see her and some other women over near the kitchens."

The Mother Abbess sighed faintly as Sister Agnes adjusted her wimple. "And you are sure what you saw last night, Sister?"

Sister Petronilla turned away from the window. "I am certain," she said. "I was watching the postern gate to ensure she returned from Lady Hinkley's. There was a man with her; I could see him standing outside the gate when she came through."

"And she had no laundry from Lady Hinkley?"

"None that I could see, Gracious Mother."

The Mother Abbess finished fussing with her wimple and made her away across the floor, looking from the windows just as Sister Petronilla was doing, seeing Andressa across the misty yard as she worked with the other nuns. Because she was so tall, it was easy to spot her among the other women.

"So Andressa has a lover," she said, but there was an icy edge to her tone. "A lover who must have killed Douglas when the man strayed too close to her. Do you suppose that is what happened, Sister? Mayhap Douglas stumbled onto something he should not have heard and was killed for it."

Sister Petronilla lifted her shoulders. "Andressa spends far too much time wandering the city," she said, disgust in her voice. "She has more freedom than anyone else because of her duties as the laundress and she has taken a lover because of that freedom. She has taken advantage of your generosity, Gracious Mother. Something must be done."

The Mother Abbess was calm, unnaturally so, as she watched Andressa go about her tasks. "Something will be done," she said as she turned away. "She will understand her place in all things or The Chaos will swallow her, too. It is something we must do. Bring her to me."

Sister Petronilla left her post at the window, a smug expression on her face because she was happy to summon Andressa to face the Mother Abbess' punishment. She wasn't happy about Andressa joining their exclusive group as it was, so the fact that the woman had proven herself unworthy was quite a joyful thing for Sister Petronilla. As she quickly left the Mother Abbess' solar, the Mother Abbess turned to Sister Agnes and Sister Dymphna.

"Bring my rod," she said quietly. "And the bindings. We shall get to the bottom of this."

The two sisters fled the chamber to do the Mother Abbess' bidding.

The Mother Abbess was alone in her solar now, waiting for what was to come. She'd been at the helm of St. Blitha for many years, and she'd seen many women during that time. Scores of them. It was rare that a nun died of old age at St. Blitha, simply because the Mother Abbess liked to play God with the women under her care, but it was something they didn't know until it was too late.

For Andressa, she was about to receive a warming before it *was* too late.

Or perhaps it already was.

In any case, the girl had gone out, at least twice that day that she knew of, both times with the excuse of delivering or gathering laundry at Lady Hinkley's fine manor home. But when she returned last night, it had been with no laundry and a male escort.

A lover.

The Mother Abbess had a lover, too, but she was well past the age of worrying over conceiving a child, so her activities were without fear. When the Bishop of Essex came to St. Blitha as he did several times a year, she would join him in the Abbot Lodge on the grounds, and they would fornicate most of the night. He chose her over younger women, because he'd had trouble in the past with nuns bearing his children. At least, they'd become pregnant, but the children were never born.

He'd made certain of it.

The Mother Abbess knew all about that, so their trysts were mutually beneficial – Aatto de Horndon, Bishop of Essex, was a tall, thin, and weak-looking man with a long tongue and a manhood that was nearly half the length of his thigh when it was aroused. He could bring a woman to her pleasure in mere seconds, and the Mother Abbess looked forward to his visits to St. Blitha. Rumor had it that he shared lovers with the king, though the Mother Abbess had never been part of that particular exchange. Not that she cared. Her life was such that she didn't care, nor was she attached, to anyone or anything.

Meaning she had little to no feelings towards Andressa and what was about to happen. If the girl wasn't guilty, there would be no regret, but if she was guilty, then there would be some pleasure in punishing her.

And then The Chaos could have her.

The Mother Abbess moved away from the window, thoughts turning away from the bishop's impending visit to Andressa. Her great Staff of Truth was propped against the wall over near the entry door and she went to collect it. In fact, she stood next to the doorway, just inside it, holding the staff, waiting for the door to open.

It wasn't long in coming.

Sister Petronilla entered first, followed by Andressa. They entered the chamber, not seeing the Mother Abbess because she was standing back by the door, against the wall. They only noticed her when she shut the door behind them.

"Andressa," the Mother Abbess said. "I understand you came back late last night."

Andressa, who hasn't been inordinately concerned when Sister Petronilla summoned her to the Mother Abbess' private solar, was now filled with fear at the sight of the Mother Abbess standing by the door with her Staff of Truth in-hand.

It was the staff that had her eye, because that was the Mother Abbess most fearsome weapon. When it was in her hand, there was always the chance that somehow, she might use it.

Andressa took a deep breath.

"I did, Gracious Mother," she said, trying not to sound terrified. "Is there a concern?"

The Mother Abbess came away from the door, using the staff as a walking stick at this point. Her movements were casual, slow, but that was deceptive. It was like watching the lethargy of a serpent before it lashed out.

"I would like for you to tell me if there is," she said. "Where is the washing you said you would collect from Lady Hinkley?"

Andressa faced her with as much courage as she could muster. There was no washing, even though she'd made a point of stopping by Lady Hinkley's late in the night, with Maxton by her side. If Lady Hinkley was asked, she wanted the woman to confirm that she had, indeed, been there. It had been a carefully executed action to cover her tracks.

"She gave me none, Gracious Mother," she replied. "She did ask me to return, thinking her clothing from the day would need washing, but she decided not to give it to me."

"Did she say why?"

"She wanted to wear the garments today for a visit."

The Mother Abbess came to stand next to her, the staff in her hand just a few inches away from Andressa.

"I see," she said. "And if I were to ask her if you had visited her, would she tell me you had?"

Andressa nodded firmly. "I would encourage you to do so, Gracious Mother," she said. Then, she glanced at Sister Petronilla before returning her attention to the Mother Abbess. "Is something wrong? Have I done something?"

The Mother Abbess' gaze lingered on her, the weight her stare so very heavy, for a few moments before turning away.

"I am not certain," she said. "Do you have something to confess to me, child?"

Now, they were getting to the meat of the situation. Andressa knew this moment would come at some point. She thought it would have come last night after she'd returned, but everything had been dark and silent. She never asked Maxton what happened to Douglas, and he'd never told her, but surely the nuns would have been suspicious when he didn't return to St. Blitha. They'd sent him out to follow her, after all.

But Andressa had been the only one to return.

Given what Douglas had said to her last night, Andressa knew that the Mother Abbess was aware the plans for the king were no longer secret. She'd known enough to send the man to follow Andressa when she left the abbey, presumably for Lady Hinkley's. But it had been far more than that, and Lady Hinkley's laundry had nothing to do with it.

She knows yer guilt, Douglas had said.

Now, the confrontation had come.

As Andressa looked at the woman, it occurred to her that she was on trial. All of this; it was a trial. The Mother Abbess was the judge and her minions were the jury. They knew she had discussed their plans and were more than likely deciding what to do about it. How they knew of her guilt didn't matter, only that they did. Someone had told them that Andressa had confessed their darkest plans to men loyal to the king.

Oh, God...

Fear surged through Andressa but she fought it. She had to stay calm if there was any hope of coming out of this alive. To pretend as if she had no idea what they were talking about was her only defense, but there was a distinct problem with that – she had never been very good at lying. Now, she had to lie as if her life depended on it, because it did. She knew it did.

She was closer to death than she'd ever been in her life.

God help me!

"Confess?" she repeated, hoping she didn't sound terrified and cornered. "I have not gone to confession today, but I shall confess to you if you wish."

The Mother Abbess ended up over by her windows, her favorite place to stand as she surveyed her empire beyond.

"I have no time for foolishness," the woman said patiently. "Tell me where you have gone and who you have spoken to. Tell me now."

Andressa held her ground. "You know where I have gone, Gracious Mother," she said. "Yesterday morning, a baker was kind enough to feed me, and then I returned to finish the laundry. I delivered Lady Hinkley's undergarments and then returned last night at her request. Where is it that I am supposed to have gone other than what you already know?"

Before the Mother Abbess could answer, the door opened and Sisters Agnes and Dymphna appeared. One nun was holding a long, thick branch that had been carved out with heavy thorns projecting from it. It was a horrifying device of torture. The other nun was carrying leather bindings, larger versions of what falconer's used to tether their birds. When Andressa saw the items, her eyes widened.

"Gracious Mother," she said, swiftly turning to the woman. "What is it I am supposed to have done?"

"Tell us who the man was who escorted you home last night," Sister Petronilla burst. "I saw him standing by the postern gate. Who was he?"

Shocked, Andressa turned to the woman. In truth, she hadn't realized Maxton had been seen and she struggled for an answer.

"A... a man I could not be rid of," she said quickly, thinking of the first lie that popped to mind. "He saw me returning from Lady Hinkley's in the dark and would not go away. I told him to go away, but he refused."

Behind her, Sisters Agnes and Dymphna were closing in. Andressa could feel it. Nervously, she tried to back away, turning so she could see what all of the nuns were doing, and she knew she was in a grave situation. In a panic, she turned to the Mother Abbess.

"Please," she begged. "What have I done?"

The Mother Abbess showed absolutely no emotion. "Someone has spoken of our command from our Holy Father," she said. "Someone has told the king's men that is our intention to eliminate the king come Feast Day. I know it could not be my faithful attendants; moreover, none of them have left St. Blitha since we received the orders. But *you* have left St. Blitha. Who have you told, Andressa?"

Now, it was all out in the open and Andressa had never been so terrified. If she could make it past Sister Dymphna, who was standing near the entry door, she might have a chance to run for her life, but she couldn't guarantee the sister, who was long-legged and fast, wouldn't catch her.

Besides... running would make her look guilty. It would make it worse when she was caught. Fighting off tears, she turned to the Mother Abbess.

"You trusted me with information," she said. "I told you I would not fail you. Why would you think I would speak of something you entrusted with me? Sister Dymphna has several nuns she is in charge of and everyone knows they gossip terribly. She has told them of what you do to women in The Chaos and they spread lies about you and they speak to those on the outside. Why not ask Sister Dymphna what she has told them? It must have been her!"

It was a well-known fact that Sister Dymphna had the inability to keep things to herself, and in Andressa's panicked state, that was all she could think to say – to try and turn the situation off of her and onto another nun. Unfortunately, it was Sister Dymphna who was holding the thick branch with the thorns, called simply The Rod, and in her rage, she swung the thing at Andressa, catching her in the shoulder.

Andressa screamed in pain, trying to move away as Sister Dymphna went after her, bring the rod down again and barely missing her. By this time, Andressa was running, and she came across the Mother Abbess' expensive sideboard, grabbing the nearest thing she could, which happened to be a pewter pitcher. It was heavy, like a hammer.

Sister Dymphna came up behind her and swung the rod again, and Andressa ducked beneath it. As Sister Dymphna staggered sideways with the momentum of the swing, Andressa came up and hit her on the side of the head with the pitcher with all her might. A dull, cracking sound filled the air as metal met with bone.

Sister Dymphna dropped like a stone.

Armed with the pitcher, Andressa wielded it like a weapon as she faced the other three nuns. "You'll not take me down without a fight," she snarled. "I will not confess to something when there are others who just as easily could have committed such an offense."

Shocked that someone they had attacked was fighting back, Sister Agnes and Sister Petronilla looked at Andressa with a mixture of outrage and surprise, while the Mother Abbess seemed oddly pleased by the display of force. She appreciated physical violence, in all forms.

"Then all you need say is you did not tell anyone," she said calmly.

"I did not tell anyone!" Andressa screamed.

It was a lie, but it was a lie to save her life. She saw no sin in lying to murdering, dishonorable women. The Mother Abbess simply nodded her head.

"I believe you," she said evenly. "And you know nothing of the death of Alasdair Baird Douglas?"

Andressa was poised to swing the pitcher again; she hadn't moved. When Sister Dymphna stirred, she was close enough to bash the woman on the skull again. Sister Dymphna fell still.

"The Scotsman?" Andressa said, trembling and cocked, pitcher over her head as if to smash Sister Dymphna's brains in. "He is dead?"

The Mother Abbess nodded slowly. "He is," she said. "You never saw him last night?"

More lies were to come, but she felt no guilt. "Nay," she said. "Why do you ask?"

The Mother Abbess didn't push her. In fact, she put up a hand as if to ease the situation. "It does not matter," she said. "Please put the pitcher down, Andressa. Come and sit and we shall discuss this calmly. In fact, the feast day is tomorrow and there is still preparation to come. We shall speak of that. All will be well now."

Her manner was calming, which had a soothing effect on Andressa. But Andressa didn't put the pitcher down until Sister Agnes set down the bindings that she had in her hands, and the Mother Abbess ushered the two nuns to her fine table. Shaken, and still terrified, Andressa reluctantly put the pitcher down, but still within arm's length should she need to get to it. She sat at the end of the table, where the Mother Abbess indicated.

With the situation calming, Andressa felt somewhat relieved but she was still on edge, still afraid there was something more to come. It was an instinct she should have listened to because as the Mother Abbess took her seat at the table, she passed behind Andressa with the Staff of Truth still in her hand.

And that was when the situation went from bad to worse.

One swing of the big, heavy iron and wood cross at the head of the staff at Andressa's head, and she was knocked silly. A second blow to the head sent her to the ground where she lay, dazed and nearly unconscious, looking up at the ceiling of the chamber and seeing the three nuns standing over her. The Mother Abbess knelt by her head.

"Now," she said softly. "If you do not understand the need for obedience and discipline yet, you will by the time we are finished with you. As for telling the king's men of our plans, it is of little consequence. Men are so arrogant to believe that a woman can do them no harm, and they certainly will never believe that nuns are capable of ending a monarchy. But they will suffer in the end, as will you. Remember that death comes from the most unexpected sources, Andressa."

The third blow from the Staff of Truth caught Andressa in the left arm, a powerful blow that sent her rolling over onto her side. As the blows from the staff and the thorny rod commenced, all Andressa could do was roll into a ball and protect that life growing inside of her.

Odd how she thought of the child at that moment over herself. To protect the child she'd tried so hard to ignore was the only thing on her mind, that inherent maternal instinct protecting the baby from blows that were drawing blood and leaving gouges in her body. In truth, she was more terrified what would happen to her should they discover the child, so maternal instincts were only part of it.

She had to hide the pregnancy.

She had to protect them both.

Curling up on the cold, stone floor of the Mother Abbess' fine solar, Andressa could hear her cries of pain echoing against the old walls.

CHAPTER TWENTY-ONE

Farringdon House

M<small>AXTON COULDN'T STAND</small> it.

He'd been away from Andressa for all of one day, and he was longing after her as he'd never longed for anyone in his life.

The morning of the Feast Day of St. Blitha had dawned surprisingly bright, in stark contrast from the heavy mist they'd had the day before, and for most days over the past few months. But something in the weather pattern had changed today and the sky was clear.

It was a beautiful sunrise that came up from the east, casting golden rays onto the land. Inside the manor home, however, there was a sense of purpose as men prepared for the coming day. Much had happened, and much still needed to happen, and there was a sense of anticipation because so much was at stake. It wasn't just a king's life, but also the life of a certain pledge who had risked her life to make sure their task was successful.

They didn't want to fail her.

The king had gone hunting in the forest of Windsor the day before, as planned, and even though the mist had been heavy well into the afternoon, he hadn't scrapped his intentions. He'd gone out with his courtiers and military advisors, and they'd hunted for several hours while Maxton, Kress, Achilles, Alexander, Cullen, Bric, and Dashiell had shadowed the group from the recesses of the heavy foliage.

It wasn't that anyone expected the nuns to make a move against the king out in the wilderness, but more as a preventative measure in case the information they'd received had been wrong and the nuns were the least of their worries. It wasn't that they didn't trust Andressa; they knew she was telling the truth. But given that the assassins after the king were of the most unexpected kind, and it was quite possible there was more than one set of assassins, Maxton wanted to ensure they were ready for anything.

Purely a preventative measure.

But it had been an odd day for Maxton as he sat in the wet forest, with water dripping down his face as he listened to the cries of the king's hunting party. After returning Andressa to St. Blitha the night before, he'd returned to Farringdon House and spent the entire night tossing and turning, dreaming of a green-eyed pledge when he did happen to fall asleep. When he would awaken between dreams, it was to the realization that he had actually proposed marriage to the woman.

And she had actually accepted.

But he'd kept it to himself. He wasn't sure how to tell Kress or Achilles, or anyone else for that matter. Not that they didn't realize that something was going on between Maxton and the pale lass from St. Blitha; they would have had to have been deaf and blind not to realize there was something more than polite concern there. It was the fact that Maxton simply wasn't the marrying kind, or so he'd thought.

As it so happened, he was wrong about that. The idea of marrying Andressa and settling down was as foreign to him as it was wonderful. He'd never hoped for a normal life as far as lives went, with a wife and heirs, so the idea that he might actually attain some peace and happiness had upended everything he'd ever known or thought about himself.

In a wonderful way, of course.

It had been a long day shadowing the king, who mostly remained under a tarp to stay dry while his advisors hunted out in the wet, and when they'd finally returned to Farringdon House that evening,

Maxton was disappointed that Andressa wasn't there, waiting for him. Somehow, he'd hoped that she would have been able to get away from St. Blitha to see him. He even thought about going over to the abbey that night, just to catch a glimpse of her, but decided against it because she would probably be asleep, anyway. He found great comfort in knowing he would see her on the feast day, and with the ending of the assassination threat against the king, he and Andressa could start their new life together.

She'd never have to go back to that devil's den again.

Therefore, there was eagerness in his movements this morning and as he dressed in a tunic bearing the crimson and gold of the royal family that Sean had provided, he found himself smiling as he thought of all of the wonderful things he would buy Andressa when all of this madness was finished.

The truth of the matter was that Maxton had been smart when he'd left for the great Quest; he'd been one of the few Crusader knights who had been careful with his money. He'd only taken what he felt he needed, leaving the majority of it with a deposit banker in London, a man who held money for some of the nobility for safekeeping and charging a small fee to hold it.

While many knights lost their fortunes on crusade, Maxton hadn't. In fact, when the battles were over and the Christian armies were heading back to their homes, Maxton and Kress and Achilles had capitalized on the situation and had taken jobs for wealthy lords in Europe, fighting their wars for them. All three of them had become quite wealthy from that venture, and whilst in Genoa, had deposited even more money with the banking system there. Being frugal men, and hating to spend their own wealth, they'd lived at The Lateran Palace while the Holy Father had paid their way.

Their hoards remained untouched.

Maxton hadn't thought much about his money since that time because there hadn't been a need, but now with the advent of a betrothed, he was thinking a good deal about it. He could easily get his money from the deposit banker in London, but getting it from the bankers in Genoa would take time. He was thinking that a trip after he and Andressa married would be in order, and he could take her to exotic places and buy her more clothing and jewels and finery than she could ever wear. The poor woman who had spent the past four years starving and living in rags would know luxury such as she could have never imagined.

He liked thinking about the things he could do for her.

A knock on his chamber door roused him from his thoughts. Nearly dressed, with the mail hood on and the tunic secure, Maxton opened the door to find Kress standing there, dressed exactly as he was. They were both in the regalia worn my men at arms and not seasoned knights, which was something of an insult for men of their station. Maxton cocked an eyebrow at the man.

"You look like the king's stooge," he commented. "'Tis shameful and degrading to be forced to wear this garb."

Kress grinned. "It was *your* idea, you dolt."

"I should be whipped."

With that, he turned back into the chamber to collect his broadsword and Kress followed, snorting as he entered the room.

"I've often said the same thing," he said. Then, he sobered. "Well, my friend. This day should prove interesting. Are you concerned?"

Maxton was fixing the leather belt at his waist. "For what?"

"For the pledge."

Maxton's movements slowed a little and he could feel his guard going down. Kress was the best friend he had in the world, outside of Achilles, but Achilles could often be judgmental about things. The man was a virtual volcano of angst sometimes, torn between his religious beliefs and what he did for a living, so somethings, he could be difficult to speak to.

But not Kress; the man understood how the world worked and didn't put too much stock in a church that had proven too many times how very immoral it could be. He also understood Maxton; the two of them always communicated well. Therefore, Maxton was thinking seriously on his reply to Kress' statement before answering.

"I must ask you something, Kress," he said. "You will be honest with me."

Kress leaned against the wardrobe built up against the wall. "I always am, Max. You know that."

Maxton glanced up from his belt. "The meeting at The King's Gout tavern two days ago," he said quietly. "It was about me, wasn't it?"

Kress' smile faded completely. "It was."

"What did you discuss?"

"The contention between you and The Marshal when it comes to the pledge from St. Blitha."

Maxton wasn't surprised to hear that. In fact, that was what he'd mostly expected to hear. "And did you come to a conclusion?"

Kress shook his head. "There was no conclusion to come to," he said. "We discussed how you have changed. The man who spent those months in the prisons of Baux and then returned to England is not the same man we have known all these years. We have never known you to be confrontational with a man of higher rank, and most especially not with someone like William Marshal."

Maxton kept his head down, adjusting the sheath on his belt. "He is a stubborn man," he said. "And I do not care what his credentials are, in some instances, he is wrong."

Kress smiled ironically, shaking his head. "We are speaking of William Marshal, Max," he said. "Mayhap he has been wrong in some instances, but he is still the greatest knight England has ever seen. His accomplishments are without question."

"De Lohr is better."

That caught Kress off-guard. "What's that?"

Maxton looked up at him. "I said that Christopher de Lohr is better," he said. Then, he waved a gloved hand at him. "Oh, I know that Chris and I have never gotten on well. The man is righteous and pious and so bloody moral that it makes me sick sometimes. But he is also unwaveringly brave, brilliantly intelligent, and unquestionable when it comes to his decisions. William is older and has therefore managed by virtue of time to establish a better reputation, but Chris de Lohr will have his moment. The man will shine in the annals of history like no other."

Kress stared at him a moment. Then, he started to laugh. "You say this about a man you did nothing but criticize the entire time we were in The Levant?"

Maxton made a face. "Because de Lohr and his brother had their noses so far up Richard's ass, when the man shit, it was the color of the de Lohr tunics. Richard could not take a piss without Chris there to hold his manhood."

Kress was far gone with laughter by now. "That is what I am used to," he said. "You bashing de Lohr at every turn. If you praise him again, I will accuse you of being possessed by the Devil and be forced to cut your head off."

Because Kress was amused, Maxton's lips were flickering with a smile. "I am not possessed," he said. "And in spite of everything, I have nothing but the greatest respect for de Lohr. He will never be my best friend, but I know he would kill or die for me, and I for him. That is the extent of our brotherhood."

Kress nodded, a twinkle in his eye. "And a most strange brotherhood it is," he said. "You two cannot stand the sight of each other, yet you would die for each other. In fact, when we were at The King's Gout discussing the tension between you and William, neither Chris nor David believed it. They could not grasp that the Maxton they've known all these years should be contentious with a superior."

Maxton's smile faded and he turned back to his sheath again. "I did not want him to send that beaten, starved woman back to St. Blitha to spy for him," he said. "But I suppose, deep down, I understand why. She is our best option for a successful mission and she has already provided us with so much information."

"Did you tell William that?"

Maxton shook his head. "Nay," he replied. "But, Kress… does everyone know?"

"Know what?"

"That I feel something for Andressa."

Kress didn't say anything for a moment. Instead, he came around to the front of Maxton, forcing the man to look up at him. He looked him in the eye.

"What *do* you feel, Max?" he asked softly. "Lust? Pity? Concern? *What* is it? Because this is not like you, not in the least."

Maxton knew that. He took a deep breath as he sorted through his thoughts. "I know it is not," he said. "Kress, I shall be honest with you – I know I have changed from the man you knew to be ruthless and heartless in all things, but I will tell you that the man is still there. That part of me has not changed. But after the incident with the Holy Father, when a man who is supposed to be the moral icon for all men and the very reason so many men died in The Levant is, in truth, something murderous, I swear to you that it was something that threw my entire life into question. I always felt like a sinner – or horrible, dirty sinner – with the vocation I have chosen. I have a talent for killing me and I have used that talent, many times. But when I saw what the Holy Father truly was, it made me question… *have* I sinned? Or is every man on earth evil, and I am no different from the rest? Is there any true good in this world?"

Kress knew all of this, at least for the most part, but it was the first time he heard Maxton put it into words. He put a hand on Maxton's shoulder.

"I knew you were searching for answers," he said. "But I did not know the exact questions. Have you found true good in this world, Max?"

He nodded. "In a pledge who is as weak and confused and searching as I am," he said. "You ask me what I feel for her? I am not certain, but when all of this is over, I am going to marry her and we are going to seek our answers, together."

Kress' brows lifted in surprise. "Marriage?" he repeated. "I never knew such a thing interested you."

Maxton shrugged. "Nor did I," he said. "But with the right woman, all things are possible."

It was a rather startling revelation as far as Kress was concerned. He knew that Maxton was feeling something for the pledge; he simply didn't know how much or how deep. Now, he knew.

"Then this is the end of the Unholy Trinity," he muttered. "The Executioner Knights will now be only two. I do not fault you for moving on to live your life, Max, and I am truly happy for you. But I am sorry to lose a brother in arms."

Maxton frowned. "Who said anything about losing a brother in arms?" he said. "As for the Unholy Trinity, that is something you and me and Achilles will always be. I will always consider myself one of the Trinity, and proudly so. It is not the end of anything. But my life will change, I hope, for the better. I would like to be happy and content for once in my life."

That was something Kress did indeed understand. He, too, had much the same thoughts on life as Maxton did, or at least he had, but unlike the rock-souled Maxton from the past, Kress had indeed secretly wondered about life and love and marriage. It was something he'd put out of his mind because he did not hold out any hope that it was attainable.

But Maxton had found it; perhaps there was hope, after all.

"And you deserve it," Kress said. "Go and get your pledge's inheritance back for her, as you told her, and live until you are old and gray and fat. But do not expect to lose me so easily; I may come live with you. Or, I may remain in The Marshal's service. I've not yet decided."

Maxton grinned at him, lifting a hand to pat him on the cheek. "Wherever you go, you know that all you need do is call me," he said. "I shall be there, wherever and whenever you need me."

In spite of the reassurance that the Unholy Trinity would always remain intact, Kress received the distinct impression that it was not to be. It was a sad thought, but one he wouldn't linger on. Perhaps like Maxton, he needed to evolve.

But they had one last, final mission, anyway.

And they would see it through.

"We have had some good times, haven't we?" Kress smiled at the memories, watching Maxton collect his helm from where it had been tossed on the bed. "I will miss our adventures."

Maxton peered at him. "Who says our adventures are over?" he said as he headed to the door. "A wife will not keep me from having more adventures."

"You think so, do you?"

It was a foolish statement, Maxton realized, as he looked at Kress and saw the man laugh. No, he couldn't imagine Andressa would be too happy with him leaving her at Chalford Hill as he roamed about the known world, killing men and making money. Besides… that wasn't what *he* wanted now. He had the live he wanted within his grasp and he wasn't going to let it go.

"Come on," he said, opening the chamber door. "Let us find the rest of the adventure hounds and get about this business. I failed to see Andressa yesterday and I am eager to see her today, in spite of the circumstances."

"Then let's go, lover. Let us not keep the future Lady Loxbeare waiting."

Grinning at each other, they headed down to the vast interior courtyard of Farringdon House where everyone was gathering before heading out. Now, the business of the day was at hand.

It was the calm before the storm.

CHAPTER TWENTY-TWO

St. Blitha

HER LEFT HAND was smashed, but she was trying to do her best with it.

As morning dawned over the winter-cold land, Andressa was already up and moving, with many things to do on this feast day.

The day had arrived.

She'd slept in her own bed last night, surprising since she was positive that she had been headed for The Chaos after her thrashing. That was the only way to describe it; a thrashing of epic proportions meant to intimidate her, denigrate her, and punish her for hurting Sister Dymphna, who was in bed and hardly able to speak of move. The damage to her skull was very bad, and she had a loss of vision on one eye, but the Mother Abbess would not call for a physic. She had one of the other nuns, a woman who tended the sick at the abbey, see to Sister Dymphna's needs. But she was in bad shape, indeed.

Yet, Andressa felt no guilt. It was one less nun to have to worry about as far as she was concerned. Moreover, she was nursing her own substantial injuries that were mostly to the left side of her body because when she'd curled up in a ball on the floor of the Mother Abbess' solar, they'd only been able to beat the left side of her body. As a result, her left foot and left knee were horribly swollen, and her left hand as it had covered her skull had been badly mashed. She knew she had some broken bones, but she could at least grasp things with her index and thumb. The other three fingers of the hand were useless.

Even so, she was expected to participate in the feast. The Mother Abbess had been very clear of that. After the thrashing, she let Andressa lay on the floor of her solar for about an hour before she had Sister Agnes and Sister Petronilla carry her back to her cell and toss her onto her bed. She'd remained there for the rest of the day and the same healer nun who had been tending to Sister Dymphna came into tend to her wounds as well. Anything bleeding or exposed had been washed with wine and tightly wrapped in boiled linen, and that included her hand. However, there wasn't much they could do about the wound on her face.

She had three big gouges on the left side of her face, by the hairline, and they had bled profusely. The healer nun had cleaned them up, so they weren't oozing, but the damage was obvious. To help conceal it somewhat, Andressa had tied a strip of the boiled linen around her head, like a kerchief to keep her hair away from her bruised face, covering up the wounds. But no amount of cleaning or boiled linen could hide the fact that she'd been soundly thrashed.

However, the fear of another beating hadn't been her motivation rise from her bed and get to work. There had been something more to Andressa's dedication to duty. As she'd lain in bed yesterday, reflecting on the situation in general, she had come to the conclusion that she was in a very important position to save the king as well as every other tortured soul at St. Blitha.

She held the key.

It was true that she was instrumental in protecting the king from an assassination attempt, as Maxton had told her, but there was more to it. So many women suffered under the hand of the Mother Abbess, and now that Andressa had been given an important role in the function of the abbey, she knew she had to do something about it. Those horrible souls who had beat her yesterday weren't going to get away with it. They wanted to humiliate and punish her, and kill those who displeased them, but no more. In the end, Andressa would have the last word.

She had a plan.

Therefore, before dawn, she was out in the laundry area where she'd stashed the dried foxglove leaves, crushing them into a fine powder with her good hand. For good measure, she'd stripped off even more dead leaves and crushed them as well, just to increase the toxicity of the poison. Once she'd finished with that, she'd gone to find the *dwale* plants and picked off sixteen fat, purple berries. Then, she'd pulled up three of the plants to get to the poisonous roots.

Washing off the plants in a bucket of water, she'd cut the top section away from the tender roots and proceeded to mash the fat, white roots in a small bowl she used when she made soap. The mashed roots were then placed in a cheesecloth from the kitchens and Andressa placed the leaves and roots into an earthenware pitcher of wine to steep, sinking the ingredients straight to the bottom of the pitcher. Her last act was to mash those sixteen berries and put everything – skins, stems, and juice – into the wine.

The more poison, the better.

It was double the amount she'd been instructed to use, but she wanted to make sure it did the job it was supposed to do. She wanted no room for error. As the very strong poison was flushing into the wine, she'd gathered two more pitchers of wine from the kitchen and used mulling spices to flavor all three of the pitchers, so that all of them would essentially taste the same. She even marked the poison pitcher with a scratch across the bottom of it, and she marked a second pitcher of untainted wine with a gouge on the handle.

It was a gouge she would tell the Mother Abbess that the marked pitcher was meant for the king, but she wasn't finished with it. Into that gouged pitcher, she put a second sachet that mimicked the one she'd put the poisonous plants in, only this cheesecloth sachet held harmless dead rose petals and dried grass. It would trick the sisters into believing that particular pitcher was the poisoned one. Only Andressa would know which wine was truly poisoned.

And that was the wine destined for the Mother Abbess.

With all three pitchers of wine ready and waiting, Andressa went about her duties of supervising the coming feast. The kitchen nuns, older women who were so bereft of all hope that they moved around like mindless ghosts, had been up before dawn as well, without the supervision of Sister Blanche. The women were boiling beef in a great pot over an open flame in preparation of the coming feast, and the smell of baking bread filled the crisp morning air.

The smells of cooking weren't unusual at St. Blitha, but it was food always meant for the Mother Abbess' fine table. Even this morning, as Andressa had worked, she saw at least four or five pledges and postulates slip from the postern gate in their morning hunt for food and she felt sorry that the smells of cooking were making those poor starving women miserable.

But it was misery, Andressa hoped, that would soon be ended.

Ironic how she had no guilt about poisoning the Mother Abbess and anyone else who drank the poisoned wine. She knew it might also be Sisters Agnes and Petronilla, but still, she felt no remorse. Murder was a sin, and she knew that, but she hoped that when she stood before God on Judgement Day, he would understand what she did had been for the greater good. Unless the Mother Abbess and her kind were stopped, more women were going to die. Murder would continue.

Andressa hoped that God would understand that.

Because of her management duties in the kitchen this morning, Andressa was able to steal a piece of beef under the guise of tasting it to see if it was fit for the feast. She had the cook add more salt to the water to flavor the meat after she'd stuffed several morsels into her mouth, feeding her rumbling belly. It was good beef, bought with the Mother Abbess' ill-gotten money, and the bread was made with the finest flour. All of it fit for a kingly feast, as the wine in the laundry area continued to leech more and more poison out of the ingredients that had been placed in it.

It was turning into a potion unto itself.

The morning began to deepen and the sun began to make its march across the sky as there was some commotion over by the chapel, specifically at the Abbot's Lodge as the Bishop of Essex made his arrive for the Feast Day.

The chapel, and the garden, filled with the bishop's men because he traveled with a massive encourage. Horses were stuffed into the barnyard on the east side of the kitchen, and as Andressa stood back in her shaded laundry area, stirring the poison wine with a stick to ensure the ingredients were melding well with the wine itself, she could see the bishop himself and the Mother Abbess, with Sister Agnes, and Sister Petronilla, standing between the garden and the Abbot Lodge.

Andressa watched the scene closely, noting that they seemed to be in discussion. She was positive that the Mother Abbess hadn't told the bishop of the directive from the Holy Father because the bishop and the king were friends, and the bishop was one of the man's advisors.

Aatto de Horndon was a loud man, obvious in manner and in mood, and he was greatly disliked by almost everyone. The Mother Abbess enjoyed a close relationship with him, probably *too* close, and the woman surely wasn't going to jeopardize that by telling him of the Holy Father's order. He may very well try to stop it.

And there was no stopping wheels that were already in motion.

Therefore, Andressa went back to work as the sun continued to rise and the day turned surprisingly mild from the icy temperatures they'd been having this season. She went back and forth between the kitchens and the laundry area, alternately making sure the food was being well-prepared and tending to her concoction of wines. In fact, she was busily tending to the poisoned wine, stirring and stirring, when she heard a noise from the postern gate. Although she knew it was locked, she turned to see what the noise was.

A familiar face was staring back at her.

Andressa recognized one of Maxton's knightly friends, dressed in full mail and a tunic of scarlet with three lions, the royal standard. He was up against the gate, looking right at her, and she could see more soldiers milling around behind him, which told her that the king had arrived.

The realization made her stomach lurch, nerves becoming evident now. Everything would soon be coming to a head and if it wasn't executed properly, it would be a bloodbath of legendary proportions that she would find herself caught up in. But the time was upon her and she knew she had to act quickly before her duties took her away from any direct communication with Maxton and his men.

Picking up a bucket, the one she'd used to rinse away the dirt from the *dwale* roots, she went to the postern gate and unlocked it.

Pushing through the gate, pretending to be going to the stream, she could see several royal soldiers milling around and a few of them turned to look at her as she emerged from the gate. So did the knight she had seen; as soon as she came through the gate, he hung back, letting her move to the stream before closing the gap and making his way to her.

"My lady?" he asked quietly, his eyes on the gate to ensure no one was watching them. "What happened to you? Why are you bandaged?"

Andressa was having difficulty drawing water with only one working hand; when he saw this, he quickly took the bucket from her and dunked it into the stream.

"It is of no consequence," she answered softly. "You must tell Maxton that the Mother Abbess will only be helped by two of her attendants today. The third one is gravely injured. The two are with her right now as she speaks to the bishop and I imagine they will continue to remain with her for the duration of the mass. One woman is fat and round, and the other woman has very dark eyebrows. That is the only way you can distinguish them, considering they are wearing the same habits."

The knight, a very tall man with enormous shoulders and piercing, dark eyes, stood up from the stream with the full water bucket. "I will tell him," he said as he handed the bucket back to her and she grasped it with her good hand. "Tell me what happened to you, my lady. Maxton must know."

Andressa didn't have time to explain everything. Besides, if she did, she had a feeling it might enrage Maxton. She didn't know the man's moods or reactions very well, but given he'd killed Douglas so quickly when she'd been threatened, she imagined he didn't have much self-control. He probably acted on anger very easily, and that wasn't something they needed at the moment. They had to get through the mass without Maxton running amuck because of her injuries.

"I will heal," she said, taking her water and turning away. "Go and tell Maxton what I told you."

"But..."

She cut him off. "Hurry, now," she said. "Tell Maxton to prepare for what is to come. Be shocked by nothing."

"What does that mean, my lady?"

"You will know when you see it."

Struggling with the weight of the water, she carried the sloshing bucket back to the postern gate and opened it, slipping inside with her water but leaving the gate unbolted from the inside. She did that for one very good reason – if Maxton and his men needed to enter the complex.

Andressa didn't even turn to see if the knight had run off, as she'd told him to. She kept her attention on her area, on the three wine pitchers she could see sitting up on table she used to lay out her dried laundry.

Setting the water aside, she checked the pitchers again, stirring the poisoned wine once more and noticing that the crushed leaves had all but dissolved, and the cheesecloth containing the mashed roots was the same color of the wine. Everything was blending quite nice. Just as she set the stick aside and covered up the poisoned wine again, she could see Sister Petronilla heading in her direction.

Her heart began to race.

Keeping calm, she bent over the bucket of water and pretended to wash her good hand in it just as Sister Petronilla approached. She casually looked up at the woman as she dried off her hand.

"I see that the bishop has arrived," she said before Sister Petronilla could speak. "Is the mass to begin soon?"

Sister Petronilla nodded. "The king has arrived, also," she said. "He is moving into the chapel as we speak. Is everything prepared as we have instructed?"

Now was the moment. God help her, Andressa was feeling more nerves than she had hoped she would. She could only pray that Sister Petronilla was so pre-occupied that she wouldn't question anything at all about the wines and their differences, or check up on Andressa's work. She turned for the three wine pitchers that were back in the shade.

"Everything is ready," she said quietly, moving for the pitcher with the big gouge in the handle. Quickly, she pulled out the cheesecloth sachet full of leaves and petals, now stained dark with wine that disguised what they really were. "This is for the king. See the mark on the handle? This will tell you that this is the wine meant for him. Give it to no one else unless you wish to kill them."

Fortunately, Sister Petronilla wasn't paying attention to anything other than the pitcher Andressa was handing her. She seemed busy and distracted, perhaps feeling her nerves for this day of days as well. Whatever the case, it was working to Andressa's advantage.

"Excellent," she said quietly. "And you did exactly as I told you?"

Andressa nodded firmly. "Exactly, Sister. I rose before dawn to complete the task. The ingredients have been soaking in the wine for hours."

A smile flickered on Sister Petronilla's pale lips. "Well done, Andressa," she said, looking her over as if pleased the beating had whipped her into acquiescence. Perhaps she could have been more suspicious of her, but she simply didn't have the time or the will. There was too much happening at the moment. "I will ensure this is the only wine the king drinks."

Andressa nodded. "It is a full pitcher, so it is enough for the feast afterwards, too," she said. "I will bring your wine to the chapel myself. It tastes of spices, as you instructed, and so does the king's wine. In fact, they should taste nearly the same, so make sure you give him the wine with the gouged handle. That is the only way you are to know for certain."

Sister Petronilla didn't question her further, about anything. It was clear that she believed Andressa had been properly punished and was now properly submissive. She simply took the wine with her, heading across the cloister towards the chapel entry. Andressa watched her go, still palming the rose sachet she'd pulled from the wine because she hadn't wanted Sister Petronilla to get a good look at it. The less she saw, the better.

Breathing a sigh of relief, Andressa called over one of the kitchen nuns, instructing her to take the third wine pitcher, the one that was only mulled but not poisoned. That would be the wine for the masses. As the woman collected it and headed for the chapel to ensure the acolytes had it, Andressa turned to the remaining pitcher, the one full of poisoned wine. She looked at it a moment, feeling no doubt at all in what she was about to do.

For every pledge, postulate, and nun who had suffered The Chaos, she would do it for them.

For ever terror and sin the Mother Abbess had committed or inflicted, she would seek vengeance.

For the beating she received yesterday at the hands of the wicked, she would seek a reckoning.

For the good of everyone at St. Blitha, she was about to play God.

There was no turning back.

MAXTON HAD NEVER really seen St. Blitha in the daylight, and now that he had, it looked worse than it did at night.

It was constructed out of a mixture of beige sandstone and gray granite, an amalgam of building materials because some of the rocks had been pilfered from an old pagan temple built by the Romans centuries ago. That meant the façade was tall, ugly, and uneven, and a growth of moss grew up from the base of it, covering the stones about halfway up with a moist, green growth.

The church itself was squat and slender, but very long, running the full length of the cloister into which it had been built. There was a big entry, double-doored, with panels that had seen better days. In all, the entire structure conveyed the same rot and deterioration that plagued the occupants inside. It looked like it belonged somewhere on the purgatory plain.

Andressa has been living in this horrible place, he thought grimly.

When they'd first arrived with the advance group of the king's contingent, Maxton had positioned himself by the entry door to the church as the rest of the men-at-arms spread out around the entire complex, covering the walls from the outside to ensure that the king was amply protected. As Maxton remained by the doors, the king's himself finally arrived and he caught sight of Sean, Kevin, Alexander, and Cullen among the king's body guards, an elite group akin to the Praetorian guard of old. It also gave Maxton an opportunity to study Richard the Lionheart's brother, a man he'd not had a high opinion of for many years.

In truth, he'd seen John before, but back when he was merely a prince, known as "Lackland" by most of the nobles in England for the mere fact he literally had no lands, no possessions worth note, and coveted everything his father and older brothers had earned or inherited. Dark-haired, and dark-eyed, with one droopy eyelid, he wasn't very tall, an oddly meek stature from a man who wielded so much power.

Maxton watched the king arrive and then shortly thereafter, so did William Marshal, Christopher and David, and Gart. The two parties mingled in the entry area outside of the church. The king greeted The Marshal amiably, deliberately ignored the de Lohr brothers because of their vast and turbulent history together, and made a point of trying to convince Gart to join his elite guard. Gart refused, so John ignored him, too.

As Maxton stood right outside the door, seemingly standing at attention as the king passed by him, he made sure to make eye contact with Christopher and David, and finally William, as they passed inside the church. He cast Gart a long look as well, watching the men file into the church for the mass to begin. Because of the king's attendance to St. Blitha, the streets were blocked off, preventing pilgrims from reaching the church, so it was a very small and very elite crowd inside. Once the king, his courtiers, and a few honored guests disappeared inside the church, Maxton broke from his position and went on the prowl.

There was a certain pledge, in particular, he was looking for.

He headed off to the west, which was the south side of St. Blitha's compound. Just past the church was the main entry to the cloister, and he immediately saw Dashiell and Bric at their posts. He made his way towards them.

"Nothing unusual to report?" he asked.

Dashiell answered. "Nothing unusual, except the door to the cloister is still locked," he said. "Wasn't de Lohr supposed to have someone unlock it for us?"

Maxton nodded, looking at the enormous, fortified door. "He was, but I do not know what became of that. He may have a man on it as we speak."

Bric cocked a pale eyebrow. "If we have to get in there any time soon, we'll have to use an ax to break the door down."

Maxton realized couldn't wait for de Lohr's man, if there even was one, to unlock the door because it was a key component to the operation. Therefore, he remembered the layout of the complex, the one that Andressa had drawn for them in the ashes and the one he'd later sketched on parchment so they could all study it. He remembered it all down to the last detail.

"As I recall, there is an entrance into the cloister compound just inside the entry of the church," he said. "It is a door used by the nuns. It is not to far from the cloister entry door, so you may be able to slip in and unlock the door without being seen. Are you willing to try?"

Young and hungry for a challenge, Dashiell nodded. "Indeed," he said. "I remember seeing the cloister entry on her sketch."

"Then go, man. Make haste."

As Dashiell rushed off, Maxton turned to Bric. "Keep watch that he returns shortly," he said. "If he does not, you have my permission to go in and save him. Just try not to make any noise and bring the entire church running."

Bric's silver eyes glimmered. "I've saved many a man before and have never made any noise," he said. "But if he gets into trouble inside of a nunnery, I will never let him forget it."

Maxton grinned. "As well you should not."

A reluctant smile spread across Bric's lips, but as he turned away, Maxton spoke. "The Marshal told me that every word out of my mouth to you would be considered a challenge, given our rough introduction," he said. "He also said you throttle men at the slightest provocation. Is this true?"

Bric looked at him, a somewhat appraising expression on his face. "Depends on the provocation."

Maxton snorted. "My first words to you yesterday were not a provocation," he said. "They were an honest assessment, given the situation. I hope you realize that. If I mean to provoke you, you will know it."

Bric faced him full-on, looking him over as if sizing him up. "So I've been told."

"Then I do not have to be on my guard with you, waiting for a great Irish fist to come flying out at me?"

It was Bric's turn to snort. "Nay," he said. "I've heard what they call you. I've no desire to tangle with someone called an Executioner Knight."

"Now I *know* you are wise. I hope that means we can discuss our mutual quick tempers over a cup of ale someday."

"I would consider it an honor."

With a flash of a grin, Maxton turned away, heading down the length of the wall as he headed for the postern gate. He hadn't moved too far away from Bric when Achilles suddenly came bolting around the corner of the wall, heading straight for him. Startled, he rushed to meet the man.

"What is it?" he hissed.

Achilles was trying to keep calm, but unlike Maxton and Kress, he sometimes didn't possess that ability. The man's talents lay in his ability to disguise himself and kill in stealth, not keep control of his emotions. As he and Maxton came together, he tried to keep his voice low.

"I saw your pledge at the postern gate just now," he said. "Max, something has happened to her."

Maxton felt a stab of fear. "What has happened?"

Achilles shook his head. "I do not know, exactly," he said. "She would not tell me. She is upright and walking, and she is going about her duties, but she looks as if she's been badly beaten. Her head and hand are wrapped."

Maxton felt as if he'd been hit in the gut. All of his breath left him and he exhaled heavily, feeling sick to his stomach. "But she *is* moving?"

"She's moving. She is able to complete her duties. And she told me to tell you that only two attendants, not three, will be with the Mother Abbess today."

Maxton frowned. "What happened to the third nun? There were supposed to be four in total."

"Your pledge said that the fourth nun is badly injured and unable to attend the mass. She also said that the two remaining nuns are with the Mother Abbess and will more than likely stay with her, even inside the church."

Maxton scratched his stubbled chin. "So they are keeping together in a group," he muttered thoughtfully. "They are not spread out, which makes our job easier. Where was Andressa the last time you saw her?"

"By the postern gate. And Max… she said you must prepare for what is to come, and to be shocked by nothing."

He looked at him, greatly confused. "What in the hell does that mean?"

Achilles shook his head. "I do not know, but the way she said it made me think that we must be prepared for anything out of the ordinary."

Maxton didn't like the sound of that. He pointed to the entry to the church, several yards away. "Go plant yourself next to that entry and remain there. I will return."

As Achilles did as he was told, Maxton made his way around the corner of the wall and down to the postern gate. There were about a dozen men at arms over on this side, standing spaced out, watching the landscape around them. He passed beneath the grove of trees as the sat scattered along the streambank, the postern gate in sight, but when he drew near, he headed for the stream itself and kept an eye on the gate, as he didn't want to get too close to it and risk being seen.

Standing next to the stream in the wet grass, he could see through the gate well enough. He could also see women moving around inside for the most part, but they were very far away. He took a few steps closer, standing behind one of the many trees that clustered around the stream, and peered out from behind it so he could get a better look at what was going on inside.

Then, he saw her.

She was talking to a nun who happened to be holding a pitcher of some kind. He didn't get a good look as the nun when she hurried away, and then he saw her call forth another nun from the kitchen area. That nun was also given a pitcher of something. Considering the nuns planned to kill the king using poisoned wine, he had an idea what was in the pitchers. As the second nun walked away from Andressa and she went back to collect a third pitcher, Maxton hastily made his way over to the postern gate and tried to stay out of sight.

It took two tries, hissing her name, before she finally turned around and saw him. Then, he could see what Achilles' had been speaking of – her lovely, pale face was bruised on the left side and he could see what looked like blood stains on her neck. Her left hand was bandage and when she saw him, she made her way towards him, visibly limping. By the time she reached him, Maxton was nearly beside himself with worry.

"What in the hell happened?" he growled. "What have they done to you?"

Andressa looked around quickly to make sure he wasn't heard. "Maxton, please," she whispered. "If they see me speaking with you, it will put everything in jeopardy. Go away!"

"Not until you tell me what happened."

She was growing exasperated. "I will heal," she muttered firmly. "We will speak of this when our task is complete. Meanwhile, listen to me now – go back to the church and wait."

"Wait for what?"

"You will know when it happens."

With that, she limped away, carrying the pitcher, leaving Maxton nearly crawling out of his skin with concern. He wanted to shout at her, furious she had not only refused to answer his question, but had walked away from him on top of it. He was desperate to find out what had occurred because she was obviously injured. His imagination began to run wild; perhaps upset with the dismembered corpse of Alasdair Douglas and knowing the last thing he'd been doing had been following Andressa, the nuns punished her for his death.

William's words came back to haunt him, then – *you could very well have jeopardized her by killing Douglas and returning the body to St. Blitha*. Maxton had known that was a risk, and damn if the Marshal hadn't been right about it. He'd acted on anger when dumping Douglas' body and Andressa had paid the price. In truth, he could only think of that as the reason for her injuries.

It was his doing.

As he watched her limp away, he wanted to rip someone's throat out and he didn't care if it *was* a nun's. He would never again stand by and watch Andressa injured, or worse, especially when he'd been to blame. But he forced himself to calm, seeking comfort in the fact that she was, as Achilles had said, upright and walking. She was limping, but she wasn't crippled. He had to cling to that comfort until he found out what had happened.

He had to bide his time.

When Andressa was about half-way across the cloister, heading for the open doors leading into the church, he snapped out of his train of thought and quickly made his way back around to the front of the church. He'd passed Bric and Dashiell along his way, noting that Dashiell had accomplished his task without being captured by the killer nuns. Or, at least Bric had saved him from such a fate. He was sure he would hear about it later, but at the moment, he had more important things on his mind as he approached the main entrance to the Church of St. Blitha.

The scene they'd been preparing for was about to be played out.

It was time to catch the assassins.

CHAPTER TWENTY-THREE

Ordo Missae

I T WAS THE order of the mass.

The Bishop of Essex stood at the altar of St. Blitha with two other priests and several acolytes, intoning the order of the mass. As Andressa stood back by the door leading to the cloister, she could see that the church really only had a few worshippers in it – William Marshal, the de Lohr brothers, and another knight she recognized as Gart Forbes. The king was also there; she knew that because she had seen him in the times he'd previously come to worship on feast days.

The king was surrounded by his courtiers, men finely dressed in the latest style, and she could smell the perfume that some of them wore from where she stood, mixing oddly with the mustiness of the church itself. Old, mossy stone smelled of mildew, creating a rather pungent ambiance.

She could also see many armed men on the perimeter of the church, big knights with big swords. She couldn't see their faces because they had their helms on, rather bad manners for being inside a church, but they stayed to the shadows for they were there to watch the king and not participate in the mass. She could also see a few men at arms back near the entry door, which had been closed, so they stood just inside the door. And she could see, clearly, that one of those men at arms was Maxton.

Somehow, she felt safe and comforted simply to see him there. She knew he would not let anything happen to her, which fed her bravery as well as her resolved. She was well out of sight, back in the shadows, but up near the altar, she could see the Mother Abbess along with Sister Petronilla.

Though it was usual for nuns to worship separately from their male counterparts, during the Feast Day, they were permitted inside the church with the men. They sat off to the side, at the edge of the sacristy, but they were in full view of the priests and the worshippers. And Andressa could see, very clearly, the pitcher of wine that sat on a table near them.

The pitcher meant for the king.

The order of the service proceeded. The *Penitential Rights, Kyrie eleison*, the *Gloria*, and the prayers from the Book of Psalms. The bishop was a loud man with a booming voice and a speech impediment, and his words echoed off the walls and up into the arched ceiling. Andressa could see the priests bringing out the large, silver chalices for Communion, and she knew that now was the time for her to act. Everything had to go smoothly.

The right wine for the right chalice.

It was as if everything in her life had built up until this moment, the time in her life when she would change the course of not only a nation, but of her life as well. No death to the king, but death to the assassins, women who had tortured her for four long years. Maxton and his men had no idea what she had planned, but it didn't matter. It would all end here and now, and she was brave enough to face it.

Her heart was thumping against her ribs painfully as she watched the priests prepare for Communion, and she moved around the rear of the altar, back in an area called the Ambulatory, where she wouldn't be seen in order to deliver the poison wine to the Mother Abbess and Sisters Agnes and Petronilla.

This one moment…

It was finally here.

"I shall take that from you."

Someone was grabbing at the pitcher in her hand, startling her as she pulled it away. She found herself looking at one of the priests that the bishop brought with him, the man preparing for Communion.

My God! She thought in a panic. *He wants this wine!*

"You cannot have this," she said, sounding frightened, but she quickly stilled herself. "The wine for the king is with the Mother Abbess. See? It is on the table next to her. It is wine straight from the barrel and has not been touched, by anyone. It is pure for the king."

The priest, a man with shaggy blond hair, looked at her oddly. "What is wrong with *this* wine?"

He was pointing to the one in her hands and she looked at it, struggling to think of a believable reply.

"The... the sisters like it sweet and heavily mulled," she said. "The king would hate such a wine. It is meant only for them."

He eyed her. Then, to her horror, he stuck his finger in it and licked it. Immediately, he made a face. "Awful," he hissed. "By all means, let them have that abomination. I will get the other pitcher."

Relief flooded Andressa. She seriously thought she might collapse from it, but she forced herself to continue onward, watching as the priest took the pitcher of the king's wine from Sister Petronilla.

There was the most wicked expression of satisfaction on Sister Petronilla's face when she handed the wine to him, and when the woman saw Andressa approaching with a pitcher of what she believed to be unpoisoned wine, she nodded her vague approval at Andressa as if to say *our mission is complete*. They were close to fulfilling their directive from the Holy Father and the expressions of contentment on their faces was obvious.

Cool, collected... *and deadly*.

Now, it was time to kill a king.

Unaware that he might have the fate of a king's life in his hands, the priest preparing the chalices made sure to keep the John's wine separate from the wine for the nuns. Since he'd tasted it, he knew it was awful, so when the communal chalices were prepared, Andressa handed over the wine in her hands and watched the man fill the nun's cup to the rim.

Then, she couldn't take her eyes from it.

Terrified she might be invited to take Communion from the poisoned cup, she made sure to hide well back in the shadows, watching everything, but ensuring that no one could see her. The priest moved to the *canon of the mass* and the *eucharist*, followed by the *Sanctus*.

Now, it was time for those present to take Communion and Andressa watched, hardly able to breathe through the force of her anticipation, as the king was the first one to receive Communion. He drank deeply of the chalice, licking his lips of the fine wine, and Andressa couldn't help but notice that the Mother Abbess, Sister Agnes, and Sister Petronilla were watching him with the expression of a hunter siting prey. Smug in the knowledge that their task was complete, they wait for the monarch to drop dead.

The king was the only one to drink from that particular chalice, which was emptied and wiped, as was the tradition. It was called the Wiping of the Chalice, in fact. Then, others were called forth to take Communion and they did, through the third pitcher of wine that Andressa had prepared for the masses, untainted and pure. The bishop drank from that cup, and so did William, Christopher, David, Gart, and a host of courtiers that had accompanied the king. Andressa breathed a palpable sigh of relief when that was out of the way. Then, came the Communion for the nuns.

It was the moment she'd been waiting for.

Andressa was back to holding her breath again as the priests gave the full chalice of wine to the bishop, who approached the nuns in the sacristy. The chalices weren't small; they were fairly large, meant for groups, but in this case, it was only three women who would be partaking. Andressa knew she'd put far more poison in the wine that Sister Petronilla had told her to because she knew that the chalice wouldn't hold the entire pitcher, nor would they drink the entire pitcher at Communion. Therefore, what they did drink had to be very strong.

She couldn't risk that they would survive it.

As Andressa watched with great anticipation, something happened that she didn't foresee – the bishop, who had already taken wine out of the Communion cup meant for the masses, also took several swallows of the spicy wine in the chalice meant for the nuns. Then, he handed it to the Mother Abbess. Given that only four people were to drink from this chalice, the Mother Abbess didn't want to waste the good wine and she, too, also took several healthy swallows. It was passed to Sister Petronilla, who drank her share, and then Sister Agnes, who drained it. There were even dregs in the bottom that she sopped up.

All of it, gone in an instant.

The bishop took the chalice back and wiped it out, handing it back to the priests who had been helping him. Andressa moved out of the shadows, grasping at the wine pitchers that were sitting near the sacristy, including the poisoned wine. She disappeared back into the Ambulatory and stayed out of sight as the bishop gave the final prayers and blessing, offering more prayers to St. Blitha on behalf of the king before finally dismissing the mass.

With the mass ended, people began to rise from a kneeling position. The strains of soft conversation began to fill the church, but Andressa could only see part of the action in the sanctuary as the bishop came away from the altar to speak with the king.

Knowing the man had ingested the poison wine, Andressa continued to watch him, wondering how quickly the poison would take effect. She'd put so much of it in the wine, but no one seemed to be reacting to it, causing to wonder if she had done it correctly.

God, what if I was wrong? What if I failed at this and now nothing will be solved, and no one, not even I, will be avenged against these murderous nuns?

What if...?

Suddenly, something happened out in the sanctuary that caught her attention. The Mother Abbess was moving for the door that led out to the cloister, but she wasn't moving very well. She seemed to be staggering a bit before finally coming to a halt, her hand to her head as if she didn't feel well.

There was a bit of commotion around the Mother Abbess as she held her head and finally put her hand to her lips. Sister Petronilla was looking to the Mother Abbess in concern, and trying to help her walk, but she, too, seemed to be unbalanced. She went to grab at the nearest solid structure to steady herself, which happened to be a table, and she ended up pulling a very fine cloth off of it and onto the floor.

She went down with it.

Now, people were noticing. Over by the king, the bishop was suddenly unsteady on his feet and as he pitched to his knees, the king's personal guard rushed forward to take the monarch away, far away from whatever delirium was happening. They had no idea what was going on, only that the king shouldn't be anywhere near it, so John hustled out of the church to the cries of 'curse' and 'the devil's work'. They last anyone saw of him, Alexander and Sean, in full personal guard regalia, were dragging him out by the arms.

The shouts were echoing everywhere.

Save the king!

As John was whisked way, some men remained in the church; Andressa could see them from her position back in the Ambulatory. She could see William, Christopher, David, Gart, and a few others, watching the bishop fall to the ground with the inability to breathe. His body was also shaking uncontrollably. Up near the altar, all three nuns were down, with the Mother Abbess on her knees as Sister Agnes lay on her back a few feet away, gasping for air.

If Andressa had wondered if she had indeed succeeded in her task, the evidence of her success was now before her. Oddly enough, she felt very calm as she watched the scene unfold. She was still holding on to the king's pitcher and the nun's pitcher with her good hand, and with the nun's pitcher being less than half full, she didn't want anyone else ingesting the poisoned wine. It had accomplished its task. Pouring the poisoned wine into the dirt of the Ambulatory, she headed out into the sanctuary.

William and Christopher were standing over the bishop as the man writhed on the ground, while a few terrified nuns who had entered the church when they heard the shouting now stood over the Mother Abbess and the two writhing sisters. Andressa walked into the light, watching the women as they lay dying, feeling nothing more than a sense of closure. For all of the evil and pain they inflicted, and for the men and women they'd so gleefully killed, it was retribution.

It was justice.

"Andressa?"

She heard her name, turning to see Maxton approaching her from across the sanctuary. He had his men with him, following him, and they were all looking around with great confusion at what was happening. When Andressa saw him, tears came to her eyes and a smile to her lips.

Her salvation had arrived.

"Andressa?" Maxton said again, hesitantly, as he came near her, reaching out to put a comforting hand on her arm. "What has happened, love? Did you have a hand in this?"

She sighed faintly, her gaze turning to the Mother Abbess and the two sisters on their backs, now surrounded by a few nuns that were trying to help them. Not strangely, they weren't trying very hard. They were mostly looking at them. She shook her head, knowing any help for the nuns was futile.

"I gave them the poisoned wine meant for the king," she said simply.

Maxton's jaw popped open in shock as he looked to the writhing bodies on the ground. "You did this?" he gasped. "*You* poisoned them?"

She nodded. "They wanted me to kill the king," she said. "I would not do it. I switched the wine so they were the ones to drink the poison. It is their own wickedness that brought this upon them. Years of pain and torture, years of men and women who could not fight for themselves… yesterday, I fought back when they tried to beat me, and these are the results."

She lifted her bandaged hand and in that instant, Maxton understood what had happened. He looked at her in utter astonishment.

"Revenge," he muttered. "You did this for revenge."

She shook her head slowly. "Nay, Maxton. *Justice*."

"And the bishop?"

"He happened to drink wine that was not meant for him."

A glimmer came to Maxton's eye as he realized what, exactly, she had done, and why. But in truth, he was beside himself with the realization. He simply couldn't believe it. All of the planning that he and his men had done, and the situation had been resolved by one small woman. Reaching out, he cupped her pale and injured face between his two enormous hands.

"And I had grand ideals of saving you from this place," he murmured. "It seems that you did not need saving. What you did... I cannot imagine a woman so brave, Andie. Not only did you save yourself, but you saved the king and accomplished what a dozen seasoned knights could not have done so easily. Utterly remarkable, my lady."

Her tears spilled over then, deeply touched by his words. The sweetness of his touch made her feel as she'd never felt in her life – comforted, appreciated, and adored.

Aye... *adored*.

"It occurred to me that taking this upon myself might somehow diminish your opinion of me," she said. "But after yesterday... after they had beat me... I knew what I had to do. You could not have punished them the way I did. Knights punishing women of the cloth would somehow sully you with the Church, no matter how righteous your cause. But this way... there is no damage to you or your men. It is over now, Maxton. Rightness for one and for all."

He caressed her face gently. "Did they beat you because of Douglas' death? It did not occur to me until after we left his body at St. Blitha that they might punish you for it. Is that what happened?"

She didn't want to make him feel badly about protecting her, because it had been the right and noble thing to do, so she simply shrugged. "They knew that the plan for the king's assassination had been divulged to the king's men," she said. "They were certain I was the culprit, but I did not confess to it. Another nun tried to beat me for it, but I fought her and injured her. In fact, Sister Dymphna is in her bed, unable to move. She is part of this plot, Maxton, and should be punished."

"I will send men to arrest her."

"It would be a good idea to…"

"Andressa!"

A howling cry echoed off the sanctuary walls, cutting her off, and both Andressa and Maxton turned to see the Mother Abbess, now propped up against the altar, her finger pointing in Andressa's direction.

Knowing she'd been summoned, Andressa approached the woman with Maxton at her side, noting that the poison was making the Mother Abbess' limbs convulse uncontrollably. Her breathing was coming in shallow, uneven gasps and when she spoke, her lips and tongue were completely dry.

"The wine," she breathed. "You confused the wine!"

Andressa looked down at the woman, feeling absolutely nothing by way of pity as she watched her struggle. She didn't even feel satisfaction. At most, she felt a sense of finality, as if the horror of her life was finally ending.

Bending over the woman, she spoke softly.

"I did not confuse the wine," she said. "I gave you the wine you intended for the king. Now, he shall live and you shall die. If you are afraid to die, you should be. All of those women you murdered in The Chaos, and the others you have managed to murder all these years, shall be waiting for you when you face God's good judgement. You have much to atone for, Gracious Mother."

The woman was looking at her with something equated to stark fear. "You… you *did* this," she said, her words slurred. "How… how could you do this to me?"

Andressa thought it was a ludicrous question, one she resisted snapping at. Glancing at the pitchers still in her hand, she carefully set them down next to the dying woman, including the one that had contained the poisoned wine. When she spoke, it was for the Mother Abbess' ears only.

"Remember what you told me," she whispered. "Death comes from the most unexpected sources. All those men and women you killed never suspected you… and you never suspected me. I hope you suffer as deeply as you deserve, Gracious Mother."

They were the most satisfying words Andressa had ever uttered. With them, all ties and all memories with St. Blitha were cut in an instant. Standing up, she turned her back on the woman completely. She could hear moaning and weeping behind her as she faced Maxton.

"If you still wish to marry me, I am ready to go with you," she said. "I realize that my actions today are most shocking, so I would understand if you would like to reconsider."

Maxton was looking at her with an expression that could only be described as joy. Pure, prideful joy. A woman so strong, a crusader for what was true and right in the world, took the greatest risk of all in seeking justice for herself as well as others. The evil of Seaxburga needed to be stopped, and she put herself in danger to do just that.

"I am the most fortunate man in the world to have such a woman," he said softly, reaching out to take her good hand. "Come along, love. You've known a life of hopelessness… let me show you what it is like to truly live."

She smiled, his words filling her as deeply as the oceans filling the earth. It was deep and vast, simply waiting for her to discover it all. That kind of joy was so out of place among dying women, and a dying bishop, but Andressa wasn't looking at that any longer. She was looking at the future, as bright and magnificent as she could have ever hoped for. As he held her hand tightly, she fell against him, affectionately, knowing that for the rest of her life, she was destined to be by this man's side, for better or for worse.

It would be just the two of them, for the ages.

"What a kind and generous man you are to those in need," she murmured, repeating words she'd said to them when they'd first met. "You knew I needed you, and I think somehow, you needed me as well."

He smiled at her, putting his arm around her as he began to lead her out of the sanctuary. What he felt for her, he couldn't put into words, but he did know one thing – she was right.

He needed her.

"More than you know, love," he said. "More than you know."

EPILOGUE

Chalford Hill, South of Gloucester
1206 A.D.

"Touch me," she whispered. "Touch me, you brute. Let me feel you."

Maxton didn't need to be told twice. Mostly because this moment was a race against time. With a growl, he picked up his wife and carried her to their bed, a very big bed that usually had three little girls in it at night, three little girls that refused to sleep in their own beds and a father who was too soft to make them do it.

So, moments in the bed with only the parents were far and few between.

He wasn't going to keep his lusty wife waiting.

Once on the mattress, he loosened the fastens on her surcoat, pulling at them as she feigned a struggle. She liked that sometimes, for him to dominate her, and he loved it as well. Whenever she called him a brute, he knew what was expected of him. He roughed her up a little bit, but it was all in good fun. Easing the shift and dress off her shoulders, her breasts popped free and he could get his mouth onto a warm and tender nipple.

As he suckled her furiously, Andressa cried out softly, holding his head to her breast as if he was a starving child nursing against her. Given that they'd had three children in five years, suckling breasts that weren't full of milk were rare these days. Not that he cared; he'd suckle her any way he could, but he didn't like leaving his children hungry. At the moment, their youngest child was almost three years of age, and Andressa's breasts weren't full of milk.

It was a thrilling moment.

Pushing her back on the bed, Maxton continued to nurse hungrily at her breasts as his hands caressed her buttocks and stroked her thighs. He loved her thighs, long and silky things, and when he gently stroked the dark fluff of curls between her legs, she thrust her pelvis forward, trying to lure his fingers into her body.

Maxton knew that and responded by slipping a finger into her tight, wet sheath, feeling her gasp with pleasure. She was very moist and he refused to wait any longer. They had a very active and healthy sex life, even with the little girls who knew no boundaries, so they had to take their opportunities when they could. Unfastening his breeches, he let them fall to his ankles and put the tip of his hard, throbbing phallus against her warm and wet folds.

"Tell me you love me, Andressa of Loxbeare," he murmured, gently kissing her chin, her mouth. "Tell me that I am your everything."

Andressa was bucking against him, trying to force him into her body. "You are my everything and more," she whispered. "Give me your son, Max. Let me bear your son this time."

Those words drove Maxton wild. He thrust into her, listening to her gasp with the sheer pleasure of it. She cried out softly as he thrust again and again, seating himself to the hilt, feeling her tight wetness around him. It was sheer bliss. Once fully seated, he held her buttocks against his pelvis and began to thrust into her.

Andressa clung to him, feeling wishing he could bury himself deeper. He was well-endowed and satisfied her every time, but she was so desperate for the man that she always wanted more. As he thrust into her, she had to put her hands up so he wouldn't push her right off of the bed with his sheer power. With every thrust, he ground his pelvis against hers and she could feel sparks when their bodies met. His lips were against her forehead, kissing her softly as he made love to her.

It was heaven.

"Mama!"

Maxton froze, looking at Andressa with an expression between disappointment and surprise.

"Damnation," he hissed. "Not now. Please, not now."

Andressa grasped his buttocks, forcing him to continue. "Keep going," she breathed. "The door is locked. They cannot get in."

Maxton tried; with God as his witness, he tried. His wife's beautiful body had him trapped, and all he wanted to do was release himself into her and feel her tight body as she released around him, too. That heavenly throbbing that was something he lived for, every day of his life.

"Mama!" Now, they were banging on the door. "Dada, *open!*"

Maxton tried to resume his thrusts, ignoring the sounds of three little girls demanding their attention, but his concentration fractured when the banging grew worse and someone started crying. He couldn't stand it when his babies cried. It was Ceri, the littlest; he recognized her voice. In his arms, Andressa started to laugh.

"My God, Max," she declared, grabbing her husband by the hair and pulling his head from the crook of her neck. When their eyes met, her laughter only grew. "There is no use in continuing this. With Ceri weeping, the entire world stops and we both know it."

He sighed heavily, a look of utter apology on his face. "I am sorry, love," he said. "But… she is so young. She does not understand why I have locked the door on her."

"She should be taking her nap, with her nurse present. Where in the world is that woman?"

"Probably sleeping, too. You know how she falls asleep when the girls do."

Andressa rolled her eyes and, giving the man a loud kiss, pushed him away from her and tossed her skirts down.

"Go, Dada," she said as she climbed off the bed. "Go to your baby girl. Make sure she understands that she is more important than her mother."

Maxton sheepishly pulled up his breeches, tying them off. "That is not true."

"It is."

"That is not fair. I had very high hopes for this interlude, as you know."

"We will never have a son this way."

"Is that all you want? My son?"

Andressa laughed as she brushed at her skirts, smoothing them. "Of course not," she said. "You are all I dream of, my love. But next time, we shall have to wait until the children are most definitely asleep and escape to some chamber where they cannot find us. Mayhap we shall go to the next city simply to be sure."

Maxton laughed softly as he watched her cross the floor. From the woman he met those years ago, that terribly starved pledge, to the woman she was today was like looking at two different people. She had filled out over the years, with beautiful, full breasts, a long torso, and a womanly shape that every man she came across noticed. Maxton had been forced to threaten and scowl at more men than he could count once they caught sight of his elegant wife with her beautiful face and delicious figure.

He considered himself a lucky man, indeed.

"We shall revisit this later tonight," he assured her, turning away from the door in the hope that his full erection would quickly die down. "I promise you, later tonight when they are all asleep."

Andressa cast him a very dubious expression before unbolting the door and opening it. Instantly, three little girls bum-rushed in, as they'd been leaning against the panel. While the eldest one, Danae, stopped at her mother, the other two ran straight to Maxton. He bent over, scooping four-year-old Melisandra and three-year-old Ceri into his arms. Ceri was indeed weeping and Maxton kissed her wet face.

"Now, now," he said. "Why the tears, sweetheart? There is no need to cry."

Melisandra, her arms wrapped around her father's neck, looked at her sister seriously. "She slapped me," she said flatly. "I slapped her back."

Maxton's eyebrows lifted as he realized the situation. "I see," he said. "Ceri, you must be kind to your sister. No slapping. We have discussed that."

True to form, Ceri ignored him. She was a blonde-haired, blue-eyed cherub who was extremely smart. She knew how to get around her father. Rubbing her eyes, she lay her head on his shoulder, weeping softly, and Maxton knew that was the end of his scolding. That was all he could manage. As he looked at his wife, who simply shook her head in resignation, another figured appeared in the doorway.

It was Cullen, clad in mail and weapons. He looked at the little girls in the room with surprise.

"I thought they were sleeping," he said.

Andressa sighed heavily. "You know better than that," she said even as she cradled her eldest against her. "No one sleeps when they are supposed to around here."

Cullen grinned; he'd been serving Maxton since the man had taken possession of his new property of Chalford Hill and was essentially one of the family now. He, too, knew that the Loxbeare brood never slept when they were supposed to. Even so, Chalford Hill was a remarkable place to raise a family, and Maxton and Andressa had the start of a big one. The fortress was also very rich property with a large castle, something that Maxton had turned into a military outpost for William Marshal.

But there was a history to that.

After the events at St. Blitha those years ago, it had been Maxton, Cullen, Kress, Achilles, Alexander, and Christopher de Lohr who had gathered the army to oust Andressa's aunt from the property, but before Maxton unleashed all of that military might and risked damaging the place, he'd had a meeting with the old woman and offered her a good deal of money to vacate the place as well as the promise he would not arrest her for stealing her niece's inheritance.

As it turned out, Hildreth du Bose was very greedy, and knowing she could not fight off such an army, she readily agreed to the proposal and vacated the castle without incident. Now, she lived somewhere in the south of France, or did the last they'd heard. In truth, Maxton didn't care what happened to the old woman and Andressa surely didn't care, so she was forgotten nearly the moment she'd left Chalford Hill.

Andressa had regained what was rightfully hers without a drop of blood being shed, but the caveat was that it became a military installation, and a powerful one. All three children had been born here, including Danae, who had been born only six weeks after the incident at St. Blitha. Maxton had no sooner married the woman and return her to her ancestral home when she gave birth in the middle of the night, quite quickly and with very little trouble, to a small but healthy baby girl.

Maxton had immediately been in love.

It hadn't mattered that Danae Eleanor of Loxbeare hadn't been his biological daughter. He couldn't have loved her more if she had been. All that mattered was that she was healthy, as was her mother, and Maxton and Andressa embarked on a new marriage with a new baby.

It was everything either of them could have hoped for.

Even now, as Maxton held two more daughters in his arms, he thought quite possibly that no man had ever been happier or more content. Life was good, and everything was wonderful, but as he stood there and reflected on his good fortune, he noticed a missive in Cullen's hand.

"What did you bring?" he asked the man. "Did a rider come?"

Cullen nodded. "You did not hear the sentries?"

Maxton cleared his throat softly, glancing at his wife, who was fighting off a grin. "Nay," he said. "I was… occupied."

Cullen smirked as he broke the seal on the parchment. "It's from the Marshal," he said, carefully unfolding it. His gaze fell on the words written and, quickly, his eyebrows lifted in surprise. "It seems that the Marshal is raising an army to go to Ireland."

The good mood of the chamber began to fade as Maxton knew what that meant – that William was asking for his sword and his support. He didn't even have to hear the words; he just knew. He looked at the girls in his arms, feeling sad as if already missing them, before replying.

"When?" he asked simply.

"Soon," Cullen said. "He goes on to say that both de Lohr brothers are part of his army, and since Kevin de Lara serves David, he will be involved. So is Gart. But isn't Gart somewhere in Devon now?"

Maxton nodded. "Dunster Castle," he said. "He has a new wife and family now."

Cullen turned back to the missive. "Savernake has committed men, which means Dash will be going," he said. "So has de Winter. That means Bric will be returning to the land of his birth to fight other Irishmen."

Maxton thought on the fiery Irishman, someone he'd come to know well over the past few years. "Bric's loyalty is unquestionably to de Winter even though his heart is in the land of his birth," he said. "This will be a difficult campaign for him. What else does it say?"

Cullen continued reading down at the bottom. "Sherry and Achilles serve William directly, so they shall be commanding the Marshal armies," he said. "But Kress isn't mentioned."

"That is because William is sending Kress into Wales for an important diplomatic mission," he said. "A marriage alliance, I believe."

"Kress is an excellent diplomat."

"Aye, he is," Maxton agreed. "Is that all it says?"

Cullen shook his head. "He asks for men you can spare to send to Ireland," he said. Then he lowered the missive. "I would like to go, Max."

Maxton nodded. "You will, as will I," he said, glancing at his wife to see that, already, she wasn't happy about this in the least. He set the girls to their feet, ushering them towards their mother. "I must speak with Cullen about this. Please take the girls with you when you go."

He kissed Andressa on the cheek, a gentle invitation for her to leave so the men could speak privately. Andressa picked up the weepy Ceri, but she didn't leave right away. She was fixed on her husband.

"Max," she said reproachfully. "Last year, you spent almost nine months in France for William. You promised you would never be gone overly long again."

He kissed her again, gently turning her towards the door. "And I will keep that promise," he said. "But I cannot ignore William's summons. You know that. Let me speak with Cullen about it and I will talk to you later."

Grossly displeased, Andressa did as she was told, taking the three little girls out of the chamber. They didn't want to go, which made it difficult, and Maxton could hear them whining and complaining all the way down the stairs to the floor below. He heard Andressa, trying to lure them away with talk of puppies. That usually worked. When the sounds faded, he finally turned to Cullen, who was looking at him with a grin on his face. Maxton frowned.

"What now?" he demanded. "Why do you look at me like that?"

Cullen laughed softly. "Because you don't want to be away from those women as much as they don't want you to be away from them," he said. "Even now, you miss your children, Max. I will be honest – I've never seen such a change in a man."

Maxton's frown turned into an ironic smirk of sorts. Ignoring the man's statement, he took the missive from Cullen and began to read through it.

"What I did not tell you was that the foray into Wales will involve me, Sherry, and Achilles also," he said quietly. "Andie does not know that yet."

"When will you tell her?"

"When I leave."

Cullen knew that was the wise thing to do, considering how attached Maxton and Andressa were to one another. She never took his departures well.

"You will note on the missive that William would like us to convene with our army at Lioncross Abbey Castle, Chris de Lohr's seat, in six months," he said. "It is clear he wants to make the crossing to Ireland after the spring thaw. But I did not want to say all of that in front of your wife."

Magnus was still reading the missive. "Six months will come before we realize it," he said. "And I shall be in Wales with Kress for part of that time. Andie is going to be quite unhappy."

Cullen knew that. He had the benefit of not having a wife, and in times like this, it was a good thing. But over the course of the past few years, he'd had the privilege of watching Maxton and Andressa, and seeing the love they had for each other. It had made him wonder if he was missing something. More and more, he was thinking that he might be. There were times when he wished he had a wife and children, too.

But not today. There was much on the horizon coming, something that a wife and children wouldn't figure in to.

"When do you leave for Wales, then?" he asked. "And I am assuming you want me to remain here."

Maxton nodded. "It will be sometime next month," he said. "The last I heard, Kevin was supposed to accompany us since his father's lands straddle the marches. Kevin knows the area we are going to quite well."

Cullen nodded as he absorbed the information. "And his brother?" he asked quietly, bringing up a rather delicate subject among their tightly-knight group. "What about Sean?"

"You know as much as I do about him."

"But what has *become* of him, Max? I have heard such terrible things about the man."

Maxton had, too. It was a sad subject for them all. "I do not know what he has become," he said after a moment. "No one does. He entered into the king's service and now has become the man's henchman. If John wants a woman, Sean kidnaps her and brings her to the king. If John wants someone murdered, Sean will do it. I do not judge the man when it comes to the abuse of men, for certainly I am in no position to judge him, but the stories of the women and children... that is quite horrific. I have heard from David that Kevin will not even speak to his brother any longer because of it."

Cullen had heard the same thing. "Speaking of murder," he ventured, "I also heard that it was Sean who was sent to find Richard's bastard son, the one the Holy Father tried to place on John's throne those years ago. Have you heard anything about that? Some say he murdered the boy."

Maxton shook his head at the horrible reputation Sean de Lara now had, worse than anything the Executioner Knights had ever suffered. At least their reputation had some rational to it, acts committed during war and conflict for the most part, but Sean's reputation had descended into madness. There wasn't anything he wouldn't do for King John, and everyone knew it.

"Confidentially, I was told that he had a hand in Arthur of Brittany's death," Maxton said after a moment. "No one can seem to locate either boy, in fact, though I believe Lothar has tried to find Richard's bastard. That's what I heard, anyway. And he has given up. It is as if they have both boys have simply vanished, with fates unknown."

"Both heirs to the throne, both missing and presumed killed by de Lara."

"Exactly."

Cullen pondered the darker rumors that had been flying about England for the past few years, many of them revolving around Sean. "They call him the Lord of the Shadows now," he said. "The man has become part of John's darkness."

Maxton waved him off. "All men must choose their own paths and far be it from us to weigh and measure what those paths might be," he said. "Sean de Lara is not my concern. My venture into Wales and Ireland is. How do you suppose my wife is going to accept any of this?"

Cullen scratched his head. "She is not," he said flatly. "Mayhap send for your father to come and stay with her while you are away. He loves the woman and his granddaughters. Why not ask Magnus?"

Maxton thought on his father, a man he'd not spoken to in many years until his marriage to Andressa. At her urging, they both went to Loxbeare Cross Castle to tell him of their marriage, and found an old and lonely old man who had been very surprised to see them. His brother, Emmett, had been welcoming, and Magnus had been surprisingly welcoming also, especially when he saw that Maxton had married.

It had been a shock that his wayward son had finally taken a wife.

Much had been hashed out the day Maxton had arrived at his childhood home. He remembered that day very well. He had spoken to his father about so many things, asking the old man why he'd never responded to his missives, only to be told that Magnus had been too overcome with sadness and despair at Maxton's absence to do it. He burned the missives, hoping that would ease his sorrow at a son who never wished to return home. He thought if he ignored the issue, it would go away.

It didn't.

Oddly enough, there was no disapproval for Maxton's reputation; in fact, Magnus had been proud of his son who had fought with Richard in The Levant, and who had returned to England and wed an heiress. So many things had been discussed during that visit, and it was a relationship that was still being restored, even more so when Maxton was informed that his little sister, Lucy, had died in childbirth with her first child a few years before.

Maxton had wept deeply for the loss of his sister.

Which was why his own daughters were perhaps so precious to him, and to his father, too. Magnus had traveled to Chalford Hill for the birth of his younger two granddaughters, and he came to visit them at least twice a year. Maxton never thought he'd enjoy a good relationship with his father, ever, but time and understanding – and the addition of four women into his life – had changed all of that.

Life, as he knew it, had changed altogether.

"Mayhap I shall ask my father to come and stay with my family," he finally said. He began to hear the cries of his children wafting through the lancet window and when he went to peer from the window to the bailey below, he could see them playing with the friendly dogs that wandered the bailey. They did so love the dogs, and the sight made him smile. "In fact, I shall go ask my wife if she would like for my father to stay with her while I am away. Mayhap that will soften the blow of my departure."

Cullen smiled wryly. "I doubt it. But best of luck."

Maxton couldn't disagree with him, but he had to try. With thoughts of his father on his mind, he quit the master's chamber where they were, making his way out of the keep and heading out to the bailey where his children were rolling in the dirt with the dogs.

A more joyous thing to see, he could have never imagined. As Maxton came upon his wife, who was standing there in a dress the color of wine, with beautiful embellishments around the elbows and wrists and neck, he took a moment simply to look at her. He couldn't remember when she hadn't been part of him, and he of her. For a man who had spent his life engaged in dark and dirty deeds, the fact that he'd found peace and love was something that still baffled him, and there wasn't one day that he didn't give thanks for all that he had, for the children that he had, and for the woman who was his entire reason for living.

For a man who had been wandering and searching his entire life, wondering if there was more to life than what he'd known, looking into Andressa's sweet face told him everything he needed to know.

The Executioner Knight had found a love story for the ages.

Finally, he was home.

○ THE END ○

Children of Maxton and Andressa
House of de Long

Danae (Duh-NAY)
Melisandra
Ceri
Magnus
Aeron
Kane
Karis
Madoc

The Executioner Knights:
By the Unholy Hand
The Mountain Dark
Starless
A Time of End

ABOUT KATHRYN LE VEQUE

Medieval Just Got Real.

KATHRYN LE VEQUE is a USA TODAY Bestselling author, an Amazon All-Star author, and a #1 bestselling, award-winning, multi-published author in Medieval Historical Romance and Historical Fiction. She has been featured in the NEW YORK TIMES and on USA TODAY's HEA blog. In March 2015, Kathryn was the featured cover story for the March issue of InD'Tale Magazine, the premier Indie author magazine. She was also a quadruple nominee (a record!) for the prestigious RONE awards for 2015.

Kathryn's Medieval Romance novels have been called 'detailed', 'highly romantic', and 'character-rich'. She crafts great adventures of love, battles, passion, and romance in the High Middle Ages. More than that, she writes for both women AND men – an unusual crossover for a romance author – and Kathryn has many male readers who enjoy her stories because of the male perspective, the action, and the adventure.

On October 29, 2015, Amazon launched Kathryn's Kindle Worlds Fan Fiction site WORLD OF DE WOLFE PACK. Please visit Kindle Worlds for Kathryn Le Veque's World of de Wolfe Pack and find many action-packed adventures written by some of the top authors in their genre using Kathryn's characters from the de Wolfe Pack series. As Kindle World's FIRST Historical Romance fan fiction world, Kathryn Le Veque's World of de Wolfe Pack will contain all of the great storytelling you have come to expect.

Kathryn loves to hear from her readers. Please find Kathryn on Facebook at Kathryn Le Veque, Author, or join her on Twitter @kathrynleveque, and don't forget to visit her website and sign up for her blog at www.kathrynleveque.com.

Please follow Kathryn on Bookbub for the latest releases and sales: bookbub.com/authors/kathryn-le-veque.

Printed in Great Britain
by Amazon